On the Tip of Her Tongue

by

Jerry Roth

Published by Aberration Press Books 2021

This novel is entirely a work of fiction. The names, characters, and incidents portrayed in it are the work of the author's imagination. Any resemblance to actual persons, living or dead, events, or localities is entirely coincidental. They often claim designations used by companies to distinguish their products as trademarks.

All brand names and product names used in this book and on its cover are trade names, service marks, trademarks and registered trademarks of their respective owners. I do not associate the publishers and the book with any product or vendor mentioned in this book. None of the companies referenced within the book have endorsed the book.

Harper Lee - To Kill a Mockingbird - Copyright (1960)

First edition ISBN: 978-1-7369804-1-5

Editing by Saren Richardson & cover and artwork by Ross Nischler

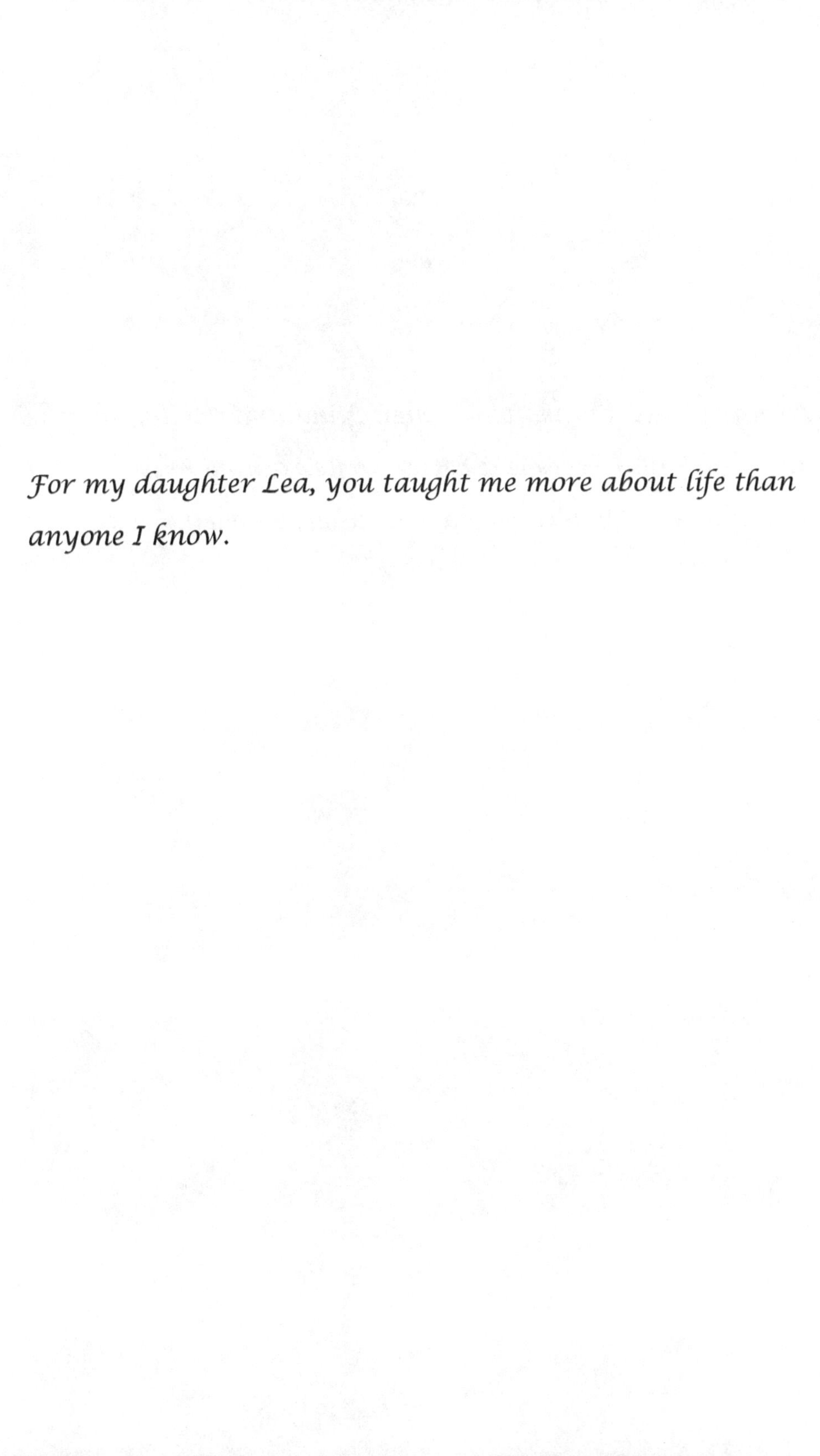

For my daughter Lea, you taught me more about life than anyone I know.

I want to say thanks to Stephen King and Molly, aka the Thing of Evil. I became a better writer asking myself: what would you do? You're not so bad either, Stephen.

Part I

"Until I feared I would lose it, I never loved to read. One does not love breathing."
-Harper Lee

Chapter One
—Nobody's born knowing—

Leather dug deep into Judy's wrists. She struggled against its resolve, thrashing like her life depended upon it, and she thought it did. The brightness from the windows stung her eyes and dug even deeper into some dark part of her brain that had never glimpsed illumination so potent. But soon, her eyes did their job, adjusting to· the penetrating slivers of light. She squinted through slits, seeing a drop ceiling's patterns with its symmetrical rows of squares continuing in all directions. The squares, covered with stains from past water leaks, resembled festers on the skin. As she shifted her head away from the ugly ceiling, a familiar pain stole her senses.

Judy stopped her movements and closed her lids like a vice. There was pain, but the feeling was more than that. There were alarm bells threaded into her remembrance, and she needed it to go away. She forced her eyelids open and did not move her head another inch. She wasn't alone in the room. Others in dirty white clothes scurried around—oblivious to her. That's what she believed until one of them spoke.

"Hello, Judy Angel." A man with a large metal necklace leaned closer. "Can you hear me, Judy?" A lady worn-down by long work hours wearing a matching uniform leaned toward the doctor.

"She's Johnny' Macklemore's wife," she said in a whisper. Glances passed between everyone in the room.

"Who are you?" Judy asked like a child, full of wonder.

"You got hurt, Judy," the man said. She watched the way the creases on his forehead rose and dove with each syllable like a puppet operated by a master elsewhere.

"How did I get here?" *Where is here?* She wanted to scan the room but remembered the pain in time—holding her body still. The flesh of the man's face shifted with each word he uttered.

"We think you hit your head, Judy. You suffered some bumps and bruises. You may have taken a spill." The man made a circle around Judy's face with his hand to bring home his point. "But our genuine concern is your memory," he said.

Judy understood the words—what he was trying to get at, and still, she didn't believe him. Something else happened—the truth slid down to her bones. *He's trying to fool me. I'm not Judy Angel.*

"How old are you, Judy?" he asked.

"Twenty-eight." Judy watched him scratch her answer onto a notepad.

"We've been in the wait-and-see part of your care. You came around earlier but couldn't recall who you were." The man looked around the room at other workers in stained medical clothes. His metal necklace, Judy then recognized as a stethoscope, glinted in the light and blinded her. "*Why* your memory has taken a hit is what we're trying to discover."

He's lying to you. Judy forced her head to turn, trying to ignore the pain. An image of screeching tires and crumpled metal filled her mind.

"I was in a car accident. That's why I'm here," she said with words that fell from her like a bag of rice spilling out onto the floor. "I remember the car—and before it hit me, I saw a little girl in the other...did they bring in another girl?" Judy's expression became terror, watching something far off in her mind. The man glanced first at the others, then back to Judy.

"We will look into that. Meanwhile, you have visitors." Judy saw his name tag for the first time and read: Dr. Otis Bain

"Can you bring in her guests?" Dr. Bain spoke to the others and they scurried like cockroaches out of the room. The words "Dr. Bain" spiraled through her mind over and over again until something flickered, then meant nothing. A light shifted, and with the change came two figures escorted to where she lay. Upon seeing them, a terror started in her belly and rose like poison begging to get out into the air. The two companions—dressed like ordinary people but on their shoulders was a horror. Judy inhaled fast and gave a roar when she saw that they had no faces at all. The features—a nose—eyes—everything that comprised a face—gone as if they never existed. *Pig's skin.* And that was the closest thing her tattered mind could come up with in its frazzled state. Judy pushed herself back against the headboard, thrashing her feet away from the creatures wearing human clothes and fleshy egg-shaped heads.

"Stay away from me," she managed to say between screams. Refilling her lungs and starting again. The doctor and his remaining minions held her down, and the faceless beings had the nerve to clutch each other like she was the threat. "Get back," she gasped with air stuck in her throat. The doctor left her side and already moved to the abominations. With her shoulder blade jammed into the hospital bed, she saw the doctor speaking—the words were soft and reassuring to the visitors. But then she heard them talk and her spine went stiff.

The voices were like an old song, and although she didn't know the lyrics, everything was right there, gnawing at her. The man and the woman, they were people she *should* know.

The folds of their blank faces pushed upward into wrinkles. Judy wasn't about to look away. The view of them didn't bring the memory any closer, but the voices caressed something hidden in her mind. She expected a part of her to open like a shoebox full of keepsakes, but nothing happened.

"Hey little Jude," the male visitor said. He didn't have a mouth, but the place where lips lay undulated up and down just the same. She studied his face hard and wanted to know who he was—searching deep for the answer. She looked back and forth between the two of them, but nothing came to her. It was hopeless until the man spoke again. "We miss you," he said. In the simple sentiment, something sparked in Judy. *Spark* wasn't quite the right word—it was closer to déjà vu. She could feel the wind leave her lungs. Butterflies flapped their wings in her belly as the fog lifted and she comprehended.

"Daddy?" He nodded his head, causing the tears to fall from where eyes belonged. She turned her head, ignoring the pain for the moment, and saw the faceless woman. "Mom?" Judy knew her, except a small part of her still held some doubt. Her mother nodded and caught up with her husband's flow of tears. Judy's face flinched, grimacing as memories flooded back. She couldn't stall them from blending—love, emotion and loss. Fragments rushed into her and she didn't stop it. Her intuition told her she couldn't if she tried.

Chapter Two
—Some skill involved in being a girl—

Caught in a dreamy car ride, Judy spied on her parents from the backseat. The car jostled her with every trundle over a pothole, and she felt the shocks dip and spring back up like an act of violence. Her parents turned from their view of the road to the backseat several times, and with each glance, her stomach churned when she glimpsed their absent features. *How did they get like this?* She wasn't ready to ask—or accept the answer that came with it. Instead, she chose to bite her tongue and stay in her seat.

The storefronts and homes of Columbus, Ohio passed her in a blur. She prayed for the ride to go on forever—to drift into a dimension where her reality was nothing more than city scenes melting into a kaleidoscope of images.

Before she was ready for it to happen, the automobile rolled to a stop in front of a ranch-style house, shoved in line next to an ocean of other shabby ranch homes. Her parents moved around the car—opening the neighborhood to her like a celebrity—ready to walk her down the red carpet. When Judy absorbed the facade of her parent's home, a strange dread washed over her. Her mother's hand was firm as it guided, and she felt her body pushing back against it, back towards the car. A turn of a chin was all she managed.

"It's okay," her mother assured. Walking through the propped door, Judy pictured it swallowing her whole—clamping her eyelids for fear that teeth would find the soft nape. Before she realized it, she stood on the faded carpet of a living room, surrounded by walls of wood paneling.

"Did I live here? I mean...was I raised here?" Judy asked. Her mother met her with a faceless nod. Framed photographs stared at her from every direction. Featureless faces matching her hosts protruded from mundane scenes. The walls themselves appeared to bend inward—reaching out to Judy like a long-lost enemy.

"It wants to hurt me," Judy said and turned to her mother.

"What's trying to hurt you?" her mother asked.

"This place—the objects. Everything in here." Judy teetered in the modest home, threatening to spill onto the worn carpet.

"Bud? Grab her. Hurry!" Judy's father obeyed his wife, catching his daughter before the floor had a chance. "Sit her down," Emily said. Bud wrapped his daughter up into his arms as if she had no weight at all and moved her onto a kitchen chair.

"I feel a little better," Judy announced, and her parents both exhaled at once. "Columbus wasn't my intended destination. I was here to okay some art designs for Johnny's newest book. Deliver the manuscript to his publisher and be back on a plane to New York. The manuscript?" Panic took hold of Judy.

"We have all your things. We placed them...right there," Emily said and pointed slowly towards a large paper bag sitting on the kitchen counter. Judy relaxed when she saw the manuscript was safe.

"How do you remember coming to town? You remember your husband but not us. Why?"

Judy shook away the question. "Johnny is' busy this week. A writer's convention took him to Europe."

"Johnny's a big deal. We've seen his books in the stores," Emily said. Judy caught a tone. *Jealousy? Bitterness?*

"I do what I can to free up his time. That's why I make trips like this one. He's got a lot on his plate, Mom." Judy believed she saw an indentation on her mother's face where eyes should be. Pools were forming, and the same was happening to her father.

"Dr. Bain warned me to stay put. He cautioned against travel," Judy rubbed her temples and tried to soothe a headache—just over the horizon but coming fast, "would it be a burden to have me in your home this week?" She looked from her mother to her father with panic on her face. Emily rushed to her daughter, throwing her arms around her.

"This is your home, Jude. I wouldn't let you leave if I had my way." Strong arms pulled Judy tight. At first a one-sided embrace—until Judy recognized her mother's hunger and squeezed her back. "Come now. You have to be hungry," Emily slid a glass of orange juice across the Formica.

Judy sat at the kitchen table, sipping orange juice, and as the stringy pulp slipped down her throat, she remembered how much she enjoyed the pulpy-style juice her mom bought for their mornings. It was the most reliable memory since her Columbus arrival inside her parent's home. She lost herself in the sheer joy of knowing something from her past. They were loving and ready to bring her back into the fold without hesitation. Bud sat across the table. Yet *still,* there was nothing in the way of a face.

"It's been so long since my little girl sat across from me," he said.

She wondered if he would cry and recalled how tears had appeared before like a magic trick. Judy wanted to speak, but without memories anchoring her emotions, she had nothing to say.

She remembered every morning she had ever spent with Johnny, but no memories of her father resonated. It was a blank slate, and that frightened her. She wondered how she had such powerful images of her life with her husband and no beautiful recollections of her childhood. Either way, she had nothing to add to the conversation and remained quiet.

"I was hoping you could join me at the pond to see if the fish are biting some time." Bud sat still as a child hearing an ice cream truck, waiting for permission to get a treat.

"Sure, Dad. It sounds like fun." Bud jumped to his feet and kissed Judy on the cheek.

"It's a date," he said, a bit too loud for the small kitchen. Judy felt sad for him, that he would be so desperate for her affection. She stood up from the table fast—too fast, finding a pain lurking behind her eyes that was there all along. Looking around the room, each inanimate object she saw shoved a dagger of this pain deeper into her skull.

The strands of agony curled inside her head, making the outside world seem bright and fuzzy around the edges. Accompanying the shrieking discomfort, Judy experienced a sudden recall. All at once, small moments shared with her mother and father came surging back into her mind. As violent as a baseball bat to the side of the head—the connections were suddenly there. Her brain swelled from their arrival.

She flexed her mind and reached out for the lost memories of her parents. All she perceived was that they weren't accessible. And in an instant, they were there. Her head ached, causing her pupils to fill with light, and she lost her balance. She stumbled next to the kitchen table, hands missing the mark, and she collapsed onto the floor with a thud. Emily rushed to her daughter.

"My God, Judy. What's happening?" On instinct, Emily lifted her child from the ground. The line dissolved between Judy, all grown up, and the five-year-old that Emily had adored many years earlier.

"A bed," Judy pleaded. Before Bud could move to help, Judy saw him. The smoothness of his face melted like lard sliding around in an iron skillet. Parts of his face fell away into nothing until a face with all the components remained. She winced when she saw the same thing happen to her mother.

"I should call Dr. Bain." Judy was already shaking off her mother's suggestion.

"I'm fine," she said, knowing it was a lie. "I need to lie down." Emily half walked and half carried her daughter to her bedroom. Judy was no stranger to migraines and often suffered from them twice a week, sometimes having to sleep an entire day before they left her. But this time, along with the pain, came comfort buried deep enough that if it had not surfaced on its own, she wouldn't have known it existed. At the start of the day, she had sat across from her father, feeling nothing except the knowledge he was her father. Within hours she had a small sample of the loving memories that *time* and nothing else provided.

She cried as her mother slid her under blankets, not because of the lost remembrance, but because of the loss. It plunged her into a profound sadness. Gone was the smooth mask that hid her mother. She saw the face of the woman who raised her and a comforting father. Gazing back and forth, she saw their human faces for the first time. Emily's face was round— soft curves formed her chin and cheeks. Judy recognized the eyes and their sadness. As Bud turned off the lights, Judy relented to the comfort of the darkness and the consent to dissolve within, slipping into a foggy sleep.

Chapter Three
—Only children weep—

Light crawled into the room. With her body drenched in sweat, Judy snapped awake and discovered flowing tears. She didn't know how long the crying fit had lasted, but her mother was by her side to witness every ugly moment.

"It's okay, girl. I'm here," Emily said. Her mother's face was intact, and she was thankful for that.

"Mom?" The bedspread slipped onto the floor as Judy swiped them away from her skin and stood up. A faraway expression captured Judy. "There's another world opening up," Judy said.

"What does it look like?" Emily asked in a calming voice. "Describe it to me."

"It's this bedroom. Not now...years ago," Judy said. She focused her vision on two separate rooms that didn't overlap—were a little out of sync. The bedroom she was in was bright, but there was another layer—another bedroom that her mind created. As her vision began, a *tunnel* formed around her like another skin.

"I see Bud, and his hands are shaking. Mother...you're crying next to him." Judy watched this happen like a rebroadcast of a television show rather than a long-ago memory. But that's what it was, a memory clear and sharper than any that came before. She was looking through her own eyes like a stowaway or maybe a disembodied soul hitching a ride. "It's me. And I'm only a teenager. It feels so familiar. A memory I somehow lost."

"What do you know about Johnny?" Bud asked.

The words emanated from Judy—resonated from her mouth. There was a vibration from her throat and tongue, but there was also a disconnect from her mind. Judy experienced fresh memories, like a speaker that received the information but played no part in its creation.

"I know I love him," Judy roared from the confrontation.

"You don't love him, Judy. You may be feeling a lot of things, but love isn't one of them. Trust me—trust us." Emily added.

"You're scared for me," Judy said. Emily clutched her daughter's hand as Judy continued to describe the vision. "I'm turning to you and Dad, and I burst into tears. You both hold me tight...and let me cry," Judy announced.

"You're right," Judy said. "I trust you and always have. I'm not ready to marry Johnny. I'll call it off tomorrow."

Reality came in a rush, and the duplicate bedroom crumbled and faded from Judy's sight. And the surrounding *tunnel* disappeared, leaving the real world in its place.

"What's happening to me?" Judy asked.

"I don't know," Emily said.

"The night I left you and Dad. Do you remember it?" Emily nodded. "I love Johnny. That much, I know. What I don't know is why I left with him when I'm sure I had decided to move on." She searched for an explanation out of reach.

"That is the one answer we never got. Your father took it the hardest when you left us behind. He wasn't the same without you here. You were a daddy's girl through and through," Emily peered at her daughter. "There is nothing I could ever do that would hurt him as much as when you walked away."

Shame and its warming sensation gave her nowhere to hide. Avoiding the subject, Judy looked around her bedroom. Rock band posters filled the walls and were the backdrop to shelves that held trophies of every shape and size. The area was a mystery, with every nook containing a secret about her past.

"This was my room? These were my things?" *But this isn't me.*

"You don't remember your bedroom?" Emily asked, already knowing the answer. Judy tried to read her mother's face—seeing her surprise. Judy waited for the past to flood back. It didn't.

"No. I don't." It was the child, long gone, that had lived a life there. The little girl's bedroom was immaculate in a way that resembled a shrine rather than a teenager's retreat. Things were clean—without a speck of dust, and she understood it was no accident.

"I spend a lot of time in here," Emily spoke from behind. "When a mother loses a child...well, there isn't anything to compare to that kind of pain." That made no sense to Judy. She recalled the way she left home—leaving with Johnny. There was no kidnap moment, no ransom demands. A young lady that was moving on with her life was all she was. *What is she holding onto in here?* Judy moved closer to the trophies that lined the room and focused her vision on one bronze sculpture with writing just below that read: OHIOANA BOOK AWARD

"I don't remember this, but it's some serious hardware." Her focus went from one writing award to another, scanning a poster of Harper Lee's *To Kill a Mockingbird*. She stopped, twitched when she saw the poster—the bottom curled from years of humidity. The sight of the poster brought something to the front. It was nothing more than an inkling, but it sent invisible fingers down her back, caressing her spine.

"This belongs to you." Emily extended a paperback copy of *To Kill a Mockingbird*. "You never let this out of your sight growing up. It was your security blanket. You read it more times than anyone—including Harper Lee herself, I bet," Emily said with a laugh. Judy reached for the book the same way someone accepted a snake, and when it touched her palm, it breathed like one as well. Emily moved to the door and out, leaving Judy staring at the paperback that held power over her. With careful movements, Judy opened the cover and saw the handwriting was her own and read: *If you're reading this, Judy Angel, you have questions—find Maddie Stewart!*

Chapter Four
—Maddie Stewart—

Out of nowhere, Maddie came in through the doorway more like a breeze than a human being. What struck Judy first was Maddie's massive hair that hung to her bottom—tight curls swelled in every direction like a lion's mane rather than hair follicles. Judy hoped she was getting better. Her parents, at least, appeared normal, and some fragments from her childhood slipped past the barrier to give her hope that everything missing would soon resurface. When Maddie stood in front of her, all hope receded.

Protruding from Maddie's face was an elongated snout with a nose a light shade of pink. Her head was slender with pointy ears peeking from the tresses of her hair. Like the eyes of a doll, Maddie's round, black eyes gave none of her intentions away. The urge to scream came over her when she realized that she was face to face with a rat. All that was missing was the fur on the face to complete the dangerous' image. The anticipation of meeting an old friend drained from her like blood from a wound. *Maybe it's a mask,* was her thought until she studied the lines cut into her friend's cheeks—into her nose.

Maddie gave Judy a crooked smile.

"Are we cool?" Maddie asked.

"What do you mean?"

"Never mind." Maddie shook her head, plunged into Judy's arms, and held tight for a long time. When Maddie withdrew, it was only far enough so that both their faces were inches from each other, nose to snout. Maddie's smile was wide as she revealed razor-sharp teeth.

"Damn it. I missed you. Living in this town hasn't been the same without you."

"I take it we were close?" Maddie raised her eyebrows as if waiting for the punchline. Maddie stared longer, cocked her head to the side, and removed her smile.

"I heard you were in an accident. You don't know me, do you?" Maddie asked. Judy shook her head. "Your mom said you were in an accident but...to not remember me—that's a tragedy." A rat's smile returned to her face without a trace of bewilderment.

"Do you remember our secret codes?" Maddie asked. Again, her questions received body gestures instead of articulation. "You were the one who taught me. We would take our favorite books and write a number, and that would be the page, then another number for the line on that page—finally, the last number would be the word. You'd write me messages so long that it took damn near an hour to decipher the code. You know what you used to call it?" Judy shook her head. "You called it following the breadcrumbs."

"I don't have any memory of you, Maddie. I don't think it was the accident, though. Could swear it was something else altogether."

"Amnesia?" Maddie's sharp smile was still present, but a little fainter around the edges. "If you're claiming amnesia, I have to call bullshit," Maddie said. "That excuse only works in television shows."

Judy gave her a shrug. The appearance of a talking rat was so distracting that Judy couldn't draw her sight away from the snout that was forming human words with such precision.

"I don't know," Judy said in the most honest tone she could muster.

"It doesn't matter," Maddie said with the first signs of strain in her voice, "You're back. You were one of my favorite people."

"Why would your favorite person leave town and never so much as pick up a phone, never write a letter, and never invite you to her wedding?"

Maddie found a chair and pushed her spine back as if punched.

"Maybe you were just too busy with that big-time writer Johnny Macklemore," Maddie said, attempting to add cheer to her voice, "I knew you were bound to get married. I just thought I'd be preordering your novels before that. Why did you stop writing?"

"Who says I stopped?" Judy asked.

"Jude, I was your best friend. I've read all your stories. If you were still writing, they would be on my bookshelves right this minute." Judy listened without an answer. "You had more talent than I had ever seen. What made you stop?" Judy nodded, throwing her sight to the carpet, then back to her friend. *My mind made her a rat. But why? Does she deserve it?*

"You're right, Maddie. If I had even a kernel of an idea these past years to put on paper, I would have. I mean, I want to...but that spark left me." Judy projected her sadness.

"Don't worry, Jude, the team is back together. We'll make things right. And that is a promise." Although Maddie's rodent exterior didn't melt the same way as she experienced with her parents, Judy had no faith in her senses and placed no trust in her perception. Maddie Stewart was a mystery and one she planned to solve.

Chapter Five
—Stillness before a thunderstorm—

Judy vaulted off the bed when the visions returned. As before, a *tunnel* formed around her, sliding the second reality on her like translucent skin. This time the vision wasn't of her bedroom. A sleepover—maybe. She guessed the girl with her was Maddie. She thought of the rat facade and the mistrust she felt in her presence. But Maddie's face was normal and young, and with the visual came more memories flooding in all around her. All the moments she had shared with Maddie seeped back inside and filled her with happiness. Even if the pain came with the memories, it didn't matter—they filled a void she'd never perceived.

Just when the dream was as concrete and as tangible as any waking moment, the edges of the reality frayed. Judy watched from the present as these younger versions of Maddie and herself talked with the volley of lifelong friends until suddenly the teenage Judy stopped talking—Maddie's eyes went round as she saw her friend. The dreaming Judy watched from afar and spotted the urgency in her friend's expression.

The edges of her sight retracted further until a narrow band of eyesight remained in focus. A fuzzy view lost the shimmery light of day, replaced by a dark shadow world where objects thrived in the hues of charcoal-muted tones. Judy's window to the world shut off, and she wasn't sure what was happening to her younger self; she was scared for her safety, but more fearful for the Judy on the other side who experienced this long ago.

She remained in the darkness, trying to be patient, and wishing she could jump out of her skin. When she finally awoke, she was in a bed, watching the ceiling through the eyes of someone else. *Young Judy.* It reminded her of waking up in the hospital, except that she was not alone in this room. Judy couldn't describe how she knew she wasn't alone, but she understood it just the same. She tried to move her body, or at least the Judy from long ago attempted to with no success.

Judy's heartbeat rose and took on a frightening rhythm when a dark silhouette filled her vision. First casting a shadow until his breath warmed her cheeks.

The figure was like a presence rather than a human. Judy watched the movements of the dark form in her mind's eye and considered them. They had the characteristics of a ghost instead of a dweller in the actual world. The Judy from this long-ago memory attempted to make sense of the dissolving consciousness, but the Judy that watched all this now recognized with horror that the form was all too human.

The intruder appeared to swell—shifting from small to large in the darkened room. All at once, the shadow was kissing her. First on the forehead, lingering a moment before plunging lower, always lower. Although her body was numb, *young* Judy recognized the pressure on her skin from the kisses. As the sensations swirled through her body, vision pulsed in and out like a traffic light—blinking its red eyes.

One emotion cut through the static of the scene, bubbling to the surface—anger. Judy experienced the violation and saw the injustice of her helpless form. Confusion gave itself over to helpless rage. The watching Judy willed her remembered body away from the dark menace, but her mind had no more power to stop it than the Judy suffering the indignity. When her outrage was at its highest point—her body jerked awake. The vision's tunnel that encapsulated her melted. She found herself standing in the middle of her bedroom.

Darkness was all around her. Memories filled the crevasses of her mind. She guessed that whatever abhorrent act that followed came after she lost consciousness. It was something so horrific, so traumatizing that it cut at her insides like an animal clawing for sunlight.

She searched in the darkness for something, anything to make the fear and violation go away. Her ideations bustled from one unsatisfying conclusion to another, but never settled on the reality of what happened— getting lost between what she discerned and what she believed. A person can make themselves believe about anything when their back is against the wall. She allowed her brain to switch to autopilot for the time being.

Judy flicked the light switch up and watched as the room took on a new feeling with the illumination. As if she had forgotten that there was an outside world since she arrived in Columbus, Judy remembered her cell phone in her purse, hanging on her closet door handle. *Johnny.* Until the random return to her hometown, Johnny had always been her champion. Without her ever having to ask, he was there to help guide her when she was alone or lost. She plunged her arm into her purse. Fingers made the movements to connect with her husband and wondered why it had taken so long to call him.

"Hello," a voice said, more than a thousand miles away.

"Hey. It's me," Judy said in a whisper.

"Judy?" Johnny acted surprised by a call from his wife, and Judy took note. "Is something wrong?" She wasn't sure how to answer and decided not to try.

"I'm here."

"Judy, it's late here."

"You're right," she said.

"Did you deliver my manuscript?" Judy glanced sideways at the lump bulging from Johnny's leather handbag.

"Yeah...it's here." Like the wind changing the direction of a sail, the conversation took an unexpected turn.

"Here? Where are you?"

"Columbus." Judy endured a twinge of shame and wasn't sure why.

"In a hotel room?" Johnny's voice stabbed.

"No, I'm at my parent's home." She noticed a rise in volume on the other end of the line.

"Why would you go there? What were you thinking?" Johnny's tone was raw, like a bare electric wire, sparking with each angry syllable.

"I was in an accident. The car, the girl in another car." The sight of the child before the collision flooded back.

"What are you talking about? Are you okay? Were you hurt?"

"I'm fine," she whispered. The phone line went silent. When Johnny spoke again, there was a renewed calmness. "Judy, it's not safe for you in Columbus or in that house." She listened to his reassuring voice with no intention of interrupting.

"Come get me." It was Johnny's turn at silence.

"I can't," he said. His speech was a faraway articulation from a disembodied spirit. Judy cried. "This convention is important to my career, important for us." Johnny could hear her weeping and pressed on. "Call a cab, get on a plane, and get home. When this week is over, I will meet you at home," he said.

"There are some things I need to figure out here," she said through tears.

"That's not a great idea, Judy—"

"You won't understand, but I'm staying here this week, and I will try to call again to check in. It's something I have to do, Johnny."

"Listen to me—"

"We'll talk soon." Before he could answer, she disconnected the call. Judy sat in her bedroom, feeling lower than she ever had. Maddie popped into her mind–*Follow the breadcrumbs.* Maddie's phrase led Judy through the room as if she were unaware of her motivations. She found her copy of *To Kill a Mockingbird* on her dresser, but here attention was drawn to Johnny's leather attaché case across the room—the sight of it made her miss her husband.

Snatching the paperback book and a pencil, Judy plopped onto her bed. *Follow the breadcrumbs.* She opened the paperback to the very last page. On the inside of the thicker cardboard cover sat numbers, and above those in Sharpie read: *Angel*
The memory and the visual of the numbers came together at the same time. A bolt of lightning from some unknown place.
Judy read: *(20, 7, 11)*

On page 20, line 7, and word 11, Judy read the word, Cal. *Who's Cal?* She continued through the first batch of numbers until she had the full sentence: *Help Cal wake up*

Chapter Six
—Calvin Reed—

It took some exertion to worm the keys out of her mother's hands and drive so soon after her accident. But with some considerable effort—begging and pleading—Emily relented. Following her mother's instructions, Judy found Cal's neighborhood. The homes were the perfect size for a wife with a bunch of kids. *My mother said he was single.*

Judy sat in her father's Chevy truck watching the surrounding neighborhood. And as the day faded into the night, she wished for a drink to calm her nerves. The taste of alcohol had vanished from her brain—she had given up drinking that many years ago. Johnny revealed to her the evils of the substance, and she *had* been happier ever since. Still, there were a few moments when the idea of a stiff drink bubbled to the surface when she wanted to release the pressure valve—longing for its calming deluge as it flooded her senses.

Judy stared at the dashboard of the old truck and wondered how she knew her favorite dessert, could solve all the puzzles on *Wheel of Fortune* and recite most of the lyrics to every *Guns and Roses* album, but couldn't remember what color Cal's hair was.

The code inside her copy of *To Kill a Mockingbird* wasn't helpful in the least. With hesitation, Judy asked Emily to fill her in about Cal—to help her understand who Calvin Reed was to her. Judy wanted to press her mother further and break down why she would reference Cal in a childhood code, but any question that came to mind made her feel stupid for not knowing the answer. Either the surrounding people were going crazy, or she was. She formed a new tactic—pretending that she knew more than she was letting on. The strategy didn't make her feel better, but it also kept her from looking like a raving lunatic. Self-deception was a Band-Aid. Still, she wanted to understand without appearing foolish.

When Cal Reed opened his door, he froze in his tracks, and a bomb went off inside Judy's head. One minute she was looking at him standing in the doorway, the next—the world faded into black like the slow dissolve of a film reel. She heard a sizzling noise and prayed it wasn't her brain. The pain told her otherwise as an ache careened through her skull. The throbbing started at the back of the neck and blasted its way behind the eyes. Judy grabbed her eye sockets, pushing into them with her palms.

"Are you okay?" Cal asked, hovering his hands around her in case she wasn't. Although she nodded, her entire body clenched as if receiving electricity. The sizzling sound kept on coming, and when she was sure the pain was too much to tolerate, the agony ebbed. Air, trapped in her lungs, escaped in a relieving gush.

When the searing pain subsided, and she could let go of her eyes, something had changed. Judy glanced at Cal and turned her head away just as fast. Cal watched Judy with such curiosity that it unnerved her, giving her the urge to lunge off his stone step, making a charge for the truck.

"Calvin Reed?" she asked with no emotion. He nodded but kept the rest of his body cemented in place. "My name is Judy Macklemore...you might know me as Judy Angel, though." Cal studied her. A smile curled around the corners until he was beaming.

"Hey, Judy Blue Eyes." The same feeling of being known without knowing crept into her senses like an ugly parasite. At first, it was massive in her chest, and then the wonder broke through her boundaries. She returned to his face, and fear took hold when she discovered she couldn't.

"Judy?" Cal's voice was distant, like thunderclaps shielded by mountains. Wrenching her neck, she saw his comforting face. Without warning, her head jerked back hard enough to crack her spine. Someone or something didn't want her to see him. Judy realized that she had said nothing for a long while.

"Give me a second," she whispered. Pivoting on her heels, she scanned the homes, cars, and empty street for anyone lurking. There was no one around, even so, she perceived someone watching her—controlling her. When she turned back, she was careful to avoid eye contact, not wanting the violent repeat of pain in her head, spiraling out of control.

Cal smiled broader, tracing the lines of her face. In his expression, Judy saw her own sadness reflected. He spotted profound pain and wanted to know everything. She was a timid bird preparing to flee.

"Are you going to make me loiter on your front porch like a salesman?" It was all she could think of to get away from his expression burning into her. His limbs came alive as if they were waiting for the invitation.

"Right. Sorry. Come inside." He motioned her through the doorway. "I can't believe you're here in the flesh," he said, lingering in the doorway. Although the home was perfect for a family, the furnishings said otherwise—modern and expensive pieces of furniture decorated the rooms from floor to ceiling.

"You never married," Judy said. More like an accusation.

"How do you know?" She pirouetted around the living room with hands outstretched but still avoiding his face.

"There isn't an ounce of estrogen in here."

"I heard you took the plunge." Judy didn't like where the conversation headed.

"What is that?"

Cal grasped the object of her curiosity and brought it to her.

"You don't recognize it?" He placed the picture frame with gentle ease in her hand. The smell of him (Irish Spring) wafted into her nostrils, threatening to awaken something at her core. "It was taken our senior year." Did she dare look at his face in a photo? *Would the thing try to stop me? Punish me?* Judy took a deep breath, swiveled her chin in the picture's direction, and inspected him in the photo. She braced for the wrath, but nothing happened. He was beautiful with blonde wavy hair and piercing green eyes.

"Who's the girl in the photo with you?" she asked.

"You," he said. Judy studied the girl's face and saw someone else. The girl in the photo resembled a sister, there was no doubt about that, but besides the features, everything was different. The red hair of her younger version was a stark contrast to her current tone, as bright as the sun. For her, applying makeup had become a constant ritual. She looked down at the clean face of a girl just beginning her life and couldn't imagine how or why she changed her appearance. *When did I look like this?* As if Cal could hear her thoughts. "You may have changed on the outside...but I bet you're just the same as I remember you." She took a moment to decide who she believed—choosing him—but wished with all her heart she still looked like that girl smiling back from the photo.

Judy focused on the image of him while he talked but feeling the make-up on her face took all her attention. *It's as thick as paint.* An urge came alive in Judy. At first, it was an inkling, but soon she was helpless to her need to get to a bathroom and scrub her face clean.

"Dinner. Have you had it?" He leveled his gaze toward Judy, and for the first time, he saw the fear seize her expression as she stared at the picture frame. With a quick movement, Cal took her arm, guided her to a chair, and sat her down without uttering a word.

"I'm okay." She read the concern in his expression and wondered what he was thinking. Everything turned weird. The idea to ask her mother what Cal meant to her crossed her mind, and then it left before it could solidify as a real possibility. Everything inside her shouted for her to remember. Cal understood her well, she was sure of it. The urge to wash her face returned.

"You've been away for a long time. I can still tell you're not okay," Cal said, daring Judy to lie. She revealed a smile that didn't fit.

"Maybe... and maybe dinner comes next," she admitted.

"Go home, get some rest, and I will pick you up for a nostalgic night on the town." She would not say no—telling Cal yes made her heart skip a beat.

"You got it. I suppose you can pick me up." She noticed her blonde curls hanging down the side of her face. The impulse to hide her hair grabbed hold. "Do you know where my parents live?" Cal leveled his face to hers and laughed. His laugh was genuine, and it caught her off guard, making her laugh despite herself.

Chapter Seven
—Mockingbird—

Suspending a box of hair dye into the air, Judy squinted to read the label—Crimson—emblazoned on the front. She slid her gaze from the box to a mirror reflecting her image and did her best to match one color to the other. Judy squinted until her eyelids were narrow slits—as if the sun shone into her pupils.

"I can't tell," she said, with Emily throwing her daughter a comforting expression and holding out photos from her childhood. Her mom's lack of input set her nerves ablaze. "It's been so damn long since I had my natural shade, I wouldn't even recognize it if it slapped me in the face," Judy said.

"Honey, I think—" Judy snapped her head to her mother. The motion was so quick that it halted Emily's comment.

"Was I in love with Cal? The guy's cute. No—he's more than cute." She squinted again, hoping her hair's shade didn't come out too light. Judy's mind drifted back to her encounter with him, wondering what kept her from facing him. Her ugly imagination blamed Cal for the incident. Like a demon in one of her novels, she loved to read.

"Are you wearing contacts, Judy?" Emily asked, breaking Judy's concentration.

"No, why would I?"

"You got your first pair of glasses when you were eleven," she said as she walked to a desk resting in the room's corner. With a gentle nudge, her hand slid Johnny's manuscript to one side. Judy tensed when the bundled novel shifted as if the friction tickled her spine. The novel wasn't the goal, and a pair of eyeglasses appeared in Emily's hand—on its way to Judy.

"Try these on." Judy stood in place, staring at her mother—with the glasses remaining in her outstretched hands. Judy held her breath when she grasped the glasses.

"These were your backup pair." The magnification caught her attention. The prescription wasn't high, no major distortion, but she realized it meant the wearer of the glasses had far from 20/20 sight. She brought the eyeglasses toward her face, feeling the sides slip over her ears, the bridge pressed against the top of her nose. The world came into view, sharp. *I needed these. How long have I needed these?* She wasn't about to tell her mother the conflict inside. Hair color became a distant deliberation as far away as thunder when the mirror reached her face. She saw her appearance with eyeglasses, and more than that, she saw deep creases in the face that age brought. The makeup had done its part to conceal the lines, and with it gone and better vision thrown into the mix, she didn't see the same person anymore. The person in the reflection had been there the whole time—hidden underneath, but there. *You can't forget poor eyesight.* The idea swirled in her head. *Who was Judy Angel? Because it sure isn't me.*

"When you were a baby, you were different. I sat for other children before you were born. Back then, it was the easiest way for a young girl to earn a few dollars. I watched happy drooling children, babies crying out to their mothers from the moment I arrived until the second I left, and everything in between." Emily hopped onto Judy's bed, pulling her down to her with a soft tug. "Not you, Jude. Even as an infant, you knew who you were and what you wanted."

"You sure I didn't have a twin? I never know what I want one day to another. Changing my mind is what I do best." Emily gave a sideways smile.

"You were not much older than six months when I first saw your single-minded stubbornness. You were *mostly* a happy little thing. But I noticed something. Every once in a while, you screamed your head off like someone was kicking your cradle." Judy listened with rapt attention. "The whole thing drove me up a wall. You can ask your father. I wrote down everything I fed you each day, what type of fabric softener I washed your clothes in, I even went as far as tracking the exact time each crying fit happened. The fits went on for a month, and I was losing my mind. One day I was picking up your baby toys from around your cradle, you were sitting there sucking on your fingers, you burst into tears so fast I nearly dropped your toy. I looked down in my hand, and it was the tiny stuffed bird. Your father bought it at the hospital gift shop the night you were born." Emily launched from the bed, slid her arm behind a row of trophies on a nearby shelf, and revealed a gray stuffed bird, showing it as a magic trick.

"Mockingbird?" Judy asked as Emily placed the bird into her daughter's hand with gentle care as if it were alive and breathing.

"Anyway, I moved this closer to you, and you quieted at once. I tested it many times, and each time this little birdie was what you wanted. Nobody believed me until I showed them. Kids have many attachments, but I never saw a baby know what she wanted so early in life." Judy looked down at the stuffed mockingbird and recognized a connection with it right away. She returned to the mirror and her reflection within.

"Be patient, baby. You know who you are, and so do I," Emily said. Studying her glasses as they sat on her face, Judy decided she liked how she looked.

"Thanks, Mom."

Chapter Eight
—O.K. Cafe—

Judy looked up at and read the words—THE THURMAN CAFÉ—on the face of a scarlet awning. Worn white bricks covered the front, giving the tiny establishment the appearance of old age. Judy caught her breath at the sight of the restaurant. Although she'd never seen the place before, every moment she lingered outside invited her in, making her feel like she found a forgotten home.

Cal watched her watch the eatery with a childlike wonder on her face. He tried to do it slyly, but she noticed. A crowd built at the steps of the Cafe, a rush of hungry patrons breaking the spell.

"We better get in there before we lose our spot." Judy nodded. Cal placed his hand on the small of her back to nudge her along. The delicate act caused a warming in her, starting with tingling in the face and narrowing of her view. Outward, she shuffled along like every other patron, but inside she sunk deep inside her head, hoping the fogginess continued.

As they entered the small building, Judy saw tables crammed so close together she wondered if there was room enough to eat.

"That's the charm of the cafe," he said as if he read her mind. "It's packed full of tables, but the food and people are amazing," he said, beaming a smile her way. "There's something I want you to see," He dragged her by the hand through the restaurant, past diners, stopping in front of a booth with a square wooden table, tucked into a corner with a view to the outside. Judy watched passersby moving to the left and right of the enormous window.

"You got me. What am I supposed to see?" Cal waved his hands to the walls and even the ceiling. Arching her neck, it took Judy a minute to make the connection. One-dollar bills lined every inch of the wall space, spilling onto the ceiling above.

"Wow," she said. Cal's smile was wide, transforming his face into teeth and dimples.

"It's a tradition for diners to come here and leave behind a dollar on the wall—signed." Judy spiraled in a circle with her face reaching to the sky.

"It's beautiful. Money wallpaper," she said in awe.

"Not as gorgeous as this." <u>Above the booth and to the left</u>—taped against the <u>wall</u> sat a dollar. Words in black sharpie ran across the front: *Cal loves Judy*

"You did this?" she asked, and he nodded. Judy took note from the corner of her eyes, careful to keep her sight safely away. Her cheeks flushed from the gesture, not unlike names etched into a lover's tree.

A waitress moved from one end of the bar to the other. Her movements were so quick—effortless to Judy, and she had a pang of nervousness as the woman approached her. The skinny server with a dirty apron pulled a pad and pencil—ready to take their order when a voice rose above the crowd and the 80s music.

"I got this one, Donna." The waitress swiveled in her shoes, already moving to another table. "You didn't tell me she was back," the man said to Cal. "It's freaking Judy Angel!" The enormous man pulled Judy from her seat and spun in a circle. *My name is Judy Macklemore.*

"Easy, Mike. You will rupture her spleen," Cal said. The owner beamed from ear to ear. He let her go, and she plopped down onto her backside once more.

"How long are you in town, Jude?" She wasn't ready for the question as she looked to Cal and smiled.

"As long as I can be, Mike." He furrowed his brows.

"I don't think you ever called me Mike." Judy was a mouse in a trap.

"That's right. You used to call him Paul," Cal said. "Because you said he resembled Paul McCartney. You remember?" She didn't.

"Sure. I couldn't remember if it offended you or not." A part of Mike's smile faded, but he nodded anyway.

"You could never offend me, darling," Mike calculated something, then his smile returned, "I'm making you a Long Island Iced Tea for the occasion." Before she refused, he was off toward the bar and back with the beverage.

"What's good here, Paul?" Judy asked when he returned. Mike gave Cal a confused glance, and Judy wished she didn't have to say a damn thing the rest of the night. Cal broke out into a fake-sounding laugh.

"She's kidding. We both want the Thurman burger." Mike pretended he was in on the joke, returning a laugh then scribbling on a pad.

"Order of Sloppy fries?"

"Hell yeah," Cal said.

"I'll put this in." Mike's smile faltered, but he left before asking any more questions. Judy was thankful and gave Cal an expression filled with sad bewilderment.

"Thank you," she said.

"Don't mention it." Cal scooted in the booth directly across from her—she shielded her eyes.

"This was our place?" He reached his hand out for hers—Judy pulled her hand back as he picked up silverware wrapped in a napkin. They both noticed her reaction but said nothing.

"Why won't you look at me?" he asked, staring at his hand. Judy saw the blur of the crowd—refusing to focus on his face. The pain happened when she looked at him and could happen again.

"Okay."

"Okay, what?" Cal asked. Judy placed both hands on the table—on either side of her Long Island Iced Tea, like a woman starting a seance. Judy turned her head and faced Cal straight-on for the first time that night. His hair was dirty blonde, his eyes were green, and his face—sculpted like an ethereal creature. Her defiance of the punishment made him even more beautiful. The sound of crackling rose over the crowd of customers. The noise wasn't in the room but erupting in her head.

"If we could make all our daily calorie intake come from Thurman's, we would," Cal said. "Try the burger." Cal motioned to the sandwich. Mike had come and gone—bringing them food without her knowing. Cal picked up his burger and stuffed it into his mouth, taking a bite too big to manage, and tried to talk with the muffled sound coming out. Each movement from him caused her pain to rise and fall in tortuous waves.

Mike came back to check on the table. "Back off, Paul," Judy said. He put his hands up and backed away from the booth. Judy grabbed the alcoholic drink with both hands and drank until she gasped for air. She went back to finish it in one gulp. Judy pinched her eyelids closed and felt in her pocket for the gray mockingbird, finding it with her fingertips, and brought the stuffed animal out into the light. She sat it next to her empty drink. When she opened her eyes, the pain vanished without a trace.

"This is more what I remember," he said and twirled his hand around her face. "For a moment I wasn't sure who showed up at my door."

"We have to get something straight," she paused, "today I realized I was a frivolous girl, and it embarrassed me," she said.

"Judy—" She lifted her hand, and he stopped in his tracks.

"It's hard to explain, so I won't. There's a lot of my past I can't seem to remember, and I don't know why. Maybe I don't want to," she smiled, "seeing how I was once a part of things made me feel like an outsider in my life."

"I liked your speech. Especially the frivolous girl part," Cal raised his hands in the air, "*To Kill a Mockingbird?*"

"You know it?" she asked. "I just read it," she said.

"I read it first then gave it to you, Jude."

"You introduced me to it?" The revelation stunned her.

"Don't be so shocked. I'm full to the brim with culture." His smile was sly, and she could tell it was genuine. Realizing that, the pain dissipated, she held the mockingbird in her hand and stared into Cal's face.

"Here we go," Mike placed drinks on the table with both hands, "These are on the house."

"Sorry about the back off comment," she said.

"No worries," Mike said. She had the urge to hide under the booth. "It's good to see you again, kid," Mike added, before leaving again. When Judy's attention returned to Cal, he was already staring at her with pride.

"What is it? Why do you stare at me like that?"

Cal shook his head.

"Sitting here with you, eating a burger, is like watching a ghost...no—it's like that moment before you wake to discover it was all a dream, facing the day, knowing the moment wasn't real." Judy slid her palm across the table and took his hand in hers.

"When I left here, I was young. I can't imagine what you see when you look at me now."

"I can tell you're having issues with how you look. But you believe that I can see the same beauty that always surrounded you. There is something deeper that weighs on you. It's your memory," Cal said.

"How so?"

He saw her discomfort and changed the conversation. "About a month before you left home for good. You came to my door, well, my parent's door, and do you know what you said to me?"

"No."

"You told me you didn't know yourself anymore. That nothing stayed the same in your mind. You went to sleep feeling and knowing one thing, and the next day things were different. You said, 'As the light hits my face, I am different.' When I think of you, that conversation always returns." Judy curled her small hand around her fresh drink.

"It has been forever since I had alcohol. I think I might be allergic."

"You serious?" he asked, already reaching for her glass. She stopped him.

"I think Johnny may have said that...I'm not sure. I get confused, sometimes." Judy picked up the large glass, brought it up to her lips, and it disappeared fast as she drank long. She slammed the glass onto the table, catching her breath. She breathed heavily, trying to laugh as she did. Cal took a long swig himself.

"That felt good," she said. "Go on with your story."

"Watching you on my doorstep that day, I was afraid for you. You shook all over. You weren't making much sense. Saying someone was watching you from a car. That part I didn't get, but the one thing that stood out for me was that you said that if you ever forgot, to give you this." Cal reached in his pocket and pulled out a locket. The small piece of jewelry did not differ from the heart necklace a father might give his daughter on her sixteenth birthday. He handed it to Judy. She swallowed hard when the locket's metal skin touched her.

"Because you were far away, the right moment to give you this never came up. But it's clear you've forgotten whatever you're trying to remember."

She gazed from the locket to him and back again.

"Right," she said.

"The whole thing was strange, but the strangest of all was this." Cal turned the locket over and showed her words scratched into its back that read: STAY AWAKE

Judy placed her finger on the hand-etched words. A sensation, slight at first but building fast, ran through her body. As blood dripped from her nose, the sight gave her a jolt—her posture became as straight as a plank. Judy studied the half-drunk glass and then Cal's eyes and he pushed a napkin onto her nose. Red flowed faster from her nose, and she saw his expression turn grim.

"Johnny was right all along." Realizing she'd ignored her husband when he was trying to save her made her feel foolish. And then she remembered his warning about her parents. The lights of the restaurant dimmed—and brightened. She squeezed the tiny bird in her hand before everything went dark.

Chapter Nine
—Otis Bain—

Light slipped past her eyelids with a direct link to the headache already working in her head. She squinted in self-defense and jerked upward from the bed.

"Take a moment," Otis said. Judy saw she was once again in a hospital room. The last time she saw the doctor, he was ugly, and this time he appeared sick—pale face—circles under the eyes, and skin near translucent.

She moved her fingers under her nose, brushing them on her top lip, and finding no blood. She released a breath of relief—for the moment, the flow of blood stopped.

"We're making this a habit. Perhaps I should pencil you in for a weekly visit with us."

"What's wrong with me? I can't remember things I should," she said, and paused, "and I'm seeing things." It was difficult for her to admit. As her senses returned, Judy wondered about Cal and how she got there.

"Cal?" she asked.

"He was here. Calvin stayed a while until I convinced him you were fine. And you are fine." The doctor's face was grotesque despite his attempt at reassurance. But it was his eyes that caught her attention. They were silvery, and she saw her reflection in them.

Judy closed her eyes, not trusting her sight anymore—searching her pockets for the mockingbird, thinking she left it behind in the café. This scared her and she wasn't sure why. When her hand touched the soft outer surface of the bird, her panic ebbed.

"In what world is bleeding and passing out fine?"

Otis considered this for a long moment before answering. "You got me. Guess that's my doctor talk rearing its head," He moved to her, placing a fat pillow under her head, and she winced at him violating her personal space. "I sprang for an MRI to figure out why I've seen so much of you lately."

Her face didn't hide her fear. "So, what's wrong with me?" He squeezed her arm, and she pulled away like his touch was the equivalent of a blow torch burning her skin.

"When I first got out of medical school, I believed medicine was like a math problem. Two times three equals six, and that's how I thought of it. I believed my patients would come to me with questions, and I would send them home with an answer from a simple formula. What an old doctor learns is that a patient's diagnosis is seldom one answer, but dozens of answers."

"So, you don't know," Judy accused.

"You'd be an excellent administrator—the hospital's version of *turning tables* in a restaurant. Thanks for cutting the fat." He pulled a chair from near the doorway. It emitted a screeching sound as the legs slid across the hard-tiled floor. He set it down at the head of Judy's bed—plopping into it as if a long day were far behind him.

"I didn't run any tests on you last time because...well, the human body has a way of working things out sometimes. If the squeaky wheel squeaks again, then we bring out the oil. You squeaked again, Judy." She considered this and allowed a glance to his face and shimmering eyes—no pupils visible. She squeezed the mockingbird harder.

"Why was I bleeding?"

"Using an MRI is a tricky thing for the brain. There is so much we don't know and can't see. We put the detective hat on for cases like this."

"I'm a case?" she asked, and the doctor nodded.

"Looking at your image, I suspect you suffered a severe concussion."

"How can you tell this?"

"The MRI is good at seeing soft tissue like your brain. If we're lucky, it will show scarred areas. Are you a recreational boxer?" The question caught Judy off guard.

"Not at all."

"The reason I ask is, I believe you've suffered from hundreds of concussions throughout your life. Scar tissue riddles your brain, Judy," Otis said.

"That's not possible…"

Otis pulled an image from a Manilla folder. The translucent photo with stark light and dark contrasts showed an outline of Judy's brain. "Bone or other hard areas show in black. Do you see this area here?" Judy again squinted and gave a slight nod. "There is evidence of damage to a region of your medial temporal lobes. Your hippocampus shows scarring with accompanying black shades. Which might explain your memory problems."

"You're scaring me."

"I don't think you are in any immediate danger, but I intend to research this further and try to get to an answer for you," he said.

"Thanks, Doctor," she said.

"Call me Otis."

"I need to ask you something…when I came in the first time…was a little girl brought in as well from the car crash?"

"You were never in a car crash, Judy. Someone found you in the Olentangy river and brought you to us. They said they witnessed you toss a piece of jewelry—a ring—into the water, climb onto the edge of the Olentangy river bridge, and jump in."

Judy jerked her hand up. A thin white line formed a band shape circling her ring finger. Judy never even noticed it was missing. The outer edge of Judy's eyes filled with tears.

"I know it was difficult to hear. I preferred to leave the detail out."

Judy shook his words away. "I don't believe you. I saw a little girl."

Otis was already scribbling on a piece of paper and extended it to Judy. "This might sound strange…but if you have things locked away inside…this person can bring it out."

"You mean a hypnotist?" He laughed.

"She's not a witch doctor. I've seen her help people in your situation. There's a chance she can help you figure out what you saw," Otis said. Judy nodded.

There never was a girl?

Chapter Ten
—Hypnotized by a gavel—

Eyeing her surroundings, Judy sat in Wendy Reynolds's waiting room studying the other patients. She wondered what led them to hypnosis. Judy rifled through magazines on a tiny table in front of her. The entire experience left her feeling silly for meeting with a hypnotist or even needing one. Returning home revealed how much she forgot. What frightened her most wasn't the absence of the memories, but that it didn't leave a discernible void in her life. Something told her there were enormous chunks gone. It was one thing to forget times in her life, and it was another thing altogether not to have a clue they were missing.

Wendy opened the waiting room door and walked straight to Judy with purpose—a hand extended well before she reached Judy.

"I'm Wendy Reynolds, and I'm so happy to meet you, Mrs. Macklemore. Please, come to my office." Judy relented a weak smile and followed her.

"Please have a seat."

"Thanks."

"I hope you won't find this out of line, but I wanted to tell you how much your husband's books mean to me. Johnny Macklemore's novels got me through so many tough times growing up. I've never come across another writer who understands women the way he does. I envy the conversations the two of you must share," Wendy said.

"I'm sure I can get you an autograph if you like," Judy said. Wendy heard the subtle tone in Judy's voice and reigned in her gushing.

"I first want to demystify hypnosis. There's no magic involved. It's a therapeutic approach to the mind. Have you ever driven home from a day of work or a brief trip, lost track of time, and not remembered how you got home?"

"Yes." Judy nodded.

"Hypnosis works in the same way, Judy. Speaking to you over the phone, I understand you want to recover some memories eluding you?"

"Gaps. There are gaps in me—in my mind. I don't expect you to fix me, and I don't even think you can, but if there's a chance to become whole, I will try," Judy said.

"An open mind is all I ask. I can guide you to what you're looking for, Judy, but I can't do this alone. What are you searching for?" Wendy leaned back in her chair.

"I've seen a car crash in my mind. I was so sure it was in a recent event. The thing is...the memory seems familiar. I can't trust my mind right now." She covered her face, touching a part of her head with her hand. Wendy reached to her desk and dimmed the lights in the room. Judy looked around her like a woman locked into an amusement ride.

"During hypnosis, you'll be wide awake in a relaxed state. Lean back into your seat and feel yourself squishing into its soft leather. I would like you to relax all your limbs, letting go of all tension. Are you relaxed?"

"I am."

"Good. Keep your face aimed toward me and direct your eyes to the circle on the ceiling." Judy did what Wendy asked, sliding her view to a small blue circle. Keeping her line-of-sight permanent was an effort to maintain.

"Without moving your eyes, let your focus go," Wendy said in a soft voice, "allow your focus to blur and let my voice resound inside you." Watching Judy, Wendy leaned forward as if the motion would somehow touch her patient's skin. "Picture the car—take in the upholstery—the texture of the seats—the sounds of the car traveling with you in it. What do you see, Judy?" Judy closed her eyelids slowly but soon felt a burning behind the eyes. Darkness turned to sunlight streaming through a glass.

"My uncle is behind the wheel. He's singing along to the radio, and I think I'm singing with him. I feel the sun coming through the window. I'm gazing through the back window and see my parents following in their car behind us. I was waving to them, excited to see them back there. My uncle turns back to see me waving at them." Judy began to breathe faster and stopped talking altogether.

"Try to relax, Judy. What's happening?"

"When my uncle pivoted to me, a car ran a red light. Rolling into our path, in front of us. He tries to turn the wheel, but it's too late. My butt is off the seat, and I feel so light. I see glass moving past my face, and I can feel something cutting into me."

"The vehicle, Judy. What is the vehicle doing?"

"It's spinning like a cartwheel. I hear my uncle scream. It's not a long scream, but I know it's him. Everything's upside down now. I can feel the roof of the car with my back for just a moment, and now I'm hitting the ground hard." Fear stole her voice.

"You are not there. There's nothing to fear. You are safe. What are you seeing?" Judy sucked in air.

"When the car hits the ground, I hear a crunch as my head hits the surface. I can't move—there's a ringing in my ears. I'm lying there when my father picks me up. I'm in the backseat as they drive away. I hear my mother talking to me."

"What is she saying to you?" Wendy asked.

"She's scared when she speaks to me. She is repeating the same thing over again."

"Saying what?"

"Stay awake ... stay awake ... stay awake ... stay awake." Judy opened her eyes and saw Wendy and cried as if she wasn't in the room.

Chapter Eleven
—Make music for us—

The bedroom door creaked, sliding inward—creating a sound like a coffin opening. The inside of Judy's room was dark, except for a sliver of light. A streetlight from next door came into the small area through the parted curtains, giving stuffed animals lining her room an angry appearance. Teddy bears menaced and a doll's eyes reflected light to appear haunted. A shadow formed as Bud walked into his five-year-old's room.

Shuffling to the far side of the room, Bud pulled a radio from under his arm and sat it on her dresser with gentle care. He slid a cassette from his front shirt pocket and slid it into the radio in one motion. Piano playing, soothing, wrapped them inside a melodic cocoon. Every movement seemed deliberate as he moved toward his daughter.

Peering through five-year-old eyes, Judy watched her father enter her bedroom. She lay there still, realizing the world around her tiny body was a blanket of fog. Judy touched the bandage wrapped tight on her head, feeling its tension, and with it a dull pain in her skull. Although she was safe in her own time, Judy worried about her younger self. Fresh from the car accident and unable to move her body, Angel lay there as vulnerable as an infant and the drama continued.

"Hey, Jude. It's just me...your daddy," he said. Judy's body twitched for the slightest moment. Bud climbed into bed with his daughter and laid down next to her. In the background, the song "Lullaby" by Billy Joel rose—*GOODNIGHT MY ANGEL, TIME TO CLOSE YOUR EYES AND SAVE THESE QUESTIONS FOR ANOTHER DAY—*

"I'm going to help you, Jude," Bud said, stroking her hair. *"We can do this together. I won't hurt you."* Bud pushed his body as close to Judy as possible. She couldn't tell exactly what his hands were doing, but the feeling washed over her was revulsion.

When he placed a hand on her shoulder and pushed his head in closer to hers, reality slammed back into focus. *No!* Judy sat up from her sweat-drenched bed with tears pouring from her. She cried in her sleep and guessed the fit wasn't stopping for a while. She tried to recall her childhood and moments with her father, and the ones she remembered were always sweet and full of comfort.

There was no way she intended to see the vision finish. *Fathers across the country molested their children. But not my father.* Pulling her knees to her chest, Judy let all the emotion cascade out of her for fear it might cause her to burst.

Chapter Twelve
—A respectful distance—

The sun made its first appearance in the morning sky as Judy pounded on the door for over ten minutes. She didn't have anywhere to go, so she kept on knocking. The neighborhood with its cracked sidewalks, aging trees, and out-of-style cars was like a different time. "Quaint" is the word locals gave the run-down little street. Sadness is what first came into her mind. Her knocks grew faster until she heard the handle jiggle from the opposite side.

A small crack appeared between the door and the jamb, with Maddie sticking her rat-like head through the opening. Eyes peered from behind matted hair, and Judy suspected it was more than sleepiness that made her appear an inch from death. Even in her condition, Maddie gave up a rodent smile that stretched her face to reveal deep laugh lines. *I'm not the only one aging.* The thought held no judgment.

"Girl...what the hell are you doing here in this part of town?"

"I suppose hanging out here on your porch." Maddie shook her head with eyes closed tight and then motioned her into the house.

"Get in here." She opened the door hard enough to hit the wall behind. "I'm half asleep." Moving into the living room, Judy stumbled over bottles of wine. A pizza box was open with its guts hanging out and spilling onto the floor.

"I think your place could use a woman's touch," Judy said.
Before she registered the number of uneaten slices, Maddie scooped the box up like a linebacker retrieving a fumble and headed for the kitchen.

"What are you doing here?" Maddie hollered from another room. Judy opened her mouth to yell back but was uncomfortable putting everything out there so soon. Instead, she sat down on a leather couch with its stuffing protruding from an arm and its fake skin peeling off in several areas.

Maddie was a hurricane coming into the living room. She picked a chair across from Judy, plopping down and coming close to overturning it, stopping her momentum at the last second. Each lady waited for the other to talk, and as the time stretched, it became more uncomfortable the longer the room stayed silent. Judy recognized Maddie had something to say that wasn't ready to come out. They exchanged awkward smiles for the third time. Judy tried to ignore the rat face that she believed wasn't there. The urge to reach for the mockingbird was strong.

"Last night was tough for me. I snuck out, so I didn't have to see my parents." Judy shifted in her seat. "I feel bat-shit crazy most of the time, but some memories are creeping back. Mostly in my· sleep."

Maddie swiveled toward the window. "What things are you remembering?" Maddie asked.

Judy took a long moment to answer. "That's a *to be continued* conversation," she said.

"Fair enough," Maddie said and cocked her head, "An idea just came to me."

"Let's hear it."

"Day drinking." Judy laughed.

"I'm in." Maddie was already on her way to fetch some drinks with Judy, wondering if she should. Judy recalled her night with Cal and guzzling alcohol in a frenzy, or at least a frenzy for her. Judy attempted to draw her memory back to when she first realized she was allergic to alcohol. She imagined her mind as a net, feeling the weight and texture before throwing it out into the abyss like a sailor hoping for a big catch.

Her memory never conjured up anything about an allergy. What she sensed was a concealed idea never fully developed but lurking like a rat behind a couch waiting for its chance to jump out. *Screw it*. Before she noticed, an entire bottle of wine was being tossed into the recycling bin.

"Isn't it weird to not have memories?" Maddie asked between large gulps.

"If it happened to somebody else, I would have said yes, but here's the thing...unless you realize the moments are missing, you go about your day as everyone else does. What scares me is...what if I never came back to Columbus? Would I have even known my past went missing?"

"I'd freak out," Maddie said.

"Strangest part—I still know myself. I'm in a deep hole gazing up while everyone else is staring down at me." Judy touched her head when pain flared and faded.

"The town hasn't been the same without you," Maddie said while pouring more wine into Judy's glass.

"Will you answer a question for me?" Maddie nodded, and Judy studied the shabby home with a slow scan. "Why are you still here? I mean...*here* in your parent's old home—living like this." Judy regretted the question even as she asked. Maddie sipped her drink, lost in contemplation.

"I'm here...in this falling-down house because of you," Tears welled in Maddie's eyes. "You're the reason I drink...stayed single...never went to college...right here waiting for this house to come down on me. The concept of it burying me alive crossed my mind more than once over the years." She returned to her drink as if it were a life raft, and Judy believed that wasn't far off from the truth.

"Hard to believe I put that much distress on you." Judy gulped deeper.

"Well...you did."

"A remembrance of you came back to me the other night. Maybe six months before I left Columbus, we got together for one last sleepover." Maddie went tense.

"How can I forget?"

"Only bits and pieces of the night came back, but there is a memory there."

Maddie tried to smile, but it died on her face. "It's funny you recalled that moment."

"Why funny?"

"The night you remember was the first time we'd seen each other in a year. Guess you could say it was my way of mending fences."

"I don't understand." Judy sipped her wine and tasted copper. Blood flowed from her nose into her glass as she drank.

Maddie spotted the trickle and grabbed a roll of paper towels. "Here," she said. Judy accepted the offered towel and pinched the bridge of her nose. "Lift your head. That's a lot of blood."

When Judy returned to Maddie, the features that had formed a rat shifted, as if made of material lighter than air. Her prolonged face had vanished—replaced by an older version of the girl she saw in her vision. The face was far too worn for her age.

"We're friends again. Let's start fresh," Maddie said.

"Why did we stop talking for a year?" Judy asked nasally through the paper.

"Time has a way of clearing out the cobwebs. I was always the reason we never spoke. I take full responsibility," Maddie said. Judy released her death grip on her nose and sat waiting for the blood to stream, but it didn't. She turned toward her friend, ready to speak when she saw something that caused her heart to skip. She reached for Maddie's arm and grabbed her by the elbow.

"Why?" Judy grabbed her other elbow, turning both outward for a better view. Maddie's wrists had deep scars cut across her wrists, not once but twice on each arm. Maddie wrenched her arms away from Judy. "Was this me, too?" Judy's gaze never wavered.

"I'm not ready to talk about this." She raised her glass and drank with tears already obscuring the surrounding reality. "You're back," Some tears fell, and she wiped away the rest, "and I can fix the past now. We both can."

"There's nothing you need to fix, Maddie," Judy said. Maddie gave her a smile that resembled a silent scream. Staring at Maddie's true face made her wonder if her appearance changed when her intention matched her words.

Maddie's massive hair was overwhelming—prominent chin and crooked nose. Beautiful wouldn't describe her, yet she had an appearance that was striking in the most relatable way possible. There were plenty of girls that made you hate them right away because of their perfect symmetry. Maddie drew the opposite effect, bringing you into her orbit.

"Just glad you're back, Jude." They finished their drinks in silence.

Chapter Thirteen
—A dull permanence—

The sunlight was the first thing that roused Judy out of her slumber. Her head was a drum, shallow and throbbing. Knowing it was from the wine made her feel a little better. When she focused, the first thing she saw was the white line that encircled her ring finger. Johnny was always patient—he was throughout their marriage. She also understood the burden of authoring his novels and dealing with a scatterbrain like her.

Her attention shifted from her hand to her nightshirt. Blood covered the neckline and turned the white cloth into a brown-colored mess. The quantity of blood scared her, and she wondered if the amount equaled her consumption of the alcohol she drank. She dismissed the notion right away after calculating how much wine she went through with Maddie the night before.

Judy sometimes hated to admit it, but Johnny was often right. It was apparent she was pressing her luck, and the drinks irritated something in her brain. *It's time to pull back on the leashes*. A knock on the door broke the silence of the bedroom and faded her worries for the moment. The door opened a crack.

"Jude?" Bud whispered. Judy pulled a blanket up to her chin, covering the dried blood and remaining still.

"Are you up, Honey?"

She considered pretending to sleep but changed her mind. "I'm awake, Bud."

He smiled. "Hearing you call me by my first name used to annoy me. Now it's the best thing in the world." Dread filled her face. "Our fishing trip never happened, and I wanted to know if you'd like to talk now," he said.

Folding inside Judy were many feelings to explore, and she wasn't ready to hear what he needed to say. If she ever would.

"I feel a little sick. Can we put a pin in our talk?"

Bud nodded. "Sure, Jude," he said.

The door closed as fast as he opened it, leaving Judy wondering how she would ever face her father again. She had no tangible reason to believe he did anything to her and yet doubt nagged at her—shut her off from the world.

The urge to get out of her blood-stained clothes gripped her. She jumped to her feet, pulled the shirt off, and threw it away like a crawling spider. Rifling through her drawer, she grabbed a concert t-shirt with the band name Skid Row across the front and the lyrics "I remember you" written on the back. Even though the shirt belonged to someone in their teens, she relished its irony as she slipped it over her head. While running a brush through her hair, Johnny's wrapped manuscript loomed next to her. Her phone erupted into a violent buzz that made her take a step back, away from the bundle of written words. When it rang once more, her hand was grabbing to answer.

"Hello?" First, a hollow electrical sound entered her ear, and soon, the phone screamed to life with a voice on the other end of the line.

"Judy—hey, it's me," She saw who it was, but a part of her pretended for a second, she didn't, "It's Johnny." Her eyes lit up when she heard his name.

"It's you?" Her question made Johnny laugh.

"It's me, sugar. I'm sorry I haven't called. It's been crazy. The number of authors here is plain ridiculous. And I don't mean just the quantity. There are real heavy hitters here. You know who I saw walk right in the hall before me?" Judy shook her head and then realized he couldn't see her. "Stephen King."

"Wow," she said.

"I paid the front-desk clerk an attractive price to get a room right next to him. Something tells me I'm going to get some amazing book ideas just being around all these writers."

"Johnny, you are every bit as good a writer as they are. Your writing is amazing. They'll be trying to steal from *you*."

"You think so, honey?"

"God, yes. I miss you so much. I'm just not myself here."

"Here, where? Aren't you back home?" Johnny asked. The answer was right there on the tip of her tongue. It sat there, smiling at her for a long time. Either she couldn't grasp her decision to stay, or she wasn't ready to accept it yet.

"I'm leaving soon, Johnny. I promise," she said, gripping the phone tight enough to cut into her palm, "I wish I was there rubbing elbows with all you fancy writer types, anyway." A genuine laugh returned from the other end.

"Bunch of shop talk...that's all. If one more panel attendee asks me—where do you get your ideas from, Mr. Macklemore? I might have to swan dive from the window."

"Jump out of Stephen King's room—the view will be better going down."

"You know I can't mess up this pretty face. Jokes aside, I don't feel comfortable with you being there. Go home," Johnny said.

"Message received. Don't stay up too late."

"Never do. Love you, babe," he said.

"Right back at you." When she heard the line disconnect, it renewed her. She was a ghost, moving in and out of other planes and not committing to any. The copy of *To Kill a Mockingbird* lay on her desk. It was much more than pulp, and it radiated power. She endowed the book with so many possibilities she didn't understand. The book was a portal to another time and place. Judy could touch her younger self, or at least her more youthful person stretched out to her.

The concept of time travel never held much weight except in the science fiction novels she bought from the used bookstores growing up. That someone could reach across time and reveal secrets to the future was laughable, bordering on ridiculous. She understood the messages in the book were from a child playing with encryption like finding a decoder ring in a box of Crackerjack. It didn't matter what she believed. Essential things never came across as accidents.

Deciding, Judy picked the book up and held it in her hands. It was as light as air, but she recognized a weight just the same. She turned to her page codes and again saw her last name written in sharpie. Angel became a new meaning for her.

"Judy," Emily said with the door swinging inward. With her focus centered on the book, the interruption half drove her from her skin. She fell back on the bed and guarded the paperback as if she suspected someone of taking it from her, then relaxed when she saw her mother.

"A scare like that could kill someone," Judy said.

"Forgive me. It has been so long since someone has been in this room. I would pass by your door like I do every day, and then I remembered you were here—couldn't stop myself."

"Forget about it," Judy said.

"A wish came to mind this morning," Emily sat down on the bed, "decades have passed, and I know you won't be here much longer...I'd like to take you out to lunch and buy you some clothes."

"Really—"

"Do this for me. If I were a better mother, I would have tracked you down years ago. Give me this, please." Judy regarded a pile of the clothes she brought with her. Most were shiny, and all made her wince with shame.

"Because my clothes are suitable for either a trip to Las Vegas or a midnight rave, I'll go." Emily wrapped her arms around her daughter, squealed, and hopped on her toes. Excitement burst through her expression. Judy wasn't thrilled as she grabbed the stuffed mockingbird from a shelf and squeezed its body.

*　　*　　*　　*

Throughout the car ride, Judy watched the town she grew up fly by in a blur. She recalled the bystander's account of her perched on the Olentangy river bridge. She had no recollection, but her imagination was as healthy as ever. A successful author as a husband isn't always easy. Many women went without, and she was lucky for her comfortable life. Emily pulled her minivan into the parking lot.

"Soak it all in. People keep telling me malls are going the way of the dodo." They scanned the structure with business signs covering the building.

"Can't argue. My purchases are all online," Judy said, "And we are waiting for what? Let's do some damage." Judy had to admit—there was nothing like the extravagance of a mall. The vaulted ceilings and polished marble screamed of the decadence long gone, a monument to consumerism.

Families walked past, and she wondered how their paths led them there. She looked different from them—similar animals yet distinct species. They moved in and out of her view like inhabitants in a zoo enclosure. Judy stroked the mockingbird inside her pocket, caressing its soft fur and soothing her fears while she did. *Do I belong here with these people? In this community?*

"Having an only child has never been a normal thing for you or us, Judy," Emily said. They sat in a seat at a table in the middle of the mall. Patrons walked past on either side of them, carrying shopping bags of all sizes. The shuffle of their feet and bright chatter surrounded them and gave them a feeling of sitting in a hive.

"I know, Emily."

"You haven't called me by my name since you've arrived."

"Sorry—"

"No, I like it. Many children were just that—children. But not you—it was like having another adult with us and discussing adult topics. You never called us Mom and Dad. That was strange for outsiders—they didn't know our relationship."

"Staying gone was wrong of me. The years went by so fast, and I never realized I was away until now," Judy said.

"Hardly a day has gone by when I haven't thought of you. Years have inched along for your father and me," Emily said.

"Hearing that makes me feel bad. I want to make up for my absence. The longer I'm here, the more I feel like myself," Judy said.

"It's no different for me." They sat in silence for a long moment. "We were happy that you found someone like Johnny to take care of you, and his success was impressive. Every so often, someone would write about one of his books—your name would come up, and I'd get excited. But a part of me wished they were writing about you. Why did you give up on your writing?" Emily asked. Judy rubbed the mockingbird with enough force to scrape off a patch of fur.

"Those answers aren't as easy, Emily. The passion for writing has never left me and will never go away. An idea will come to me. Sometimes in the morning—taking over my mind like a flame. I can see the entire story in my mind—the characters—beginning to end just like when I was a child; by the next day...all gone."

"How's that possible?" Judy shrugged.

"Maybe muses exist, and mine is having fun with me."

"It's something else," Emily said. Judy let up on the mockingbird for a second as something clicked. She wasn't sure what it was, and it contained the cloudy form of reality right before waking as the dream-world dissolved.

"Stories. I feel them inside me. Locked away, but still there—but trapped. They're my babies. The ones I never had, and they're calling out to me," Judy said.

"We can figure this out, Jude."

"That's never been said out loud. I've considered it a thousand times, but I was afraid that Johnny might think I was crazy."

"Crazy will never describe you. You're brilliant, and we will find your stories and find your voice again. I promise." Emily's words comforted her even as they sounded like the sentiment parents gave their children when they saw they were powerless to help. Because of a change of scenery or the dip into the Olentangy river, either way, Judy sensed a shift taking place. Something frightening was crystalizing, spreading toward conscious thought, and enveloping her like a blanket. She welcomed any change.

Chapter Fourteen
—Secret knothole—

The paperback copy of *To Kill a Mockingbird* sat in the center of Judy's bed like a living, breathing thing. From childhood, the book held so much authority over her, and its power increased since she's been away. *Follow the breadcrumbs.* The words splashed against her skull as if someone else besides her spoke. The book was a wild animal that she grabbed with a quick ability as if she were taming it with her hands alone. Her grip tightened further, feeling the creases in her palm. Opening it was like a foolish idea that made no sense. The book lay untouched a thousand miles away for decades, and she suspected it was speaking to her.

Judy had to know. She spread the pages away from the back cover and saw the familiar handwriting, the handwriting of Angel. A new code sat waiting for someone to solve its riddle. Where would Angel lead her? What could a teenage Judy have to say to her after all these years? Her heart raced when she scanned the words: *Where Boo Radley hid gifts*
At first, the words made little sense until they did. Judy remembered the knothole from the story in the book and recalled Boo Radley hid gifts for Scout and Jem in the knot of an old dying oak tree. *A secret knothole. But how does this apply to me?*

Judy turned her head around in the child's bedroom for a clue or anything that might give the riddle away. A framed picture of a tree hung on the far wall. It was a thin cherry tree in full bloom. She shook her head and continued her search. It wasn't enough, and she guessed it might not even be inside her home. Feeling discouraged, she glanced back to the breadcrumbs. Judy lost her breath when she found more words and allowed the giddy moment to capture her as she read: *Always Start From The Beginning*

She hurried her decryption through the book and jotted down each letter until one word appeared: C-L-O-S-E-T

Her mouth spread, revealing teeth—a smile the lips couldn't contain. She was a woman possessed, bouncing off the bed with the closet in her sights and swinging the door open wide. Studying the walls, she found nothing but plaster holding up every wall. She began tapping behind clothes with nothing to satisfy her search. Her gaze fell to the large rug covering much of the floor except two inches from each wall. The two visible inches were wooden. That was all she needed to excite her imagination. Her hands shook when she coaxed the edge of the rug away from the wall. The soft fibers scraped against her fingers as they rolled the thick fabric into a larger and larger tube. With the carpet safely aside, she saw the wood planks lined side by side and in the center, a knothole.

The knot watched her as she watched it. The mystery in the hole threatened to suck her down inside and swallow her up like a hungry black mouth. Sliding a finger inside the knot, Judy expected the space narrowing as it clamped down on her, but it remained permanent. With a quick motion, the board flew upward and away from the floor.

Out of the hollow space, Judy slid a business card with worn edges. Part of the card turned a shade of brown from years of age. She blew the dust off the front, revealing an address with a set of gray angel wings hovering beside it. Below these were three monogrammed letters: AAU

She tried to connect with the address or the monogram and came up empty without even a flicker of recognition. A roadmap was peeking from inside the small hiding place, curled up toward the sky. When she brought it into the light, red ink circled several home addresses with the largest circle resting in the middle. Something white reflected in the shadowy area. Hands reached deeper, feeling their way until she grasped the object, and when she pulled it free, her eyelids opened wide. She held in her hands a stack of loose copy paper three inches thick. The top sheet of paper had two typed words in the center: DESERT LILY

Her head swiveled out of the closet and into her bedroom. After a moment of searching, she found what she wanted and stared intently. It was an antique typewriter sitting next to the window. Her grandmother used it to write to her grandfather when they were courting. Having the memory at her fingertips made her smile. Leafing through the typed manuscript brought back the evenings she spent writing it there in the bedroom. The story wasn't there, but she could imagine herself typing away. One idea led to another until she was experiencing it for the first time in so many years. It had been her nightly ritual, lost to her until that moment. She smiled again and touched her upper lip to find it damp with blood.

Judy found a handkerchief on the floor of the closet and brought it up to her nose. Before she wiped, she saw something brown on one side of the white cloth. Dried blood alarmed her senses. The handkerchief was there since the night she left so long ago. *My nose bled back then?* She wiped and watched the bright red liquid spread next to brown and didn't know what to think. Her first conclusion was a brain tumor, given the amount of blood loss in the past few days. *Wouldn't Otis Bain have found a tumor?*

Her mind returned to her novel. She marveled at the ocean of words as she fluttered the pages. As the years fell away, she'd grown to believe her opportunity to complete a book had passed her by, and yet in her arms now was the proof that she had the ability. Judy cried. Writing was the one thing she had always wanted to do, and there was hope again. She leaned back against the wall, escaping into her words.

Chapter Fifteen
—Foolhardy schemes—

The warmth of her coffee radiated through Judy's hands and burned her lips as she attempted to drink. She blew several times at its surface and went in for another taste. A knock at the door broke Judy and Cal's attention from each other, and before he could answer, the door swung inward. Maddie flew in like a hurricane.

"I'm here now. The meeting can begin. Coffee me," Maddie said with way too much energy. Cal handed her a hot beverage as she hugged Judy, then moved to do the same for Cal. There was a hesitation before she gave him an awkward embrace.

"Haven't seen you since high school," she said to Cal.

"Been a while," he said. Maddie tilted her head down at her feet.

"What did I miss?" Maddie asked. Judy noticed the strange interaction between Cal and Maddie and filed it for later.

"Last night, I read a novel I didn't even know I wrote, and it floored me." They saw the tears forming that she already tried to conceal. "It's hopefulness on my part...but I think it was as good as a Johnny Macklemore novel."

"Believable. You're an amazing writer," Maddie said.

"You always were," Cal added. Sipping her coffee slow, Judy decided how she would recruit the help of her two friends.

"My *ask*, tonight, is big. A hand is reaching across time—reaching out for me." Her friends said nothing. "The teenage Judy is a mystery to me. I guess I'm a different person now, but she wants to tell me something important."

"Reaching out...how?" Cal asked. Judy tapped her feet on the wood floor, giving her time to consider the answer.

"She's talking to me through my copy of *To Kill a Mockingbird*." Cal swiveled to Maddie, and he struggled keep a straight face. Judy noticed the glance.

"Go on," Maddie coaxed in a soft voice.

"Imagine if you didn't know how you got to where you are? Memories are like a web connecting where you began. I don't have that—not even sure when I lost it, but it's lost. I know how this will sound—she sent me codes that are leading me."

"Where?" Cal asked and sat back into a chair before he fell.

"Leading me to what I've forgotten. It's as crazy to me as it is for you. If I didn't stumble across my old book, I would have just gone back home content in my ignorance. I have a glimpse of what disappeared. An Angel is guiding me." Judy pulled the novel from her sweater pocket and extended it to Cal. The book held so much value that handing it over was difficult for her. Cal spotted the codes in a woman's delicate handwriting.

"Where exactly these clues from my Angel will lead me is impossible to know—not sure I can do it myself. Business always took Johnny away—and I don't want to go it alone anymore."

"You don't have to," Maddie said.

"I'm with you, too," Cal added. Judy found she was holding her breath before they answered. Air rushed out with relief.

"First off, I'm a Daphne and not a Velma." The sudden absurdity of them diving into a Scooby Doo mystery made them laugh sudden and hard.

"I'm a real detective, so I can't be Shaggy. What would others on the police force think?"

"You don't know what this means to me," Judy said.

"My help is way overdue. What is our first step?" Cal asked, a map landing in his hands even as the words fell from his lips.

"We start here. Angel circled this address for me to find." Maddie traced the red ink with her fingers.

"We go there tonight," Maddie said, tightening her lip, forcing a smile, and then reached over and hugged her friend once more. Judy didn't think her friends believed her, but it was all right with her if they went along for the ride to get to know the new Judy—see what makes her tick. There was no expectation that her book would lead them to anything other than a little girl's fantasy.

*   *   *   *

The car ride was about possibilities for Judy. What would she find at the circled address? She wanted to convince her friends that the link to her past was real, but the night's destination was the actual test. Where the map led would tell her whether the book's codes were nothing more than an impossible coincidence or the first step to reclaiming her life, if not her identity.

Judy watched Cal in the driver's seat several times. She imagined a life unlived. Instead of Maddie in the back seat, it would be their children talking or singing behind her. She shook her head as if clearing cobwebs. *You chose differently.* Judy stole one more glance at his beautiful face and saw kindness—or was it patience? Judy was a woman in need, and she suspected his approach to her came from that angle. Still, he was there sitting next to her—walking a tightrope into God knows what.

A song came on the radio. "LULLABY" by Billy Joel. Cal snapped to turn it to another station when Judy grabbed his hand.

"Wait," she said. Jarred by the quick grasp, Cal turned to her in surprise. "Think I like this song." His hand went back to the steering wheel as the melodic tune expanded in the car. Blood dripped from her nose and the *tunnel* came alive around her like a cocoon.

Cal was a young man, sitting in the car his parents gave him for graduation. His face was smooth, with none of the lines that years brought with it. Judy peered out of her teenage body at Cal with a love she couldn't describe. She adored this man next to her and every second they were alone was precious. Getting away from the parents and doing adults things together made her feel like her life with him was beginning.

After a moment, she realized she was seeing double. The Cal from long ago was driving in the sunlight, but this image was transparent enough to show the current Cal doing the same task with the sun setting

59

around them. The effect was a trippy doubling sensation that made her dizzy, until she tried to focus on one Cal or the other, and she was astonished to find she could do it easily. She switched from one reality to the other like changing the channel.

She was happy to be with Cal in both, but there was an allure to the years-ago scene that called her back. It thrilled Judy to see what it was like with Cal or more to the point, what she was like with him.

Deep inside the memory Cal swayed his hand, sunshine glistening off his young skin, and caressed her cheek. The smell of his skin entered her nostrils, giving her several other glimpses of times together. The first kiss— sharing of a meal—hearing the words "I love you" falling from his mouth.

"You're bleeding," Cal said. The words caused Cal's teenage form to morph with hostile speed back into his current image. The *tunnel* reality faded like it always did. Judy adjusted her eyes back to the failing light of day. She wiped at her nose, sensed the wet liquid, and imagined what it would be like to kiss him.

"Thanks," she said in a timid volume. Cal's eyes were back on the road, and Billy Joel's piano was ending. She stared at him, thinking about their first kiss, and the feeling she experienced at the café. The intimacy of her vision sent an embarrassing rush through her. There was so much she wanted to ask him, but Maddie was within earshot, and she locked the questions away for later.

Cal's car slowed its speed and came to a halt near a curb. They surveyed their shabby surroundings. These were older homes that used materials from a by-gone era. Although the structures were sound—dense wood, the rest of the facade—antiquated by the day's building standards— plaster instead of drywall—fuse boxes instead of breakers—asbestos siding as opposed to modern vinyl. The mostly ranch homes were in various degrees of decay. Some had roof issues while others required new windows. The neighborhood was a melting pot of aging sadness that got worse every season, she guessed.

"That's it, right there." Cal pointed at a white home across the street. Even as darkness slid in, they could tell the white of the siding had mildew forming along the bottom giving the house a dirty appearance like pants dragged through the mud. Cal pulled a revolver from inside his jacket, opened the cylinder to note the bullets, and closed it just as fast.

"Let's step back," Maddie said from between the car seats when she saw the gun in Cal's hand.

"Just an insurance policy...can't go in without some protection," Cal said with a wry smile. Judy furrowed her brows. "That didn't come out as I intended."

"Well, until we know what we're up against, keep it in your pants," she whispered, leaning next to his ear. She looked down at his lap, so briefly that it was their experience alone.

Cal froze with Judy already opening the car door to exit into the night. With her companions following, she walked unafraid toward the darkened house.

Edges of cracked concrete seemed to reach up to snag her by the shoes and might have accomplished the task if she hadn't seen the danger a millisecond before. Cal moved to get ahead of the group and made a stop for cover behind a tree. Maddie bumped into them both, mistaking them for their shadows.

"Maddie—this is serious. Don't bumble," Judy said with hushed words.

"Sorry," Maddie matched her volume. All windows in the home were black, with no figures seen behind.

"A covert tactic will not work if you intend to see this through tonight. I say we take a few days, maybe a week, and case this place until—"

"Absolutely not," Judy cut Cal off and spoke loud enough to make all three study the quiet block. "Neither of you know what it's like to walk around like a blank domino tile with no future and no past, and this is my only chance," Judy said.

"Don't be so rash, Judy. Patience," Cal said. Judy shook him off with the front door in her sights.

"You said you were with me. Well..." Judy leveled her face inches from his, "are you...with me?"

"Yes. I'm with you," he said, craning his neck to the front door. "Full frontal assault it is." Cal motioned for the ladies to follow as he crept up to the home first. As they glided for the door, Cal patted his pocket, as if to feel for the hardness of the gun. It was there, and he looked relieved. Standing inches from the door, Judy pushed Cal aside so she could be the one to knock.

Judy closed her hand into a fist and pounded on the door as hard as she could, making the wood shake. A hollow sound reverberated inward. Maddie took one step back as the sound of footsteps met the inside of the door. Although they were waiting for the door to open, the speed it propelled caught them off guard.

"What do you want?" A tall man with greasy hair yelled out at them from the open doorway. His voice thundered onto the porch and caused Cal to reach for his gun—a reflex. Shriveled would describe his body, despite his massive frame. An image of a grape maturing to a raisin popped into Judy's mind; it was as if something had drained his insides. Maddie was already moving back off the porch.

"Answer me!" His voice rose, taking on a maniacal tone. They stood shaking like visitors of Oz. Judy spoke first.

"We'll just take a second—"

"Get away from my house. If I have to tell—"

"Frank," a woman's voice matching his ferocity came from deeper inside the interior of the home. For the first time, the man filling the doorframe appeared vulnerable—his expression resembled a dog waiting for punishment. As if by magic, Frank disappeared from the door, and a woman took his place.

"Come in," she said. They followed her inside when their bodies told them to run for the car and its safety. Moving to the center of the living room, Frank retreated to the far side like a dog trying to choose whether to attack or flee.

"I'm Sue. And you are?" As the words tumbled from her mouth, she answered herself, "You're Judy Angel." Frank made the connection and pushed forward like a nipping hound.

"Get the hell out of here. We don't want you here," Frank said.

"Shut up, Frank," Sue's voice found a new level of intensity. "Get out of the room. Now." Frank had more to say, but his face went blank, either from her volume or her tone. He left the room, resembling a person with things left undone. Judy studied Frank as he left and then turned to Sue.

"Do you know me?" Judy asked. The sides of Sue's mouth turned upward, a grimace instead of a smile.

"Everybody knows the wife of the famous writer, Johnny Macklemore."

"Okay, you may know my husband. How do you know me?"

Maddie placed a hand on Judy's shoulder.

"Let's get out of here. She's some obsessed fan," Maddie whispered. Judy considered her comment and shook her head while never breaking eye contact with Sue.

"May we sit?" Judy asked. Sue nodded and motioned to an aging living room set. At this, Maddie's body seemed to stiffen in fear. Judy took her hand and jump-started her locomotion. She sat her friend down on a couch like a mother might a child. Sue watched all this with fascination.

"I'm *your* mother, Judy," Sue captured their attention, "Johnny Macklemore is my son," she said.

"Frank and Sue," Judy whispered. The wheels turned.

"Guess this meeting was overdue. Wouldn't you say?"

Judy could do nothing but nod.

"Been years since Johnny visited. When he did, you were never with him," Sue leaned in closer, "Why is that?"

"Not sure," Judy said.

"Suppose it doesn't matter. You're here now." Judy had so many questions about Johnny's childhood, and they would come and go over the years, but for the moment, she went blank. She flailed internally, trying to grab the words like a drowning person might for anything substantial.

"Sue—"

"Call me Mom, please." Calling a woman, she met only seconds before "Mom" was ridiculous, but since her arrival in Columbus, she was in the land of the absurd.

"Mom? What was Johnny like as a child? Did he always want to be a writer? What did he write? When did he take it seriously?" The barrage of questions came from nowhere. Or they were there all along, hovering just out of sight and waiting for the opportunity to ask.

"Until his books made the news and the bookstands, I never knew he was a writer," Sue said and reached in her pocket, slid a cigarette from a pack, and put it to her lips. A lighter was not far behind. With the fire touching the tip, she breathed in strong and blew out fast.

"He's sold so many books collectively. How's that possible?" Cal asked. Sue inhaled again and shrugged.

"Never saw him so much as write a to-do list," she said. The cigarette's tip burned bright orange at her mouth. "One thing Johnny possesses is motivation," Sue said.

"How so?" Maddie asked. Sue never turned to her but answered just the same.

"No one adapted to their surroundings like your husband. If he wanted to learn something, nothing would get in his way, ever. Frank and I figured he might have a photographic memory—he kept so much and so fast." Things became clear to Judy for the first time in her life. Their marriage worked because they were opposites. Johnny possessed the memories she lacked and was there to make sure she wasn't alone in her void.

She peered at the white band wrapping around her finger where a ring once rested. A spasm of regret ached in her chest. Judy imagined the support given to her through the years, and within a brief time without him, she had become lost.

It was easy to consider their relationship as a crutch, and it was dawning on her that Johnny supported her. Judy's resolve to retrieve her past remained firm, but she didn't want to lose the awareness of who helped her when she didn't have solid footing mentally.

"The reaction of your husband to our arrival...why?" Maddie asked. Sue considered this as she stared over her shoulder toward where Frank departed and back to the group.

"Trust doesn't come easy for Frank. More than once, fans· have tracked down this house. Suppose the childhood home of a famous writer carries some value." Maddie nodded.

"I just felt like he recognized me," Judy added.

"He also drinks too much," Sue said in a whisper, "some days are better than others. Today—not so good. You drink, darling?" Judy shook her head.

"Rarely. Have little tolerance for the stuff," Judy said. She recalled her recent brushes with alcohol and the blood that flowed from each occasion.

"Good. Nothing more than nasty medicine. If you ask me, when you drain a bottle, it drains you," Sue said. Judy bet the woman saw many drunken nights living with Frank. Although Sue was a sober type, she shared the greasy, worn-down quality of her husband. Scanning the interior of the home gave Judy a sense of visiting a different era. The furniture and decorations were of excellent quality. There was a pretty penny spent on the furnishing many years before. Yet there was resignation in the surroundings—someone stopped caring.

"The three of us always hear a drinking lecture when Johnny visits," Sue remarked.

"Three?" Cal asked. "Johnny has a sibling? Never read that in his biographies." Judy was curious about this too, but what caught her attention was Cal's fascination with Johnny Macklemore. His knowledge of her husband struck Judy as odd.

"Wouldn't be awful for you to know the truth. I don't want the press nosing around. I want to protect Johnny," Sue said. Her posture slumped into her faded corduroy chair. "We have another child, older than John. A daughter, Tessa."

"Can I meet her?" Judy asked. Discomfort in Sue's face transformed how she saw the lady. They sat for a long time, and Judy assumed an answer wasn't coming.

"Yes...just you," she said. Sue was already up and walking deeper into the ranch-style home. Maddie and Cal threw Judy helpless expressions as she ran to follow her mother-in-law. She smelled perfume wafting off Sue. At first, she deduced nothing of the smell until she made the connection. It was the same fragrance she wore, and the one that Johnny always gave her. Sue halted in front of a bedroom door and turned to her.

"Discretion...that's all I ask," she said. All Judy could do was nod as Sue opened the bedroom door. With Sue entering and Judy following, she got her first glimpse of Tessa. She was leaning against her headboard, staring off into the distance. Hair matted across Tessa's face, giving her the drowsing appearance of a woman either heading toward or away from sleep.

"Hey, sweetie," Sue said in a gentle voice. Tessa never moved at the sound of her mother.

"What's wrong with her?" Judy whispered. Sue adjusted Tessa's footy pajamas. Although they fit, they were unsuitable for a woman her age.

"She fell sick," Sue said. The bedroom was an odd mix of children's toys and teenage distractions decorating the bedroom. Judy saw the living space for what it was, a snapshot of a girl's transition from child to woman. As if on a leash, she edged closer to her lying sister-in-law—testing her distance with Sue watching.

"May I?" Judy asked. Sue nodded. Judy swept Tessa's hair away from her face and mouth. Tessa never stirred, with eyes that perceived nothing.

"Turning sixteen, Tessa started forgetting things. It was humorous at first. Events from the night before slipped her mind, or the names of friends and family would vanish from her vocabulary. The doctors flirted with a diagnosis of Huntington's disease but settled on juvenile dementia."

"Does she know we're here?"

Sue's face went serious.

"As a mother, I want to think she does...the thought that she's trapped in a shell looking outward with no way of communicating might drive me to madness though, if I put all my eggs in that basket. The truth is somewhere in between. Things surely break through, but I'd wager it isn't too often," Sue commented.

"There's no cure?" Judy thought of her own Swiss cheese memory.

"If there was hope, it hasn't been around here for a while."

"How has Johnny dealt with her illness?"

Sue stroked her daughter's hair like she was a baby doll.

"You've seen Johnny's compassion. He always looked up to Tessa—he adored her. When we first noticed her symptoms, Johnny begged to stay by her side to sleep on the floor next to her every night he could. He was so devoted to her, and it tore him apart to watch her fade away."

Is that why you stayed with me for so long, Johnny? Did you take pity on me because of your sister?

The account of her attempted suicide came back to Judy and how she stood on the Olentangy river bridge and chucked her body into the water. It seemed unimaginable. *Simple answers were always the case.* In a moment of clarity, she chose to not be a burden any longer.

She was sad for the girl in bed and understood she was in the same boat. *How long would it take for her to lose her memory completely?* She had no way of knowing. Intuition screamed that the journey was long. Where did that leave her? *With the same fate as Tessa*, she guessed.

"Johnny's taking care of her medical bills, right?"

"My boy is taking great care of us," Sue said. Judy snuck a quick peek around and wondered how that was possible. Money hadn't touched the home in decades, and she had an inkling Tessa had no visitors, ever.

"I'm happy to hear that. I want to get involved if you'll let me," Judy said.

"You're family, dear. Always welcome," Sue said. Judy hugged her and again smelled the perfume on the woman's clothes. Walking out of the bedroom, she turned back to Tessa, who never moved an inch during the entire visit. The existence horrified her, sending a chill down her spine.

It was ridiculous, but her instincts told her to take her sister-in-law with her. Judy didn't find out Tessa existed until that day, and there wasn't any evidence of mistreatment to the woman—still, the need to take care of her was intense.

She told her goodbyes to Sue, and they moved toward the front door when Judy stopped.

"Judy, what is it?" Cal asked. She twisted to Cal and Maddie.

"Wait here," Judy said and headed to the back of the home, following the same path Frank took after their arrival. This part of the house was dark, and the hallway led to another living room in the back section. When she walked into the room, it smelled of beer and who knows what else. Her first sight was of a television flickering a sporting event. Frank sat in a recliner as close to the screen as possible. He didn't stir at her approach and as drunk as he appeared, she doubted he could hear her steps.

"Frank?" He turned to her as if she caught him in the shower.

"What do you want? Why are you in here?"

"When I arrived, you knew who I was and still wanted me gone. Why?" Frank regarded her with something other than anger for the first time. He gave her a smirk as if to say you are asking the right question. Frank leaned closer. That's what she waited for—but he dropped his body weight toward her. The alcohol was working on his motor skills, and she noticed.

"I've heard of you...don't know if you're involved," he said with slurred speech, "you may not believe someone like me, but alcohol helps. It's the only cure you got," he said.

"The cure for what?" she asked. The smell of beer was strong in her nostrils.

"We all think of ourselves first...don't we?" He returned to his waiting beer. "I'm always ready. I pride myself on being prepared."

"Prepared for what?" He laughed, and the creases in his face deepened with the jovial outburst.

"You aren't a threat unless you're the best actor in the world. You don't have a clue. Do you? Maybe I will let you in on—"

"Frank?" Sue materialized in the doorway. "Does it give you pleasure to play with a woman? She's our family. You can drink as much as you want but crawl into a hole and leave the rest of us alone," Sue said. Coaxing with a gentle pull, Sue moved Judy away from her husband. Judy pushed the hair from her face and took a deep breath.

"Forgive him for his behavior. He's not around people much anymore," she said.

"It's fine," Judy said. At the door, Sue hugged her for the last time.

"You come to visit us again, and I promise to keep Frank sober." Judy nodded and left the Macklemore home.

The car ride home was quiet. Judy couldn't get over how the destination turned out to be Johnny's family—her family, now. The red circle, outlining the address, was too ominous to be nothing at all. The streetlights went by in a blur, causing a strobe effect that soothed. She couldn't get over the image of a grown-up woman in a child's pajamas. The sight of the kid's room—the blank stare that wanted to move—to do anything except remain motionless. It was too much to bear—a prison inside her mind. Things so horrific didn't show up in her worst nightmares, and she was sure the images would soon.

Cal stopped his car in front of Maddie's house. Although Maddie was still shaky from the night's experience, she refused Cal's escort and promised to talk soon. Judy had noticed her smile when it turned out that Frank and Sue weren't the Manson family, and she might survive the quest. An adventure might be just what Maddie needed. Judy suspected her friend spent most of her waking moments inside her drab home. The reason she shunned the outside world was still a mystery. Maddie was out into the night air and that was good. The mission to resolve Judy's mysterious past gave her—gave them all—a reason to be together.

*   *   *   *

Cal scooted into a parking spot in front of his home. Emily Angel's car shone in their headlights a second before they went out, leaving her borrowed transportation again in a blanket of darkness. The air was brisk the way Ohio weather got right before Halloween. Residents might as well toss a coin any morning of October to decide whether a jacket was the smart move. Unfortunately, Judy didn't choose wisely, and she shivered from her lousy planning.

"I know the right thing to shake that," Cal said.

"Shake?"

"I have some amazing Sumatran blend coffee that I've *been* saving well over ten years for your visit tonight." The absurdity of the statement made her laugh despite her mood. She glanced at her mother's car, dark and lonely, and back to him.

"One cup...then I have to get this antique tank of a car back to my parents." Cal flashed her a smile and fumbled into his pocket for the house key. He showed it to her like a dog retrieving a bone. She gave a "great job" smile and loosened her exaggerated grin before she appeared maniacal in the sparse-lit night.

His movements to open the door resembled a normal human being, and within a few gestures later, the door was open, pushed inward with a nudge, as Cal extended an arm to enter. She watched this and did just that. The living room was dark when Judy entered. Cal, from behind, clicked on a switch. Lights from several parts of the home illuminated the small room and made an ottoman standing in her path visible before she toppled over it.

"Our feast awaits in the kitchen, mademoiselle," he said in the worst French accent possible.

"If you don't do that voice again, I'll join you," she said.

"I'll have you know...I studied with the most learned French educators in all of France to perfect this accent," Cal said with a grin.

"No wonder the French hate us."

It was his turn to laugh as he stuffed a coffee filter into the maker, scooping the grounds right after, and snapping on the power button. She watched the clear button turn an orange-red color. Before she could protest, he pulled a pizza box from the fridge and slapped it on the kitchen table in front of her. When he opened the cardboard box, it stunned her that the pie was untouched.

"Get back, vampire," she said, teasing. "Who can resist a pizza?"

"Tell me why we make a pizza round, place it in a square box, and cut it into triangles?" Cal asked.

"Even I've heard that one before."

"You're talking to a bachelor. I buy two pizzas and eat the second the next day. It is now the next day," he said, grabbing a slice. "Nuke it?"

"Kidding me? Nothing in the world better than cold pizza," she said.

"I know. Had to know if that was the same," Cal said with a sad smile. The feeling that Cal understood something she didn't revisited her.

She didn't like it and pondered throwing him an expression of disgust but shoved the tip of a slice in her mouth instead.

"So, a cop, huh?" Embarrassment transformed his face, and she noticed.

"Detective Calvin Reed at your service," he said.

"I honestly didn't mean it as that sounded."

"No, it's fine."

"A Boy Scout is what I would peg you for, Cal. Even if I didn't lose my memory." she smiled to get him to smile back, and he did.

"Helping others was...my path. Becoming an officer was just logic playing itself out in front of me. My first plan when you left was joining the military."

"What went wrong with that plan?" she asked with a mouth full of dough.

"The recruitment office saw me way more than once during those days...I guess I wanted to be here in Columbus just in case." She studied him the way a child might watch a kite take air and soar skyward.

"In case of what?"

"Know what? It might be a sin, but I think I need to microwave this one. It's too cold on my teeth."

"Wimp," Judy said. The pizza was spinning in the microwave before she had the chance to react. He pulled out the microwaved pizza, flopped it onto the table. The top of the cheese glistened from the grease with the topping wilting from an overnight in the refrigerator.

"Memories might be sparse for you, but they are too many to count from this side of the table," he said. He pretended to consider his slice before taking an enormous bite. Remnants of cheese stuck to his chin, and he wiped at it several times until satisfied with the results.

"Cal... I'm sorry you think I somehow abandoned you. Trust me when I say I can read that on you. The thing is—choosing Johnny was not a reflection on you." An uncomfortable laugh escaped Cal.

"If I didn't know any better, I would swear you rehearsed that line for years," he said in a harsh tone.

Judy went silent. Gazing off in any direction, Cal wasn't in view. She saw nothing at all—then, she focused on the photos that hung on the walls. Judy swiveled her head around to see as many of them as she could. A breath came out hard when she realized she was holding it too long. The frames contained pictures of her—alone with Cal—or with other people, but always her. With little focus, the images appeared normal enough.

When she saw her face repeated in one photo after another, it caused her heart to race. Still hurt from her words, Cal never noticed the scrutiny she gave the shrine, built around him, in the modest home. She remembered their visit to Sue and Frank's and the words he said to her. *Johnny has a sibling—I never read that in his biographies.* Cal saw the fear in her eyes.

"Judy?" She remained still. He leaned across the kitchen table until she put a finger up into the air. The gesture was a visible warning, but it could also be a motion for someone to say *one second while I collect myself.* Whichever way Cal took it, he stopped in his tracks and retreated from their neutral zone.

"Reminiscing over a lost love isn't what this is about, Cal." She no longer saw him—lost in contemplation. And her only thought was self-preservation.

The part of her that wanted to escape into the night caused her hands to shake. The other part, who wanted to know the answers to the void that was her reality, caused her hands to clench into fists. She gazed down and remembered how she was before she knocked on her mother-in-law's door.

"You know a lot about Johnny Macklemore, don't you?" she asked, leveling her face to his and wanting any reaction he let slip. He gulped, pulled the half-eaten slice to his lips, and instead threw it back onto his paper plate. He sniffled into a napkin and gave her a sinister grin.

"I know a lot about Johnny," he said, returning her gaze.

"Between the two of us, you're the cop," she spat out like a slapping hand, "but I'd bet you have a box or a wall, maybe more than that, covered with images of Johnny. Newspaper clippings—book signing dates—a lock of his hair?" Cal sat there, stone-faced.

"I have a huge box," he said. "Would you like a beer? Because I'm having one." Beer was out of the refrigerator and in his mouth like a baby receiving a pacifier before a tantrum. His admission was unexpected, and she had nothing to do but stare at him as he downed a Bud Light way too fast. He hadn't finished the beverage, but he was already on his way to replace it with another. She sat there dumbstruck by his rush from sobriety. He drank another one down fast and grabbed another. The carbonation caught in his throat, causing him to give a painful belch.

"Obsession is the word I would use as well..." He wrapped his arms around his head like a boy practicing a school tornado drill, "There's no way for me to explain without sounding...crazy," he said, punching the air. "It wasn't supposed to happen like this," he said.

"I'm going," Judy said, as toneless as a robot. Cal placed both his hands up into the air like a traffic cop directing a car to a stop. She saw this and did as instructed without knowing why.

"Are you happy? He provides security. How about happiness?" She couldn't remember someone asking her the question before, and it had an impact, skewing her thinking. Living with a thriving artist left little self in the equation. Even if Johnny had time for her, the busy schedule of a writer pushed other, less essential tasks, to the side. A new book became the primary focus within the writer's sphere. *Guess I'm in his sphere.* Cal's question hit home, but if she told him so, down the rabbit hole they both fell.

"Johnny was there for me when no one else was. Loyalty isn't even a strong enough word to describe him," she said. Judy imagined him enduring her even as the memories vanished. Tessa's blank face popped in again. *What a patient man.*

"No one else was there for you...because you ran away," Cal shouted.

"I never ran," she said, and wondered if she did, "I moved on." She saw him flinch and realized it's what she wanted...she didn't want to see it through.

"Take me out of the argument." Cal leaned on the table, moving closer. "I never met a girl who was as close to her parents as Judy Angel."

"Macklemore," she corrected, and he nodded.

"In over ten years, how many times did you visit your parents?" He waited for an answer that never came. "A call?" Judy turned away. "A note...to see if they were still alive?" Judy returned a watery stare his way and didn't want him to see her tears, to know her weakness, but that was out the window. She could argue with anything he threw at her except her parents. Judy didn't have a piece to that puzzle just yet. Many ideas floated in and out as she fell back to a vivid dream of her father's late-night visit. She pushed the thought away so fast, squeezed her eyes shut tight. *One thing at a time, Judy.*

"And what did I ever do to you that kept you from picking up the phone?" Cal asked. He backtracked to himself, and she was glad for his retreat.

"Writing has always been my identity. Maybe that was my attraction to Johnny."

"You heard Sue just as I did. He never wrote a thing in his life before you left with him."

"Maybe I was his muse," Her comment came out more flippant than she intended.

"You're the writer...and you always were." The words broke through her defense. "Words—phrases—getting lost in the stories...your stories. When I called you each morning, you'd say you fell asleep on a book or with it on you. More writing talent came from you than anyone ever. Tell me you didn't feel that spark when you read your words the other night?" She remained silent. "Writing for you wasn't pretend, or a child's fantasy of what you want to be when you grow up. You were about to spread your wings and fly because of your writing." His onslaught made her weak. Johnny was a good man, but she also knew that she once lived in words. She could tell the passion by inspecting her bedroom in her parent's house. "Think I wasn't afraid I'd lose you to a writer's world? But I would not hold you back. Has Johnny?"

"The car's got to go back to the parents," she said, pulling herself upright. Cal reached over the table in one quick motion. Her eyes went round. He clutched her necklace and turned it over to reveal the carved words: STAY AWAKE

"Take your advice, Judy Angel." Showing her the scratched words was aggressive, assaulting her senses, and afterward, getting up and stumbling toward the door had the dreamy quality as if she suffered from a punch.

He said something from behind her she didn't try to hear. Falling through the door and taking the porch steps two at a time, Judy breathed in the fresh air and understood October's genuine power—like a bucket of ice water hitting her face. Her mind swam with every word Cal had spoken. There was a scary value in hearing an inner dialogue falling free from the sky like throwing knives into the air without regard to where they landed.

Chapter Sixteen
—One evening after supper—

Judy wanted nothing more than a good night's sleep. She decided on a healthy dose of Benadryl—hoping to fade all her invading thoughts of her father. Instead of a peaceful rest, Judy's vision began as they all had since coming to her city in Ohio. The translucent *tunnel* grew on her like a creeping fungus. Her memories were Polaroids that revealed the events enough to remember, even as the light-sensitive plastic of the photo faded with each passing moment. She believed that was what memories were, a slice of time captured unharmed and deteriorating ever after. Sure, her memory was faltering faster than others, but everyone's recollections ended up in the same place. With life, no one gets out alive, and the remembrances go first.

Although she was getting the hang of experiencing these fresh memories through Angel, the troublesome part was figuring out her age right away. An attitude was the first sign to hang her hat on. When she was a teenager, the feeling was love or excitement, or even lust when she drew back to ones containing Cal. When she inhabited her younger Angel this time, things felt dangerous.

At one point while experiencing another memory, she peered out of the body of her six-year-old self—a solid year after her car crash. It struck Judy as odd how quick and precise this younger self was in the vision as compared to how lethargic and muddy her thinking was right after the accident. *How could I have progressed with such speed in that short of time?* She wondered if the recollections were trustworthy. Memories injected through the syringe of a dream world had some extra ingredients. But she was a woman drowning, reaching out for a lifeline. Who was *she* to question anything that delivered her some essence of who she was?

Understanding her visions was akin to tightrope walking, despite that, she was learning to navigate the reality like she had done it before. Riding a bike came to mind on the outside, even though she was aware it was nothing like riding a bike. Even as ordinary scenes played out for her, the terror that dreaming contained stayed with her always. The terror was irrational like dreams or nightmares—full of adrenaline.

More evidence she was finding her balance on the tightrope came when she sensed the illusion. She was breathing, and she felt that—the bedroom was warm, and she felt that, too. She recognized the blood flowing over her top lip, with some going into her mouth.

In the vision, Angel sat in the kitchen with her parents—both were there. Emily was younger with no wrinkles touching her skin yet, and although gray was attempting to infiltrate her brown hair, she carried a youthful image that she now missed so much from her mother. *Did I cause those wrinkles and gray hair to take over? I hope not.*

The woman standing in front of her was substantial—full of life. Emily scooped up an egg and shuffled it onto a plate next to an already waiting slice of bacon. Little Angel cut into the body of the egg like a surgeon might. The yellow liquid oozed from it, and she was already dabbing it with the corner of a buttery piece of toast. Even as she saw this as a non-event, she relished it all the same. *I used to love eggs over easy.* The texture of the juicy eggs going down coated her throat and filled her in every way possible.

"I love breakfast for dinner, Emily," Judy heard her tiny voice squawk between bites.

"Make sure you eat every bite." Angel washed down the bread with orange juice, making a slurping sound and working hard to catch her breath after.

"I bet you can catch more fish on a full stomach," Bud said, rounding the table and sitting in a chair next to Angel.

The adult Judy sitting in her bedroom, jerked involuntarily at the sight of him. Her control of the vision ebbed—replaced with the image of her on a rollercoaster, strapped in awaiting gravity and the helpless plunge.

"So...I won't see you two until late into the night?" Emily asked as she made her plate of food last and sat with her family already in the middle of their meals.

Bud swallowed before answering, "I'd bet on that. There's an art to fishing. I intend to teach her the right way," he said and tossed a sideway smirk down to Angel. The younger Angel didn't acknowledge this subtle gesture from her father. But Judy saw it, and it frightened her.

As she watched, they continued to eat, and time became a factor for Judy. She didn't want the meal to end. Finishing up meant...*what did it mean? Where was Bud going to take her? Was it fishing?* There was something deeper inside that grasped the answer, and it pleaded for her to stop the event or delay it. But the incident already happened. Spectating to her past was all she could do. The slow trickle of regaining memories was torturous even as another part warned that getting the memories restored or knowing what she lost all at once might be dangerous for her brain. *How can I know such a thing?*

The car accident that damaged her came back into her mind, the one her parents had withheld, and again she wondered how she came back from that trauma. The kernel was small, but it gave her hope to know that if she made it back from that, she could make it back from the situation she faced. *It isn't impossible.* Her heart raced when she noticed her family clearing the last scraps from their plates. Angel was tipping the bottom half of a glass of orange juice and making a lot of noise.

"Ready, Jude?" Bud asked. Angel nodded and maneuvered her petite body from the wooden kitchen chair. Judy saw her mother turn away to tend to the dinner mess. *Stop them, Mom!* Judy was screaming for no one to hear. Emily continued to straighten the kitchen while Bud prepared to take Angel out into the night. He placed a coat onto Angel, buttoning each large button on the wool peacoat. When he climbed inside his jacket, he extended a hand that Angel took. *Mom. Please turn around.* As if she heard the voice years into the future, Emily turned around. Judy saw her face with no fear or apprehension. *Are you blind?*

"You two have fun tonight. Catch and release only. I don't want something stinky sitting in my sink when I wake up," Emily said. Bud leaned in and, still holding Angel's hand, dragged Angel along for the ride. He kissed Emily's cheek.

"Don't wait up."

"Don't wait up," Angel repeated in her smaller voice. Emily smiled at both with Bud leading her away. *You're just watching her go.*

*   *   *   *

As they sat in her father's car, the scene became a jumble of shadows and images. She supposed Angel was drifting in and out of a doze that made her freshly gained memories just a haze. Gauging time was hard as the driving went on and on. The darkness in the backseat was her world except for the occasional illumination from a streetlight accompanying a soft drone of the engine, and tires lulled both Judys. The iridescent light of the dashboard threw odd squiggles on the car ceiling's liner.

She stared at them for what was an eternity until the car slowed. Angel was shaking off the sleep as the car came to a complete stop. Bud leaned over the backseat toward her.

"Ready for this?" Angel nodded, slow. "Don't be afraid. I will never hurt you, Jude." She nodded again. As if it were a magic trick, Bud exited the car and appeared next to Angel's car window like an apparition. He opened her door, and she hopped onto the pavement. She was still clutching the fishing poles.

"Leave those, Judy. You won't need them tonight," he said. Judy had enough—more than enough. Judy wanted her memories back, but at what cost?

Angel obeyed and placed the poles back into the car. Judy saw the child wanting to keep them or keep the fishing date instead of the lie Bud told her mother. As he pulled her along toward a building, she couldn't make out because of the light, Angel looked down. Judy saw the pavement was red brick, laid in opposite directions crisscrossing and had a logical pattern until another section took on another design. The brick scheme made no sense and added to her discomfort. Judy went deep into her body to recognize the bed she was laying in and jerked her muscles. Although it was in her mind, Judy hoped it would translate to her physical body. *Wake up.* She didn't want to see the rest. *Wake up, wake up.* Bud moved to the door and disappeared as if the building ate him alive, and Angel was next. *Wake Up!* Judy focused her conscious mind on stirring her body, and before she was ready, the body jerked enough, and the vision dissipated—the *tunnel* dissolved. She wasn't all the way awake, just somewhere between the dose of sleep and brutal clarity of reality.

Light seeped in again, and she was so grateful she didn't receive all the memories of the night yet. And the speed they were arriving showed that they would come whether or not she liked it, and she didn't like it one bit. The vision made her feel more than embarrassed—it made her feel foolish, smiling at her father each night without knowing the truth. From the first day she saw him at the hospital, Judy had called him Daddy, and the word drew such endearing images that it now made her nauseous.

Why am I staying here? I can afford an expensive hotel. The answer that came back every time she wanted to move to a hotel or skip town altogether was the same—her mother. Emily was an innocent bystander to what her father did to her. There wasn't a doubt that Bud was the reason she left home and never returned. He was also the reason she had decided that a life with Johnny, a man she didn't know, was the best option.

As her thoughts churned faster than she could analyze or even deal with, they hardened Judy. And still, she couldn't bear to hurt her mother any further. There was too much at stake to bail on the whole situation, even though her intuition screamed to stop. A confrontation with Bud was on the horizon, and she also expected that when it happened, there would be no coming back from it—no more home—no friends—and depending upon how her mother reacted—no more mother.

Out of the corner of her eye, she saw the stuffed mockingbird on her nightstand. She leaned over and scooped it into her hands. She sat it on her stomach. It stared back at her with its beady eyes. *My father gave this to me*, she thought with disgust. *I made too many decisions because of him.* She picked the gray bird up and caressed the faux fur, making the tiny hairs flow one direction or another with each pass of her hand.

She squeezed the mockingbird tight, hopped off the canopy bed, and made her way to the closet, holding the business card with the letters AAU emblazoned on the front. Things she needed to discover were waiting for her. The night's vision was a reminder she would not like what she found, but why else was Judy there if not to become whole for the first time since she left with Johnny.

Judy's fingers closed around the business card as if it were a rose petal she hated to see destroyed. A part of her was familiar with the business card; it had much more value than she could ever describe. Her Angel left that for her to find and follow. Maybe Angel was the sole person she could trust. Maddie was a good friend, but Judy trusted herself—her Angel.

She considered Cal and his motives, whatever they were, and wished she had heard him out before storming away like a child into the night. As the past trickled in, it was hard to deny that she was still a child, stunted by her great escape so many years before. If she had dealt with the past instead of running away—the words *running away* performed cartwheels in her. That was her theme or her weakness. Did she always want to run away? Did she still have the option?

Judy snapped off the tags on one shirt Emily bought her, wiped her bloody nose with the sweater she had taken off, and slid on the new one, feeling its starchy unwashed skin against hers. The mockingbird and the business card remained in her hands as she glanced over at Johnny's manuscript lying neglected on the desk. This duty was the first one Johnny ever gave her regarding his writing, but she found other things that needed more attention. *When I get back tonight, straight to the publisher it goes.* Satisfied with her promise, she left her room, heading for the front door.

"Haven't got to see you much since you been back," a voice said from behind. "I'm missing you," Bud said. His voice made her skin crawl.

"Soon," she was calmer than she believed possible.

"Okay."

And with that, she was outside and away.

* * * *

When Maddie answered the door, the smell of alcohol was strong in the air. Judy wondered if Maddie bathed in it as she consumed it each night.

"Come on in," she said, like a mouth full of cotton. "Where's Cal?"

"Cal is no Calpurnia," Judy said. Maddie looked puzzled. "She's a character in *To Kill a Mockingbird*." All Maddie could do was nod. "You mind if we get going soon? I want to stay out in the October air as long as I can," Judy said.

"Yeah." Maddie backed away and headed for the bedroom. Judy heard drawers open and shut several times.

"Is Mystery Incorporated breaking up already?" Maddie shouted from another room and returned to her friend for the answer.

"Not sure yet," Judy said. "Guess I'm mulling over whether it's him or me that has an issue."

"It's the devotion that ruins the sauce," Maddie said, leading Judy through the doorway and locking it once she was clear. "I never had that problem myself, but I'd imagine you'd wonder what his motives were, putting someone before himself."

"Right. Maybe Cal is Calpurnia," she said and laughed. Maddie shot her another puzzled expression that didn't last as long.

"If I had to describe myself...cynic would walk to the front of the bus. One fact kept bubbling to the top—the defining characteristics always shine through. Since we were kids, Calvin Reed had been and always will be a Boy Scout, and you know that. I don't know what Cal's done. What I know is, whatever he did, it was with good intentions," Maddie said, piling into a worn-out car. "Are we going to get a new Fred?"

"No," Judy said in a pouting voice.

"Good...there aren't many out there like him. Where are we going?" Judy lifted the business card.

"Here."

Maddie nodded and pulled away. Their conversation was light during their ride, and Judy was happy for the long gaps of silence. More than once, Cal invaded her head. She regretted the way she treated him and leaving him out of the day's adventure. *I'll make it up to him.*

"If this card leads us to a third cousin of Johnny Macklemore, I'm going to be pissed," Maddie said.

"You and me both." Judy leaned her head against her passenger window, watching the people of Columbus driving or shopping—living out their lives as she spied on them from her cheap seat. One street blended without effort into another with no discernible differences, until something changed. It was the scenery, but it was more than the aesthetics that caught her eye and made her sit up straight in her seat.

"Where are we?" Judy asked, swiveling her head to spy through all the car windows.

"It's called German Village. It's kind of a world unto itself." Judy had no trouble believing that—enthralled from the first sight. The typical wooden structures that made up most of the city didn't apply there. Brick of every size and shape overwhelmed her faculties. The street itself was red bricks, carved and arranged so tight that she couldn't detect any gaps between the millions of cubes.

Stone churches, hand-carved by masters hundreds of years ago, reached high into the Ohio sky. They lent themselves to fortresses rather than homes or businesses. Although brick was the primary material used in the neighborhood, no two structures were the same. The builders had used some bricks pressed like smooth marble while others had the rough, rustic charm provided by some long-ago artisan.

Her heart sank at the sight of everything around her. There was history—a past that wanted to reveal itself to her. Some homes were like normal Brownstones, and certain unique homes appeared like castles meant as a barrier to protect the inhabitants. There was a character German Village had—shaped by antiquity.

Above all these things, Judy perceived something else that was indescribable. Something you found in the soul. It was astonishment, but more than that, there was a coming-home feeling as if she belonged there. A spiritual part of her, resting below the surface, allowed the view to enchant her.

"This place is amazing," Judy said.

"I guess so," Maddie agreed, driving on but checking in on Judy every few moments. The streets were beautiful—that she could attest to—still, Judy's reaction was childlike. Pure—undiluted rapture. Judy pressed against the window hard enough to leave a mark.

"Do you visit this area a lot?" Judy asked, not drawing her attention away from the outside world.

"Yeah. The crème puffs at Schmidt's Sausage Haus down the street are to die for, in my opinion. They had me acting like a crack addict for a while." They continued their ride, twisting and turning down the one-way streets of the village. The businesses morphed from one innate structure to the next until an image captured Judy's attention. Before she realized she would do it, she screamed.

"Stop the car." As if it were a warning that she was about to hit a child or a stray dog, Maddie slammed on the brakes, and it caused both to feel the hardness of the dashboard.

It was a Victorian-style home, converted into a business. On the front of the establishment hung a red banner: The Book Loft

"I know this place." They exited the car with Maddie nodding until she realized Judy didn't know she was there and stopped.

"Yeah, you would…you spent nearly every cent you ever had in this place and dragged me here far too often. It's an oddity here in Ohio," Maddie said.

"How so?"

"It's our version of the Winchester mansion."

"I never heard of it," Judy admitted but kept watching the bookstore.

"The original site used to be a saloon," Maddie said. "Owned by a couple, Maureen, and Oscar. The story goes, he turned into a werewolf, and if they didn't keep a candle burning, he would return to claim her."

"Seriously?" Judy asked.

"Here is where it gets weird. Years later it became a business for a young spiritualist named Amelia. They said she conjured a demon in the basement. And once it arrived, she didn't know how to rid the world of it.

So, she kept building rooms to confuse the entity. And that's why there are 32 rooms in *The Book Loft*. Amelia figured out a loophole that would keep the ghosts away. The legend says it remains trapped in the cellar."

"Then what?" The story enthralled Judy. "Until her death, Amelia had workers constructing additions that were unbelievable. Halls that stopped for no reason—rooms with dead-ends. You name it, and she built it, hoping to fool the spirits, and throwing them off her trail."

"Did it work?"

"Some say yes, and others claim they got to her."

"Why are you telling me this?"

Maddie pointed to The Book Loft. "Inside that bookstore is thirty-two rooms that defy logic. No two rooms are the same. Some paths and hallways are not much wider than a small child. I got lost in there once before I got the lay of the land, and I'm sure others experienced the same when it wasn't so busy or near closing time. I believe there was magic in that place and I think you thought so, too."

Invisible strings pulled Judy toward the bookstore that called to her with Maddie's story ringing in her ears. Dread washed over her when she tilted her head down. In front of Judy lay a sidewalk made of red bricks *laid in opposite directions, crisscrossing* just like in her vision the night before. She froze in place.

"Judy?" No answer. "What's happening?" Maddie was a faraway voice as Judy scanned the intricate brickwork, following the path to the face of a building. Tilting her head upward, she took in the concrete monstrosity. The building had the aesthetics of a bastille with its rounded corners. The once-white concrete had turned a dark gray that made her think of the movies featuring dank dungeons. There were hundreds of small square windows lining the exterior that didn't seem to serve any purpose except to impose itself onto anyone watching.

On autopilot, the two ladies shuffled to the front of the building. Judy glanced to her feet and recognized the same image from her vision the night before—like a glitch in the software that spat out the same sight twice for good measure.

She took a hesitant step as if the building could spring to life and devour loiterers. She adjusted her glasses and trained her eyes on a deteriorating shingle that dangled from a single chain—its partner hung and swayed around the front of its body, greeting her with its feeble arm. On the sign were the same Angel wings decorating the front of the business card. She fished it from her pocket and brought it up, lining it side by side with the shingle. Unlike the card, next to the wings were three large words: ANGEL AMONG US

"This is where Bud took me...instead of fishing...we ended up here." Maddie smeared the windows to see inside.

"Your father took you here?" Emotions came on fast, but Judy held them back. "This place hasn't been open in—hell, I don't know how long," Maddie said. "It's been boarded up a long time, though." The longer they stood outside, staring at the shape of the building, the more it resembled a prison.

"He lied to my mother...me too, I guess...brought me here in the middle of the night." *Why did he take me here?*

"What did he do?" Maddie asked, a hair above a whisper.

"That's what I want to find out. I need to know everything about this place," Judy said, clenching her teeth.

"I know someone," Maddie offered. Judy turned to her, burning into her with such intensity that it made Maddie take a step back.

"Who?" The question came with such speed that it caused Maddie to take another step away from her friend.

"She was a friend from high school." Judy heard all she needed to hear and was already planning.

"Send directions to Cal and have him meet us at your friend's home," Judy barked. As they moved to leave, Judy gave *The Book Loft* one last wistful peek. *Some other time.*

Chapter Seventeen
—Beckoning in the moonlight—

October skies were often gray in Ohio, and tonight was no exception. A brisk wind howled. It was an icy knife whipping at any skin, not bundled. Moonlight, full, and round, shone overhead and made the shadows into small, husky creatures tagging along for the ride. The tall build of Cal made more significant from his diminutive shadow clinging to him.

"Had no clue this place even existed," Cal said, out of breath from a mixture of his hike and the frigid air circulating in his lungs. The area was next to German Village and was a sad reflection to its neighbor. Although they built both areas around the same time, this one never had the fortune of experiencing the gentrification that German Village enjoyed. Instead, the homes appeared to be in the throes of an incremental death from neglect.

"You girls need to stay close to me," Cal said. Maddie flashed a look of disgust that Cal never saw.

"We can handle ourselves," Maddie countered. Cal raised his hands as if to say he surrendered. He kept a wide berth, orbiting Maddie, and planted himself in front of Judy.

"Should we discuss last night?" Cal asked in a hushed tone. She shook him off.

"It can wait," Judy said, smiling. Her forgiving signal caused his posture to loosen even in the frosty night.

"Okay, we're here."

"Where is here?" Judy asked. All faces turned toward her.

"Her name is Becky..." Maddie rubbed her hands together like starting a fire, "and the thing is...well, nobody knows the history of German Village better than her—"

"The catch?" Cal thundered.

"She's...unusual," Maddie admitted.

"How unusual?" Judy asked.

"Very." Maddie witnessed the group wilt. "She's a good person...just eccentric."

"How do *you* know her?" Judy asked.

"She went to our school. A friend during my wild times," Maddie said and took a deep breath, then knocked on the door. Paint peeled in several spots and noticeable warping rippled along the bottom from snowy winters. They exchanged uneasy glances. "Harmless," Maddie reassured. The door swung inward. Her hair was long and blonde, but so frizzy that Judy suspected it painful to tame every morning. She wore faded jean-overalls that Judy was sure hadn't been sold in stores for many years.

"Come in. Come in," Becky said in quick succession. When they entered, she slammed the door as if to keep out a stalking wolf—the door missed Judy by an inch at most. Becky wasn't a small woman, and when she walked in the older home, the floor expelled a creak with each step she took.

"Please sit," Becky said, talking fast. Judy wondered if the coffee was the culprit or some other chemical enhancement. The home on the inside differed from the aging exterior. The décor was sparse but neat. Becky took pride in her home, and Judy took note.

"Nice to meet you...Maddie told us all about—"

"You don't remember me, do you?" *Not again.* "You wouldn't, and I wouldn't expect you to."

"Sorry, I don't," Judy admitted.

"High school wasn't among my greatest accomplishments. You...had school figured out. Maybe better than some teachers," Becky said and let out a howl of laughter, leaning in and nudging Judy to emphasize the strength of the joke. They passed nervous laughs to each other. "By senior year, you were already the school's Virginia Woolf." Becky craned her neck to Cal. "She was an English writer."

"I know," he said, with too much force that Becky never noticed.

"One of my last important papers—it helped me get the diploma— you proofread for me."

"I did?" Judy asked, surprised. Becky nodded as fast as she did everything else.

"The red you left on that paper..." She rattled her head back and forth, and it hurt Maddie to see her do it. "Most high schoolers would not have had the guts to shred someone's writing like you did me," Becky said and leaned in again, and this time without her cackle, glided her face to Judy's until their noses touched. Judy became still, like a doe alert to sudden movement. "You tore it apart. I saw nothing like it before or since." Judy swallowed as Becky broke their invisible barrier. Arms went around Judy as Becky pulled her in for a hug. Judy recognized her powerful grasp and wagered she had to use her frame to keep the lights on and food in the fridge. She melted into her embrace, knowing she didn't have a choice, anyway. "I'm positive you're the reason I graduated." The group relaxed.

"Happy I could help," Judy said.

"I still have it somewhere if you want to see it," Becky said and was already moving to find it when Judy stopped her.

"It's okay... some other time." Becky sat back down.

"To this day, your corrections are a reminder of what someone can accomplish...and all those red marks let me know how much I didn't learn through school. Either way, you affected me, and I want to do whatever I can to help. When Maddie told me you needed me, I fell over."

"Guess we're adding Velma," Cal joked. Maddie pierced him with a look.

"Maddie says you know a bunch about the history of German Village. We need to find some answers."

Becky put up her hands to quiet the room and dropped them into her lap, palms up.

"Place your hands on mine."

Judy hesitated, and Maddie motioned her to follow the directions. Judy clenched her jaw, extended her hands, and rested her fingers on Becky's. A slight jolt and nothing more came from Becky as her eyelids clamped shut. They all sat still without knowing what they were awaiting when Becky spoke in a voice that was different enough to alter Cal's expression.

"There are gaps in you I've never seen in a person before. I can feel the walls inside you. Computers have firewalls keeping one area separate from another. I feel this in you. Something is dividing your brain."

"What is it?" Maddie asked, scooting hip to hip with Judy. Becky never acknowledged the question and continued.

"You haven't lived up to your potential. You are only now coming to terms with your choices, and whether you know it, you will make changes. There is pain—a shame for a family member. You're blocking yourself or me from that." Judy pulled away like she was touching an open flame with her eyes popping open. "This is a noble cause. I feel good about joining you in your quest," Becky remarked, adjusting to the light.

"What was that you were doing?" Cal asked, skepticism creeping into the words.

"I practice psychometry."

Judy leaned into Maddie's ear and whispered. "Did you tell her anything about me before we arrived?" Maddie shook her head.

"It's different from scrying. Scryers use objects like crystals or sometimes a crystal ball to see things. With psychometry, I gain knowledge from touching things around me."

"How does it work?" Cal asked, enthusiasm spilling across his face.

"Anyone can do it if you practice a lot."

"Yeah, right." Cal scrunched up his face in disbelief.

"No...really. A seer must tap into something out there in the world like some superhuman antenna. I trained myself to feel the power that objects give off."

"Objects give off power?" Judy asked.

"Sure, sometimes we endow the objects with the power from our emotions, pain, or maybe death. I get the distinct feeling that some things have the power of a residual spirit. But I don't think it's as simple as a spirit. I think what I interpret is energy. We give or take our energy from things all the time and never even consider how it leaves a mark on items or people. When we say positive energy or good vibes, that's what it means," Becky said.

"And you can do this anytime you want?" Maddie asked, drawn into the conversation.

"I admit I was showing off a bit for Judy, but it's what I'm good at, so I couldn't help myself."

"So, everything has an energy that's readable?" Judy asked, reaching into her pocket.

"No...most things don't."   Judy presented her plush mockingbird. Becky considered the item perched in the center of Judy's palm. It was too much like a test, or she feared what she would find, but when Becky took the toy, she held her breath as it contacted her skin.

She brought her hand and the bird back onto her lap, her body went limp. No one made a sound as all attention went toward Becky. Eyeballs shifted back and forth fast behind closed lids. Judy remembered the cat wall clock with the eyes that moved in sync with the seconds passing.

"The person who gave you this...there are powerful emotions tied to it. Your feelings are changing the ingredients I feel, but underneath all of it is love. You got this when you were born. I can see your child spirit in my mind's eye." Becky opened her lids and handed it back. "That's all I can see." Judy tried on a smile.

"Thank· you," Judy said, hugging Becky with no provocation. The outpouring of affection made Becky shine, and it was easy to tell she had little human contact.

"Maddie said you· wanted to know about German Village," Becky said, as they all gathered closer like a campfire yarn about to begin.

"Living so close to the village for so many years, I couldn't help but absorb the stories and legends. German Village is the jewel of Ohio, and Nathaniel Deville was the founder. After the revolutionary war, our government was rewarding those who stood with colonies against the British."

"I've heard of General Deville, or maybe I saw his plaque somewhere," Cal interjected with Becky nodding.

"He received just under four hundred acres that are the German Village we now know. Although Columbus was the capital of the state, it wasn't much to look at back then." Becky reached for her plastic bottle of Coca-Cola on a nearby end table, spun the cap off, and guzzled hard with fizzy air expelled as she withdrew. Her arms jiggled as she returned it to its resting place. "Nathaniel built his home, more like a mansion, in the center of his land. It still exists as the Deville Castle. There is some mystery surrounding why he abandoned the castle—rumors of a tragedy in the home, and some call it haunted and the name they give it is Blood Manor. Either way, he sold all his land except for a small section for farming, which he left to his son. I think most of the Deville family died years ago. I read a story of Nathaniel's last descendants, Ben, and his wife Lily, dying in a house fire on the same farmland with their son as the lone survivor."

"That's terrible," Maddie said.

"Cursed," Judy added.

"There's no doubt in my mind. Anyway, Nathaniel sold most of the land to immigrating Germans, minus a few acres he kept for himself. Soon after, Nathaniel moved to Columbus, trying to forget whatever happened in his past but never living within German Village again," Becky said.

"What happened to the child who survived the fire?" Judy asked.

"From what I understand, the boy Robert Deville grew up and became a Columbus police officer."

"I know Robert Deville well. He's the best detective on the force," Cal added.

"These were things I've learned over the years, but when Maddie called and asked me about the building you saw today, I dug a little deeper and found something fascinating," Becky said, returning to her bottle of pop. The time she spent gulping more cola, the three couldn't control their anticipation. Cal spoke first.

"Out with it. What did you find?"

"The building, the one with the wings, was owned by a Deville. The older brother of Ben, the farmer who died in the fire. I guess the building had been in the family for generations. The oldest brother, *Brice Deville*, rented it out for other businesses to use. And that's where it gets a little fuzzy. I've found nothing else yet," Becky said with sadness.

"Seems like a lot to me," Maddie said.

"Doesn't sound like much to me," Judy said with frustration threaded through her tone.

"A dead end's a dead end. Not much left for us—" Cal began.

"We visit. Tonight," Judy said, cutting Cal off.

"Hold on—"

"Cal, you're a cop, and I know this is risky for you, but I'm closer to the answers than I've ever been. We'll let you off here." She was remorseful for putting him on the spot and was going to, anyway. Cal stood staring at Judy with her staring back. In the center of Becky's home, Cal nodded. Judy wrapped her arms around Cal and held him for a long time.

*　　*　　*　　*

The group was getting larger, and the car rides were becoming more interesting with the addition of Becky. Judy couldn't believe she intended to break into a building. *What would I be willing to do next?* Becky's patterns of speech were off the charts—fast, often rambling, and always fascinating. Judy saw Becky's exuberance for, and it showed in her knowledge and her love of life.

Jealousy spread its tentacles over Judy. The life of a writer needed exploration to grow in every aspect. Even though Becky had written nothing since the paper Judy graded for her, there wasn't a doubt she was part of the world.

A few twists and turns away from Becky's place, and the car rolled to a stop. Becky applied the brake and saw her red taillights throwing glowing red on the street signs behind her, reflecting in her mirror.

"Keep driving. We don't want people to see us. Drive to the back," Judy said, waving her hands like a traffic cop, ensuring a constant flow. There was something ominous in the way she wanted to be invisible. It was dark except for the moon, and it was the moon that spoiled their chance to be undetectable. In the back seat, Cal studied his hands holding a pry bar

93

and gauged the weight of it. The crow bar's implications went way further than the heft of the steel. Maddie sat next to him, and with some hesitation, he drifted closer.

"This could go bad for me," he said. Maddie regarded him with a mixture of sadness and sympathy. "My job—pension."

"This won't change who you are...not on the inside," Maddie assured. "The world isn't black or white. Good people can do terrible things. It won't make us bad. Trust me." The car came to a stop, and the pry bar didn't seem as heavy.

The back part of the building blocked the moon, blanketing the group with precious darkness. And the blackness that enveloped the building perpetuated the structure's form as a forgotten castle among the shops and bistros. It's as if it were hiding or protected by the nearby structures—hiding in plain view.

"There was more..." Becky stopped cold.

"It's okay," Judy coaxed.

"There's a community online that passes information about this place. They trade horror stories and superstitions related to this place. Ignore is my first rule when I find anything unbelievable except..."

"We can deal with it," Maddie said. Becky appeared unsure whether to continue.

"From the safety of my home, I was sure it was bullshit, but standing here in its shadow, I don't know."

"We'll help you decide," Judy said, placing a hand on her shoulder.

"The consensus that I've seen says that whatever this place was...whatever its purpose served..." Becky closed her eyes, "hunting children was what I found buried in the web." The wind howled loud off the brick facade. "Locals called this place, *The Angel of Death*."

"What's in there?" Cal asked, gripping his prying tool for protection. Becky shrugged.

"According to the threads—the owner rounded up children who were too weak to resist and brought them there. And for what? I don't have a clue, and neither does anyone else. I'm afraid to go in there," Becky said, tilting her head in shame. This time each placed a hand on her.

"You have an ability that's amazing. I didn't believe it existed, and we need it, Becky," Judy pleaded. Becky considered this.

"Go ahead, Cal," Becky said. Cal walked to the back entrance. The door was the robust steel variety used by businesses that needed things protected.

"It had never been a bank or anything so official, so why the fortified door?" Cal asked.

On either side of the intimidating entry was crumbling concrete. The years of neglect caused the once-hard material between the door and the wall to deteriorate. He spotted a small crack and poked the tip of the pry bar into it with one jab. He hesitated for a split second and then pulled the bar toward him with all his strength. There was a shallow cracking sound that was the door coming out and away from the wall. It was also the sound of something breaking inside Cal. Doing the wrong thing, even for a just cause, wasn't in his nature. The crowbar was heavy again, and he let it drop to the ground as Judy opened the door. They filed inside the Angel of Death.

The dankness of the interior was hard on the lungs. Rot mixed into the air they breathed. Without climate control or proper circulation for so many years, it gave the inside the smell of a tomb. The smell heightened their anxiety even more. They shuffled onward—their feet pushed leaves, sticks and dirt that should not have found its way in along with them. Judy pulled flashlights, bought at a Walmart before they arrived, and passed them out. Lights roared to life in the dusty hallway. The cloudy mist surrounded the beams, transforming them from harmless lamps into eerie light sabers.

The tile was the industrial type found in most hospitals. Judy recognized it as a hospital. *But how?* Moving further in took forever as time slowed, and their apprehension grew. The belly of the beast had them, and they all kept peeking back toward the entrance as if the door were closing its hungry mouth, sealing them inside for good. Moving to the front of the group to take the lead, Cal slipped into his detective role, like sliding on a glove. He wasn't afraid and had his gun if something went down.

The hall gave way to rooms, with the largest of them to their right. The dirty floors echoed with each step, throwing the sound off the walls, and mimicking the sound of children's feet, close but always out of sight. Halfway into the room, the group pushed closer to each other, more from instinct.

Flashlights covered every surface of the room until they all settled on one spot. On the far side, opposite the door, was a wall of monitors, nine in all. The screens were of the tube variety, large with their bellies curving outward the way newer sets never can. The monitors had the aesthetics of a cube but on a grand scale.

"It looks like a Rubik's Cube I got for Christmas one year," Cal said, "I remember twisting each side for weeks until I gave up and peeled off the stickers to solve it and then placed it on a shelf to draw dust forever."

Straying from the safety of the herd, Maddie migrated to the monitors. She found a switch on the wall next to them. Without thinking, Maddie toggled the switch up. Lights flickered as the tubes warmed, hummed, and turning the room bright as noon. Bouncing from one screen to the next, they saw examination rooms.

"They watched them from here," Judy muttered.

"Doing what to them?" Maddie asked.

"Question is, why does this place still have power? It's been empty a long time," Cal said.

"Someone's paying the utilities on an abandoned facility?" Her own words surprised Becky.

"Let's check out the rooms," Judy said, like they were checking if the dryer stopped. Her enthusiasm had the reverse effect on them as they lagged. The door of each room had enormous windows for someone to peer inside.

"These are examination rooms," Maddie said. Scratching, loud and frantic, stopped them all in their tracks. The sound came from the walls. The noise had an insectile quality, but it was too big for things that small to emit. Judy turned her head toward one door. Although dirt covered the glass of the door, it fell away with a few swipes from a hand. Pressing her nose onto the glass, Judy directed the flashlight inward, illuminating the room. Inside sat a medical gurney in the center of the room with a chair planted next to it.

Judy noted it wasn't an ordinary chair, but the La-Z-Boy recliner type a man would station in front of his television to catch all that week's sporting events. Whoever sat there planned to be there for a long time. Judy pointed her fingertips—touching the glass.

"You see them—straps?" Still fastened, like keeping an invisible patient restrained, were nylon straps with buckles on the ends. Straps, thick and meant to hold someone or something secure while...

"Becky?" Judy spoke, and the sound of her own voice seemed to return her from a location somewhere far off. Becky acknowledged her name with a flinch, and Judy didn't blame her. The row of rooms would lead none of them into a peaceful sleep that night. Becky darted to the door, holding her hand just in front of it. Touching any surface inside the Angel of Death was foolish. Except for turning and heading for the door, she had no options left to her. She grasped the handle, awaiting an image that didn't come. The door opened as if no days had passed since its installation. In the room, they followed, orbiting Becky as she went to work.

Coating the room was a thin layer of dust. The examination room didn't share the acrid smell of the hallway, and the group was thankful for the short reprieve from the odor.

"There is a lot of pain in this room," Becky said, spinning around the chamber with arms outstretched like antenna pulling in energy. She hadn't locked in the way they saw her earlier. Becky moved as if she were trying to discover the origin of a chilly breeze invading her home. It wasn't unexpected when she moved toward the hospital bed.

She allowed her palms to hover over the straps. She shook her head slightly and guided her palms toward a pillow at the head of the gurney. Seemingly satisfied with its placement, Becky pushed her hands against the pillow.

"They're fighting...against the straps. They don't understand the straps. Their little bodies—pressed hard against the bed. They struggle, but it's useless," Becky said. Judy brought her hands to her mouth to stifle a scream. Maddie moved in close for support as Becky's eyelids popped open. She saw something that wasn't in the room. "It's a little girl—maybe five or six—she's crying."

"Can you feel or see what she does?" Judy asked. If Becky heard her, she never let on.

"Blackness. The girl's thoughts—they're muddled. She's there but not...coming in and out like a turn signal. She knows she's afraid and can't even voice her fear." Maddie interlaced her fingers as if to pray for the girl long ago and far away. "I'm seeing more now—too many to count—every color, every size. They share the same fear, the same pain. I'm feeling something new,"

"Can you describe it?" Cal asked, speaking into her like she was a fast-food intercom system.

"I see what they are looking at...who they are looking at..." Judy moved closer to Becky.

"Who do you see, Becky?" Judy asked. Becky broke away from the bed and backed against the wall for support.

"I saw you," Becky said, pointing to Judy. "Through all of their minds—hundreds that visited this one room alone—hundreds saw you."

"That's not possible," Judy clutched her chest and believed Becky was wrong.

"Fear was in their hearts when they regarded you. What did you do to them, Judy?" Everyone turned to Judy. The abandoned building, the old smells, and the horrifying hospital beds were all forgotten for the moment.

"It wasn't me," Judy protested. Becky nodded.

"It was you, Judy Angel."

Chapter Eighteen
—Entered that wool of hers—

Judy awoke to a knock on her bedroom door. The light was too harsh, and the actual world was as she expected it to be. The knock came again, and this time she pulled her comforter over her head, blocking most of the light except pinholes in areas where the fabric was wearing.

"I don't want to talk," Judy said in a muffled voice. The door opened a crack, squeaking with the few inches.

"Jude...you have guests," Emily announced. Judy gripped the comforter tighter—
The sound of footsteps circling her bed rose in the room.

"Go away." The door closed again, and she was furious that her mother let people into her room without permission. She lay there until a woman spoke.

"You can't stay in there forever," Maddie said.

"Watch me." A foot dragged, and then a butt hopped onto her bed next to her.

"Are you actually in my bed?"

"Not exactly in it..." Cal said with a smile peppering his voice, "more like on it."

"Well, get off of it," Judy said, matching her tone to his. Another voice, not so recognizable, spoke.

"Something I want to say to you, Judy," Becky added. Judy considered it and resigned her hope of avoidance. From underneath, she slid the cover off her face. Light touched her cheeks, and she didn't want Cal to see her tussled hair and anything else out of place.

Judy's cheeks warmed, and she hoped he didn't notice a change in her color. Their expressions weren't leering and had none of the coldness she expected. They were quite the opposite, and it made her doubt her experience from the night before. Judy had lots to say but would never talk first.

"I've known you the least..." Becky said, wavering at the foot of her bed, "when I touched you last night—I sensed no malice in you." Judy bobbed her head.

"We are not in this for us," Cal said, and his phrasing hushed them. "You are the missing piece in our lives, and we never would think you would do something bad to children—"

"The idea is crazy," Maddie said. Judy sat up in her bed, squeezed her bent legs until her knees propped up her chin, and tilted onto her headboard.

"If I'm honest—" Becky begged with Maddie waving her off.

"No...go ahead. I want your honesty," Judy said. Becky gave a subtle nod and continued.

"I'm not boastful when I say that I have a gift for psychometry. I have never been wrong before."

"What you saw, I can't explain," Judy said.

"I saw a child, and that's what you were...and a child can't be responsible for what they do. Or told what to do." Becky's reassurance soothed her anxiety. "Last night was sleepless for me, so I did the only thing I could do...research," Becky said.

"Hope you're ready for this," Maddie said, leaping onto the foot of the bed. They all gathered around Judy like kids at a slumber party instead of grow-ups dealing with an ugliness unraveling around them.

"Child experimentation was the business of that clinic. People who lived in the area weren't clueless. Still, every time I followed a rumor, I found a dead end. Someone has worked hard to cover any trace of what was happening inside." In another room in the house sat a man who had the answers she wanted. Her stomach dropped, thinking about the confrontation. "Caught one break," Becky said. "Found a tax return online that had the clinic's address. It was a nurse. She was in her twenties when she worked there, and the time frame matches up." Judy couldn't hold back a grin.

"Great work," Cal said, sharing a smile with Judy.

"I found a working phone number for the nurse, Virginia Mathers." They exchanged glances, and no one spoke for a long time until Maddie broke the ice.

"What do we have to lose?" Maddie asked. Judy shook her head with nothing to offer. Becky reached into her pocket, pulled out her phone, positioned it into the center of the mattress, and dialed the phone. Maddie extended her hands out from her side. They each folded their fingers into one another's—connecting into a circle like a modern séance with the glow of the cell phone instead of a crystal ball. Nervous scans passed between them as the phone's speaker came alive. The phone blared a hollow, tinny sound out in the bedroom and floated toward the ceiling like the fumes of a bonfire. A ringing began, and they all predicted its interval until a click interrupted the rhythm.

"Hello," a tentative voice answered. The group sat in the dead air, waiting to see who will talk. Becky pointed to her chest with raised eyebrows—nods all around.

"Virginia Mathers, right?" Becky asked in her best salesperson voice. The pause was now on the other end of the line.

"Yes. Who is this?" Becky placed her digit finger to her mouth to hush.

"Virginia, my name is Becky. I came across some information that you can help me with," Becky made a face to the group.

"Information?" On the other side of the line was a frightened woman.

"Virginia," she repeated to put her at ease like a friend calling about the weather, "I know you were the attending nurse at Angel Among Us. Don't let that scare you off the phone...you are the only one that can save a woman's life." The pause was so long it signaled a disconnect. "Virginia?"

"Sill here," Virginia said in a quiet voice that also had the salt of many years of smoking.

"First, this call isn't to place any blame about what happened there in the past. Any broken laws from back then will stay between you and me." Shame hovered over them for remaining quiet during the exchange.

"What blame do you think I should shoulder?" Virginia's voice came alive for the first time. Anger was good, and Judy expected the emotion would spill her story.

"What I did...I had to do," Virginia said.

"I don't think you were completely at fault," Becky added with an upturned tone. Judy marveled at Becky's technique. Her gift for reading people was impressive to witness as she pulled Virginia's strings with perfection.

"Make me a villain if you like—I won't wear those clothes, though."

"I think we got off on the wrong foot, Virginia," Becky said in a soothing—singing voice. "Can you tell me about Brice Deville? What kind of man was he?"

"Brice was an odd fella, no doubts on that score," Virginia said. "But he meant well...we all did."

"So, he just supplied the funding for the clinic?" Becky asked.

"No. AAU was something he cared about, and he spent his last dime to see it through." Virginia sounded like she jumped through the phone. Walking her conversation-tightrope caused Becky to perspire, and she wiped the sweat from her forehead and cheeks.

"You and Brice still talk?"

"I see him from time to time." They heard in her voice the subject of Brice brought her down. Cal jabbed with his head toward Becky to continue down her path.

"Does Brice bring up the past with your visits?" Another pause.

"He would if he could..."

"Why doesn't he, Virginia?"

"Brice can't speak anymore and hasn't spoken in a long time."

"Tell us...me what happened to him," Becky demanded.

"The same thing that will happen to me if I talk about this any further," Virginia said. Judy spiraled her fingers around each other in circles to keep her on the line.

"Don't hang up, Virginia. Someone's life is on the line. If you hang up, they lose their last hope." Judy held her breath. "Virginia?"

"Still here," she said, and Judy exhaled.

"I thought it was a joke at first...with Brice, I mean. He forgot things—conversations from the day before—procedural practices that he studied for years. The names scared me..."

"Names?" Becky prodded.

"Brice forgot the names of the workers in the clinic, and some he knew for a long time."

"Alzheimer's or dementia?" Becky offered.

"Those were easy conclusions for Dr. Bain to jump to, but I never believed—"

"Dr. Otis Bain?" Judy asked. Becky shook her head with desperation.

"Who is that? Who spoke just now?" The fear returned to Virginia's voice. "If you aren't answering, then—"

"The person in need of your help," Judy said.

"Your voice...I know your voice. Judy Angel?" Judy nodded and realized Virginia never saw the gesture.

"It's Judy Angel." She weighed the option of telling her it was her maiden name and let it go.

"God bless you, Angel."

"So, you know me from the clinic?" Virginia laughed, loud and unexpected.

"You're the Angel Among Us, Judy," Virginia said with a newfound spirit.

"What were we doing in AAU?" Virginia was thinking the question over.

"Why don't you remember? You lost your memory—didn't you?" Judy nodded, but this time spoke at the same time.

"Yes. Why?" Judy's words came out like bullets. There was no response on the other end.

"We are all friends of Judy, and we are trying to help her put the pieces of her life back together," Cal said.

"Pain isn't a strong enough word to describe how I feel for you, Judy. If you're losing your memory...it's already too late for you. They've gotten to you."

"Who has gotten to her?" Becky asked with no answer returned.

"You don't understand. I'm getting some of my memory back."

"Nose bleeds, am I right?" Her statement hushed everyone.

"How do you know that?" Maddie piped up.

"Immersion into forgotten surroundings will restore lost memories—alcohol."

"What about alcohol?" Cal asked.

"When Brice realized he was spiraling into oblivion, he drank...a lot. His nose bleeds increased, and so did the memories he once lost." Judy was in silent agreement. "He wasn't a man who could drink forever. It wasn't in him to pickle himself—so Brice lost the battle, and the slow fade overtook him. What scares me, besides sharing his fate—it's the fear that he's still in there, somewhere. And I think he is still in there," Virginia said through tears. Judy recalled Tessa and her sad prison.

"Can't you help me?" Desperation seeped into Judy's words.

"Stupid advice is coming your way," Virginia said after a long pause. "I'm not saying to get smashed and stay smashed, Judy, but treat alcohol as a prescription while you are searching for answers. Every hour or two, down a shot—never enough to get a buzz. I think drinking too much, too fast, could rupture something in your brain. That explains the blood."

"Maybe alcohol could cure me," Judy said with hope shining through.

"It can't, Angel. You're in an ocean, and it's a life vest. It will help you for now, but not forever. My theory from watching Brice—keep a low dose of alcohol in your system all the time. Set the alarm at night and do it around the clock, and it will buy you some time." Maddie cried and seeing her tears sent Cal down the same path.

"What other details? What went on at Angel Among Us?" Judy asked.

"Offering answers is what I could do. God knows I spent a lot of time at AAU. But my answers would leave you asking for more, and I don't think you have that kind of time left. No one knows what went on in that facility like you, Judy Angel. Except maybe..." Virginia trailed off, lost in her struggles.

"Maybe what?" Becky prompted.

"Otis Bain began the program, and he learned as much as you. He, unfortunately, is less likely to spill his guts than I am. He knows the threat more than you and me both. If I had to guide you on a course, Otis Bain is that direction," Virginia added. The conversation drained every ounce of energy from the room, and it was visible on every face.

"Thank you for helping me, Virginia." Cries rose on the phone, soft but distinct.

"Angel is the most appropriate name I've seen a person receive. I've watched you deliver miracles to this world, Judy Angel. My heart cries out against the fate that awaits you. You deserve a life—a meaningful life. Good luck, Judy," Virginia said, and with a click on her end, her voice disappeared. The four on the bed released each other's grip. The vitality in the room vanished as if a trance ended and the spell broken. Each face glistened from sweat.

"Otis Bain has our answers," Becky said.

"If he's as skittish on the subject as Virginia thinks, I have to confront him alone," Judy said. They sat there for a long time without speaking.

"Forgive me for doubting you," Becky announced. Judy pulled her across the bed for a hug.

"There's nothing to forgive and a lot to doubt still," Judy assured Becky. An unreality that forces conspired to destroy those connected to *Angels Among Us* hung in the air thick. In a day, the facility went from *The Angel of Death,* and now—Judy didn't know the truth but meant to find out everything from Otis Bain.

Chapter Nineteen
—Calming turbulent seas—

Judy waited outside of Otis Bain's office, going on two hours. His office hours were over, and Judy knew he was playing the waiting game until she left. A hospital nurse leaned over a waiting room desk every so often to give her the evil eye. *I can wait all night.* Otis seemed to have come to the same conclusion, darting his head out of his office, spotting Judy in a chair, and motioning her inside.

Without greeting her, Otis shuffled around a small steel desk. His gray hair, what was left of it, drooped toward his ears. He pushed the strands back into place and tried on a professional smile for Judy while she repositioned in a chair in front of his desk. The doctor's face was a roadmap of the things he saw over his lengthy career.

"Thanks for seeing me, Doc," she said, attempting to keep her end of the conversation light and cheery a while longer.

"Sure...I will say that I rarely agree with appointments, so last-minute, you know? If I did this for everyone, I'd be sleeping here. Are there more symptoms you wanted to run by me?" Judy drew out a metal flask from her pocket, unscrewed the lid until it fell. A chain caught, causing the top to clink—metal against metal. Judy tipped the flask upward to take in whatever was inside, and her throat worked with the substantial gulp—breathed in and perceived the burn of the alcohol on her tongue.

"Excuse me, Doc. I was late for my Rx. Nurse Virginia's orders" He studied her—enthralled by the display. There were questions written on his face he would not ask, and that was a good start for her. "Why did you have me visit a hypnotist? I mean...that isn't the thing a medical practitioner jumps to first with recommendations," Judy said, fastening the lid back onto the flask without turning back to him. He was a statue in posture, watching her as the wheels inside him turned. She leveled her gaze to him as if he appeared in the room by magic in the instant their eyes met. She cocked her head sideways. "You seem so familiar to me, Dr. Bain—"

"Otis, please call me Otis." She detected his nervousness.

"Okay, Otis. Have we met before? I guess you have one of those faces—full of character."

"Can't recall us meeting before this week. But I see so many patients," he said, returning the volley, both knowing where this conversation was heading. He squinted, a subtle change in his expression, but Judy caught it no matter how small.

"Would you be shocked if I told you that we knew each other very well?"

"That would be shocking, wouldn't it?" Otis had no intention of giving up the game.

"Imagine, if you can, not knowing who you are—your past— friends, family and passions. All gone. What if you woke up one morning and were a blank slate? What would you do to bring back the parts that vanished from your mind?" His stare intensified as she spoke.

"Truthfully, that sounds horrible. I must get somewhere now. I'm sure we can schedule a follow-up to discuss your trouble, and maybe—"

"Where do you have to be at this hour?" she demanded.

"I have night shifts at Reclamation Correctional Facility and I'm late to boot," Otis said, launching from his chair. Judy slammed the flask, bottom first, onto the top of his steel desk. The sound was loud and harsh enough to drive Otis back into his seat. Keeping her hand where she made contact, Judy shifted her body over the top of the desk—hovering like a cat about to pounce.

"If you get out of that chair again, I promise I will strike more than this desk." He saw her desperation. His frame shriveled into his chair as he relented.

"Very well, Judy Angel." Without a smile, she slinked back into a chair, her butt leading the way.

"Sorry," she said.

"You see a frail old man in front of you. And it's true, but I started my medical career walking from home to home, miles every day when house calls were part of the gig. And after that, I ended up working for the prison. I've seen my share of outbursts—yours wasn't out of line."

"What am I involved in?" she asked.

He stood up, and this time she didn't react as he walked to a file cabinet, rifled through a dozen files, and brought out a Manilla folder.

"I've done things I'm not proud of—illegal but not unethical. As far as the law was concerned, I suppose I'm as guilty as any criminal. A higher purpose caused me to stray from my oath, and not a day goes by when I don't wrestle with some aspect of my choices." Otis handed her the folder. "They say bartenders are therapists—maybe they're right. A doctor, with an extensive career in a community, has the burden of omnipotence. You hear of surgeons having a *God complex*—trapped knowing that they have power over life and death, and family doctors are like that. Patients share their hopes, fears, hatred, and indiscretions. We immerse ourselves into the fabric of the lives of everyone we treat. And yes, I will die, keeping some disturbing and tragic secrets that I've collected over the years. Humans—we aren't able to keep them alive forever."

Judy opened the folder—rocked by the graphic photo of a girl with her skull broken inward—eyes bulging. Judy brought her hand up to her mouth. "Can't imagine that's easy to see," he said. The girl in the picture was of her.

"Passing along information of the car accident in your youth was never my dilemma—you believing it happened when you arrived here last week was." She scanned all the information, darting from one sentence to the next as fast as her ability to focus.

"Brain damage," she whispered.

"The worst I ever saw. The impact was in your hippocampus area—memory, Judy." Tears blocked her view of the medical report. "Wheeling you into the emergency room, I gave no hope you'd survive—months after your recovery, I never believed you'd have a normal life." She swiped at her cheeks with the back of her hand. "You proved us all wrong."

She gave a sarcastic laugh with no humor.

"I can't remember yesterday," she said, breaking into full sobs. *More secrets for you to keep.*

"The memory loss you suffer...is not from the accident," Otis said. His voice was quiet, as if he hoped she didn't hear, but she did.

"Explain."

Otis again found the comfort of his worn executive chair, plopping into its leathery center.

"Angel Among Us..." he gestured to her, "was my brainchild. The clinic started from humble beginnings—a staff of two nurses, me as the medical doctor, and Brice Deville financing the operation. The things we did in the first few months were miraculous. Scratch that, miracles abounded during that time. I'm a man of science, always have been and always will be but that period in my life...I sensed God's intervention. I didn't know what it meant to know there was a God and to believe it. Those were the *salad days* for you and me, Judy."

"I don't understand," Judy said, forgetting the tears.

"People of faith take for granted what I didn't know—what I didn't have a clue about."

"What didn't you know?" she asked.

"Opening up your world to goodness brings something else with it...darkness. There isn't one without the other. There was a light over us—it was pure and must have *been* like a beacon taunting the darkness. Evil seeks to destroy any shred of purity."

"Who?" He shook her question away.

"Before we planned it, our clinic, with a meager staff, grew to include over thirty. I...we were on the brink of something great when the first cases began. Then, employees never made it into work. When we tracked them down, they would say they forgot to come in—others forgot they worked there altogether. It was like a plague spreading through the facility. I didn't know what to make of it. I saw fate undoing all of our work, or something was restoring the natural balance of things we had no business messing with."

Judy pondered Brice and his slip into a strange stupor.

"Brice?"

Otis gave a quick nod, avoiding her gaze. "Over twenty workers in total lost their minds," he said.

The way he phrased their condition sent a chill down Judy's spine. She never considered conscious thought as something lost or gained like the weight on a scale. "The workers are scattered around Ohio facilities right now. Lost souls."

"But why? There has to be a why," she said.

"The rest of the staff not infected, quit. You left Ohio and never turned back." The comment hurt, and he saw her pained expression. "Blame is the last thing I think of when you enter my thoughts. Judy...you were like a daughter to me—an angel who showed me there was more than money, more than education. You revealed the universe has grander plans for us."

She wondered what role her father played in everything. The conclusions that flooded in made her feel sick.

"I'm not brushing you off or telling you lies, but I have urgent business at the prison." He stood up and awaited the flask hitting the desk which didn't come. When he stared down at her, she was a wrecked woman. He walked over, pulled her to her feet, and wrapped his arms around her. His aftershave—*Old Spice*, she wagered—filled her nose, and she remembered his embrace. The connection was distant, like a ship bobbing on the vast ocean, but she spotted it there all the same. "Reach out again, and I promise to tell you all that I know."

"Promise?" she asked in a way a child needs assurance. He smiled a warm smile that made her believe.

"It's a promise. And take it easy on the medicine," Otis said and was out of the office. Judy remained there lost in a trance and couldn't put the puzzle together. She slid her hand into her pocket. The soft fur of the mockingbird comforted her once again. Bringing her phone to the light, she dialed. The usual sound of the telephone attempting a connection whispered into her ear. A man picked up.

"Hello?"

She cried again, wondering if she would ever run out of tears.

"Daddy? I'm ready to go fishing."

Chapter Twenty
—A climb inside the skin—

Fluorescent tubes crackled overhead when Bud flipped them on. They moved into Angel Among Us, and he went to every switch hidden in the dark. She watched him navigate through the building like someone who's spent their share of hours under the roof. Age was catching up with him, and she wondered what this man had meant to her during her childhood. He carried himself with strength, and even his walk offered confidence in the man he became. Although anxious, Judy was ready to see Bud Angel, not the name of the father figure, but the man that stood before her.

"Sad to see this place so disheveled," Bud said, continuing to illuminate lights as he went. "It was always a bright and cheery place. It was the rumors that were the hardest for me to bear. The things they would say about this place—I hated it."

She had to admit—the clinic appeared much different without the shadows and threat of danger clinging to it.

When the hallway ended, a large reception desk, not unlike the ones found in a conventional hospital, stood desolate. Ignoring the desk altogether, Bud pushed left to another hallway. He passed each office, calling out the names as if they were still inside working away. They reached the end of the hall. A painting sat on the wall of a girl sitting with her father while he read to her.

"Here we are," he said. "Berthe Morisot...French impressionist." Judy connected to the painting right away. The artist's strokes gave the scene a dreamy quality. They were in a garden as the father was giving her lessons. "You placed this painting here. You said it felt perfect," he said with pride.

"What do you mean, here?" She glanced up at the painting to see his point. He moved as slow as a magician, revealing a trick to his audience.

Bud slipped his hand under the bottom of the painting—she saw his hand working there—searching. An audible click cut through the silent hall. The wall, trimmed with fancy wainscoting, fell away. The wall, now a door, opened to another room.

He wasted no time entering and lighting the room as he ventured inside. A place, hidden from the world, made Judy hesitate. Pushing the apprehension away, Judy willed her legs to move, and they obeyed. The wall was only a foot thick, and still, she imagined passing into another dimension and disappearing through the threshold, just out of sight, as if he had crossed over. A few more steps inside and she saw him sitting in a chair next to a bed, calm as a marble statue. The concealed room was a bedroom. If her room at her parent's home was the example of a childhood bedroom, this was the grown-up version. The desk, made of expensive wood, sat in a corner with a pricey computer perched on top. The computer was a Macintosh, and although it was decades obsolete by the day's standard, it was way too expensive for a teenage girl to afford.

"Your home away from home," he said. She twirled around to keep from missing a single detail of the secret chamber. She collapsed bottom first onto the mattress and thinking how soft it was. Her childhood room has plenty of books, but nothing compared to the amount that lined every wall in the space.

"This is where I took my writing to the next level," Judy said, caressing the leather spines of several books in her impressive miniature library.

"When you weren't working, you were writing," he said.

"Bud? Why was this room built for me?" she asked.

"Patience...I will tell you everything," he said, patting her arm. "Just after your fifth birthday. You were so small. You were in a car accident—"

"I just saw the medical charts," she interjected, with him nodding.

"The doctors didn't say, and they didn't have to—they didn't expect you to..." Bud turned away to compose himself, "You'd have to be a parent to understand seeing your child the way you were. When your mother and I brought you home from the hospital, you hardly ate—your ability to speak vanished. Your sweet child's voice never stuck in my mind until I couldn't hear it anymore. You lay in your bed all day, and if not for us feeding you, your mouth wouldn't move." His eyes glossed over. "Not sure who took it harder, your mother or me. To watch you grow and learn—watching your personality bloom right in front of us day after day, year after year, then to see it brushed aside in one day. You were a happy, intelligent little girl..." He let Judy take his and hand fold it into her own, "six months later the doctors said nothing hopeful. You needed around the clock care—your mother and I took turns. I picked the night shift. You wanna know why?" he asked. Emotion overtook her as she bit her lip and bobbed her head.

"When you were asleep in my arms, you were like every other child." He couldn't stop the tears any longer. "In the dark—listening to you breathe—soft murmuring sometimes. You were perfect and complete. I was selfish, and I understood what seeing you during the day was like for your mother, and I forced that burden on her..." Bud buried his face into his hands and cried.

"You're not selfish," she comforted. Still hidden behind hands, Bud shook her comment away.

"The situation wasn't perfect," she added.

"Growing up, men didn't have emotions, let alone show them. But the day you were born was the day my heart was born. The problem is, having a heart brings so much pain into your life." They sat there for a long time, saying nothing.

"How did I come around, Bud?" The first hint of a smile returned to his face. Creeping into the corners of his mouth, but still a smile.

"Like the car crash that brought you to the state you were in, your recovery was a total accident—a happy accident, though," he said. "My favorite musical artist—hands down—is Billy Joel. I always played Billy's music around the house, and I always liked his faster-paced stuff. But this day, I let the album play out instead of picking and came across a song called LULLABY. The lyrics were about you and me. There is an underlying sadness in his voice that spoke to me." Bud wiped away the remaining wetness from his cheeks. "That night I went to your bedroom as I always did...this time I brought the lullaby. I can't swear I noticed anything that first night, because it was like a dream, and that's what confused me," he said.

"What did you think was a dream?" Her curiosity was getting the better of her.

"Maybe the music, maybe something else. I think the song was a fuse. When we fell asleep, I heard your voice—the first time since before the accident." She moved closer, wanting him to finish and trying not to interrupt his recounting with her sobs. "I dismissed the first night...it was the second night." Bud looked to be conjuring up the story from somewhere far away. Judy couldn't stand the suspense any longer.

"What happened? What did I do?"

"You talked to me...in my head—our heads. My body was sleeping, and my mind was awake with yours. Your voice was the start. And then I saw a garden blooming from the darkness. I watched plants and trees form out of thin air as the environment sprung up around me. I realized it was my memory of a time we shared an outing. Overcome with déjà vu, I saw a world come alive. And there you were—my little girl—walking and talking, just as you had before the accident."

"We understood each other?" she asked.

"Yes. You said you saw your mother and me every day but couldn't answer—couldn't make your thoughts turn into words or make them into movements. I asked you how we were communicating, and you didn't know, at least not then. But I found out much later that you could pull memories from me. The garden that we visited became your sanctuary or starting point to rebuild your damaged brain. I didn't know what you were doing at first."

"What did I do?" He gave her a sly grin.

"Rebuilt your brain from my memories—filling in the gaps— rewiring yourself. I don't know the technical terms—Otis would know better than me. Along with damaging parts of your brain—memory parts— other areas of your brain had increased in size. One section shrunk, and another grew. I was happy to talk to you, even if it was only during sleep. What I didn't know was you were recreating the branches of memory a little each night. Months later—you spoke to your mother out loud. I was glad you spoke to her first. She needed it more. Your speech wasn't perfect, but you got better and better until one day, I noticed you were moving your fingers and toes. It took a solid year of us sharing our dream world, only one year, and you were back to us. We weren't the kind of parents who could let go of a child. When you left us and never came back—never called—it devastated us. We lost you all over again."

Guilt seized her, and she didn't push the sensation away because she realized she had it coming. She deserved every bit.

"Sorry," she said, and was all she could say.

"You're back now. For however long we have you...we have you."

She lunged for his waiting arms, melting into him, and imagined all the work it took for him to bring her back to their world. After a long time, she pulled away but wished for it to go on and on.

"This is all incredible...but what does my accident have to do with this place?" Judy asked. Bud looked nervous for the first time, squirming in his seat.

"For the longest time, I believed the ability to heal the brain through sleep was *my* gift. Until..."

"Until what?"

"One morning, when you woke me, you were excited when you told me about a time we spent together fishing, and I couldn't recall ever doing it. You said it was only once, but it was an amazing night. The memory eluded me—disappeared."

"How do you explain it?" she questioned.

"When you borrowed memories to restore your own, you sometimes removed them from me as if they were never mine. That's when I realized we had to be cautious and learned the true extent of your powers. You had to learn how to copy the memories like a Xerox machine instead of yanking them free. It was hard, and you got it wrong many times—still, your mind was incredible and strong. You soon mastered the art. It was something you said that resonated with me, and I couldn't shake it. You told me how awful it was—stuck inside your own body—own head. That made me think of all the other children who found themselves in the same pit," Bud said and reached for a picture frame on her desk, plucked it with one hand, and gave it to her. The photo showed the two of them in front of the building they were inside.

"Look at us. I was so young," Judy said, studying the image.

"We both were. But you were so wise. I think when you were remaking your memories, you may have gleaned something from me that made you much more mature than your age would let on. Anyway, my idea was to help others with your gift. I found Otis Bain, and he found Brice Deville—and we were off to the races."

"I wish I could see myself helping those children," she said. Bud swiveled in his chair, clicked the Mac power button, and located the files marked: ANGEL OBSERVATIONS

"Here you go. The videos are not much to look at, though," Bud warned. The video file opened in a small box on the computer screen. Judy was ten years old and outstretched in a La-Z-Boy recliner. In the same frame, a girl, smaller than Judy, lay strapped into a hospital bed.

"How did I do it?"

Bud shook his head. "It was a mystery to me. If you grasped it, you didn't tell me. You've had endless conversations with Otis about it. Perhaps you told him."

"What's that?" Judy directed her finger in between the two figures on the screen. Bud leaned, focusing on the spot she pointed at and shook his head.

"I don't see anything," he said. Judy stared at him in disbelief and back to her younger self. She saw the room filling with a yellow substance that appeared to be fog containing electricity. The mist had tiny ripples like waves darting up and down and circling the two in the observation room like a giant vortex. A thin white tendril in the shape of an arrow drifted from the mist. It surprised Judy how the mass of the fog was yellow, and the tendril, still connected to it, was white. *There's intelligence in that.* From above her body, the tendril shot into her head like a fuel pump nozzle inserted into a car. The child's body twitched from its insertion.

"You saw that, right?"

He squinted.

"No. I don't, Judy."

With the white branch still intruding on Judy's body, another white vein was floating over to the resting child until there was a perfect bridge between the two.

"This is incredible."

"I wish I could see what you're seeing."

"I'm tapping into her mind with my own," she conveyed. The section of the umbilical cord closest to the outstretched child turned green and moved toward Judy. "I'm pulling things from her conscious or unconscious mind." The entire tendril turned from white to green as it reached Judy. Another slight jolt.

"I saw you flinch," Bud offered.

"I'm getting her memories." From Judy's head, the connection was turning white again and changing the green as it went. This time the girl on the observation bed jerked as the memories returned to her.

"You saw that, too, right?"

Bud nodded.

"I think I'm extracting her memories and creating new branches inside her." Without notice, the tendrils withdrew, and the fog above faded as if it were never there. The two girls in the video remained asleep, and nothing more was visible to Judy.

There was something about the video that itched her brain, and the answer eluded her. Judy exited out of the video and spotted an icon on the home screen with the words: JUDY'S NOVELS AND MISCELLANEOUS

Judy saw the file containing novels and recognized her heart rate rising. She filed that information away for later and turned back to her father.

"This was how I helped the others," she said in a soft voice, stunned by what she witnessed.

"For years—countless kids," Bud said. "Their injuries trapped them, and you set them free."

"But how did I do it? Where did this gift come from?" She sought-out his eyes. Bud tilted his head toward the celling as if the answer awaited there.

"Jude, the only explanation I have doesn't make sense."

"Try me," she urged. Bud licked his lips.

"It's like when the senses of a blind person develop around their disability. Their hearing doubles or their smell increases. When a part of your brain stopped working, another part took over. That's what I believed."

"Bud...I need to know about this cagey disease that afflicted the staff and myself when I arrived."

"Malamarkus. You were first to give the disease a name. The skeleton Lord of death, you said. The truth? No one knows anymore. By the time we noticed what was happening, we were powerless to stop it. Some of us cried conspiracy. A group was trying to stop all the work we've been doing. I guess something like *Men in Black*—using neutralizers on our brains to destroy our organization from the inside. I heard those exact scenarios," he said, shaking his head. "Others swore the outbreaks were biological...something in nature that was trying to reset the balance we threw off. I'm in that camp. We know so little about the brain—how can we know there aren't self-defense mechanisms fighting back?" he said. Judy brought up the image of the white beams that made a bridge between her and the injured girl and how they changed color like a battery icon showing its progress.

"If that were true..." Judy pondered the notion that nature had such human intelligence, "then we are talking about a higher power?" Bud shrugged, "Are we referring to God or some natural occurrence?" she asked.

"That's the real question. You worked here for over a decade which is why we built this room. You were spending more time here than at home, and you needed a place to unwind."

"Right...why so many years later? Is there something that's spread from one brain to another with the mental link?" she muttered. The image of the tendrils returned.

"There is something physically that we can't see or measure that's being gained or lost through your process," Bud said. "Is something else passed along beside memories?" he asked. She shook her head.

"If that were even possible, why did the staff get infected when they never underwent my procedure," she asked. "Did they?"

"Not at all. I never saw you work on anyone but the injured," Bud assured.

"We're stuck then?" she said, dejected.

"For now. Only for now." Bud wrapped his arms around his daughter.

"I feel horrible for not coming to you sooner. I can't trust my thoughts," Judy said.

"No. You're back in the game. I can see it in your eyes," he said, and she nodded.

"I can't let myself forget...I have to *stay awake*," Judy admitted.

Chapter Twenty-one
—There's just one kind of folks—

The bedroom door creaked, slid inward, and created a sound like a coffin opening. The inside of Judy's room was dark, except for a sliver of light. A streetlight from next door came into the small area through parted curtains, giving stuffed animals lining her room an angry appearance.

Teddy bears menaced and a doll's eyes reflected light to appear haunted. A shadow formed as Bud walked into his five-year-old's room. Judy suspected she was reliving a vision as the *tunnel* fortified her body, except the edges weren't as fuzzy as she peered through Angel's eyes. Her father was already heading toward the cassette player with Billy Joel in hand, fresh from his shirt pocket. She saw the hopeful expression painted on his face. *This must be the night after he first heard my voice.*

He was either so full of optimism or desperate to hear his girl speak again. One thing was obvious—Bud was a man on a mission.
She watched her father, noticing the fog in Angel's mind, but also understanding that there was a person in there. Bud moved closer to his daughter until he pressed his body to hers. In the background music rose—
GOODNIGHT MY ANGEL, TIME TO CLOSE YOUR EYES AND SAVE THESE QUESTIONS FOR ANOTHER DAY—

"I'm going to help you, Jude," Bud said, stroking Angel's hair, "We can do this together. I won't hurt you." He pushed his body as close to her as possible.

Judy's view went from a misty child's perspective to a bright green garden, lush with plants. The scene was both familiar and alien, as if it were a garden on another planet.

It was part memory and part child's imagination of what a garden resembled. Everything was perfect in the way a plastic display of fruits and vegetables copied the objects but lacked the subtlety of actual life.

Angel opened her eyes, and Judy saw the same tendril from before, now connected to her father. The coil was as white like the one she saw from the video file earlier, but this one was feeble in its size—matching the strength of its user, she guessed.

Within a few seconds, she was back in the garden, now with her father sitting opposite her. He had the same perfect appearance that the garden presented. His face was what her mind couldn't recreate with accuracy. An automaton was the word to describe this projection, but damn impressive for a five-year-old that suffered from brain damage.

Back and forth, they spoke. The language was rudimentary because of Angel's age and her inability to maintain the projected surroundings. Doing both at the same time proved challenging. She was spinning plates and keeping them up was a victory. Although her vocabulary was years beyond her age, she hadn't yet gained the layered context of an adult. The sentences between both Angel and her father were short, but she recognized the exuberance in the long-awaited reunion.

Judy perceived the push and pull of her younger self. She was learning a new trick that promised to bring her back to the world, and after a small taste, she was hungry for the possibilities that lay before her. Bud was critical to the process, but he was nothing more than a vessel for Angel to draw from, and she understood this on some level. As she fed her mind, power radiated from her, and Judy suspected that she used only a small portion of her skills. In that beautiful, horrifying period, Angel was a parasite absorbing knowledge—memories. The danger became apparent. *I drain memories...like a vampire.*

Angel was on the precipice of something new and monumental, but Judy, older and more experienced, recognized something only a grown mind could. Bud was at her whim. He didn't know it—the risk was something he couldn't predict—but she saw the threat. Angel was a giant stroking a tiny insect with its small, weak structure. She could become a wrecking ball, bashing him inside without a thing he could do to stop her.

The vampire idea had more credence than she first admitted. Because he opened his mind to her, she had the run of the house. He invited the vampire in, and once you do such a thing, there is no going back.

An anxious voice screamed that the act was wrong, and she calmed that internal voice by telling it she was coming back from the brink, and he wanted to help her. Still, he couldn't know all the implications of his decision any more than the girl in kindergarten drinking from him the source of life, like a juice box.

Allowing a damaged girl, only a toddler, to wield such power was maddening. Bud gave Angel a loaded gun and stood in front of her, hoping for the best. Her love for her father was overflowing. In the deepest part of his knowledge, he must have realized the risk. She guessed he didn't face it, but he was an intelligent man, and he walked toward danger.

Copper, metallic and harsh, entered her mind, and at once, she pictured her body, deep in paralysis, draining blood. And like a spark, the blood made sense. Weight fell off her shoulders. The empty spaces in her became whole. Not all, but some, and that was enough for her—for now. The father-daughter conversation within the garden was ending. Angel gorged on the memories. It occurred to her that memories are the building blocks of life, at least with creating the self, and they were everything that made up a soul. Judy identified their value better than anyone.

The garden faded away. When Angel woke, she saw her father sleeping next to her. She had jumbled thoughts, which hadn't changed, but there was a clarity that wasn't there before. Her mind was a pair of glasses, caked with mud and grease. They had wiped away a thin layer of the gook. *That's how the clinic worked.* Each session was wiping away a thin film, done over and over until one day...you were back from the murky waters. You popped your head above the surface for your first breath of fresh air.

Chapter Twenty-two
—Enough food to bury the family—

From the back of the diner's kitchen, food on trays kept coming. Judy had to arrange, then rearrange the center of the table to accommodate all the entrees they ordered.

"If not for you all..." Judy scanned the table, filled with friends. "Not sure how I'd end up, but you guys rescued me. When this is all behind me, I want to fly everyone to my home to stay for a while. My treat."

"You have a pool to dip in?" Becky asked.

"Right next to our living room," Judy mentioned.

"You have a swimming pool inside your house?" Maddie asked with disbelief painted on her face.

"Yeah...sounds weird saying that. We have a bowling alley, too." Judy threw a cringing expression. They all erupted with excitement.

"It wasn't my idea, and I don't use it—think I've thrown one ball down its lane," she said. "If Johnny saw you were taking care of me the way you have, he would shower you with more than a banquet from a diner. I know he will love you all the way I do." She raised her glass of pop to her three friends, and they followed suit.

"Shouldn't that be alcohol you're drinking?" Maddie teased. Judy patted her coat pocket.

"Medicine's always close by," Judy said.

"No way in hell can we eat all this food," Cal said, scanning the tabletop, not seeing an inch of daylight between dishes.

"I'm going to do my damnedest to take care of these. Everything looks so amazing. Thank you, Judy," Becky said.

"It's the least I can do—dragging you out into the night." Judy wanted to fill in her friends about everything she'd discovered, but her true intention was to have a normal day—and she wanted to be a normal woman. Her pursuit of finding herself was chugging right along, and that was the problem—she was a dog on a leash, and they were running to keep up. She grasped their commitment to help her, and nothing came close to her appreciation. Family and friends were out her reach for so long, and now she had everything.

Except for the description of white strands shooting out of Judy's head and connecting to others, they were excited to hear what she learned, and even added to the story with things they unearthed. As always, Becky was the most animated of the bunch. She was a parade float preparing to fly away at any second.

"Tracked down the owner, Brice Deville," Becky said between bites, "he's in a sanitarium rubbing the two marbles left to him together. Except he's not the owner of the AAU anymore."

"New owner?" Judy asked, pushing away her plate and scanning the diner as the lunch rush took hold.

"It was something Cal said when we went in...he wondered why it still had power. I know landlords want to keep vacant properties humming through harsh winters—frozen pipes—moisture seeping into walls during hot summers. But there was something unusual about the utilities running full speed ahead. The problem was—there's nothing to track down. The county courthouse has property records for every structure in the city—these are public records that anyone can access. And there was no owner listed," Becky said, situating a slice of pie across from her.

"Impossible," Cal said, "you can't bury records like that—at least I've never seen it."

Becky raised her eyebrows and plunged her fork deep into her apple pie's crust.

"Maybe it's a ghost building," Becky said, "We entered another dimension—because the rest of the neighborhood saw the place bulldozed years ago."

Maddie threw a wadded-up napkin in her direction.

"Stop reading those science fiction books. Your imagination is getting the better of you," Maddie said. "There's an answer—we just have to find it."

"Unlike the rest of you, I did some actual police work," Cal said and pretended to polish a badge that wasn't there.

"Well, holy shit. Step back, ladies. I think Cal's head will fill up this room," Becky said in a fit of laughter. They all joined in except Cal, who was deciding if the comment was good-natured or not. He gave a tentative smile.

"I'm only fucking with you. Tell us your info, Boy Scout," she teased. Her comment wiped the smile from his face.

"I found some patients who you helped at *Angel Among Us*. Grown with families of their own, and let me say—if you wanted to run for Mayor, these people would plant a sign in about a million lawns for you. The impression you made, Judy—ten out of ten in the inspiration department," Cal said, tipping a cup of coffee back.

Judy wondered how the lives of her patients, kids when she met them, detoured from sorrow to whatever life they led. A component of her wanted to talk to them—find out who they became. Another part understood this as a foolish daydream. She wasn't a doctor, and they weren't her patients in any legitimate way. *I was only a meddling teenager.*

"One woman described a playground that you would meet her at every day," Cal said. "Ring any bells?"

Judy shook her head.

"Another man swore that you were on another planet with him...Saturn, I think," Cal laughed. "He said it was months of you talking to him until one day he could sit up in bed with no help and turn to face his family—one story was crazier than the last. However, you did these things—you changed some lives in that place," Cal said.

Becky squeezed Judy's arm.

"We are proud of you. We were friends throughout our childhood—you never told me about any of this. I would have bragged my head off if I could do what you can," Maddie said.

"I was her fiancé, and she never told me either," Cal thundered. The table went quiet.

"We were engaged?" Judy asked. Judy saw embarrassment wash over him. An image popped into Judy's head and was only a flash come and gone before she could describe it. The image was an engagement ring. Blood spurted from her nose, and Maddie came to the rescue with a spare napkin. Judy dabbed.

"The bleeding is scaring me," Maddie said with worry in her voice. Judy doubled down on the tissue, shaking her head with a hand still holding them in place.

"Good thing," Judy muttered through a bulge of paper covering her nose and mouth, "I know why I'm bleeding—discovered the reason within a vision."

"What causes it?" Becky asked.

"Memories," Judy said, laughing, "hard to explain—when a branch—neuron or whatever gets restored, the bad parts become severed." The diner erupted with noisy patrons scooting tables and chairs and talking loud at the height of the noontime shift. Everyone stared at Judy. "A stroke was what I first thought...it had to be. It crystalized last night. I was seeing something that already happened to me, and BAM...blood started flowing." She pulled the flask from her pocket and took a swig as if no one could see her. "And it's the alcohol that propels my remembering. Like the night we drank at The Thurman Cafe," she glanced at Cal as he nodded. "Or the night I drank with you, Maddie."

"Then Virginia was right, more than she let on," Becky said.

"Yes," Judy agreed, "She was right about overdoing it with drinking too much alcohol. My thought is my brain would hemorrhage if I drank too much, too often. I think I dodged a bullet on that count," she confessed. Judy stared down at her feet, and the table went quiet. "This trip revealed two things to me...I want to help others like I did when I was young. I've never been as happy as I was when I found out what I did for those children. Suppose I was that way back then, too. Wanting to always feel like that...part of the community."

"So, what's the other?" Cal asked.

"I want to write again," Judy said, like a child talking about Santa Claus. "My dad is bringing home my computer from the facility." She showed a toothy grin to her friends. "Seeing my writing will be the thrill of my life. I have a good husband who is a brilliant writer, but I have dreams of my own."

"Good for you." Maddie cheered.

"When you are a famous writer, don't forget about us again," Cal said. His blunt joke drew a laugh from everyone.

"I have something to say." All heads turned to Becky. She twisted a napkin in between and around her fingers in nervous movements.

"The three of you were good friends at various times in your lives. When we were in high school, I ran with the cool kids." She dropped the napkin and made air quotes with her fingers. "Thing is…they weren't the cool kids, and I discovered that soon after school. Looking back, I would have done anything to be friends with you guys. And if I can call you my friends now…I'd be grateful."

"That was so sweet," Judy said.

"We were the nerds. You'd be bored," Cal confessed.

"Speak for yourself," Maddie interrupted, "I was not a nerd."

"We'll stay in touch this time," Judy promised.

"When are you leaving?" Cal asked with a somber tone. Judy flashed Cal a smile without teeth.

"I board a plane tomorrow."

"What about the rest of your memories?" Becky asked as desperation seeped into the words.

"I've gone as far as I can here. I need to finish my healing at home and reclaim my life."

Becky nodded, tears glistening on the edges of her eyes.

"Don't forget us," Cal said. The standard sentiment that people use all the time became way more important.

"Never," Judy said while shaking her head. When she stood, they all did, embracing each for the last time. No one wanted to be the first to let go.

Chapter Twenty-three
—People see what they look for—

Bud put Judy in a bear hug with Emily wrapping her arms around them both. Their forms filled Judy's small bedroom.

"Our home feels different with all of us here," Emily said, squeezing tighter.

"One last big breakfast tomorrow before your flight," Bud said, wagging a finger her direction. "No excuses." She tossed him a salute, and her parents moved toward the door and turned back. She wondered what they were seeing. *The teenage girl that shared the same walls so long ago?*

The night was more difficult than Judy expected. Bud and Emily needed more time with their daughter, and she understood it as well. Breaking away again was bearable because she resolved to return as often as she was able. Johnny's novels were selling well, their finances were on cruise control, and he had a machine around him managing his daily book business. For the first time in her life, supporting Johnny's dreams wasn't a priority. Any guilt she carried about seeking her career path drifted off her like a silk sheet. She was free to be selfish for a change. The world was brand new to her. She held no illusions that Johnny's literary world wouldn't pull her in when it chose, but that was okay.

Behind her desk, smaller than she remembered, Judy sipped a glass of wine. *Wait until I tell Johnny that I have orders to drink.* He's going to love that news. The irony made her laugh as she powered on the vintage Macintosh and watched it crackle and buzz to life. She didn't remember the computer, but the appearance captured her imagination. She imagined pounding away late into the night. Spinning thread into gold.

The phrase was silly and made her feel inadequate about restarting her writing career. The bottom of a mountain was where she stood and meant to climb every inch to reach her goal of becoming an actual author.

Sliding the mouse, Judy placed the cursor on the file labeled: *Judy's Novels and Miscellaneous* and clicked. She held her breath and imagined what stories her fresh young mind had conceived. Twelve rows of files appeared one after the other. Judy exhaled so long that her lungs hurt and thought her ribs were rubbing against the lining of her stomach. All at once, she went from too much air to not being able to catch it.

The files sat there mocking even as her focus blurred. First, from anxiety and then from the tears that leaked from the sides. Lids slammed shut hard, causing the liquid to stream down her cheeks. She was trying to make sense of what she was seeing. It was right there in front of her, and yet the meaning didn't hit her. Judy squinted at the screen—lines skewed left and right as she tried to focus. Sobs took over her body in convulsive jerks.

Her body was in the bedroom, safe, but her thoughts were outside, thrashing, and twirling out of control. The implications were beyond what she could fathom, and with every connection, another would fall, tumbling like dominoes. The chain reaction was already underway. Everything had changed. Her phone rang, and she edged back from it as if it were a bomb about to detonate. A name—bold and prominent, populated its screen: JOHNNY MACKLEMORE.

Blood rushed to her face as she moved toward the blaring device. She placed the phone to an ear and listened.

"Judy. Are you there?" Johnny barked. She made no response. "I can hear you breathing on the line. My publisher said you never delivered my manuscript. What the hell is going on?" His voice was so high that it hurt her ears, but she kept the phone tight against her head.

"I know what you did," she said in a hissing tone—silence on the opposite end.

"Didn't I tell you to leave? I warned you, Judy," he said, dragging out her name to taunt. She was in the middle of a game that started way before that day. *How can I win if I don't know the rules?* Her mind went blank except for the first thing that popped in.

"Fuck you, Johnny." Her defiance caught him off guard, and his imitation of a congenial man melted away.

"Judy? I am...coming...to get you," Johnny said, strangling each word.

Her eyes went wide. She snapped the phone off and propelled it onto her bed like it was a snake that crawled into her hand without her knowing. She gazed up to the ceiling and let out a primal scream that started in her chest and finished in her mouth.

In that roar was everything she had experienced, learned, and found out she lost since returning home. Judy's scream didn't stop as much as drained from her like a balloon. Falling to the bed, she stared at the computer screen and cried. Bud and Emily scrambled in, searching the room first for an intruder, then settling on their sobbing daughter.

"Judy?" Emily prompted. Judy shook her head, tears streaming down to the floor. Emily checked her daughter for injuries, saw none, and embraced her frantic child.

"Talk to us. What's wrong?" Bud prodded. She pointed to a row of names on the monitor.

"Every bestseller that Johnny wrote..." They followed her finger to the screen. "They were my novels. He published every single book I wrote!" Her parents didn't understand at first. Judy ran and picked up her novel and hurried to her desk, where Johnny's manuscript remained wrapped. She tore away the brown paper covering the novel to reveal the title: Desert Lily.

"The son of a bitch didn't even change the titles." Weeping threatened to derail her voice again, and she presented the two manuscripts next to each other. Mirror images. Grabbing the mouse, she hovered over each file. "Year after year, Johnny published my novels," Judy said.

"But how?" Emily asked. Bud and Judy exchanged suspicious glances.

"Johnny didn't even know the room that this computer was in even existed," Bud argued.

"What room?" Emily asked.

"I will fill you in later," Bud said, speaking to Emily.

"I thought I was a failure," Judy whispered. "He let me go on believing I was a failure—calling my novels his." She sniffled loud, slapped the tears off her face, and nodded her head at no one in particular. Gathering clothes from around the room, she slipped them on and reached for a jacket.

"Where are you going this late at night," Emily asked.

"I need the keys. Can I borrow the car?"

"Sure...but. What are you planning to do?" Bud asked. Judy extended her hand and left it there until Bud dropped his car keys into her palm.

"Johnny is on his way...I intend to find out who he is before he arrives," she said and was already out her bedroom before they had a chance to protest.

*　　　*　　　*　　　*

The Columbus city skyline loomed large through the windshield. Buildings jutted outward from the middle of Ohio's Capital city. The car ride for Judy was one of the loneliest of her life. The miles went by, and as they did, she recalled the day she arrived, her delusions of a car accident that didn't happen, and the truth Otis offered. Suicide was like a far-fetched notion and now she wondered what she saw that drove her to the act.

Her mind drifted to the night that started it all, the night she left home forever. The memories were foggy as usual, but she always held onto the reassurance that she, above everyone else, wanted to walk away from her family and start a life with Johnny Macklemore. She wasn't as sure of anything anymore, except he stole her dreams and lived out the life she wanted right there in front of her. *Did he take pleasure in my jealousy—my sadness? He must have seen my spirit crushed and did nothing*. The emotions hurt her chest, digging deeper and deeper as the anger and self-pity burned in her like a furnace. Her routine of pushing the ugly thoughts away wasn't working, or she was past that ability. Hurt gave her memories a good foundation, and she relished their stark clarity. She refused to hide from anything ever again, no matter what pain it inflicted.

A mad rush to action swept her away, and now with some distance, she wondered how the night would end for her. Over the years, she built up an image of what a wife was. Filled to the brim with sacrifice—support and suffocating a part of herself for the betterment of the relationship.

They had shared decisions like two sides of a mathematical equation that gave each partner the right answer. At least that's what she believed. And now she pondered how many of her paths were ever choices. There was no bottom to the possibilities, and it threatened to drive her insane. She arrived a blank slate, and that terrified her. But not as much as discovering what he had done to her.

When the wheels came to a stop, Judy stared at Johnny's childhood home. The place filled her with dread. His mother, Sue, passed as amiable, but as she was slow to learn—*trust no one*. The next link in the chain ran through Johnny's house, and it led to Tessa. Of the three souls inside, Johnny's sister alone held the key. Judy's mind skidded back to the night she met Tessa, lying in bed, trapped in a world no one understood. But Judy understood everything.

Moving from the vehicle, Judy copied the same path as her first visit, except this time instead of heading for the front door—she imagined the floor plan as if she were inside. Judy followed the perimeter, hoped she chose the right window, and placed a pry bar, the same one Cal used the other night, under the window. She prepared for a loud crack and pried. The window slid up with no sound and she was happy to find it unlocked. *Things are finally going my way tonight.*

Hoisting her body onto the window ledge, she shimmied through the opening. She pictured the house like a hungry mouth taking her in, swallowing her whole. The image was unexpected, threatening to force her back outside if not for the slimmest need to disobey. With eyes not yet adjusted to the dark bedroom, Judy planted her foot on Tessa's carpet, and half expected Frank and Sue waiting for her in the room. In her imagination, they were standing by the window as if they had awaited her break-in since her visit. When both feet were solid on the floor, she tilted up and saw no one in front of her. She exhaled the nervous air.

With her back to the window, streetlights invaded the room from behind and helped her eyes focus with each fuzzy shape having more precise edges. A dresser became a dresser. A desk became a desk—and the bed materialized in front of her like a magician's illusion. The air was much warmer than outside, and that gave her some comfort as she occupied someone else's living space. Because the home was older, each step emitted a squeak from the worn floorboards. Without considering the floor, Judy stopped her progress and placed her feet down softer and more deliberate.

A child's dollhouse, built to the exact specification of a Victorian home, rested in the room's corner. A trickle of light gave the tiny building a haunted facade, and she expected miniature ghosts to shoot from its door. She was thankful it remained a child's toy, dark and silent.

Shuffling her feet instead of walking to lower the chance of a board releasing a moan, Judy made her way to the bed with Tessa stretched out on top. Tessa had outgrown the single bed as her form assumed all the areas of the mattress. She resembled Snow White scrunched into one bed belonging to a dwarf. Even in the dim light, Tessa's blonde hair tussled all about, appeared rich and beautiful. Judy recognized a beauty queen when she saw one, and Tessa, although older, belonged on a stage with a crown. The benign face of the woman was one that a mother wanted and caused a father sleepless night trying to protect. Prettiness was a description Judy heard throughout her life, but it was undeniable that Tessa owned different DNA than the common girl. She guessed that her exterior alone threatened the ladies around her growing up, and she conceded her own insecurity as she spotted the sleeping beauty. Kneeling next to the bed, Judy brushed the hair away from Tessa's face and leaned closer.

"I will bring you back, Tessa," she whispered and allowed her body to fall back into a lying position to match Tessa's. They were identical, with one on a bed and the other on the floor. Two things came to Judy's mind— how to fall asleep at will in a house you broke into, and how the hell she would relearn how to use powers she hasn't used in decades and didn't until recently even remember she possessed.

Her task appeared daunting as she lay there, squeezing her eyelids closed so tight that veins wanted to burst. *Just relax and let yourself drift.* Her body obeyed. Tendons loosened with the limbs becoming limp—heavy, and soon her thoughts followed suit until a calmness spread throughout her entire frame. She didn't think about it until much later, but her shell remembered the technique, even as her conscious mind didn't have a clue.

One second, she was awake in her sister-in-law's bedroom, and the next, she was falling into a black void, and sliding off to sleep with an agenda that made all the difference in the world.

She recognized a seam that she never noticed before. It fascinated her it was there at all. There was a divide in her sleeping mind that presented two paths. She understood now that one led to a deeper slumber while the other was where she could do the work she intended to do that night.

The division was only a thin veil, and she wondered if anybody could see the two paths and believed they could if they trained themselves or knew what to look for with skilled perception. She also imagined that the pull to a deeper sleep was too irresistible to pass up for everyone. Besides, how many people were entering sleep to work? *No wonder no one saw the veil.*

Judy guided her presence toward the road not taken and floating that direction even as she was aware her body was stationary. As she drifted, her skin changed temperature. It was as if she was entering the vacuum of space. Passing through the veil was altering things in the physical world, and it frightened her to know there was more involved than just her thoughts alone. If the astral journey affected her body, it meant injury could happen along the way. She was like a live wire in the new plane.

It wasn't as if she was happy or unhappy—instead, she was an antenna—super sensitive and ready to receive. Her fear doubled. Judy couldn't put her finger on the sensation except for someone placing a sensitive hearing device next to a person preparing to scream. It was anxious anticipation making her heart beat faster.

A chill covered her, and she still went further into the veil. Something was different, and she stopped drifting. A thought shifted into focus. It was of veterans that came back from war without a limb and still perceived its presence even after it was long gone. They swore they could move an arm no longer present as if it remained in an invisible realm, gone but still there somehow. That's how it was for Judy. She had hundreds of limbs surrounding her, and although she didn't see them, she tested their grip like a person trying to open and close a hand. A comic book character she saw once flew into her mind from nowhere—Doctor Octopus, Spiderman's villainous enemy. Her heart raced as the connection solidified into fact. Inside this expanse, her entire essence became the act of either pushing or pulling. Freedom thrilled her.

What do I do next? A connection. I need a link. Judy closed her eyes inside a body that had already closed its eyes and reached out for Tessa. A thrust of an invisible tendril, snapping out for what appeared to be miles even as their physical bodies were but a couple of feet apart. The long distance ended, and she connected to Tessa—soul to soul. She remembered what Bud told her about Angel taking memories away from him, and she didn't want to traipse around in Tessa's subconscious like a bull in a China shop.

Another vital step rushed in—a world for the two to share. Whatever skill Judy had for world-building was knowledge she had long ago, and the training wheels were back on the bike. The power every child takes for granted, imagination, was what she needed to use to get her world up and humming. *Where would Tessa feel most comfortable?* Magnifying her thoughts, she settled on Tessa's bedroom as the perfect meeting area. Walls formed around them and the hint of items that lined them. The walls faded back out as she tried to get a handle of keeping the visuals of her projection alive.

The images faded in and out like a light on a dimmer switch. Judy focused on searching for a grip to make the visuals stay put. It took several attempts before she discovered the process required splitting her concentration into smaller thoughts. The idea was impossible until she tried, and it shocked her to see she could do it easily. Each task was like placing shirts on a clothesline. She formed a mental picture then put a clothespin on top of that image, and it stayed where she wanted. Judy marveled at the capability of a mind.

As the bedroom went from a translucent structure to a stable-enough form, Judy placed a clothespin on it, and moved to her new task of filling it with Tessa's precious items: bed, dresser lined with knickknacks, posters on the wall, and the dollhouse in the corner.

She placed more clothespins on the images to cement them into reality. A realization that she didn't account for everything in the room became clear but her first attempt at the enchantment impressed her senses. There was still one apparition left to conjure, and that was Tessa. Nervous energy took over, and she was afraid to make it happen. Summoning a human being with a conscious of their own was a lot different from imagining inanimate objects. *This is why I'm here*, Judy thought, and pushed through the panic.

First, a shadow appeared on the bed, followed by a solid outline edge of the same shadow. It became apparent that Judy needed to use all her invisible limbs to pull Tessa's form into her constructed room. The effort to wrangle the body and mind of an individual was much greater than she expected. Designing rooms and items were like lifting a ten-pound dumbbell. But creating a functional person in the same space required lifting a one-thousand-pound dumbbell in comparison.

She focused her concentration like a magnifying glass, and Tessa entered her bedroom world. When the process was complete, Judy placed another mental clothespin on Tessa and found she needed little concentration to keep her there with her.

Tessa wore the same baby-doll nightgown she saw on her when she arrived next to her bed—her blonde hair brushed to perfection and tied up with a scrunchie. The feature that got Judy's attention was her eyes. Tessa's eyes were the bluest Judy had ever seen. They resembled the blue of a tropical sea, piercing in a way that made her feel self-conscious to have them gazing her direction.

Tessa wasn't a static image without life, and Judy discovered she was looking around her surroundings, exploring everything. Tessa hadn't undertaken the simple task of exploration in years. Judy recognized the exhilaration the woman exuded at the sudden liberty come true.

"Tessa?" Judy asked and heard her own voice reverberate in the constructed space. Tessa froze as if she hadn't realized there was someone else with her. Her head moved like a robot up toward Judy and stopped. The expression was curiosity but also fear. Judy couldn't decide if the woman was afraid of her or attempting to talk for the first time in forever. Lips moved without sound, and Judy wondered if Tessa had the ability anymore until sound rose.

"—really here?" Tessa managed. Her voice was like a phone cutting out. Some words made it through while others remained in her faraway place. Tessa had to employ some concentration of her own to take part in this mental communication.

"In your mind...think about your mouth making the words," Judy instructed. Tessa nodded with genuine fear.

"How...my here?"

"Better," Judy said. "Imagine your throat pushing out the sounds."

"Who are you?"

Judy smiled at the question.

"My name is Judy. I'm your sister-in-law, Tessa." The woman raised her hand to her mouth and studied her hands as if they belonged to someone else.

"It's okay. This isn't real."

Tears filled Tessa's eyes, and Judy bet that the Tessa resting on the bed was crying.

"I remember when I used to move. It was so...ago...long ago," Tessa corrected. "I stopped trying."

"I understand," Judy said. Tessa peered at her moving arms once more.

"When you can't move...or speak...you let yourself drift into the fog to hide from the anxiety of not being able to. And after you push yourself into that place for so long...it's hard to come back...even when you want to," Tessa admitted.

Judy nodded and reached out for Tessa's hand and found that her hand felt like a real hand. The typical human interaction thrilled Tessa, and Judy took that for granted.

"How did you end up stuck inside yourself?" Judy asked and guessed Tessa hadn't thought about it in quite a while.

"John...he did this to me," Tessa said, as much to herself as to Judy. The admission caused tears to flow down her cheeks.

"What did he do?"

"He was my little brother, and I loved him," she said, "I was a teenager with my focus...I didn't have time for him. Maybe that's why he did what he did."

"Did what?" Judy asked in a panic. Tessa gave her a weak smile.

"I was like many other girls...I was a daddy's girl. You could say I had him wrapped around my finger, and John realized that, too. I suppose that was his source of jealousy. My relationship with my dad was what it was, and I never analyzed it or even questioned what others thought of it— what Johnny thought of it. Mostly, I only focused on my teenage life—the boys who liked me, going to high school football games on Fridays, what clothes I would wear the next day at school. These were the things that stole my attention. My little brother was not on my radar...guess that's where things went wrong," she said.

"How did it begin?" Judy coaxed.

"The way everything does, I suppose...slow. Household chores were the first. My parents gave us things to do around the house. Things my dad told me to do before and after school vanished from my mind. He'd come home from work and get pissed I disobeyed his orders. These were things I swear he never told me. It went on like that for some time until..."

"What?" Tessa closed her eyes.

"Soon, homework assignments forgotten—meetings with friends or boys were never kept. I got the backlash when all these happened, but I couldn't prevent anything or help my situation at all. My dad brought me to a doctor, and they said nothing was wrong with me." Tessa's form appeared to shrivel as she described her past.

"I'm sorry," Judy said.

"Me, too. My memory never got better. It deteriorated until I could no longer remember common things like tying my shoes—putting on make-up—even my dad's name eluded me. How have you restored my memory?" Tessa asked in a hopeful tone.

"Tessa, I haven't. I believe I'm talking to your subconscious mind. Below where your memories branch out. The core of who you are."

"I'm not fixed?" Judy shook away the question and saw the desperation in Tessa's expression.

"It's okay. After I find out everything about how you got in this situation, I will work to help you. I promise," Judy assured.

Tessa sobbed when reality hit her.

"How do you know your brother did this to you?"

Tessa continued to cry, and Judy let her. Living in the imitation world felt safe, but Judy remembered where her body was on the outside and prompted Tessa to speak.

"I need you, Tessa. How do you know it was Johnny?"

"It's difficult...fragments here and there...not sure what was said, but...my feeling says Johnny told me."

"Okay. I want to reach in and find those memories if I can. Is that all right with you?"

Tessa gave a slight nod.

"I'm new to this. I can't protect you from what you see. It will be like a live experience for both of us, okay?"

"I understand," Tessa said. Judy wondered if she did but took her at her word.

"I know you can't remember the details, but I want you to think about him revealing himself to you. Feel yourself hovering over those moments."

If bringing the projection of Tessa into her world was like lifting a one-thousand-pound dumbbell, then diving for her buried memories and bringing them to her conscious level was the equivalent of one hundred thousand pounds. Even though the task was all mental, it had a physical component she didn't understand, like flexing a muscle. Her tendrils were firm on the memory, but they wouldn't budge with her usual effort. *I bet six-year-old Angel would have no problem.* She loosened her hold, if there was such a thing, and started again. This time Judy imagined her tendrils were arms, strong and muscular. At first, she didn't think it would help, but the trick of the mind began pulling the memories from the depths of Tessa's brain.

Limitations of her thinking forced her to perceive the act as if they were coming from the bottom of the sea. Tessa and Judy both sank into the images.

"Is this normal?" Tessa asked.

"Not sure what normal is at this point." Tessa was in the same bedroom they were occupying. Although her condition had progressed past her ability to use her muscles, Tessa could shift and focus around her. *Trapped in her body*, Judy thought.

They heard the door opening with Tessa straining to move her body without achieving the goal. Tessa scanned the room until a boy came into view. They saw Johnny enter her line of sight. He was skinny and young, no more than a middle schooler. It was the eyes that struck Judy—not the eyes of an adolescent. Behind them was wisdom, and they hid something else she couldn't plan, but it scared her to see it all the same.

He tilted his head to match Tessa's.

"Baby Tessa. Isn't that what Dad calls you?" His expression turned to disgust, "How's it feel in there?" She did not react as he began stroking her hair, except for the goosebumps that rose on her skin. "Dad loves you...and he can keep on loving you, but you won't know it. Every night I come in here to take a little piece of you. I keep what I want and throw away the rest. I'm close, Tessa," Johnny said, stretching, so his mouth was right next to her ear. "They will have to feed you and pull the shit from you the rest of your life." This surprised Tessa, and he revealed a toothy grin. "Still there...not for long. Goodbye, Sis." The memory ended and Judy saw Tessa had been crying the whole time.

"Maybe I deserved this. What did I do to Johnny?" Tessa asked.

"There is nothing you've ever done to deserve what he's done to you," Judy said.

"So...if this isn't real, I'm not real?"

She didn't know how to answer. Judy Angel, who had worked at the clinic long ago, was the one to ask and, more than likely, the one person who could help Tessa.

"All I can say is that it isn't hopeless," Judy said. "It's hard to explain...I'll come back for you, Tessa."

"Where am I?" Tessa asked, panic rising.

"You're safe. With your parents—far away from Johnny," Judy said. "I want you to remember one—"

Breathing became hard for Judy. Tessa mirrored her fear.

"What's wrong?" Tessa asked as Judy gripped her own neck, trying to understand why she couldn't breathe, and the answer washed over her like freezing water. It was her body. She broke away from the world she'd created to see Frank crouched over her, hands around her neck. His face contorted into a mask of anger and he squeezed Judy's throat tighter. Could she have fought him off if she'd seen him come into the room? *A question for some other life.*

Frank smelled of Budweiser and sweat, mixing into some terrible, hostile cologne. Judy and Frank's bodies were in the same room, but Judy was watching the outside turn into a fog while Frank showed his fury. His fingers were his instruments delivering his wrath. Judy moved her mouth with no sound passing her lips. She closed her eyes, for the last time, and reached out to Tessa to tell her she was sorry. Frank gripped tighter.

Tessa's body jerked hard. Her movement was close to an involuntary flinch, but it caused her head to rotate on the bed, shifting to the side—staring at Frank. Her gaze captured him. The sight forced his hands up and off Judy.

Judy gasped in the air like someone breaking the water's surface. She had stuttering breaths like a child after a panicked crying fit. Frank brought his hand toward his face, studying them as if covered with Judy's blood and returned his gaze to his daughter on the bed. Her irises, although not animated, stared at him. Judy pushed against the wall and was getting enough air to slow her breathing to a normal range, rubbing her neck to get the horrible feeling of choking off her skin.

"Tessa hasn't moved in...so many years," Frank said, watching his daughter as if she could sit up and talk at any second. Judy tried to speak, but her throat wouldn't let her. Instead, a loud hiss came out. She swallowed and made another go of it.

"Wasn't hurting her," was all Judy could manage and went back to stroking her neck. Frank's head swiveled toward Judy, and he saw her for the first time that night, at least without red-hot anger. His expression softened.

"Tessa is the one thing in this fucking world I love," he said. Judy nodded with pain, tears streaming. "I check on her every night—talk to her. She never speaks, but I pray she can hear me. I used to think my voice would bring her back. I gave up on that years ago, though. This is our routine—each night." He returned to Tessa. Judy had considered him a mindless monster, but that wasn't the case. Frank was the mirror image of her own father. He lost his little girl in the same way Bud lost his daughter, and he suffered—with no end in sight.

"When I saw someone in here..."

"I...know," she squeaked out. "What *really* happened to her?" Judy already had an answer, but did Frank? Large palms covered his face to hide his shame.

"Caught Johnny in the same spot you're in now. He was talking—more like taunting her. That was the last time he was alone with her."

"How did he do this?" she prodded. He shook his head.

"Don't know...still doubt it sometimes. It's too unbelievable."

"Try me." He scanned her face to discover her intentions.

"Same time as she was losing her memory," he turned his attention to his daughter as if he were talking to her alone, "I started to forget things. But I was sure that something wasn't right. After a month, I saw a pattern."

"Pattern?" she asked.

"Yeah. The night that I drank—my memory was fine the next day."

"And?"

"And the nights that Johnny slept outside the house. It was too late for my daughter, but I started drinking every night." Judy sympathized with the man that drank himself into oblivion as a defense against his son.

"You haven't stopped since?" He gave a pitiful shake of the head.

"Johnny doesn't come here anymore. When he visits Sue—they do it away from here—away from Tessa. I make sure of that. Drinking isn't protection—like it once was. I drink to stop my pain. I came to terms with that a long time ago," Frank turned from his daughter, "my drinking is to stop my thoughts," he said in a whisper.

"Thoughts?"

"If I don't have enough in me before I visit her at night. The urge to put a pillow over her head—end her suffering visits me."

She released a nervous nod.

"My existence is keeping my son out of my head and not killing my daughter." Frank cried. It was strange, but Judy placed her hand on Frank's shoulder to comfort him moments after he had tried to strangle her life away.

"Guess I thought you were finishing what John couldn't," he said.

"Johnny convinced me I couldn't drink alcohol," she laughed with no humor, "now I know why." Judy faced Tessa. "She's beautiful."

"Yes."

"What happened to you...what happened to your daughter—Johnny has been doing to me our whole marriage...I was here for answers and nothing more." Frank stood.

"Well, you got them. You can go now," Frank said. Judy nodded for no one to see as Frank had already turned and left the room. Judy bent down and kissed Tessa on her cheek. Pain exploded in Judy's back from a powerful blow. *Frank returned to finish me.* Agony spread down her spine like wildfire, driving her to the ground. Another came down, this time across her shoulder. The second one wasn't as solid with the impact glancing off her. Judy spun around to see the assailant. Sue stood over her with hate on her face and a Louisville in her hands.

"How are you going to explain killing me to the police?" Judy asked. Sue was in the middle of another swing when the question made her pause.

"You...dumb girl...you broke into my house. I bashed her head in, officer before I realized it was my daughter-in-law." Judy *never* doubted her plan for a second. If she didn't act fast, that statement would be in the paper next to an author's picture of Johnny Macklemore. Sue was as angry as Frank, but something was different about her. Frank was trying to protect his daughter, and Sue was trying to protect...

"You haven't acknowledged your daughter once," Judy said through a gasp, the ache still alive. Sue glanced at her daughter, awake and staring at the same spot Frank occupied earlier.

"I saw her," Sue said with venom.

"You knew," Judy said. Disbelief transformed her features. Sue forgot about the baseball bat, and Judy was grateful for the recess.

"Johnny takes care of this family. I'm responsible for an invalid and a drunk—and he checks in on us all. He takes care of you well, from what I've heard, you spoiled bitch," Sue said. Judy wanted to form a plan of escape. Except, she couldn't help but take the bait.

"Johnny doesn't give—he takes," Judy said with equal venom. "He's a vampire that's sucked the life out of your family." Judy suspected the interchange gave something for Sue to think about, or at the very least—she was working on an argument because her sight drifted. Judy observed the open window from the corner of her eye, making no sudden movements. Sue meant to kill Judy as much as Judy meant to get out of the house. An impulse to run toward the window took hold—Sue trained her eyes on her, and she was vermin backed into a corner.

"See what he did to Tessa?"

"What's done is done," Sue said with no emotion.

"You're no better than him," Judy said. An ugly laugh spewed from Sue.

"Is that right? He was killing you, but slow. I won't do that—I promise." Sue lifted the baseball bat over her head. The wood made a whooshing sound as it cut through the air, and Judy had time enough to tense before she felt the impact of the bat. Her eyelids clamped tight but the wood never made contact. Judy's eyes sprung open to see Frank wrestling with his wife.

"Get off me, you motherfucker!" Sue screamed. Frank tried to manage Sue in his drunken condition. He switched from holding her to holding the flailing bat—back and forth.

"Get out!" he wasn't asking, but roaring—a sound that blasted off the small bedroom walls and got Judy moving.

"My Johnny's coming home," Sue blurted out to Judy while struggling with Frank, "you can't hide from him." Judy squared up the window and dove through the opening with no regard to what was out and below. Nothing but hard ground stopped her fall, but that was okay. Sue was still hollering from inside, but the words weren't registering, and Judy couldn't care less. She was out and safe. *What the hell is safe anymore?* She went into a full sprint. They were not likely following, but she saw enough movies to know you didn't stop until you were long gone. As she drove, her thought landed on Tessa. With every mile away, she missed their connection, and she regretted leaving her behind in her house of horror for a second time.

Chapter Twenty-four
—A permanent fiancé—

The knocking on Cal's door was so loud that he considered bringing his gun for the briefest of moments. Drowsiness won out, and he opened his door unarmed in his boxers, as vulnerable as it gets. Officers on the force were at the mercy of the job, he noticed. A sentimental sap of a cop saw enough thieves, abusers and liars day after day—year after year—to alter their personality. By his estimation, the transformation was inevitable, the longer you were a servant to the public. *It's the lying that has the most effect on a person's cynicism.* He would concede that everyone lied from time to time. He heard untruths ranging from white lies to huge conspiracies.

It's the constant bombardment of the lies that turned a happy-go-lucky police officer into a person suspicious of everybody and everything. Old ladies tell stories about why they speed—drunks explain how they were right in slugging the other drunk next to him after their home team loses.

When you run into a cop, Cal discovered, you are already figuring out your lie. This was heavy on his mind when he found out that Judy was close to a saint. Happy surprises about someone's character didn't happen so often on his watch anymore. By the time he got off work until he fell fast asleep, he wished he had another night to spend with Judy. Not in a restaurant, and not with the crew. What he wanted was Judy all to himself. Even as she was heading back to her fancy life with Johnny Macklemore, he wanted it.

Sleep's foggy blanket smothered his senses with the pounding on the door continuing. The knocker was persistent as he swung the door open, and he prepared himself to tear into whoever woke him at such a late hour. He froze there, no words. Judy stood in the doorway. There was more of a chance of a door-to-door salesman working into the wee hours of the night than Judy perched on his stoop. Hovering in the doorway with nothing but his boxers on, Cal remembered his robe in another room. He shrugged his shoulders and went to the door. A contest to see who would speak first was in full swing. Cal broke the ice.

"What are you doing here? Your flight was the earliest," he said. She stared at his green eyes, ignoring every word. His disheveled hair fit into what the youngest generation called a *Tousled* look.

"You're still in love with me, aren't you?" Judy asked.

"Yes," he answered without hesitation, "I always—" Judy moved to him—grabbed both sides of his face and pressed her lips onto his. The action was so unexpected that Cal didn't return her kiss until a few seconds later. She pushed him into the room with lips still locked.

"Where's your bedroom?" she asked. Cal pointed to another section of the house without a voice. She smiled, nodded, and found his mouth again with her own. Two bodies entwined—they navigated the room until they were on his bed.

"What about Johnny?"

Judy shook her head.

"I'm not Judy Macklemore," She kissed him deep. "I'm Judy Angel." He pulled back and fixed his emerald eyes on her. "I'm your Judy Angel," she said.

They spent the night exploring each other. With each touch, it was like relearning everything they once loved about the other. Several times Judy flinched from the bruises Sue had inflicted on her back, but Cal was patient. Judy knew that for him it was setting things right that had been wrong for so many years. He showed no blame or resentment held for her leaving—he appreciated the second chance that most people in the world never got.

For Judy, it was about fulfilling something her soul was telling her. The old Judy thought such things were stupid or adolescent nonsense. Her circumstances taught her to listen to that quiet person inside. It was that small voice that came to her rescue. With this step as the first, she pledged to trust her intuition.

Drifting off to sleep, Judy believed she was in control for the first time since she was a teenager. Judy planned to leave Johnny because of his betrayal. But the guilt of taking another man into bed wouldn't go away. Did it matter why Johnny did what he did? The question nagged at her and begged for an answer. Not because she hoped to find out that Johnny was a good person deep down or that his reasons were noble. She already made her mind up on that score. What she couldn't live with was the thought that her entire life was for nothing, wasted.

The news over the years reported children abducted from their families to spend days, or even years, in basements. Her heart went out to the kids living a real-life horror show with a detached sympathy, never knowing she was one of them. The *why* kept returning, no matter how convincing her resolutions for a new life were. The past wasn't like the fading feelings of a sad novel, replaced by the next one in line. Her suffering would grow with every new memory—getting reacquainted with Judy Angel meant fresh wounds that needed attention. Tomorrow was for rebuilding. She lay with who she believed was the love of her life. True love was thrilling, romantic, and somehow not intended for her. As sleep coiled itself around her, an idea formed. *I deserve it.* Without realizing it, the *tunnel* returned faster than it ever had before.

The ring shone bright enough to blind Judy. First impressions were important, and the green sparkle appeared perfect in every way. She remembered the celebrities on television showing off their flashy golf ball-sized rocks and thinking how fake they looked. Even If Cal made the money, it took to buy such a ring, she wouldn't want it. It wasn't practical. She held out her hand and admired the ring's beauty.

"If you don't blink soon, your eyes will dry up," Cal said.

"You only have yourself to blame for any degeneration I suffer at the hands of this amazing thing. It could alter my writing. No one with happy endings writes anything of substance," she said.

Judy regarded the recent memory with much more excitement than before. She realized she was now in bed beside the man in the memory, and her stomach had the rare butterfly sensation she acknowledged was precious and seldom.

Peering through her eyes, Judy saw Cal's face without the lines that time brings. The shade of green found in his eyes was spot on, and there was something else... Cal was full of hope for his future. Fresh from his proposal, his life trajectory was on track for happiness. There was sadistic uneasiness knowing that the engagement wouldn't last, and his world would soon spin out of control. Johnny took her from her love, no different from Cal, except she didn't have a constant reminder of the loss. *It must have been unbearable for Cal.* The irony was, she left Cal even though she was a pawn in Johnny's plans.

"Engagement lunch?" Cal asked.

"Yep...Thurman's," she blurted. "Paul needs to see this hardware while I can still lift my arm."

Judy was inside her younger self, feeling what she was feeling, but she couldn't deny that she was jealous of her bliss. It was ridiculous to envy a memory, more because the memory was hers—but there she was, a bystander viewing their contentment like a stranger. By the time the couple parked in front of *The Thurman Cafe*, she was heartsick.

The scene inside the restaurant played out as she expected it would. Mike and a few others she didn't recognize hugged them—patted their backs—raised glasses to toast, and when they made it to a booth for lunch, both were on cloud nine about the engagement. Cal lifted his menu to decide which item was suitable for his celebratory feast. And that's when Judy's stomach sank.

In Judy's peripheral, someone was there staring, and the attention wasn't just of a curious gawker. This person's body faced the young couple who were unaware. Judy watched—unable to turn away—discomfort saturating her skin. The urge to wake up, avoid the vision altogether, was strong. It was too late—the person's face came into focus. Johnny Macklemore was grinning a maniacal grin. She had seen that smile many times, but it was now menacing in a way that she couldn't—or wouldn't— admit during their marriage. He sat there smiling at her, then stopped and turned his head toward Cal. His face changed from jovial to disgust as he studied Cal from top to bottom. Her body was tingling with the inkling that someone was watching, and yet she never caught his gaze, too excited about her life event.

When Judy guessed Johnny would turn around, he did the unthinkable—walked toward them. Safe in Cal's bed, Judy's heart raced as Johnny's form grew with each step. Judy Angel peered up at Johnny Macklemore, and then he spoke.

"I couldn't help but hear you two talk about your engagement," Johnny said to both, but only gave his attention to Judy. "I'm so happy for you."

Johnny was young and thin as a rail but with baby fat still dwelling in his cheeks—no more than a freshman in high school. He extended a hand, and she took it out of habit.

"Thank you...ah..." she said. Johnny gave another maniacal smile, a little muted this time.

"Johnny," his body was still opposite Cal. "You're beautiful, and capable, I'm sure. Your guy doesn't know how lucky he is," Johnny said.

"I actually do," Cal interjected and extended a hand of his own. A momentary expression of disgust flashed across Johnny's face but was gone as soon as it arrived.

"I'm Cal."

Grasping that he had to shake, Johnny reached behind, still facing Judy, and shook—turning back like it never happened.

"It was a real privilege to meet you..." His hand was back on Judy's.

"Judy Angel...well, soon to be Judy Reed," she said, smiling at Cal. She lifted her ringed finger for proof, breaking eye contact with Johnny. He nodded. The hitchhiking Judy was familiar with the sour expression and saw it for what it was—jealousy.

"I wish you luck...maybe we'll see each other again sometime," Johnny said.

"Maybe so," she said and shrugged. Johnny's gaze lingered a moment longer on Judy. He left the table without as much as a glance in Cal's direction. The couple exchanged frowns.

"That was weird," she admitted, "should we invite him to our wedding?" she joked.

"Yeah...I don't think so," Cal said with a laugh.

The memory halted fast with the *tunnel* snapping off her body like a punch with its exit. When Judy awoke, she was still in Cal's bed. Facing him, she yanked her mind back from him when she saw he was watching her sleep.

"What are you doing?" she yelled.

"Sorry...I couldn't help but watch you sleep. You're beautiful." She melted a little.

"Even when I snore?"

"Especially when you snore," he teased.

Blood dripped from her nose. He reached to his nightstand, grabbed a tissue, and was already cleaning her before she knew what he was doing.

"Did you have one of your dreams?"

She nodded.

"Was I there?" he asked and wiped the remaining red away.

"You bet you were. It was the morning of our engagement. You remember?"

"I remember it all," Cal said. She wondered if she should mention the way Johnny showed up. They had a good night that made her feel normal—loved, and she didn't want to ruin that.

"Probably shouldn't ask you...because I gave it back. Did you keep my engagement ring?"

His face went serious. He jumped to his feet and fished his hand inside a jewelry box. As he walked back to the bed, Judy detected the return of the butterflies. He nestled close to her in bed, positioning it in his hand, and revealed it to her.

"May I?" she asked in a delicate tone. Cal nodded and watched her pluck it from his hand. She held it up to the light and watched it sparkle. "It's beautiful. You chose well," she whispered. He shook her comment away.

"That ring chose you."

She gave him a crooked smile.

"The history of it meant nothing until all this sleuthing began with our little crew."

"I don't understand," she said, scrunching her face.

"I was searching for the right ring for months...and trust me, money hadn't kept me from buying one. Nothing told me it belonged on your finger. That's the only way I can explain it—frustrated with my hunt, I passed an antique store and went inside it. Remember...I'm the rational one. When I approached the jewelry case, all the other rings disappeared."

"That's cool, but unless you mean literally disappeared, why is it so strange that you chose this one?" He took a deep breath and stole the ring back, staring into the emerald.

"The owner blathered on about its history. He told me it belonged to a wealthy woman. He added colorful details like—she was one of the first *enchanters*," he made quotes in the air, "found out that was another word for a witch. Anyway...he told me her name was Sarah Deville," Judy was astonished. "Right. Wife of the founder of German Village, Nathaniel Deville...and his ancestor owned *Angels Among Us*, who helped you." Cal swallowed the ring up in his palm like a magic trick, feeling proud of himself.

"Wow," was all she could say.

"Cool story, huh?"

"Amazing."

"Becky is not the only one who's spooky." Cal paused for a long moment before speaking again. "Do you know what's causing your visions?" he asked.

"No. I have lots of guesses—just no definitive proof," Judy said.

"What's your best guess?"

All her answers came out jumbled into categories like intuition—facts—assumptions—and every degree in between. But she gave the question a shot.

"Breadcrumbs," she said.

"Breadcrumbs?" he repeated back to her.

"Yep. Before I ever left home, I think I was trying to stop myself. I know it sounds weird." He tilted his head.

"Every detail about your return has been weird. I was squarely in the skeptic column until you came back into town—suppose I can uncheck that box now," he said.

"My copy of *To Kill a Mockingbird* must have been my first attempt by my unconscious mind...and these visions are warning me..."

"About?"

"Johnny," she said, "He's behind everything. If I have any chance to save myself before he gets here, I have to know what his powers are."

"Powers? Like yours? How's that possible?"

"I don't know. But I've seen what Johnny's done to his sister, and he can do a lot more than that, I'd bet," she said.

"Listen to me. I'm an officer of the law. I can deal with Johnny," Cal bragged and swept her hair from her face. She smiled.

"How gallant," she said. "Cal...the tools we need to defend ourselves from Johnny are not physical and maybe not even from this world. I can't explain my abilities any more than I can explain what he can do. I've lived with a bad person, and I'm coming to terms with that, but if we approach him wrong...he can hurt us in ways we can't imagine."

"Whatever you need...you know that Judy," Cal said.

"I do. There's one more thing I debated telling you," Judy said. His face took a worrying turn. "In my vision last night...Johnny was there, too. I didn't know him then, and I don't think it was the first time he was watching me...or us."

"Johnny planned to take you away that far back?" Cal asked.

"That's what we have to find out. It may be our way out of this." Cal raised his eyebrows to show his uncertainty.

"Seems unrealistic," Cal said.

"I've left the breadcrumbs for me to follow, and it got me this far— the key is my memory. The answers are there if I can access them...we'll be one step ahead of Johnny Macklemore."

Chapter Twenty-five
—Proceeding on the dim theory—

Millie Bain passed out cucumber sandwiches like she was dealing out a hand of euchre. Judy's mother used to make them when she was little. She found it funny what she remembered and what she didn't. If Johnny was behind her gaps, then she guessed her recollection about vegetable snacks was not on his short-list of threats to remove. Judy wanted to laugh, and if it were in a comedy, they would find her on the floor in a fit of guffaws.

Maddie took a sandwich and bit down, but Becky had a more cautious approach to the pickle-filled appetizer. She reached for one, sniffed it as a canine does, and slid a corner into her mouth. No sooner had her teeth cut through—the food was back out and into a napkin. She folded up the tissue like it was nuclear waste and turned up her mouth in disgust with no thought of Millie.

"It's such a pleasure to see you after all these years," Millie said, pouring tea in every available cup. "You've grown up."

Judy gave a nod of respect even as another person spoke of an absent past, for her at least. The niceties that people spewed out as a courtesy were wearing thin. It wasn't the old woman's fault, but Judy was always in a game of catch up or charades trying to figure out what people were referring to and discerning their intentions or ulterior motives in a conversation were out the door. She had no hope of reading into what people were saying when her memory resembled Swiss cheese.

Otis sat opposite the ladies in uncomfortable silence, manufacturing a fake smile in all the right spaces in the exchanges and nothing else. His wife rattled on, and he never tried to stop her, but the distaste for their unannounced and uninvited visit appeared on his face. Judy didn't care. She was an empty vessel, and he was someone who could fill her once more. She took his constant avoidance of her, like a parent hiding the truth, as an insult.

With Millie in the room, Otis didn't plan to speak with honesty. *Save for the AAU clinic itself—he kept Millie in the dark.* Judy wondered if Otis saw the unraveling of the clinic and everyone involved as a dirty secret that didn't need to touch his wife. Judy was in self-preservation mode and although she understood Otis's misgiving about the past, her need for a future outweighed the old doctor's desire to shield his better half.

After the second cup of tea, Judy gave Otis the Thousand-Yard stare that told him either the tea party was ending or prepare to invite Millie into their ugly affair.

"Sweetheart?" Otis waited until Millie turned. "I have two things... medical-related to speak to the girls about," It was clear Otis had done this often. Like seeing a cue from a movie director, Millie was already packing up her tea. "I'll be out of your way in a second," Millie said. "It was so good to see you again, Judy. And nice to meet you, girls," she said, and went into some other room in the house. If she didn't know any better, Judy would bet Millie was under his mind control. Millie left, but Otis allowed the room to stay quiet in case she was still within earshot. Otis was about to speak when Judy wrangled the opportunity.

"We can see you are uncomfortable with our intrusion. I'd say I'm sorry, but it wouldn't do any good. I think lives are at stake, or we wouldn't be here," Judy said. Her speech was just the medicine he needed.

"What do you require from me?" His blunt question dashed their hopes of getting an undefended dialogue. His guard was up, and that had to change to help her. Becky had a gift for strategic questions and proven capable right away. Judy tilted her head to Becky, and her friend responded with a nod too slight for Otis to acknowledge.

"Doctor Bain—" Becky began.

"Otis, please," he corrected.

"We think her husband," Becky gestured to Judy, "Johnny Macklemore, shares Judy's unique ability to reach into minds." Otis was unimpressed. The women swapped glances.

"Why is this not a surprise to you, Otis?" Judy asked, and Otis didn't answer.

"You're a smart man," Becky offered. "You think the further you get involved—the more trouble will splatter onto you or maybe Millie."

"From what I've heard, you've helped a lot of children have normal lives. You once did the right thing...don't stop now," Maddie urged. Otis was unmoved.

"I get it. You have people to protect as we do. But last night I visited Tessa Macklemore—a woman my age who could never get married—or have her father walk her down the aisle," Judy's own life came to mind. "And I never got to have children and watch them grow. And if I thought I would be the last person hurt by Johnny from here on out...I would walk out that door with no regrets," Judy said.

"Can't swear Johnny had anything to do with Tessa," Otis said, "I suspected." Relief washed over Judy, and the room itself appeared to exhale.

"What pointed to him?" Judy asked, hoping to keep him talking.

"Her parents brought her to see me...it was during the last gasps of Angel Among Us. They were desperate, as you might expect, to find a cure.

"Did you examine her?" Maddie asked.

"I examined the girl. But her case was unusual at the time. You and I have worked on many cases of brain damage," Otis turned to Judy. "The markers were different for Tessa."

"Unusual for the time?" Judy asked.

"Tessa, just like you, had scar tissue throughout her medial temporal lobes. Patients with brain damage have scar tissue the same. Don't get me wrong. But the number of spots is consistent with professional fighters and not teenagers like Tessa. My experience tells me they are from concussions," Otis said.

"I think we know better...they aren't concussions," Judy said.

"Let's not be so hasty," Otis cautioned. "If you coaxed out broken or lost memories in a person, the way you have, their brain would look much different from someone who was doing the opposite."

"Johnny?" Maddie asked. Otis shrugged.

"If you ripped a memory from a person like a grape from a vine. What would that look like inside you? Like you went ten rounds with Mike Tyson?"

"I think so," Otis said. "We used to talk about your process of healing," Otis said to Judy, "and you mentioned it was like watering a delicate plant—enticing the memories to grow new neurons." Judy nodded her agreement.

"That example feels right."

"Now imagine seizing a memory. That act would be violent—severing neurons—leaving black areas...the same ones I saw in both you and Tessa. If I didn't know better, it would resemble a person who hit their head hundreds or maybe thousands of times."

"What the fuck?" Becky blurted. "How can you do that to someone?"

"Because they can," Maddie added.

"It's about control," Judy said. "When you add or remove memories, you change how that person thinks or what they believe—like my books he took from me. Think about it—why would I knowingly live with a person who stole my novels and called them his own?"

"Make you forget you wrote them," Becky was thinking out loud.

"That's exactly what Johnny did—kept me subservient. He was more subtle when he worked on me. With Tessa, Johnny was a wrecking ball—smashing without caring about the aftermath. With me, he surgically removed the memories that improved his life," Judy said.

"But how did he do it?" Becky asked, "You possess this gift...like one in a billion chance. Then Johnny having the same ability? That shit doesn't compute."

"Maybe the reason you have visions holds the clue," Maddie said.

"Hypnagogic hallucinations...more than likely," Otis interjected. "Humans have two kinds of memory—episodic. That's your past events—a timeline. And semantic memory, which is your general knowledge—colors, shapes—how to tie your shoes or ride a bike. But hypnagogia is the bridge between the two memories. Have you ever heard of the myth of Charon?" he asked. Heads shook all around. "He's from Greek mythology. He's a ferryman who carries the souls across the river Styx—he lives in the divide between the living and the dead. When I was in medical school, Charon was what helped me understand hypnagogia. It's in this state that you can access things from both sides of your memory, Judy."

"And Johnny's experiencing this as well?" Becky asked.

"No. Johnny's on the opposite spectrum. If he's stealing memories, he is choking with memories that are not his own—the bridge or hypnagogia becomes corrupted by memories. His visions won't be his own, and the more he lives with other people's memories—he cannot discern reality from hallucinations. Plucking thoughts from a person is a skill he learned, but I suspect releasing those memories is a whole other talent he may not possess."

"So, the memories are rotting him from the inside?" Maddie asked.

"In theory," Otis said. "It's the difference between possessing a power and knowing how to wield it. Instead of visions coming to him in his sleep, a nightmare world warped his mind."

"So, I might heal myself through my dreams?" Judy asked, hopeful.

"Yes and no," he said, "Without intervention, you'll gain a sliver of recognition every so often, nothing to hang your hat on." Judy thought about their last conversation, and an idea occurred to her.

"Help me regain my past," Judy said.

"What do you suggest?" Otis asked with a suspicious tone.

"Be my Charon. Allow me to use your memories as my own. Act as a life vest and—"

"Out of the question. What you ask is too dangerous...and not for you, but me." The outright denial stunned Judy. "I know what your father did for you—the sacrifice he made for you was amazing and irresponsible," he said.

"You told me I was like a daughter to you," Judy pressed.

"Judy, you are...but I have a daughter and grandchildren. You do not understand how powerful you are and what you could do to someone, even by accident. I often wonder how Bud was before he attempted to bring you back. What memories did you destroy to heal yourself? I bet he gave up a major part of himself to get his little girl back, and I understand that. Still, I can't risk cherished memories of my family. At my age...it's all I have left. I'm sorry," Otis said with sadness.

"Coward," Becky said. Otis lowered his head.

"No. Otis is not—he's right. It's too risky," Judy said and got to her feet. They headed toward the door, feeling defeated when Otis spoke.

"One last thing. Tessa had scar tissue in her medial temporal lobes, just like you—she also had damage to her primary motor cortex."

"And?" Becky asked without patience. Otis never faced her and instead kept his view on Judy. "The functionality of a human being depends upon that region of the brain," he said.

"What's your point?" Judy asked.

"If Johnny did that to Tessa—it's a vicious act—destroying her ability to move...imprisoning her. I want you to know what kind of person you're facing." Otis wasn't wrong. Every additional detail she learned about Johnny frightened her. And she knew she had to confront him alone, or he'd never go away. Judy nodded and left Otis Bain's home wiser but feeling more isolated than before, knowing that her nightmare was beginning.

Part II

"Memories warm you from the inside. But they also tear you apart."
-Haruki Murakami

Chapter Twenty-six
—Johnny Macklemore—

The rental car was nice, but there was a better one—he knew it, and so did the girl behind the counter. *She recognized you, Johnny—putting you in your place.* He clenched his hands, feeling nails dig into his palms, not deep but enough to remind.

It was the way Judy hung up the phone. *That fucking bitch.* It bothered him. And he was sure she was off the rails. It wasn't the first time, and he imagined it wouldn't be the last—but this time was different. *You're making something out of nothing, Johnny.* Still, he saw how things went sideways in a hurry if you weren't careful, and he wasn't careful. *The moment she called from her parent's house, I belonged on a plane to collect her and clean up the mess.* He nodded to himself.

From the very first moment he met her, Judy was always a persistent woman, and he saw no change coming over the horizon. When he sunk her into the ground, Johnny would chisel the word *stubborn* on her headstone, he guessed. It was okay with him—he relished a challenge. There is no victory without an adversary, and Judy was what drove him to greatness throughout their marriage. Sometimes it was her reminders he was a talented writer and other times—it was her minor acts of defiance that got his juices flowing. They worked well together, and he supposed that was why he was so successful and why he had to get her back on the leash. He imagined what her family had been filling her head with this entire time. He gave a heavy sigh because he alone understood the work it would take to bring back his Judy.

Through his car window, Johnny watched the Columbus neighborhoods pass by fast, and fast was the way he liked it. He had never been as happy as the second he escaped the city forever. Ohio was a working-class state with working-class people, living out their lives in quiet desperation. The neighborhoods they resigned themselves to, resembled their character—small and shabby. These were the people that read his books, but they were not the people he ever had a desire to rub elbows with at parties. He acknowledged that it was Ohio, Columbus, who helped launch his writing career. The city was so desperate to call something or someone their own that they flocked to him like a moth to a flame.

It was this same adoration that pushed him further away from his hometown as the blush of success landed. Although he kept the same publisher from the city to visit his mother, he returned home less and less. Johnny refused any Ohio conferences, appearances or book signings that tried to lure him back. The city became a distant past, and nothing made him happier. That's why he allowed Judy to deliver his manuscript. His mistrust sending anything electronically and disgust for the city. Both set the events into motion, and now he's paying the bill.

When Johnny's luxury sedan—black, he always chose black—slowed to a stop in front of Bud and Emily's home, he flicked at his hair and adjusted his suit jacket—how he carried himself was important, above everything else. Even as he prepared to walk to the house and collect Judy, curtains parted, and blinds from several windows rose.

There was a walkway made of concrete that led from the curb to the front door. Johnny wouldn't call the house expensive, but he saw the house was well-maintained for the neighborhood. Bud was a meticulous man—one of the few things he admired about him.

His stride was full and confident as if they were expecting his arrival, as his fans did on the book circuit. The idea was silly, but he enjoyed the fantasy more than what awaited him. He was there to retrieve what was his and nothing more. He tracked the movement inside from window to window and saw the front door shake and open. A face peered through the screen door as if he were an assailant brandishing a gun and waving it around on the front lawn. *They are so pathetic.*

Before he reached the porch, in need of repair, the metal screen door swung out. He was already smiling as broad as his cheeks allowed. *I must look sweet to them.* Judy was the first to walk out onto the porch. Johnny's smile widened. He noticed her friend Maddie following close behind like the caboose of a train. When he saw another woman exit, he mistook it for her mother except it wasn't. The woman was heavyset and by the look of her clothes and hairstyle, he was sure she preferred ladies to men. He regarded all of this and still plastered on a salesman's grin.

"Hey, Jude," he said in a tone that dripped honey. "Grab your things. I was hoping to get a bite to eat before our flight," he said like a ventriloquist keeping his expression static. The big woman shifted diagonally in front of Judy like a checker piece blocking him from his wife. *Who the fuck...do you think you are?* His smile remained.

"You're a thief, and the lowest kind," Judy said. "You're taking that flight alone." His face glided from all three women. One shrunk from his gaze, but the other woman in overalls puffed up her chest.

"I hate drama," he said, keeping things light and breezy. "I reserve those emotions for my novels."

"You mean *my* novels?" Judy didn't hide her contempt.

"Now they're your books, Jude? I have never seen you write one word. Except on a check...that I provided."

"They were mine, and you stole them," Judy said. His smile left but didn't stray too far away as it was back in a flash.

"How did I accomplish such a thing? I suppose I had you write at gunpoint?"

"You stole them from my mind," Judy said with Johnny laughing.

"That's a new one. You haven't been taking your medication. Have you?" Sadness took over his countenance. Becky's stance was less defiant. "Guess she didn't mention that to you, fine ladies."

"That's a lie," Judy let her outrage spill out with her words. His statement shook their unity, and he loved it. He stepped forward.

"I will bring you home and keep you safe. I promise," he said. Judy was considering this and offered a step of her own when Becky spoke.

"Which medication is Judy currently on, Johnny?" There was a long pause.

"Her medication is none of your concern. And you are?" Johnny sputtered and waited for a name.

"Becky. What's her ailment? Diagnosis? How about her doctor? I'm sure you know the name of the doctor who's been treating her, right?" Becky said, releasing her words in a sarcastic melody.

Fuck you! Johnny's dam cracked, and he wasn't about to give them the satisfaction of watching him lose his cool. His manufactured beam never left, but it existed with more force than when he arrived.

Johnny's calm demeanor mesmerized them, and Judy the most. He used the right words with her because he exuded safety. She found the quality comforting, and he could tell. He lifted his hand out toward Judy. It was a soft, beckoning gesture.

"You're a fucking liar," Becky said. Johnny lowered his hand from the Mack truck that just went through. "You know what they say about liars, don't you, Maddie?" Beck asked and gazed at Maddie with a smile forming.

"No. What do they say, Becky?" Maddie joined into the conversation.

"They say lying gives you a small pecker. You must tell us, Judy. Does he have a small pecker?" Becky asked. Judy smiled as Becky broke the ice, and they all were themselves once more. "Don't leave us out here in the dark, Johnny," He ignored her, forcing a smile that appeared out of place. "Has all the lying shrunk your cock?" Becky taunted. Johnny could not restrain himself any longer.

"You have a filthy fucking mouth, you know that?" Johnny said with eyes fixed on Becky. She gave a broad smile, and his stomach dropped. *That's the reaction she's trying to elicit.*

"Blame the Columbus public schools. I don't have the sophistication of a world-renowned author. But you aren't an author either. Are you?" He allowed himself a glance at Becky and right back to Judy.

"Cal will be here," Maddie whispered to Judy but not low enough. *They are trying to stall you.*

"It's interesting what you did with your hair. And the glasses...really?" Judy couldn't help but reach for her head. Johnny edged in and leaned. "You don't belong here, Judy. You are better than this." The confident grin returned.

"Hey, Johnny? Why don't—"

"Shut your fucking trap," he snapped to Becky, and she saw the raw anger. "You know I hate this place. So, get in the car now." Judy considered this and took one hesitant step in front of Becky.

"My days with you are over," Judy said and hoped every syllable stung. "You stole my family from me. For what? Did you ever even care about me?"

Is there an answer that will get you into the car?

"Nobody gets me as you do," he said. His lines were well-used. *But if something works, you go back to the well...until the well is dry.* The image of his sister entered his mind for the briefest moment. He told her the same thing once, except his sister was aware of the person he was, a little too well. He considered his relationship with Tessa a complete failure, even as he believed he wasn't to blame for how it ended. In his estimation, it's always the parents who fail the children. Their love didn't blanket the kids the same, and they were okay with that—he wasn't.

He tried to get his point across to his father more than once. He then turned to the bottle. It was sad to see his old man pickle himself rather than fix his issues. So, he did what he had to do—turned his attention to Tessa. She ended up more resistant than expected, and he wondered if Judy was going down the same path. *It doesn't look good for her. You might not save her this time.* He extended a hand again with more authority this time like a consequence of disobeying was drowning.

"Right now," he said as if reprimanding a naughty dog. "The car." Her friends saw Judy flinch. Becky found a place between the husband and wife.

"She's not going anywhere with you, limp dick," Becky said. She had the girth to stand her ground, and he bet with a mouth like hers, she'd seen her share of confrontations. The temperature rose on his face, and it wouldn't surprise him to discover his cheeks had turned an angry shade of red. What irked Johnny was the way Becky spoke to him—such disrespect. People in his world did not talk to him like that. *Another reason to get on a plane and leave this state behind.* A big lady or not, these were still women, and heated aggression wilted flowers. Instead of stepping toward his wife, Johnny lunged like a basketball player posting up against a defender.

In shape was the last thing Johnny thought Becky was, and yet she moved like an athlete. Before Johnny could make the short distance between him and Judy, Becky was already in front of her friend like a female Secret Service agent. The move was unexpected. Squinting was all he could do as her arm waited in the path of his throat. His momentum moved forward, and although he wasn't a big man—average—he was large enough to make it difficult for a sudden stop.

When her hand met his neck, the collision sent a shock through his gullet inward. With an open hand, her palm closed tight around his throat. The effect was hard and immediate. The jarring blow to his Adam's apple sent a choking spasm of pain through his body and left him gagging out of reflex. What neither Johnny nor Becky realized was a burst of images passed between them both. Stunned by the energy, they each fell back as if a resistant magnetic strength repelled them.

For Johnny, it was a hand with eyes that probed within him, seeking—searching. Alien was the first word that jumped to his mind. There was a mystical numbness that accompanied the interloper. There was also something old in the invader as well that he couldn't describe— wisdom, surrounded by darkness, but wisdom none the less. Two forces met inside him, and like a white blood cell that attacked any foreign bodies—he pushed her out of him. His instinct warned that she brought something out and left something behind in the haste of retreat.

"What the fuck are you?" he said, already expecting a migraine with its initial throbbing taking hold.

"What the fuck are *you*?" Becky countered. Johnny stepped back again with no intention in his movements. His body moved, and he obeyed.

"What did you do to me?" Johnny asked in a panic. Becky didn't answer and instead trotted closer to him and pointed her head toward Judy.

"What did you do to her?" she screamed. And that's when Johnny understood what she saw inside him. His skin went clammy, and fear was real, for the first time since he was a small child. "I saw what you did," Same anger, same tone, but this time, a mask of hatred consumed her features.

"Those are my thoughts...you have no right," he bellowed. Becky shook as she searched her surroundings for something to grab—something to swing—something to bash. Her gestures were far from universal, but his intuition sent him moving backward even further from the porch and Becky, who was raging. The migraine, he presumed, was ravaging his head in the mere seconds after their contact.

"You think you got away with that?" she screamed.

He was right for what he did and didn't need to defend himself. But to hear it said out loud—through the air—to his face. It was unacceptable.

"That is private...between my wife and me," he said, still backing away. Becky followed his retreat.

"Between you two? She doesn't remember, does she?" Becky whispered in a voice that was like razor blades slicing the air. "You made sure she would forget." She was out of his head, but there was a residue that lingered. It was like a fragrance wafting in the air. It was putrid, causing him to gag.

"You're a damn witch...aren't you?"

"Yes. I'm a witch—and I will curse your soul—bastard," He could stand the throbbing in his head no longer. Johnny darted for his sedan, clamping his hands against his temples.

"This is only the beginning, bitches," he moaned without ever turning back. In one uniformed motion, he was in the car, starting it, and peeling away from the scene and the cause of his anguish.

*　　*　　*　　*

The pain made it difficult for Johnny to drive. Forty-five minutes later, he arrived at the Renaissance hotel when the trip was no more than twenty, tops. Several times he stopped by the side of the road to gather his thoughts and wait for the massive throbs to subside. They never went away, but the intensity at least withdrew enough to get moving again.

He needed a bed and darkness, and he could recharge his batteries. *What did that bitch do to me?* He couldn't be sure about anything except that he needed to rest. The black and white vampire flicks he watched as a child came back to him. The head vampire protected their coffin from the coming of the light.

If you listened to your body, which most didn't, it whispered its orders. That was the problem—whispers are persistent. Johnny's body was screaming its orders, and he understood, at least on some level, that if he discounted the need to rest, it meant the end. Fortunately for him, he called ahead and made reservations to speed up the check-in process.

A girl who was too young to hold a job worked the front desk. She babbled on about the history of the hotel which she was more than proud to relay. Johnny nodded at the right pauses, or at least imagined he did. It was hard to tell with the persistent ringing in his ears. The girl continued her onslaught of words by moving to the usual banter about how she read all his books—an inspiration—same bullshit that, under normal circumstances, he could tolerate. His etiquette was ending, and he wasn't sure if the conversation's thread and his nodding in the right places were out the window. The girl transitioned to the prevailing custom that all these better hotels required, the spouting of what other celebrities have made their stay with them.

He hated this part because he knew damn well the moment his stay ended; he would be the celebrity example right alongside Arnold Schwarzenegger. The latter stayed here during the *Arnold Classic* this year or the politician Fred Ricart. She even threw in his campaign slogan, *We're Dealing*, for good measure.

The small talk never ceased, and he must have said as much because the girl went quiet, and her face was sullen like a child taken to the woodshed. That was okay, and his politeness was working against what his head demanded. Johnny snatched the hotel keycard from the irritating girl—heard her instruct a direction toward his room, which he ignored, and staggered down a hall. Johnny studied the card number and the door numbers—back and forth like a drunken sailor. He was in a horror movie where the character was moving down a hall that never ended—perpetual motion. Johnny was on the brink of collapse when the door, his door, appeared like an oasis he didn't trust until he inserted his card and heard the blessed beep followed by green lights erupting on the door handle.

The room was dark, and he kept it that way, trudging into the room, dropping his suitcase wherever. He plopped onto the bed like a dead fish. Because his body ran hotter than most others, he never pulled the bedspread to cover himself. The stillness was working already, soothing his aching head. The visions would come—they always did. He couldn't remember a night when his sleep was undisturbed throughout. And he also admitted they were getting worse—longer, harsher, and they were bleeding into his daytime thinking.

He learned long ago how to pluck thoughts from others while they both slept. It was a trick that made him his fortune and the same trick that would kill him. He sensed that down deep into his bones. Like an alcoholic making their resolution to slow or stop their behavior, Johnny did the same with his trick of the mind.

He made a vow not to use his ability after the writer's conference. Did he have the willpower to stop before the conference? He'd like to think so, but the talented authors gathered there were incredible. *A goldmine of novels was there for the plucking.* The royalties on all his past novels, movie rights and television series would guarantee a comfortable lifestyle if he never used his powers ever again.

It wasn't about the money, at least not all the way. The allure was taking stories from the biggest names in the business. They had all donated their novels to Johnny over the years, and he wished he could thank them for their contribution—to his reputation and his bank account. The critics, mostly, wrote love letters about his novels. Not because they were all genius, but because he was the rarest of all writers, one that could change his writing voice so drastically from book to book. It was the uniqueness of each line—style—and dramatic beats that kept the readers coming back for more. And although some of his books, Judy's contributions, had a similar voice, most others varied, and the readership relished the departures.

He had over fifty more books resting in his head, waiting to land onto paper, and that was the rub. When he collected thoughts, memories, or even novels, he couldn't release them. They cluttered his mind like a closet too full to close. They pushed out his thoughts or, even worse, mingled with his own to make some Frankenstein-belief that he never intended to take to heart. The top of his list of worries was not knowing when it happened, and he supposed it didn't matter, anyway. What could he do except give up collecting?

His mind was at full capacity, threatening to overflow—malfunction. And here he was back in Columbus to clean up *the Judy mess*. He had no illusions. Fixing the situation with his wife would require collecting and banishing thoughts from everyone Judy had infected while she was off the rails. The task ahead was daunting, and he was sure that it would change him forever, but what choice did he have?

Judy belonged to him, and she was his responsibility. The person he was alone, at night in the dark, didn't comfort him. And collecting meant he would like himself even less after the dust settled. It was his humanity that fell by the wayside, and with every memory entering, another of his own became absorbed into the stew. If he considered it, and he didn't often, the punishment was fitting. His greed for other people's knowledge was altering and corrupting whoever he once was.

The headache was receding, replaced by a numbness that he welcomed. Johnny's thoughts were his own again, without the accent of distress, jumbling his options. A plan was already forming, as natural as thinking of the breakfast he will enjoy. Becky had blind-sighted him and risen to the top of the charts so fast that it consumed him like an open flame devouring wood. She couldn't collect, not like Judy or himself, still...there was an act of intrusion or violation when she touched him. Ability to collect, for him at least, needed his host to be asleep, and himself. It was a tricky dance that left him physically vulnerable, but inside their mind, he had total control.

Becky's gift of reaching inside someone while wide awake scared the shit out of him, and nothing scared him. It was an unnatural talent, based in mysticism, or she was tapping into some spiritual realm—selling her soul to wield power. Either way, she was an obvious danger that he needed to deal with if he hoped to get Judy out from under them. He had Becky in his sights for sure, but she wasn't the logical target. *The bond between them was strong.* He had a better idea in mind.

The cover of night was essential for collecting, and that was good because he needed to sleep. The visions were drifting. It wasn't the one Becky invaded, and he was thankful for the reprieve. Few of the visions were warm and pretty, with most containing gut-wrenching memories, but the memory Becky gleaned was torture on several levels. As he melted into sleep, the images came in from some other part of the brain. *The collective unconscious,* he once thought. They were sharper each night and becoming as vivid as his daylight reality, and that was what worried him. When he recognized the gist of what remembrance was to come, it relieved Johnny. *Something unimportant—no emotions to sap my energy.* An instant later, he was within the memory as a passenger once more.

The memory was familiar, or a variation of it. There were many like it, and Johnny sometimes got confused as the visions became like wallpaper. He made a game out of these certain memories. *Which book is Judy excited about now?* The sooner into the vision that he picked the right book, the more credit he gave himself. *There was no escaping, so why not get entertained as it ran its course?* They were at their home in New York—maids bustled to get their lunch out of sight, and he was trying to read the paper, hoping to see an article written about him. It was fluff, mostly—his rise from nothing—the self-made man (this-can-be-you) spin. It stroked his ego but accomplished little else. Beyond the money he received from writing novels, the self-congratulatory peripherals were the upside.

"Johnny?" Judy covered the distance of the Great room with a full run, stopped hard, and breathed in and out, catching air. "You will not believe this," she said, blushing with excitement.

"Try me," he said. Johnny observed himself lowering the paper to show he was listening.

"I haven't had a great idea for a novel since we got married. And I thought the lack of inspiration would be forever," Judy shook her head fast with reckless abandon. "Not anymore."

"You mean you will finally contribute to our income?" he said with laughter. Judy ignored his jab and continued.

"It's a coming-of-age story—"

"Is this a completed idea? I mean...have you envisioned a beginning, middle, and end, or is this in the early stages?" Johnny remembered the question and its importance. Other times when she came to him with an idea, it wasn't as well-formed as she led on. During his collecting, it turned out to be useless fragments or stories with no concrete narrative. It annoyed him to no end.

"I got it all. I even know the title. Desert Lily," she said, spreading her hands out into the air like it was coming to life in between them, "Damn it. She said the title of the book before I could guess." It was her best book idea because it was so personal. His readers would eat it up. The critics were in awe of how he spoke from a woman's point of view with such authority, and she was his secret weapon.

She rattled on, and he half-listened from there onward. He didn't have to listen—late that night—while she was fast asleep, the novel would be on its way into his mind. The system wasn't foolproof even after it transferred to him, close though. There were missing filler scenes that he would complete himself. More times than not, those scenes his editor had to fix for him, anyway. Not to mention, he discovered many parts didn't come out right because she never had the chance to improvise them. He had to laugh, thinking about how he would give her hypothetical questions about her scenes and what the characters would do—she always came back with some great stuff. He always came out smelling like a rose.

Deep into their marriage, he considered allowing her to finish and publish a book of her own, back when his softer side had a hold of the wheel too often. Better judgment won out after he realized it was the long droughts that motivated—spurred her on to keep writing. Judy believed it was her writer's block that kept the stories away, and when an idea arrived. Judy was a beast at formulating every detail. He had to admit that his books were more intricate and thoughtful when an idea arrived as a miracle to her. What would the public think if his wife authored a novel with his exact style and voice? There were ways to explain it, but none were worth the trouble and effort. Johnny was fine with how things were rolling.

"When did this flash of brilliance come to you?"

Judy considered this.

"Two days ago. Right before I fell asleep."

Johnny nodded.

"Just as soon as you finish your manuscript, I'll pass it along to my publisher," he assured. Anything he wanted to say, he could. Her last few days and all the memories inside were a wisp in the air after that night. Her face was so bright, and he was glad he could give her that moment. She lunged into his lap and hugged him so tight that viewing the scene again— he remembered her thankful grip. She sat there with a grin, imagining all the possibilities that lay ahead.

Chapter Twenty-seven
—By force without consent—

Judy sat at her mother's kitchen table across from Becky and Maddie. They had been up late talking, and it showed in their postures.

"I feel like shit...but tell me I don't feel as bad as you two," Becky teased.

"Worse," Maddie said, scrunching up her face, "much worse." Becky flicked her off and laughed.

"Thanks for staying with me last night," Judy said, regarding both with a glance.

"You're kidding me. I stumbled into a real-life supernatural thriller with villains and all," Becky said. "It beats the hell out of psychometry readings with bored homemakers any day of the week."

"If only your clients knew you were the real deal. You could charge twice the price," Maddie added. Judy was pouring coffee all around and pushing milk and sugar to the center of the table.

"Help yourself," she said, and they did. "What do I do now?" Judy spoke into her steaming coffee and watched her reflection inside.

"He's not going to stop...ever," Becky said.

"How do you know?" Judy asked. Becky gripped her cup a little tighter. The girls noticed the pause, and that was enough to draw their attention.

"Becky? You are not afraid to speak your mind. What is it?" Becky volleyed her face to both and cleared her throat.

"Yesterday, when I got between you and..."

"I remember. What about it?" Judy coaxed.

"When my skin touched his...I read something and debated all night whether to say something. I mean you are leaving him anyway and—"

"Tell me. I want to know," Judy said, placing a hand on hers. Becky nodded, but hesitation was still alive in her expression.

"I know when you peer inside someone—it's more cinematic than the way it happens for me. At least that's my impression. I get fragments that I luckily get to put together like a puzzle," she said, bursting with sarcasm, "But what comes along with the images are emotions—the feelings I drew from him about you was horrific." Becky sipped her coffee to prevent a crying fit. "He has your memories locked away inside him. And he guards them like his treasure—his gold." She paused again.

"It's okay," Judy said. Maddie attempted an understanding smile to encourage.

"Have you ever wanted children?" Judy nodded. The answer upset Becky, and there was no hiding it. "You should have had children, Judy."

"I'm confused," Judy admitted.

"I saw the times you were pregnant..." It was clear enough for Judy to get the drift, but she chose not to comprehend, and Becky didn't blame her. "Maybe four or five times—couldn't be sure about that. Your smiling face was there, and... each time, he convinced you to get rid of it. He realized you wanted a baby. I think if you had a baby together, came the obligation to treat you like a person—he wasn't about to do that."

The truth hit Judy like a shovel, first in the chest and then in her stomach. She grabbed her belly and wept.

"I feel like a part of me got it somehow," Judy said. "Maybe a mother always knows." Maddie found their hands and squeezed tight as Judy shook without control.

"He made you believe it was your decision. Even blaming you when he saw how destroyed you were every time. When he couldn't deal with your grief any longer—he took the coward's way out and wiped your mind clean of the whole incident, until the next time," Becky said.

"Did I deserve this?" Judy asked through tears. Becky and Maddie both stood and wrapped their arms around her.

"You did nothing. It isn't your fault," Maddie said. Judy nodded, but the words weren't relieving the pain.

"I have a good feeling why you made the leap off the bridge. I'd bet these memories came back to you." They sat in silence.

"Please don't let me go back with him," Judy begged.

"Not while I'm alive," Becky said. They sat there for a long time, saying nothing. They saw Judy's hurt, and being close was all they could offer.

"You remember your book? The one where you left clues behind?" Becky asked.

"*To Kill a Mockingbird*," Judy said.

"You still have it?"

"Yeah...sure, hold on," Judy said. She left the room and was back without the worn paperback.

"I can't find it," Judy said with fear in her voice.

When Emily entered the room, she smiled at everyone and headed to the sink. Emily's behavior was atypical, and Judy noticed. They exchanged concerned expressions.

"Good morning," Judy directed her voice to her mother. Emily turned to Judy, then back again. It was the smell that got Judy's attention, followed by the flames rising from the steel sink.

"Emily?" Judy shouted. "What are you doing?" All legs made it to the sink and saw her paperback burning. Judy doused the book with water, but it was too late. The cover became embers.

"Why?" Judy asked her mother. Emily reached for a butcher knife standing upright in a knife block. As the sharpened utensil slid out of its home, it made a scratching sound as she pulled it clear. They all turned to Emily.

"Emily?" Judy asked as Emily drew the knife outward, hovering over her left wrist. She formed a smile that leaned toward an unhappy grimace and brought the blade across her wrist in a downward slashing motion. THWACK. Judy didn't want to know that skin had a sound when it separated. Blood poured as Emily shifted the knife into her other hand. The gesture broke Judy from a horrible daze, and she jumped onto her mother to stop her from cutting her other wrist.

"Call 911," Judy screamed. Maddie fumbled with her phone, trying to steady her hands while she dialed. Judy held her mother tight as Becky pressed a kitchen towel against the wound and elevated Emily's arm.

"An ambulance is on the way," Maddie announced.

Judy spoke to her mother, "Why did you do this?" Emily shook her head, and Judy was sure Emily was unaware of her actions. But she realized who was responsible. They all did. Judy sat there waiting and spied her copy of *To Kill a Mockingbird* covered in ash and blood.

When help arrived, they stabilized Emily on a gurney and placed her in the back of an ambulance. Maddie and Becky said something to her as she climbed in with her mother—she registered their voices as murmurs, way off in the distance. An EMT shut the back doors, and they were off. *What hope do I have if Johnny can do this?* The question was reasonable, with no one to answer. She tilted her head toward her mother on the gurney, and she was staring back at her.

Judy adjusted her glasses and remembered back to the realization that she wore them and didn't know it. *Was that to keep me from reading or trying to write?* The answers were coming into focus. She couldn't stop Johnny from hurting the ones she loved. She could defy Johnny, live with her parents, and divorce him. Judy wanted to start a life with Cal, but she didn't dare dream that was a possibility. None of these options would keep Johnny away.

The way she saw it, two choices presented themselves. Take her own life or go back with Johnny, which amounted to the same thing. *And if I went back to Johnny...who's to say I wouldn't have a recall and end up back here at some point—putting them right back in danger?* Her head dropped into her hands. Watching her mother slash her wrist was a memory she didn't want. A raspy voice spoke next to her.

"Judy?" a voice said. Emily was staring at Judy and had been for a long time. She wasn't born with the ability to read minds, but a mother saw their children and understood what they thought as no one else could.

"This is my fault," Emily said. Judy saw tears running down her mother's cheeks. They were making damp circles on the gurney's cloth sheet below. Emily was crying the entire ride to the hospital, and Judy never noticed. She didn't wail or sob—she lay there—quiet in her suffering.

"I brought this to your doorstep," Judy said. Emily shook her head, throwing tears from her face as she did.

"I'm your mother. I should have protected *you* from him."

Judy considered this and thought of Johnny and couldn't help thinking of the children she lost. If he didn't stop there, where would he stop?

"This was bigger than both of us," Judy said. Her remark was empty, and that was all they had to comfort each other, empty reassurances. Again, Emily shook her head.

"On our anniversary, about five years after you left home. Your father and I felt more like ourselves—and it was hard to get to that point, let me tell you. You left a large void we couldn't fill no matter what. Well...like I said, it was our anniversary. You know I don't drink—never have. But that night I did.

"Your father bought two expensive bottles of champagne, and I swear I drank one and a half by myself," Emily chuckled. "It was one of the first times I let loose. We talked about you, and for a shimmering moment, it didn't hurt to speak about you—guess it was the alcohol. When I think back, it was as if we were putting you to rest—in a way. It was our anniversary, but we used that time to give ourselves closure. You were out of our lives, and you weren't coming back. That was the night we accepted it." Judy joined her mother with tears.

"I'm so sorry, Mom," Judy said.

"Please...let me finish," Emily begged. Judy held her mother's hand and nodded. "The total experience was cathartic. Except that night, I had a dream—I thought it was a dream. It was the most lucid dream I ever had. It was the time of night when I'm asleep, but that night I had things to do for your PTA, and it had slipped my mind.

I got up in a panic to knock it out, then headed right back to sleep. That was my intention. Instead, I heard a noise as I passed your bedroom, except the lights were off. As my eyes adjusted to the dark, I saw you thrashing in your sleep. I turned the lights on and rushed to check on you. Your arms flailed like you were physically fighting somewhere far away. I called your name and shook you, and it did nothing. My first thought was a symptom of your childhood accident that had come back.

"That's when I heard another sound, and this time, it was close. It sounded like a snake seeking warmth under your bed. I backed away from you and the bed, slow. First, I saw a foot, and I couldn't believe someone slid from under your bed. It wasn't a man but a boy, nearing eighteen was my guess. When he rose to his feet, he was already hovering over you with a knife against your throat. He told me that if I screamed, you were dead. I remember the fury on his face. I didn't doubt him. He instructed me to move to him, and he pressed his blade closer to you to show he was serious."

"He doused a rag with something, and he handed it to me. Put it over your mouth and nose, he said. I didn't move—frozen in place. There was an urge to scream to your father, but he was so close to you. He touched the edge of the knife to your skin and told me it was my last chance. I did what he said, and that was all I remembered. The person in your room that night was Johnny," Emily said.

The revelation stunned Judy. She let go of her mother's hand and found her own, rubbing them together. She was seeing the outside but lost in thought.

"When was this?"

"It was the night before you left us," Emily said. It all made sense to Judy. She recalled back to her vision of telling her parents she wanted to leave and deciding it wasn't the right thing to do. *Johnny didn't take no for an answer.* What stood out was the frightened expression on her mother's face that evening.

"But I will never forgive myself for not flying to New York and bringing you home. When the memory returned, it was five years later, and I thought if you needed me, you would have called before then. I let it go," Emily said and closed her eyes tight, expelling tears.

"Johnny was hoping for that, too, and you couldn't have known." Emily whimpered.

"A mother worth anything is at your doorstep..." Emily said. "I saw your face tonight. I don't want to lose you again. Not like this," Emily pleaded.

"Alright, Mom. I promise," Judy said and leaned over the gurney and hugged Emily tight. She wasn't all the way convinced about her choices but continuing to fight was what she owed her parents. That's what she planned to do, except something else brewed; Johnny had wronged her by cheating her out of a normal life. While she was unaware, Johnny devised plans and schemes, and he beat her at every turn. It was about time that she had strategies of her own. She held her mother tight, but her brain was off somewhere else.

Chapter Twenty-eight
—Every tool available—

Brice Deville lay in bed, a prisoner in his body. Pictures of family members covered the walls. Some photos were crisp while others had the patina of decades. To Maddie, it was like a visual timeline played out around them.

"Becky's not picking up," Maddie said, "she always picks up."

"We'll try this without her," Judy said. The three of them had become inseparable. Cal was a different story, and what they were, she needed to face sooner or later. She was aware of replacing one man for another was foolish and had little chance of success. She also understood Cal was her original path, interrupted by Johnny. The girls were something else altogether. The girls formed a protective wall around her, and their devotion was miraculous to Judy. She had seen female relationships grow in movies or heard about them in social circles, but never experienced it before now.

"Maybe Otis was right. I don't want to hurt the guy," Judy said. She regarded Brice with sympathy. Maddie stood beside her and watched him as if he were as interesting as a waterfall.

"Not sure there is anything more you can do to him. Plus, you're not trying to pull memories to heal yourself—you're just nosing around in him. We're here to talk to him if you're able and find answers if you can," Maddie assured. Judy nodded, unsure.

"Call Becky one more time." Becky had become the group's strength, and Judy depended on her most of all. There was something about a woman who took shit from no one that was comforting. Becky was like a lighthouse that let you know she was there and kept you safe from the rocks.

"No answer," Maddie said. Judy didn't need Becky for what she was about to do, and yet she wanted her close.

"Listen, Maddie. You don't have to do this. I'm not sure of the danger," Judy said.

"I trust you. You can do this."

"Okay. Let's go. I won't be able to get started until all three of us are asleep," Maddie nodded. Judy wasn't sure if she was ready.

"You'll be careful while you're in there? I mean...you won't sever anything by mistake?" Maddie asked.

"I'll be more than careful," Judy said. "Can't pretend I know how to control this, but my intuition tells me that altering anything inside the mind takes a lot of willpower. When you are doing something in there—you know you're doing it," Judy said with a smile. "Ready?" She knew Maddie wasn't, but she nodded. The video her father showed her helping the child flooded back. There was an important detail she wasn't seeing because her mind wouldn't let it go. Judy shook her head at the sad condition of her mind. A task awaited her without training, or without a safe path to follow. She clamped her lids shut and let her worried thoughts fade.

When they were all asleep, Judy reached out and sensed them in the room, making her body an antenna. Her visuals were a black screen, and the challenge was making the connection. It was amazing how much the human mind was like a computer. Her first idea was to recreate the room Brice was asleep in, but she also questioned how natural the surrounding was to him. On the fly, Judy thought of *Angel Among Us* and began projecting the facility. It was his home away from home and it would serve as a less jarring return to the world.

Satisfied with her created universe, Judy found the space between her and Maddie. The tendrils were reaching, and her thoughts had their heavy weight once more. It was easier, this time. *Like riding a bike*. Three dimensional Maddie entered the illusion and sat in a similar chair. Maddie's features were astonishing.

There was an artistic component that she never dreamed existed. Maddie believed she was breathing, so her chest moved—she understood humans blinked, so she did that, too. Engrained in humans was a mind's tether to reality if traits and characteristics followed along like a shadow.

There was a symbiotic element that Judy didn't account for or couldn't. She pulled the image of Maddie from Maddie, but her friend was aiding her with all the nuances that made her alive. Maddie spun around her virtual environment.

"This looks so real," she said, touching each of her arms. "This isn't so bad," Maddie admitted.

"Listen," Judy warned, "We don't know what Brice remembers or doesn't. We must be delicate with the information we give or ask. Okay?"

"Sure," Maddie bobbed her head up and down, distracted by where she was.

"The way Johnny operates, as far as I can tell, he either extracts memories or he severs them as he did to Tessa. When he takes them, they aren't there to access, but if he severs them, I will have to go deep, but I can get to them. Going by what Otis revealed, Johnny's separating the memories in the primary motor cortex area and disabling their mobility." Maddie shrugged.

"You lost me a few miles back," Maddie said.

"Just hold on." Judy plunged her feelers deep into the void. Although Brice Deville was a mere two feet away, Judy perceived the divide as miles away. The closer she was to Brice, in this other world, the more the tendrils vibrated. To Judy, it was his power—life-force, or whatever it was, radiating energy as she clasped him. The distance or time was much greater to reach him than it was to draw him into her created space. The reasons were a mystery, containing some universal truth. She imagined the connection produced a shared energy stronger than hers alone.

When Brice completed the trio, the shared space bulged like a breathing lung and then righted itself. He was an older gentleman with salt and pepper hair. Judy saw the lines on his face that came with age, but she bet they formed from joking and laughter rather than from unhappy times. His response mirrored Maddie's. He soaked in his surroundings, marveling at the construction of the smallest details.

"Hey, Angel." He didn't just smile at her, he beamed with his entire face. "I knew you'd find me," Brice said.

"That makes one of us," Judy said. His expression faltered, but like a rubber band, snapped back. "I know we know each other...but..."

"He took your memory, too," Brice finished her sentence.

"How much did he steal from you?" Maddie asked. He turned to her as if having a second person deep in his mind was a natural occurrence.

"Hard to tell. It's hard to miss what you don't know is missing," Brice chuckled. Judy nodded to show she related to his situation.

"You're handling this well," Maddie said.

"I was just thrilled I didn't contract some Alzheimer's or Malamarkus. That was the gossip around the facility," he laughed, turning from Maddie to Judy. "What kept my hope alive was seeing you do amazing things through the years. You were miraculous—and here you are." A grin exploded on his face.

"About that...all the years of honing my skills have vanished. Me visiting with you is the current extent of my ability," Judy cautioned. His expression turned solemn.

"Then you're here for some other reason than a rescue mission," he said.

"I'm afraid so. This visit makes up my second attempt, and I have someone stalking me."

"Johnny Macklemore," he said. Judy and Maddie gasped.

"You remember?" Maddie asked.

"I think I was his first. Whether you remember, I was losing my memory for months. It turns out he was practicing on me—getting it right—or wrong. I found this out later, from the man himself, that he had camped outside my home night after night."

"You spoke to Johnny in person?" Judy asked.

"More like this." He spun around the imitated room. "But he talked to me, as we are now,"

"Do you know why he did this?" Maddie asked.

"Are you talking motivations or a reason?"

"Both," Judy blurted. He nodded, noticing her impatience.

"It was you, Angel. He was doing it for you," Brice said. "Honestly, I was at the AAU a lot as it was getting off the ground, but as the years passed, Otis became the day to day, hands-on administrator. And let me tell you, over a thousand patients came through the facility. Many brain damage cases were of the young, not to say the ages didn't run the gamut. There's no way I would invest my time into every patient the way you and Otis did. Hell, we saw so many people throughout the decade, the faces blurred." Judy was waiting for a point that was never to come. "Johnny was one of your patients," he said.

"I healed him?" Judy asked. She was more interested in something far off, lost in thought.

"A fall brought him to us. A broken skull, according to Johnny."

"This makes little sense—but why concentrate on her?" Maddie asked.

"He was in an abyss—from nowhere comes a light—a hand pulls him to the surface. Judy was his savior." He shifted in place. "Years passed after you helped, but I think he became transfixed on you and couldn't let you go. Building you up to the point of obsession," he said.

"He hurt so many workers. Why go to that length?" Judy asked.

"I—we—were in his way. It was your dedication to helping others. If he eliminated your passions, your distractions...he could isolate you."

"He was hunting me," Judy whispered, "driving me away from the safety of others."

"He was young, but I could see from the beginning that his wiring wasn't right. His pleasure came from the act of taking. His goal was to get you, and anything in the way fueled that fire."

"Still doesn't explain how he's able to do what Judy can," Maddie reminded. Brice shook his head.

"I couldn't tell you. Like I said, I was Johnny's first, unless he was using it on others. I don't think he was all that proficient with his gift yet," Brice said. Judy thought of Tessa defenseless in the same home with him.

"How can we stop him?" Maddie asked, with Brice already shaking her off.

"Kill him," he said.

"Yes," Maddie agreed.

"He's not the type to stop. Perhaps because of his accident or the personality he was born with—Johnny will never bend for you or anyone. Extinguishing his fire is the lone chance you have to rid yourself, all of us, of him," Brice said.

"I can't," Judy confessed.

"Why?" Maddie asked. "I don't want to kill anyone, ever. But Johnny deserves to die."

"Johnny has my memories. Who I am or who I was—they're locked away inside him. If he dies—they die with him. I will lose them forever," Judy said.

"You think he's just going to give them back? Sorry I took them—here you go?" Maddie said. "Johnny will never part with them. And if Otis is right, he's not even been able to shed them if he wanted to," Maddie pointed out. Judy drooped her head.

"The only chance you have of defeating Johnny is to master your ability. You were a finely tuned instrument when you were at the facility. I do not doubt that a Judy Angel at the top of her form would scare the shit out of him. My advice is to regain your skill and find his vulnerability," Brice said. Both ladies nodded.

"Thank you, Brice. And I promise I won't leave you here. I'll bring you out," she said, and thought of the same promise she made to Tessa. Her list of souls to save, because of Johnny, was growing.

"Johnny thinks of himself—you don't, and that's your edge, even if it feels like a weakness," Brice said. Judy nodded and released the tether between them. He soared back to his body, and she pictured a fish caught—snagged by a hook and then thrown back into the water. The friends sat, staring at each other in an all-too-real room. Brice's guidance was sound, but Judy still did not understand how to turn his advice into a plan. Johnny was a treasure chest of memories, and she meant to open him somehow, some way.

Chapter Twenty-nine
—Mutual defiance made them alike—

The bedroom lights were still on in the room. Although exhausted, Becky couldn't imagine not turning them off when she went to bed. She retraced her steps the night before leading up to getting into bed. Turning the lights off didn't ring any bells. It didn't mean she didn't forget—it just meant it tired her. A clock resting on her dresser read 4:15, and her perception told her it was midnight. She could neither pull the covers over her head nor get up and flick the switch—both options annoyed her. Weighing her choices, she pushed her bedspread aside and stopped. Someone was watching, and the sensation ran through her body.

Managing her movements slow, she swiveled her head to a chair next to her bed. At first, she saw nothing out of the ordinary, and that was good. Goosebumps rose on her arm as her focus cleared enough to see a figure sitting motionless in the chair she believed was empty a moment before. The figure never stirred until she spotted the form in the small bedroom. She leaned toward her nightstand, clicked a lamp, and glared at the chair. The added illumination exposed Johnny sitting there as immobile as a statue with a smirk decorating his face.

"Hey, Becky," Johnny said. Becky slammed her back against her headboard. The wood rocked, and her head hit hard enough to leave a mark. "How are you?" His tone was benign, like he ran into her at the grocery store. She remained motionless. If she stayed that way, he would disappear—that was her scrambled thinking. She sat there for a long time. She didn't speak, and he didn't speak. They were in a stalemate. The problem was, he wasn't going anywhere. He wasn't a hallucination and *was* there. It became more tangible when he turned his head to stare at her.

"You and I are a lot alike, Becky," he spat out her name like a cuss word.

"Why are you here?" she demanded. He leaned closer and folded his hands into one tight ball.

"That's a wasted question because you know why I'm here," he said. "If it were me...I'd ask what you will do to me." Still pressed to the wood.

"Are you threatening me?" she wanted to sound strong and accomplished it—but not quite.

"You have no idea what you're involved in," he said. Becky watched his knuckles turn white from the pressure he applied. If she didn't understand before, she got it now. He wasn't there to put a scare in her— she was in danger. Her wheels were turning when she glanced at the closed bedroom door. Johnny slid a long knife from somewhere unseen. It glimmered in the dim light thrown from the lamp.

"This will find you before you touch the door handle," he promised. He was one step ahead, and it occurred to her—*he's done this before.* Becky couldn't think like a victim. She had to talk her way out of the situation if she hoped to live. Surprise, fear, and panic dulled her reasoning and left her thoughts jumbled. Her phone rang on the nightstand.

"I'd let that ring. How can you see inside my head?" he asked and kept the knife within view.

"I was born with it," Becky said. She had to keep him interested— keep him talking. "Until I was a teenager, I believed everyone could do it."

"I didn't like it," he said. Becky nodded, not wanting to continue down that path.

"Fair enough. You go your way. I go mine," she said. Johnny's face contorted as if he was within an internal conversation. Becky seized upon an opportunity.

"I can tell what you are going through," Becky said. His head snapped, and his concentration went from wherever his mind *was* to Becky. His demeanor changed from passive to animalistic in the time to rotate his skull.

"What am I going through?" His facial features strained from straddling between the conversation with her and the unseen one he was battling. A horrible image skidded into her head of an entity fighting to get out of his body. He wasn't in his right mind for manipulation to work, and as far as she could tell, Johnny was unstable. She had nothing to lose.

"Your mind is being corrupted." Leaning back into his chair, Johnny placed the hand that held the knife on his knee as if settling in to hear a campfire story. His countenance changed, and that was the best she could hope for under the circumstances. "Every time you bring in memories from others, you can never release them," she said.

Her words fascinated him, and she saw it right off. The subject of their chat was one he wanted to have with someone his entire life—the singular discussion that eluded him. The distracting dialogue competing with her—pushed to his background.

"It's written on your face. Each time you take a thought or memory, you're losing yourself." Becky didn't see the door. Instead, she allowed her peripheral sight to linger on the area as she spoke.

"Continue," he whispered, trying to coax her forward. She swallowed hard and contemplated which words could set her free and which would seal her fate. Johnny was an unexploded bomb.

"What if I can help you?" He leaned in.

"With your mystical powers?" His line came out condescending. Becky shook her head, choosing each word with care.

"These memories are cluttering your mind. And although you have been able to use Judy's mind as you please, you haven't been able to tap into how she can banish these collected memories with success." Becky had his full attention. She pretended to shift in her bed as she peered at her bedroom door handle. An unlocked door meant that it would give her another second for her escape when the time came.

"Yes," he said without being aware he was uttering the word. Becky hit the mark and found his desire. A lucky guess—maybe, or she read that in his mind when she touched him the day before. Often, the details she gleaned from someone never materialized until she tried to put them into words. He confirmed her fears. Judy was an asset to him.

Besides having a live-in author to steal from, he needed her to relieve the valve in his brain. And his mind was getting worse with every use of the dark ability. Judy had kept the secret for years, and down deep, she understood it was keeping her alive. Without it, she would be no more useful than anyone else he left in his wake. Johnny placed his free hand onto his chin as if to say, let's hear this.

"She trusts me. I can talk to her—"

"Talk to her?" he interrupted. Becky made a miscalculation. "I've spent over ten years trying to pry knowledge from her," he trembled with anger, "and a long weekend with you, and it will all come floating out. Is that what you're telling me?" he asked. To speak or not to speak, that was the gamble.

"You'll spend another ten years without me...if you make it that long," Becky said and held her breath. Johnny collapsed back into his chair, slumped his shoulders, and assumed a relaxed posture. Her phone rang once more, and she turned, released the air she held captive, and was already forming another plan.

Johnny catapulted his body onto the bed. He drove both knees into her stomach and leveled his weight onto her chest. One of her arms was under him and pinned against her frame. He found the other arm and secured it so that the hand holding the knife had a free range of motion. If he painted a mask of terror on her, it would never match her absolute fright.

"There are talkers and doers. Judy and I are doers...you are a talker. I haven't forgotten how your whore mouth spoke to me yesterday," he waved the blade in the air.

"If you do this, you'll get caught. Crime scene investigators will always find the DNA," she said. Johnny smiled with no humor.

"Take a gander at the clock." Becky did as he said and saw that it read 4:15 the same as when he arrived. He twirled the knife in small circles in the air as if to say, hurry and figure it out.

"I'm asleep in my car a block away," he said and inserted the knife into her mouth. He cut away her tongue in one swipe. She tried to scream and couldn't figure out how. A moment later, he disappeared from the room. The thin layer of reality that existed through their conversation dissolved into the actual room.

Becky was alone in her bed with blood pouring from her mouth onto the sheets below. In her mind, the blood belonged to someone else. She glanced at her hand and saw a tongue—her tongue torn from her mouth. She had done it to herself.

Chapter Thirty
—Change of venue—

Judy and Maddie stood in the shadow of the Columbus police headquarters. Columbus, like other cities throughout the Midwest, tried to shed its small-town reputation. Judy heard people call the capital city a cow town more than once, but now, witnessing the enormous building, Judy saw the changes right in front of her. The classic *Ghostbusters* movie came to mind with its pivotal scene finishing in an ornate building reaching toward the heavens. The police station even had its version of the gargoyle in the form of guardian lions protecting the structure as they filed up the stairs.

There was a crowd around the entrance. Some photographers—writers—only twenty, but Judy made an educated guess why they were there. More than a bystander than anything else, but she was in the peripheral of many of Johnny's articles and news interviews. Would the press recognize her as she walked past? It was possible, but she doubted anyone would make the connection. The wife of an author had its own set of humiliations. You always attended the balls but were never the guest of honor. She learned early on to drop any expectations and remember that she was there for support. If the wife of an established author was an inspiring writer, forget about it. Interviewers would step over you to get to the husband. Judy realized it was all about publicity and money, but it still hurt.

Cal waited by the door with a grin two miles long. *That's the definition of a schoolboy grin.* Coming out of his daze, he spotted the press and slid into his official role. He stood between Judy and the story seekers. She threw one last glance toward the writers as she reached the threshold. One writer had a flash of recognition, and she saw his shoulders slump when he realized she was safely inside. She smiled at his childlike behavior of missing a quote or photo at the very least. *I have to get out of here somehow.*

Cal ducked them into an empty section of the building away from prying eyes. Maddie looked over at Cal, seeming to see his facial expression as he looked at Judy and put her hand up to her mouth to hold back a laugh. Every feeling Cal had for Judy was visible with no facade within sight. If Judy was as lovesick as Cal, she did a better job of covering it in public.

"We have Johnny," Cal said, as if he'd captured Bigfoot. "He is in an interrogation room," he said.

"Did he confess?" Maddie asked.

"No. And I don't think he will." Cal had already described the ugly details of how they found Becky over the phone, and he treaded light from then on.

"This is not my case. Still, I'm friendly with the lead detective," Cal said. "Speak of the devil."

Robert Deville and Scott Sedge arrived on cue. Detective Sedge was an older gentleman, but he had a youthful quality that gave off the warning that he was a man who could handle himself. Detective Deville was more of a live wire, and Judy could tell that adrenaline was his drug of choice even as she detected a Boy Scout vibe about him. Cal made the introductions.

"Robert Deville?" Judy asked. Robert returned a respectful nod. "You're related to Brice Deville," Judy commented.

"He was my uncle...is my uncle. He's been sick for years," Robert said.

"Your family has a lot of history in the area," Maddie said. Judy saw an expression on Robert that made her nervous. He seemed uncomfortable talking about his family, and she remembered what Becky said about Robert's parents and how he lost them in a fire. She also remembered Maddie's comment about the Deville family curse. She guessed any family with a long history has some bad patches threaded through the family tree. Robert didn't want a recap of the past, and she couldn't hold that against him. Detective Scott Sedge extended a hand to Judy.

"It's a pleasure to meet you, Judy," His smile was bright and genuine. "It distresses me to hear about this business with Johnny Macklemore. My wife turned me onto his books years ago—hooked ever since," he said.

"Everyone has their secrets," Robert interjected.

"Thank you, detective," she said.

"Please, call me Sedge, and he's Robert," Sedge said and pointed to his partner. "Here's the thing...when we picked up Johnny from the Renaissance hotel, he said he'd been asleep at the time of the assault. We questioned the hotel's staff, and—he went up to his room early, and they never saw him leave," Sedge saw Judy's miserable reaction. "This doesn't mean he didn't slip out in the middle of the night. It means they didn't see him leave," Sedge cushioned the blow. "Becky was lucky to be alive, and we didn't get much more than Johnny's involvement to go on. We'll be able to get more from her when she recovers," Sedge said.

"We brought Johnny Macklemore in as a favor to Cal and nothing more. The man's a revered author—almost a God in Ohio. And you have more motive to lie than him," Robert added. The turn Robert took in his tone stunned her.

"The things Cal said aren't adding up," Sedge said. "When the authorities arrived at Becky's home, they had to bust their way into her home. Every door and window—locked from the inside."

"It also didn't help that Becky's wounds appeared to be self-inflicted," Robert said. Every fiber of Judy wanted to scream at how Johnny did it—how he invaded her mind and assaulted Becky, but she knew they would never believe her.

"We questioned him. And let me tell you, he's a stand-up guy. He seemed even nicer than his television interviews..." Sedge trailed off.

"But he will walk," Judy finished his sentiment. Both detectives nodded. Cal stepped closer to Judy.

"They agreed to allow me a crack at some questions," Cal said.

"But you watch your step," Robert thundered. "If a hair is out-of-place afterward, the department will have to pick up the pieces."

"I understand. There could be a backlash if a famous writer remains locked up without evidence," Cal said.

"Cal's the best interrogator in the department," Sedge announced, "He's a Goddamn lie detector. I'm not bullshitting about that."

"That's all we can do for you," Robert said, looking Judy up and down.

"You think I'm lying," Judy said.

"It's not for us to decide," Sedge countered. But Judy saw the truth in their eyes.

"Good luck," Robert added as he fell in line behind his partner already walking away. Cal took a breath and smiled at Judy.

"Ready for this?" Cal asked. Judy nodded, and he led them upstairs through the building to the holding cells.

"It's just a strategy, but I would like you to watch while I'm questioning him. Anything you can pick up could benefit us. Is this okay with you?" The night they spent together, his arms around her—his smell that mingled with all her senses—kept crawling back and had been since their encounter. Judy pushed the images as far back as she could, knowing that they would return stronger than ever.

Fear sat in the corner, dressed as a one-night stand. They haven't talked since they made love, and she didn't want to check in on her feelings. She saw the situation as a house of cards. If she moved slowly, she could add another card—build up the foundation.

Cal led the ladies to a door at the back of the station. Judy's idea of where she was within the building became jumbled. She understood why when he opened the door to the room. Builders must have wanted the area to blend into the rest of the surroundings. The room had a door, but it didn't appear to be leading anywhere. A room that didn't exist led to a small space with a chair. Although there were light switches, Cal never went for them. They met face to face with a mirror that extended the entire length of the wall.

"Make yourself comfortable. We'll start in a minute," Cal said, already closing the door behind him. Through the glass, opposite them in another room, sat Johnny Macklemore. He turned to the wall of glass and stared. His gaze swept across the two-way mirror and stopped in Judy's general area. *He can't see me—there's no way.* She doubted the reassuring words even as they came to her.

"Is he staring at us?" Maddie asked in a whisper.

"No. Johnny can't." His focus contradicted her statement and sent shivers through her body. He forced her to avoid his gaze. As if tuned in to their frequency, Johnny turned away. The invisible string snapped.

"I feel strange about this," Maddie said.

"Just relax," Judy said in a calming voice, but witnessing her friend's anxiety rise. A door on the other side of the glass opened as Cal slipped in like he was late for a meeting instead of grilling the man who stole his love. The sight of Cal caused Johnny to sink into his chair. Judy didn't see nervousness in her husband—she saw outright terror. She couldn't count on memory, but she was sure she'd never seen that raw emotion on his face or in his demeanor before. Maddie noticed it. They traded curious expressions, thrown by the sudden weakness of a person who prided himself of his exterior fortress. Cal moved to a chair across from Johnny and gave a wink to the mirror and the women behind.

"The famous Johnny Macklemore," Cal's words flew like bullets.

"That's right," Johnny said in a confident voice. His frame spoke something different. "Let me go. So, why aren't you?"

Cal dropped his hands to the table that divided them and jabbed his head forward. Johnny reacted with a backward lunge of his own.

"You're very nervous, Mr. Macklemore." Johnny shifted in his chair and glanced at the mirror once more.

"Not at all. Why would I be?"

Cal smiled, and the subtle gesture surprised Johnny.

"He's scared shitless of Cal," Maddie said.

"Yeah...but why?"

Cal slid a pen from his jacket and scribbled something on a piece of paper resting in a Manilla folder. Johnny watched it all with interest.

"In my experience, the number of innocent people brought into this building for questioning is low. You may be within that group, except for the information I have says you disagreed with the victim a day ago? Is this correct?" Cal pretended to be reading this from the folder and allowed Johnny to see the motion.

"She may have been there, but my conversation was with my wife and no one else. Like I told the previous detectives, I don't even know the woman. I'm sorry she got hurt, but I have my things to take care of, and all of this is interfering," Johnny said.

"Do you know who I am?"

Johnny didn't answer.

"I mean...I'm close to Judy. We were engaged. You know that, right?" The mirror and its reflection transfixed Johnny. "Look at me," Cal thundered, and Johnny obeyed. "How is it possible that you and I have never met until this very moment? Or have we met?" Sweat beaded on Johnny's forehead.

"Is that what this is about, Cal? Did Judy leave you for me?" A confident grin made its first appearance on Johnny's face. "You think you could give her the life she's used to living with a cop's salary? You have nothing to offer her—or really, anyone," he laughed and was himself again. Overhead lights flickered and dimmed, before flashing faster and faster. Maddie saw the surge and spun to Judy.

"Did you do that?"

Judy shook her head.

"I wouldn't know how." They both swung their heads to Johnny. "He's dangerous. We have to get Cal out of that room," Judy said. The two men stared at each other, ignoring everything around them. Judy realized that for Cal, the standoff was overdue, and for Johnny, it was inevitable.

The lights above shone brighter than their bulbs should allow. A high-pitched squeal grew as if it came from the air itself, and it was spreading through the room. Eyes locked onto eyes, and if either of them noticed the changes taking place, they never let on. Judy wanted to cover her ears. It occurred to her that the sounds emanated from both men— inside their heads.

"Johnny's trying to kill him!" Maddie screamed. The table separated Johnny and Cal in the spatial distance, but there was a discreet link between them as solid as a wooden board. Their faces contorted from a pressure that was building in both. Judy got to her feet and slammed her hands against the two-way mirror. Solid or not, it shook, giving off a twangy reverberation that roared louder than the high-pitch shrill.

Judy continued to bang, feeling each impact vibrating her arms with pain. Soon, the penetrating sound drowned, faded altogether, and the connection between the men melted. The wooden bridge turned soft and evaporated entirely. With the mental conduit gone, Judy's last hit stirred them back into their surroundings. This time everyone in the room wore a mask of fear.

Sweat beaded on Cal's forehead, then dripped down his cheek.

"Can I go now?" Johnny asked. Cal stood and came close to falling as he did. With weak knees, he made it to the door, pounded twice against its metal skin, and dodged the door as an officer swung it open.

"Get out," Cal shouted. When Johnny stood, Cal smiled when he saw Johnny's footing wasn't so stable. Before Johnny ducked out the room, he gave one last glimpse at the mirror, and Judy was sure he was peering straight at her. And then he vanished, and that was enough for her.

By the time Judy and Maddie made their way around to the rear doorway of the interrogation room, Cal was on the floor, the door propped open by his body.

"Are you okay? What just happened?" Judy asked. He gave a feeble shake of his head.

"You got me," Cal said. They helped him to his feet. "Can you find your way out? I'll call later."

"Yeah. You sure you will be okay?" Judy asked.

"Go home and lock the doors," he said. Judy smiled and was turning when he pulled her back for a kiss. She didn't resist the embrace. "We'll get him, Jude," he said. She smiled but didn't believe him.

As they moved toward the exit of the building—Maddie spoke but all Judy could think was Johnny's powers were more than she could ever fight against and hope to win. She wondered if she was in the same position many times before and always relenting to his will. Through the front entrance, Judy saw something that made her feel stupid for not expecting. Johnny was there, fielding questions from the press.

"Let's go," Judy said. She grabbed her friend by the wrist and tried to hurry past before...

"Judy?" Johnny called before she could sneak by. He caught up to her.

"Just leave me alone," Judy begged.

"Not until you're home safe with me," he said in a sugary tone.

"It's over. Just deal with it, Johnny," she said, and he laughed.

"You don't get to make that decision. You're lucky to have me, and you'll see that soon enough," Johnny smiled at Maddie. "The person she can trust is her husband. Isn't that right, Maddie?" He opened his mouth to speak but he saw the press edging closer. "This is your last chance to come with me. I'm not responsible for anything after this."

"Never," she said.

"I warned you, Judy." Johnny sneered and walked away. But Judy froze in place—Maddie stared off into the distance.

"Maddie?" Her friend wouldn't face her. "How does Johnny know you?" Judy's wheels were turning, but there weren't enough dots available to her to make any visible connection. Maddie was already crying when she twisted back.

"You've seen me...I've worked to make things right," Maddie said through tears.

"Maddie. What did you do?" Judy asked with more force. Without knowing, Judy had a death grip on Maddie's wrists until Maddie yanked free.

"We weren't friends anymore—it had been over a year since we even talked," Maddie wiped away tears. "Remember when I said you were the reason...I did nothing with my life?" Judy nodded. "You were moving past our friendship. You were already a brilliant writer. I didn't even fucking know about you saving brain-damaged children then," she said with disgust. "You had everything, Judy. Even had Cal." Judy rushed back to the first night they all got back together and how awkward their greeting was.

"You wanted Cal?"

Maddie nodded, and Judy thought of the first time she saw her friend. The rat face flew into her mind. *You were a rat.*

"Since grade school. Cal never once looked my way—and you...he fell for in an instant. You didn't even have to work for it!" Maddie raised her voice. "By the time I got the courage to approach about my feelings for him—it was too late for me. He let me down easy...it was Cal. I'm sure he didn't even tell you."

"I couldn't say," Judy admitted.

"He didn't. But I'd had more than enough of you. I spent the next year moving on. I couldn't compete with Judy Angel if I tried. So, I didn't. The one thing that didn't go away was my bitterness. I heard of your engagement, and I can say I wasn't happy for you. The opposite, I imagine. Drowning in my bile, someone showed up and pulled me to the shore."

"Johnny?" Judy asked.

"He promised me happiness—revenge. He promised me...Cal," Maddie's sobs were stronger than ever. "It was a bargain with the Devil. He didn't tell me about his plans, and I didn't care. I did much later, but it was too late—for you and me," Maddie said and pulled away with Judy holding on tight.

"What did you do?" Judy's face contorted with thoughts of Maddie's rat face.

"I gave Johnny you,"

"But it was my mother—" Maddie shook her head.

"Your mother let him take you, but it was me that introduced him to you. I led him to you."

"I don't remember that."

"You wouldn't!" Maddie screamed, yanking her arm away from Judy, and ran.

Chapter Thirty-one
—Pride in their talents—

It wasn't a surprise when her vision came this time. The *tunnel* wrapping around her body was an old friend. Mastering the return of her memories bordered on impossible, but she prepared in the same way a dog readied himself for a boot from a bad owner. There was no way to keep the memories away, so she just let it wash over her. A part of her, a dark corner, needed to see this vision above the rest. The betrayal had aged ten years, and it was a fresh indignity.

She was watching through Angel's eyes like an old pro, and this time, she wasn't taking everything at face value. When she entered Maddie's bedroom, her friend was greeting her. At the first go-round, Maddie's behavior wasn't out of place, but with a second viewing, Judy saw her nervousness. In front of her was an anxious girl who prepared to sell her friend off to an evil man.

The anger rose in Judy. What she uncovered about Johnny gave her evidence that the wheels were in motion well before the night's events. Still, she regarded this vision as the pivotal moment in her life where everything changed forever. Her life was cruising along down the path she chose. So much work went into a future life after high school, and Maddie obliterated it in one night. And with her friend's insecurities, she allowed Johnny to strip her of everything she was as a person.

She recognized the happiness of Angel spending time with a friend she hadn't seen in a long time. Angel wasn't without her apprehension. There were awkward chunks when she just wanted things to be like they once were. *That was my weakness.* They put music on from their past, and Maddie's plan chugged right along.

"It's so good to spend time with you again. So much has happened this year. Whenever something happened, I would think, *I wish I could share this with Maddie*," Angel said.

Judy caught something she never saw before. It was in Maddie's expression—a flicker of anger or jealousy. Angel was speaking, but Maddie was in another headspace that involved deception. *Rat!* Maddie was bolstering her decision to deliver her to Johnny. In the limited time, there was a way back, and her inner dialogue was firing at full speed to either retreat or stay the course.

Don't do it, Maddie. Judy escaped into vivid images. When she realized that all this was in the past, anger gained another foothold. The one-sided conversation continued for the girls. In her mannerisms, Judy saw Maddie decide to go through with her plot.

She wanted to hide her face from the rest and already understood the lack of plasticity of the visions. And it was more than that alone; there was something else at work with the memories that were coming back. They seemed like random memories when she had arrived, but now she accepted them as clues from her subconscious. Survival instincts kicked in, and the brain's instinct to adapt and return to reality was way stronger than she gave it credit for. Her mind was trying to fill in the gaps of the missing pieces and trying to create a full image out of the fragments she had to work with to no avail.

The one-word answers that Maddie was offering ceased. She went quiet, and Angel even noticed the change.

"Girls like you can't always get what they want," Maddie said. Angel stared at her friend in confusion. "Not this time."

"What are you talking about?" Angel asked.

Maddie's bedroom went from a harmless teenager's room to something attempting to swallow her whole. Angel didn't understand her friend, but alarm bells were ringing. Maddie sat there with a vicious smile, waiting for something that Angel wouldn't like. Angel stood, and Judy sensed the fear firing on all cylinders. Maddie made no move to stop her, wearing the same horrible smirk.

The bedroom door opened, and Angel saw a teenage boy enter. He was younger than her, but he walked with a purpose that didn't match his age. There was an intention written on his face that chilled her and stopped her in her tracks. The mixture of youth and knowledge seized her like a deer in a headlight. Curiosity was getting the better of her, making her watch out of fascination rather than fight for her life. Judy, watching from a safe distance, saw all of this unfold and understood how it happened—how it could only happen this way.

Beyond the advancing teen, Judy fell into despair by acknowledging the inevitability of her past. When her memories were scarce, she believed her timeline was fluid or easily changed. Watching the worst passage of her life revealed, Judy accepted her fate, and with her acceptance, she wanted her memories back. *They belong to me.*

Johnny pressed her onto Maddie's bed with aggression that Angel had never encountered in her short life. The new experiences culminated in a dreamlike state, furthering her apathy for the danger that threatened. While Johnny secured her, Maddie remained as still as a portrait.

"Don't just stand there," he whispered, but with fury in his voice. Maddie held an amber glass bottle with a liquid sloshing inside. The bottle was as innocuous as any found at the local pharmacy. With someone pinning her down, the harmless-appearing bottle became far more sinister. Maddie was in the throes of second thoughts about her involvement, but Johnny wasn't letting her off the hook. "This is your last chance. I'm not responsible for anything after this," he said to Maddie. His words were like a gut-punch. He uttered the same ones in front of the police headquarters, and she tried to imagine their conversations before this night and what he must have said to keep her in line.

Maddie was back on board, and she was moving again. She soaked a cloth with a clear liquid. The fabric absorbed it with more overflowing and leaking onto the carpet. "Careful inhaling that shit," Johnny cautioned. If she heard him, she never let on. Maddie moved closer. Angel's heartbeat was pounding in her chest as her best friend covered her mouth with the medicated cloth. Somehow Judy still empathized for her friend, who was damning her to a life of slavery for the next ten years—it didn't make sense, but there it was.

Before her eyes closed that night, Angel saw Johnny smiling—his task accomplished because of a jealous teenage girl. A haze was overtaking Angel's thoughts, and with them, the fear was ebbing. The last thing she witnessed, decades after the fact, was Maddie standing beside the bed crying. She understood Maddie's stunted life—why she lived alone. And why she tried to make things right.

Chapter Thirty-two
—Interfered with your reasoning—

Columbus, Ohio had a tainted, wicked quality, Johnny observed. People walking the streets were menacing, and he wanted the safety of his walled home—tucked inside his gated community. There was a stench to Becky's neighborhood that Johnny couldn't remove from his clothes. He knew he was above these common people in the small communities. People either chose a new car or a new house and never both. Both would mean getting what you wanted, and most did without what they wanted. For a man that did whatever it took to win—he saw their behavior as drone-like, and he hated it with all his fiber.

Tonight, health was his primary concern. He was deteriorating faster than he ever remembered, and his outing with Becky proved this to him. Every year of his life, with the ability, Johnny saw the range of his tethering grow and expand. When he first learned to use his powers, he needed to be within a few feet of his host. With some practice, he could extend that distance to over a few blocks, which became useful not to get caught or interrupted while collecting.

Changes were apparent. He attempted to tether onto Becky from his usual range, and he couldn't. At first, he thought his powers were disappearing, and that sent him spiraling. What was he without his gift? *Like everyone else.* A block away was the furthest he could sleep safely in his car and still reach out to her. Although he accomplished the connection, it was a makeshift bridge that led to a shabby recreation of the surrounding. *That fucking clock.* A detail he never had to worry about five years earlier. It was the intricacies that strayed from his focus and the aspect of collecting that he beat himself up about when he didn't get things right.

A thumping in his head was ongoing. He was sure his encounter with Becky brought on the attack, but the pain accompanied by the ringing in his ears never left. The intensity rose and dove through each hour and lingered like a black cloud that followed his every step. Whichever way he threw the blame, collecting memories was at the heart of his decline. When the rubber met the road, he had two choices—stop collecting or remove all the memories he'd collected over the decades. Both options were a realistic way back to his old self, whoever that was.

He was a flame burning twice as bright, and Becky was all the proof he needed. His visit with her flew off the tracks. He planned to scare her for sure—to make her think twice about crossing him. The world went fuzzy. A side effect of a full collection was wrong decision making. When he was younger, poor decisions would ebb in and out like normal lapses in judgment, but now he couldn't say that with a straight face.

What he referred to as the *overload of memories*—saturated all his conscious thoughts until he had to pick through hundreds to get to his own. The job of deciphering between his memories and the ones he took in was tedious. Patients with extreme cases of OCD describe how the constant re-thinking of every detail becomes overwhelming. And that's how he lived most of the time—exhausted.

As the wrong thought matriculated in, he had to throw them back out into the abyss until the right one—*his* thought—made it through. It was easier said than done. Sometimes it would take a dozen attempts before he was sure the thought belonged to him. Cutting corners was a way around the exhaustive weeding out of inappropriate thoughts. The downside was the Becky situation happened.

The whole task of living became a chore, and with each fresh memory collected—more plates to keep spinning. Often a plate would hit the ground if he weren't careful, and Becky was one of those plates. It was an annoyance—he wouldn't argue with that, but in the scheme of things, Becky wasn't important. To Johnny, Becky was a loudmouth bitch who had it coming. And if he didn't intervene in her life, someone else would. She was an unpleasant woman, and he realized why she was living alone.

A block away from Bud and Emily's home, Johnny wondered if his brain was thumping out of his skull. Most of the day, the pain never rose beyond a dull ache behind his sockets. He eliminated all activities in his mind—his strategy vanished. Judy's betrayal disappeared, and he found that just picturing a foggy black television screen did the trick. Even his car ride to Judy and her family used only the bare minimum of his faculties to navigate the roads.

Judy's defiance, although not unexpected, became more difficult to reign in than he expected. The little parlor trick with her mother and the butcher knife made a striking scene, but it didn't budge his wife's thinking. The problem was that Judy was off the rails, but there was no way to tell how much she was off the rails. He'd spent a lot of time burying the memories of her parents. *How much of her childhood memories came back?* If enough didn't return, she wouldn't have a strong connection—the need to protect them would be less, and more motivation would be necessary.

The unplanned horror scene with Becky was foolish on his part. Judy never witnessed the trauma of Becky, and they haven't known each other long enough. *So sloppy, Johnny.* The ringing in his head changed to a rhythmic buzz that made him think his eyeballs bulged in time with the pulsation. His actions hadn't motivated Judy so far, but that would end after tonight.

He found a parking spot in front of a random house without exterior lights blazing, and far away from a streetlight. The area was as perfect as he could hope for under the circumstance. He had a knack for planning to the point of ridiculousness. He wasn't sure if it was the constant droning in his head or the muddiness of his thinking as of late, but his pre-planning was suffering. The fastest way to slip up—to get caught—was to fly by the seat of the pants. The last thing he wanted was a cop tapping on his window to find out why he was asleep in a car a block away from where a crime took place. Johnny lived and died by the principle of *always have an alibi.*

The haze was gaining ground and chipping away at his safety nets. The thoughts were coming in too fast to stop. He sighed, shook his head, and folded himself into the rented sedan's backseat. Another reason the girl behind the counter of the car rental pissed him off. The car he wanted had a nice, roomy backseat. *That fucking jealous girl.* He tried to find a comfortable position for the work that lay ahead. He shifted his body several times before he found an arrangement that was relaxing enough to drift off to sleep.

Johnny counted himself lucky that sleep came to him fast. He'd practiced nodding off for so long that it was as natural as throwing a ball or swinging a bat. As the collection's static grew over the years, the ability to fall asleep at the drop of a hat was his saving grace and the skill that saved his life more than once. He was asleep but still aware of his body resting in the car—the homes that lined the streets—and even tiny nuances such as the wind or a blinking streetlight far off were on his radar.

He stretched out his vines first skyward, then moving out into the open space of the neighborhood. Judy was easily recognizable to him—radiating energy maternal in its familiar signature. Along the way, the grasping vines passed homes with others sleeping. Each person had their unique pull that beckoned the vine, like an organic form of magnetism. While there was no air involved, denying a connection with the random people stole his breath.

More than once, he compared sending out his vines to fishing—trolling for souls to connect onto—to snatch. If there weren't dire consequences to overfilling himself with memories, the hobby of casting his line out into the world and bringing back treasure would be at the top of his list. The few occasions he allowed himself to do such a thing was at his latest writer's conference. There were too many talented writers to let the opportunity slip by. After two days fishing, more like whaling, for novels, he put a stop to all his gluttonous behavior. He didn't leave himself a reserve, and he was paying for his indiscretion ever since.

Johnny was getting closer to Judy, and it was amping up his senses like gasoline onto an open flame. There was an urge that straddled his vine as the distance between it and the host fell away. Judy wasn't awake, but he was sure she was feeling his approach in some forgotten corner of her mind. *There she is*, he thought as his vine passed into Bud and Emily's home. Because his vine was invisible to anything but the hosts, it cut through everything physical and clamped down upon Judy. He sighed with relief when he made the bridge with his wife on one side and him on the other.

There were times throughout the years when he attempted to tread lightly inside Judy. Most psychiatrists affirm that the mind is a fragile environment, and Johnny would agree, but not in the way they think. The laws of physics did not rule his ability to change the things inside her. Instead, it was a matter of will, his against hers. She wasn't aware she was playing the game, and it made things a lot easier—there was no fair play in his game, but that was okay with him.

Removing Judy's mental ability and how to use it was the first thing he helped her with when they got together. He had no choice. She was way too strong, and her dexterity with the mind was second to none. Competing with her one on one was out of the question. When he met her, she was colossal, and in comparison—he was a dwarf. His skills improved over the years—a small percentage better, but the gap between the two was laughable.

Perhaps if Judy were to show him the ropes, train him how to wield his powers, he could eliminate the memories that were corrupting his brain. The problem was Johnny was too afraid to drop her veil. She was like a tiger you had to release from its cage to help him. The fear was releasing her, full of her memories, ready and willing to use. His lack of options maddened him.

Subterfuge was the name of the game, except it yielded nothing other than frustration. Even as he soothed a giant to sleep, she was still too sturdy, and any information remained locked in a much better vault than his feeble tools could open. The impractical portion of Johnny wanted to just shut her down like his sister. Watch the lights go out from the inside and piss on her ashes. That option was becoming the lone route if he couldn't get her back on the rails. Being hauled into the police department and then questioned by the pretty boy had all resulted from her big mouth.

The anger rose in him, and the branches of his vine were ready to dim her shades forever. It was only the push of a mental button, and she—and his troubles—would be over. What if you can get her secret to emptying your collection? His body, a block away, wanted to scream to the sky. Instead, he screeched his displeasure inside his wife, and Judy reacted with a flinch in her sleep. He smiled at the small victory. *It's time to bring you home, Judy.*

He moved with purpose, allowing his tiny branches to sweep through her as if he were caressing her brain instead of searching for what he needed. His exhilaration was at an all-time high since he was back in his hometown. She was pliant—open to anything he wanted, and he wanted a lot. A pliable Judy meant he got the answers he desired. His first plan was to erase her memories of her time there, but hoping he could gain much more, taking the memories became secondary.

Other memories were bombarding him—countless misperceptions left him second-guessing his certainty again. *Focus on getting Judy home. Worry about the rest later—when you have all the time in the world. I will*, he told himself. His branches traced the spot where her newest memories were born. Whether to sever them or remove the memories altogether was the hardest question of the night. As the events of this week suggested, cutting them wouldn't last. The other alternative meant taking in more memories and debilitating his health even further. He couldn't risk her exposing him to anyone else, the authorities most of all.

Johnny willed the surrounding branches into recent memories. His temperature rose as it always did right before the information transferred to him. The weight of the task was light as a feather with his practiced skill, but he discovered he couldn't budge the cargo at all. As if cemented in place, Judy's mind was untouched. *It's not possible.* The other time someone blocked is progress was when he tried to tap into his father. *It doesn't make any sense—Judy doesn't drink alcohol.* He attempted several more times. His body temperature rose higher than it ever had and still, nothing.

Anger consumed him as he released the vine from Judy. He wanted to hurt her, lash out, and make her pay for keeping him out. She called her skull her own. But for ten years, it was his domain. He screamed, and this time he wagered that his body, laying in the sedan, was joining in the chorus.

An idea occurred to him. Even if it arrived from somewhere else and was a part of the jumbled messages that got through his filter, he didn't care. The futility of not correcting his wife was too much to bear. The lesson he learned from his incident with Becky was less and less crucial. He wanted to strike out at Judy for blocking the rights of a husband.

His vine, still in Judy's home, became an antenna receiving everything around. It searched until it found what it wanted—it didn't have far to go. It slid to the other side of the modest residence—the vine attached to Bud Angel. Rage took control, pushing out everything else and all rational thoughts away. He let the pure emotion influence his actions, not attempting to stop it.

As the branches spread out within Bud, he coaxed them deeper than he often tried. He led his mind into the darkest reaches of the brain. Doctors called the region amygdala, but to Johnny, it was *the Terror*. When he was young and stumbled upon the dark part of the brain, he stayed out of other people's minds for months after. Johnny learned that when he gazed into *the Terror,* it gazed back, reflecting his fear.

The brain had always been a playground to Johnny from the minute he received his gift. But *the Terror* was the single place where he questioned God. If there was such a being that created him and everything he saw, why would he make such a pure evil place as *the Terror?*

The amygdala so disturbed him when he came across the region, he bought a medical diagram of the brain to see what it looked like. The area was unimpressive, no bigger than an almond, unless he passed its threshold—the mental landscape encompassed miles, and if he weren't careful, he could get lost—time was different there.

Everything that kept a human alive waited in *the Terror*. If he tried to see the area from a scientific point of view, it contained the things that reminded you that fire hurts, bees can sting, to run from danger—and all the other instincts that had kept men alive from their earliest steps on the Earth. He was sure it was the oldest part of the brain that made a person a person with dark secrets waiting to be untapped for those who weren't afraid of what they would find. If he were to say it out loud, *the Terror* was just an ancient version of the unconscious. But locked away, he was sure *the Terror* had its thoughts alien to its host.

The danger of entering *the Terror* was how it left its mark. He soon understood that the things you saw weren't just images. A tar pit came to mind as he realized that everything inside clung to him and bled into his conscious mind, altering the aspects of who he was without him witnessing the change. The worst parts of what a human *was*, lived, and breathed in *the Terror*, and it scared him.

He brought Bud into a mental representation of his bedroom. He was sure his skill in creating a victim's self-image would rival even Judy's ability. Bud was there, sitting next to him with a receding hairline—liver spots—and eyes in the beginning stages of glaucoma. Every detail—plucked from Bud's memory of his mirror the day before. He sat there proud of his creation as if he were a God forming a human being from the air itself.

Bud blinked several times but refused to marvel at Johnny's construction efforts. The older man was no stranger to the imitated world, and Johnny learned this from the memories he liberated from Judy. If there were a soft spot for Bud, the sacrifice he made for his daughter would leap beyond the rest. Judy never witnessed the extent of the destruction she caused in her father as she used him to find her way back. The brain damage, caused by her car accident, was catastrophic, and the havoc she caused was not much less in comparison. The gaps in his recall resembled Swiss cheese.

"Why didn't you tell Judy about what she did to you?" Johnny asked. Bud stared as if he were alone. "She fucked you up to save herself," he laughed with no humor. "The appetite of a little girl," he added. Bud turned his head away and understood he was Johnny's prisoner. "Shredded your mind and left you far behind," Johnny prodded.

"Rewiring her brain never made her yours," Bud said. "I wasn't there, but I bet she fought you every step of the way." The projection of Johnny's frame tensed before he could stop it, and Bud took pleasure in seeing it. "The only way someone like you could get a woman like Judy is to steal her."

"You know nothing about her anymore, old man."

"I know she's getting the better of you. Why else would you come to me?"

"Her entire childhood centered on her abilities. When she took memories, how did she release them?" Johnny's expression became childlike. Bud nodded and sat motionless with his hands folded.

"I tried the carrot—didn't work. You're the stick. After Judy sees what I do to you, she'll beg me to come back," Johnny said. Bud showed fear for the first time. Johnny sensed Bud had a plan and before he could stop him, he spoke.

"Hey, Judy. Since you've been back, we haven't found the time to connect like we once did. I want you to know how proud I am of you and the woman you've become."

"What are you doing?" Johnny demanded.

"He needs the secrets of your ability to survive. He stole your memories...let him drown in them, Jude."

"Shut your fucking mouth," Johnny roared.

"Don't let your anger for what he's done to me lure you back to him. Stay safe and stay awake. I love you, Angel," Bud said through tears. His message to his daughter enraged Johnny.

"You think she will ever see that? Never. I will never let her see your last moments. And whether you like it or not, I will take her back from you," Johnny said. Bud's face turned stoic—he was ready for whatever came next. Hatred for the stubborn older man flared in Johnny, and he had no more use for him. He would risk his worst fears to punish Bud. His brainwaves were buzzing in and out, stirred up by his anger, and he didn't fight them anymore.

Hundreds of conflicting thoughts collided with his own. So, he stopped trying to figure out if he was right or wrong. He spread his branches out toward *the Terror* and sensed when he was close. If the old man got one thing right, it was the word rewiring. Johnny thought it was the perfect description of his process.

The basis of his work on others hinged on creating a fresh path from a certain emotion. In the most complex cases, it was a belief he was creating. He rewired people more times than he could count, but he never had the path derive from *the Terror*. *The Terror* was the closest thing to a monster, and he avoided it all his life. He wasn't even sure how it would work. Would *the Terror* leak into Bud like a poisonous gas? Would Bud go off like a bomb, infecting all his senses? From his conscious to his unconscious and everything in between?

Another part of Johnny, a now quiet section, screamed restraint. *If you destroy her father, will you be able to control her?* The thought got through the static, but it was as if someone was speaking through a damp blanket—muffled and far away. It held none of the urgency the other voices possessed.

If he would do it, he planned to do it all the way. He began his patches, first from *the Terror*, and then connecting the other end of the lines to other parts of the brain. The work was tedious, but he relished something so novel. His job continued as he created one line after another until he was sure every region of the brain would receive a large dose of *the Terror*. Although the paths were invisible to the naked eye, he saw them there all the same—a miniature electrical system—feeding him from the amygdala. *A fucking work of art*, he told himself when he completed his task.

"How I wish you could tell me the feeling. But I wouldn't want to be you or step a toe into you after it begins. One of life's little mysteries, I guess," Johnny said. Bud's face stayed passive right until Johnny opened the pathways to each line. "Goodbye, old man. I'll take care of your daughter." Before Johnny could detach the vine, he experienced *the Terror* spreading throughout Bud. His best description would be of a slimy crawling that wanted to devour everything within reach. A flicker of sympathy tried to bubble to the surface. Johnny stuffed it back down, released the vine, and enjoyed the whoosh of his conscious mind slamming back into his body. Before he even reached his shell, he needed the comfort and safety of his bed back at the Renaissance hotel. He imagined it would take more than a day to recover, but it was worth it. He smiled when his mind and body reunited.

Chapter Thirty-three
—Majority rule is a person's conscience—

Bud Angel was the strongest man Cal had ever met and seeing him lying in a hospital bed showed how vulnerable they all were. Emily sat in a nearby chair dozing, her arm with a fresh bandage wrapped from a hospital visit of her own, and Becky rested in a room down the hall. Refusing to give up, Johnny had turned every one of Judy's friends and family into the walking wounded. Cal wondered if Judy had a circle of friends in New York that met with the same ailments because of her husband.

All evidence of the tough facade Judy kept up for the sake of her mother, melted away. When she turned his way, the dam broke. Even as he scooped her into his arms and tried to reassure her, her crying continued unabated. Seeing her father damaged was too much to bear. *Part of Johnny's plan.*

"I know who was behind this, but what happened?" Cal asked. Judy buried her face into his chest and shook her head.

"When I found him...I saw no one like that before," Judy's sobs stopped her speech cold. "my dad was writhing in pain. He was crying, Cal. Bud saw something—feeling things that weren't there."

"What did Johnny do to him?" She shook her head.

"It wasn't natural—the way he was acting was more like an acid trip. There was no consoling him or bringing him back to reality. He screamed and clawed at the air until the moment the EMT sedated him. I think he'd still be thrashing even now if they hadn't," she said. "He hurt my dad," she said, weeping. A helpless feeling swept over Cal, and some ugly thoughts came into his mind for the first time in his life. He squeezed her tighter and fought off thinking of the ways to stop Johnny for good. The worst mistake of his life was allowing Johnny to leave Columbus with the woman he loved, and he would not let that happen again.

Over his years on the force, he'd brushed shoulders with some bad dudes a time or two. He was no stranger to the horrible but clever ways criminals disposed of people. The lengths some would go to get away with murder were frightening and ingenious. Did Johnny deserve to die? There wasn't a doubt in his mind. *Could I go through with it?* The question lingered in his mind and needed an answer at some point.

"I promised Becky I would visit," Judy said while wiping tears. "Will you go with me?" Cal nodded and watched Bud sleep. His mentality switched back to its default, and he envisioned ways to stop Johnny by legal means and came to the same dead end. He held her as they moved to Becky's room. When they got inside, Becky was sitting up in her hospital bed—her mood threw them for a loop. Becky smiled and waved like she was there to get her tonsils out and not fresh from surgery to get her tongue reattached.

"Hey, Becky," Cal started, and she gave a weak smile. Judy grabbed her hand and brought it up to her mouth, kissing it.

"I'm so sorry this happened," Judy said. Becky was already reaching for a notepad resting in her lap and went to work before turning it toward them: *Not your fault.*

"It sure feels like it," Judy said. "Is there anything you can tell us about your experience with Johnny?" Cal asked, hopeful that Johnny slipped up. Becky scribbled: *He's sick and getting worse.*

"Sick how?" Judy asked.

It's his decision making. Johnny's unhinged and dangerous. Judy nodded. Becky went back to her pad when they heard a knock on the hospital room door. Maddie stood there using the door frame for support. Her face was red and puffy.

"Is it okay that I'm here?" No one spoke. Cal made a move to Maddie when Judy grabbed him by the arm. He gave Judy an expression of disbelief, and she answered by shaking her head. The room remained quiet for a long time until Becky wrote on the notepad and lifted it for Maddie to see: *Why are you here?* Maddie edged into the room—they knew she waited for them to tell her to stand by the door. No one did.

"What I did to you," Maddie glared out of the hospital window as she spoke, "was horrible, and I'm a horrible person."

"I saw the night you let Johnny take me over," Judy said. The admission was like a slap to Maddie's face. She took a step back and nodded.

"I tried to back out of my decision to help him—days earlier, and Johnny wouldn't have it. I didn't know what kind of person I was dealing with, and I soon found out. I met with him and told him I wasn't going through with the plan. He became furious. So, I walked away from him and thought it was over," Maddie cried. Becky added to her note: *Go on!*

"The next morning—it was my mom. She didn't remember me. I was horrified. I was a stranger to her in one night. He took her away from me because I refused to give him you. He told me her memory would return if I helped him, and I did."

"Did she remember you again?" Judy asked.

"Two days later," Maddie said. "I'm ashamed of what I did now, but I was also sorry when it happened. Seeing his powers firsthand, and I couldn't live with my choices. I told him I'd go through with it if he wiped away my memories after." Maddie fell into soft sobs.

"Let me guess. He erased nothing?" Cal asked. Maddie continued to cry as she shook her head.

"I watched him take you from Cal...from your family. I had to live with it every day. That son of a bitch wanted me to remember what I had done to you. I saw interviews with Johnny and you, and it was horrible that I did nothing to help you. The years went by, and every time I tried to do something for myself—I didn't deserve good things in my life."

"You're right. You don't," Cal said.

"He manipulated a teenager," Judy said. "I can't forgive that girl who hurt me because she's long gone. I just need time." Judy said. Maddie nodded and retreated to a corner. Cal could tell Judy was softening but was not sure he was ready to forgive Maddie so soon. It impressed him that Judy could rise above the betrayal, but in her place, he didn't think he could.

"You okay, Cal?" Judy asked. Cal shook his head, turning away in anger. Becky made an entry onto the notepad and flipped it around: *Found something out.* They gathered around Becky as she penned more: *I tracked down the sale of Angel Among Us. Any guesses who bought it?*

"No way," Judy said. Becky nodded and returned to her writing: *The seller was Otis!* Becky circled the doctor's name several times.

Chapter Thirty-four
—Worrying about the next world—

When Otis Bain returned home, the strange car parked in the driveway sparked an urge to throw the shifter into reverse, head back onto the highway, and take some time to think. He ignored that reaction and did none of those things. Otis dodged every bullet that Judy threw at him—but there was something different in the air that wasn't comforting.

From the outside, everything appeared peaceful, but when he entered his home, things would change. Millie was crying, and Judy was holding her hand. It wasn't a good sign for him. He hung his coat on a rack and turned to his guests, stretching time.

"I gave you every chance to come clean," Judy said.

"You did...I just wasn't ready," Otis admitted.

"If we leave here tonight without answers...our next stop is the authorities," Cal said. Witnessing his wife sobbing, all Otis could do was surrender a nod of agreement.

"Please tell us that Johnny threatened you," Maddie said.

"He didn't have to do any such thing...I knew what he was capable of before he approached me," Otis said.

"How did you know that?" Cal asked. Otis located a chair and crumpled into it.

"I think you've heard from others that there was an epidemic that ran through the AAU facility," he said, focusing on Judy. "That was true and...you caused the infection." Cal stood up and headed toward Otis.

"Watch your mouth," Cal said. Otis raised his hands for defense.

"Hand to God," Otis said.

"What are you talking about?" Maddie asked. Cal took a step backward but was still hovering as a reminder.

"You were a miracle, Judy. The things you did helped a lot of children—or at least that's what we thought," he said, regarding Millie with apprehension. Otis wasn't ever planning to tell his wife the specifics, and more than that—he regretted the way she would find out. "Years later, I discovered that when you helped others, you were causing...mutations," he said.

"This is ridiculous. I don't believe a word this liar is saying," Cal boiled with anger.

"You are welcome to believe what you will. You came to me for answers. I never came knocking on your door," Otis reminded.

"Let him talk, Cal," Judy said. Cal slid into a chair like a dog scolded and folded his arms.

"Thank you. Helping people has its rewards, but I wanted to find the root of your ability so we could help patients of brain damage on a larger scale. You were always generous with your time and never squeamish about the poking and prodding in the name of science, but besides showing some activity in certain regions of the brain, we never had a clue why you possessed your skills. We went back and checked in with the ones you helped and what I found..." Otis shifted in his chair and glanced at Millie, hanging on his every word. "The parents of the recovering kids—some were telling me stories."

"Stories?" Judy asked. Otis nodded and kept his eyes locked onto Millie.

"They were showing unusual symptoms. One mother told me that her son often read her and her husband's thoughts. She described going over her Christmas list in her head while he was watching television, and he blurted out his excitement for what he was getting that year. Another family—and I'm not making this up—swore their child communicated with their pets, long rambling conversations that went late into the night between this child and their dog. Those were the mild cases I came across. Some abilities appeared dormant while others..." Sweat ran down the doctor's forehead. They watched him wipe the sweat away and saw more take its place.

"What did you find in the others," Judy asked.

"Those...I tracked down in prisons—foster homes—juvenile detention centers. You know better than anyone the responsibility of such a powerful ability." Judy nodded in agreement. "Because we didn't identify this phenomenon early, the children had no one to help them understand their gifts or the dangers of using them against others. Their gifts isolated them from friends and family, forcing them toward the worst behaviors. Many of your patients have done unspeakable things, Judy. Because not all injuries were the same and delivered to the same parts of the brain, no two abilities were the same. No one person had the same skills with their mind. But one thing was sure, they all had the potential for a lot of power," he said.

"An entire army of Johnny clones," Maddie commented.

"Why didn't you tell them? Why didn't you warn anyone?" Millie asked her husband. Otis lowered his head.

"He's a coward. Otis saw what these kids could do, and he turned the other way to spare his own family," Cal said. Otis turned to Millie as she was already shaking her head in disbelief.

"No, he's right, honey. But I was thinking of you and our babies." Millie turned away.

"How could I have done all this?" Judy asked.

"I have theories, but solid evidence has eluded me. When you reached inside someone—when you rebuilt tissue and pathways, you left a mark. You altered them—opened something up—I don't know for sure."

"These are ticking time bombs all over the city...maybe the state," Cal said. "After you healed and altered Johnny, he became obsessed. Who's to say more won't become fixated on her? There's no telling what they will think," he said. Judy couldn't breathe.

"Johnny is our biggest threat right now. We deal with him and then figure out what to do about the rest," Maddie said. "What is your connection with Johnny?" All heads turned to Otis.

"Johnny came to me a few years ago. He was already a popular author by then and explained that he was a patient of Judy's. Did I think he was responsible for the rash of memory loss in the facility? No. I didn't. Did I think he had some ability? Sure, and I thought it was the reason he became an author. I was happy that one of the affected used their ability for something good…"

"He stole Judy's books," Maddie said.

"I didn't know that…AAU fell into my lap after Brice got sick. When Johnny offered to take the facility off my hands, I was more than happy to rid myself of the whole damn thing," Otis said.

"What you mean is wash your hands clean of any responsibility," Cal added.

"I cared about Judy. And I cared about every person who came through the facility," Otis corrected.

"Just not anymore, right?" Cal asked. Otis avoided Millie's gaze.

"From what my father told me, you were a person I loved and respected. We did a lot of good together, and our intentions were pure in the beginning," Judy was talking to Otis but facing his wife. "Your deceitfulness has broken my heart and my trust. Look at Millie," she said. Otis hesitated but turned to his wife. "You have kept her in the dark as much as you have me, is there anything important you're leaving out?" He swiveled his attention to Judy.

"You were aware at one time—don't think you know it now, though."

"Know what?" Judy asked.

"How you and Calvin met. He was one of your patients, too." The air went out of the room, and a hush fell over them.

Chapter Thirty-five
—Sickness and little things in between—

Johnny Macklemore was nervous about his last session with Angel. There were things he wanted to say to Judy, and he wasn't sure how he would pull it off. His time with her was like being born again, and although she was close to him in age, she gave off an air of intelligence that was enthralling.

Judy always met when him right after he left the amusement park. The place was one of his favorites, but he wondered why she never came earlier so she could enjoy the day with him. Johnny spent the first few minutes of each session telling her about Whipper Wheel or the Toboggan ride. She always smiled and said how glad she was to know he had fun, but she had things to do. *Next time*. He didn't hold it against her for not coming, and he blamed his shyness for not interacting with her enough. It took three sessions before he built up enough courage to say more than a few words to her, unprompted.

Her work with him was nearing completion, Judy explained, and that inspired him into talking to her. He couldn't figure out how he could improve if he never talked. But she assured him he was almost perfect. The compliment was confusing, but it also made him feel so special. *Almost perfect.* He allowed the phrase to tumble through his head all that week until the words became something even more than their intention.

Life before Judy had little meaning for Johnny. The early sessions that Judy spent with him were a blur of sounds and images that he couldn't remember. The harder Johnny tried to draw out their first times together, the more they floated away. It was so aggravating that most attempts to focus his mind on those initial sessions ended with him crying into his pillow. He didn't understand why his last few sessions were so clear and vivid, and the first one was so fuzzy.

According to his parents, going back to school was in his future. They never said why he wasn't in school, and that bothered him. He heard they used lockers in middle school with combination locks and all. And when each bell rings, he had to use the combination in time to get his books out of the locker before the next class started. The whole thing overwhelmed him, like a spy having to crack a code before the place exploded. Then they told him he would start the fifth grade again. The news angered and disappointed him in equal amounts.

His days at home were a jarring kind of reality. His father's focus was on his sister most of the time, and although his mother spent a lot of her time with him, she treated him like an invalid, always hovering—adjusting—and her baby talk was infuriating. He struggled to understand why a mother still talked to her son like a two-year-old when he's going into middle school.

It was unfair that his sessions with Judy were ending, as he was discovering himself through her. He needed more time with her, but he didn't have a clue how to make that happen. What bothered him the most, when he allowed himself to think about it, was Judy didn't feel the same urgency about not seeing him anymore.

As *almost perfect* continued to flash in his head, something crystallized. It wasn't his thought or even his memory. He plucked the thought from Judy's mind like an apple from a low-hanging branch. The idea bounced around in him, and he was unaware of how it got there. The thought belonged to Judy, and it was so personal that it even had a scent to it—no...a feeling was a better description. It was all Judy, and when he accessed it—he sensed a warm glow.

Were there others? He closed his eyes and concentrated on the inside of his head. Startled by his discovery, Johnny soon sensed a muscle, not unlike fingers, which existed in his mind. He flexed the muscle—other thoughts came to him in a whirl of images that overlapped. When he focused harder on a certain thought, it appeared by itself and clear, replaying like a recording. That was for sure the happiest single moment of his life. It was the divide between a child, often ignored, and a child with the potential to make his life whatever he wanted.

When he replayed the thoughts, he saw that he had quite a few from Judy. Without even knowing, Johnny had collected many of Judy's reflections over the expanse of their time together. And although the courage to talk to her, the way he hoped to, never happened, he still collected some of her intimate thoughts like rare stamps ready to frame.

How he brought in the thoughts was a mystery, but the one thing he was sure about was he wanted more. Anxiety rose and dipped in his stomach as he readied himself for their final meeting. He had a speech all prepared and was sure he would never have the bravery to say it out loud. The speech didn't matter—what mattered was his feelings behind the words. He tried not to think about how important the last session was to him. If things didn't go right, he would never see Judy again. He hadn't a clue where she lived, the school she attended, nothing. Their relationship teetered on their weekly meetings, and he wanted to stretch those infrequent intervals into something more meaningful.

As usual, after a day of enjoying his favorite amusement rides, Johnny met with Judy. She was sitting on a nearby picnic bench and using a straw to sip fruit punch from a juice box. Every time he approached her— she was holding the same drink. The sight comforted him, and he even went as far as making his mother buy the same punch at the store the week before. Drinking his juice box in between their visits did the trick for the first few days until the fourth day when its impact waned.

"Hey, John," she said. He noticed that her smile was as vibrant, but her words mechanical and as if she were drowsing somewhere far off. The reasons made little sense, but that was fine because they were together. He wanted to tell her he had some of her memories, and they were precious to him, but didn't. A deeper part of him wasn't sure how she would react to knowing that he borrowed them.

He was positive the information wouldn't bother her, but he wanted to wait until their relationship bloomed. They would sit back and joke about how they became inseparable with it all hinged on her private thoughts. When he imagined their future conversations, butterflies tickled his stomach. Because it was their last day together, Johnny absorbed every detail to save for later. Something disturbing struck him about her expression. He peered into her beautiful face and couldn't notice anything out of place. And still, a nagging continued. For sure, it was in her expression, and he couldn't shake the feeling no matter how hard he tried.

Discovering the invisible muscle in his mind changed things, and he wasn't sure how. Their meeting was the same, and yet different. He searched his feelings and came up with nothing that completed the puzzle. Then he spotted a gesture from Judy that made his blood turn cold. It was there the entire time, and he had ignored the aspect. The smallness of the motion was easy to overlook, but once he saw it, he couldn't unsee it. It mocked him.

A fraction of a second, nothing more, Judy's left eye closed as if something got in. A particle of dust—a gnat—he wasn't sure what it was, but the gesture repeated after a few minutes of conversation and then once more in a continual loop. His heart was racing, and he tried to slow it, but his mind was running at the same speed, so it was useless to do anything but give himself over to the panic.

When he stared at her mouth, the words weren't matching the movement of her lips. How often do you notice someone's lips when they talk? The more he stared, the more disturbed he was by how the two didn't sync. He saw the lips, now along with the repeating eye twitch, and he saw his world spinning. Judy noticed.

"John? Are you okay?" Judy asked, and for the first time during the meeting, her expression was natural and present. He shook his head to clear the cobwebs and nodded.

"I'm fine. Just a little dizzy," Johnny admitted. The tremor of Judy's eye kept re-running in his mind. On the edges of his view, something else begged for his attention.

The invisible muscle came to the front of his mind again, and by thinking about it, he flexed it like a hand—a vine was more precise. He tried pushing the vine out of his body and saw he could do it with little effort. With apprehension, Johnny guided the vine toward Judy. With the vine, he could feel her close, but when the invisible appendage crossed to where Judy was, he sensed nothing. Johnny didn't understand and allowed his body to find Judy. Before he realized he could, the vine tracked her down far from where Judy sat on the bench, sipping on a straw.

Space, as he understood it, made no sense. Armed with a new tool, Johnny told the vine to touch Judy, and it obeyed. With a bridge formed between the two, he was aware of a finer tool that protruded from the vine. These small tools were full of sensitivity, and he guessed they were both reaching out and sending information back like a pulsating heart. When he told these tiny branches to move, they did—inside Judy. When he entered her, it was like a jolt that both hurt and soothed.

He was frightened and exhilarated by being inside Judy, and her not suspecting that he was in her made it even more exciting. The secret was intoxicating in its raw disobedience. It was a voyeuristic pleasure that he never conceived as a possibility. The vine spun in circles, trying to make sense of the alien territory that he could now access. The challenge was splitting his thoughts. Could he be both in her body and talking to her at the same time? If she noticed he couldn't keep up with the conversation or his expressions went dull or who knows what, she would discover he was trespassing inside her brain.

"I asked you a question," Judy said. Johnny's vine froze.

"I'm sorry. What did you say?"

"Did you like the amusement park?" He considered the question, and he tried to recall the rides he rode that day with the experience eluding his grasp. He sat there in bewildered silence. *She's going to catch you inside her. Say something—say anything.*

"The best time ever," Johnny said. Her smile came back, and he noticed her twitch returned. Johnny ignored both as he escaped back into her mind. Coming away with memories of her the last couple sessions was a surprise, and he wanted to figure out how he accomplished something so mind-blowing. He dialed up his concentration, and his branches were right where he left them. What memories did he want to take? The choices appeared endless as he pressed his branches against a part of her brain. The area produced conscious thought, and it was ongoing like a radio program. Johnny listened for a moment: *I need to get to The Book Loft—they have something I ordered. Maddie might spend the night—if she gets permission.* He listened with his new superpower, as giddy as a child on Christmas morning. The thoughts were incomplete, coming out as shortcut fragments, but it was thrilling to gain entry. *This kid is making this job harder—he lacks imagination. Don't worry, Judy—last time with him—then you're done.* Johnny's jaw dropped open.

Johnny withdrew his branches and vine in that order. He experienced the shame of being in her without her permission. Then, the embarrassment of hearing her words about him. *She thinks you're just another kid. Nothing special or perfect.* If she was talking, he stopped listening. The thinking was another thing he wanted to stop, but he couldn't. Judy was happy their time together was ending. The feeling made him want to strike out—to show her he wasn't just another kid.

Resentment turned into anger, boiling in him so fast that he never saw it coming. His mental muscle was stronger and more potent than before. He pushed his vine onto Judy, and it clamped tight onto her. The branches never hesitated as they scoured her brain. He wasn't sure about the region, but he found some memories he believed were fresh, the night before he was sure. In the memories, Judy had been up late writing a section of her novel. *She's a writer.*

The exact way to remove her memories wasn't apparent, but the anger helped fuel the trial-and-error process. The branches were the key, but they didn't have the strength he needed to make it happen. He imagined a powerful person. He-Man, Master of the Universe, jumped to the front, and he pictured the strong man lifting memories. To his surprise, they rocked and then budged. They were sliding into his vine on the way to him. Despite the anger that still simmered, he smiled because he didn't need her permission.

When they entered him, it was like fresh air brushing against his skin. They were like a recording but filled with emotions. Taking memories was like taking a piece of that person in the most realistic way possible. He got the essence of Judy. Anything she was feeling, thinking, hungry for, sad about—was there. It was all there in that slice of memory. Although the memory was her reciting the words from her book, there was so much more hiding within—he loved it. Johnny had a part of her to keep forever. She was talking, and this time, he tuned in.

"It's time you and I say goodbye, John," Judy said. When Johnny scrutinized her face, the eye twitch went away, and her mouth synced with the words again. One second, she sat on the bench with the juice box in her hand. Then Judy's image faded. He couldn't understand what he was seeing. Was she disappearing, or was he? He tried wrapping his mind around the glitches in his vision when the entire world went black.

When he opened his eyes, a nurse was shaking his body. Tilting his head, he saw straps around his frame as he lay on a hospital gurney. Johnny couldn't remember how he got there, but he believed the amusement park didn't exist—never had. Judy was there, staring at him from another chair. He noticed her expression was warm but distant, like she had other thoughts on her mind. *A slumber party*.

"Have we been here the whole time?" he asked. The nurse was loosening his straps.

"I thought it would be easier to visit you at your favorite place."

"How...how do you know it's my favorite?" Judy smiled.

"I've been asleep? Every time?" Johnny asked.

"You sure have," Judy answered. Desperate to understand what was real and not, Johnny searched within and found the memories he took from her. He let go of a deep breath. He had to be asleep to steal memories—they both did.

"Can I ask you a question," Johnny asked. He could tell she had already checked out but pretended interest.

"Sure."

"What did you do last night?" She smiled. He could see her wheels turning from the question. Judy's face went blank, and it was his turn to smile.

"Not sure. I must have fallen asleep early," Judy gazed into the distance and found nothing there. Her memories weren't a copy, they were the originals. The realization that he saw things about her that she didn't was like icy rain on a hot, summer day—thrilling. He wasn't powerless anymore, and although using his ability meant being asleep, he saw a future all laid out before him.

Chapter Thirty-six
—At the expense of a human life—

To see Maddie at her doorstep was hard for Judy to swallow. A debate raged within until she relented and opened the door. Maddie read the ambiguity in her face.

"Thanks for letting me in," Maddie said. Judy avoided her gaze, holding the door wide.

"Sure," Judy said and then shook her head. "Honesty is all I have left. I forgave you before you showed up at the hospital. Pretending it's all in the past isn't as easy for me," Judy admitted.

"I get it. My sorry isn't enough," Maddie said. Judy walked into the living room and plopped down on the couch as Maddie followed.

"Did I remember wrong? I don't remember you telling me you were sorry," Judy said.

"I am sorry...sorrier than anything in my life. The reason I kept the truth from you was my shame. Plain and simple." Judy wasn't sure how to accept her contrition. They sat in quiet for a long time, hoping the bitterness would evaporate in the silence.

"Have you talked to Cal?" discomfort transformed Judy's face.

"He's called. A lot actually, but..."

"Why won't you accept his calls?"

"Logically...I know Cal's nothing like Johnny. Just knowing they were both my creations..." Judy shook her head. "This power—whatever it is or wherever it came from, it changes people. What if it changed Cal?"

"You'll get no argument from me. What I will say is, Cal was born honest. Cal has loved you since he met you," Maddie said.

"That's what frightens me. Is it me Cal loves, or is he drawn to me because I saved him? Does he think he owes me a debt? It's hard for me to trust at the moment," Judy stared at Maddie and laughed.

"Yeah," Maddie agreed.

"Where's your mom?" Maddie asked.

"She's sleeping at the hospital with my dad," Judy said. Maddie moved next to Judy and sat as close to her as she could. "I just wish I could help him," Judy said.

"I've given you every reason to hate me. And...that's why I'm here." Judy wanted to edge away from her friend but held her ground.

"What do you mean?"

"Your father made the sacrifice of bringing you back. Whether he understood the danger to him, he chose you over himself. He's not able to be there for you this time. But...I can." Maddie studied her hands.

"How can you help?"

"I want you to use me. Do whatever you have to—unlock your memories and fight Johnny." Judy laughed without humor.

"You speak to me as if you know what you're asking," Judy said, not meaning it as a slight, and it still came out that way.

"I played my part in stealing ten years of your life. I allowed you to live with your abductor—pretending I wasn't the cause—drank to forget it, but there was no forgetting my sins. Your return was my second chance. I saw the concept of redemption as a fairy tale that belonged in romance novels until you came back to us. If I don't fix what I've done to you, there will be nothing left of me anyway," Maddie said with tears. Overcome by her sincerity, Judy hugged her friend.

"Maddie, what my father did for me when I was young took months. I'm afraid we don't have that kind of time, even if I agreed to let you help. I don't know what damage Johnny has done to me. But the state I was in when I arrived tells me he stole everything from me. And what's left in there will take a lifetime to fix—if ever," Judy said. Maddie considered this and lit up.

"What if," Maddie paced the floor in front of Judy, "instead of reclaiming memories of times in your past, only focus on your abilities?" Judy stood next to her friend, lost in inspiration.

"That's brilliant," Judy said, and began pacing.

"We'll streamline the entire process. We rebuild anything to do with how to use your powers, and we can worry about the rest later. You'll be able to stand up to Johnny. And who knows—maybe take your memories back, when you're able, when you're stronger," Maddie said. Judy couldn't stop smiling.

"That's a perfect plan," Judy said, and Maddie saw a smile fade.

"What?"

"That still leaves the matter of you. To rebuild me in such a short span would cause chaos inside you. Not to mention damage things I won't be able to fix," Judy said.

"Shut up," Maddie screamed. Judy froze. "You are doing this for me, and all I want in return is one thing."

"Tell me."

"For *you* to keep me as a friend and truly forgive me. I don't even mean right now—just someday," Maddie pleaded. It wasn't easy, but Judy nodded.

"Good. Let's get busy," Maddie said.

*　　*　　*　　*

More than once, the novel *Frankenstein* came to Judy's mind when Maddie stretched out on her childhood bed. She tried to push the similarities aside, and they kept returning. It didn't matter the reasons for tampering with the natural world. Once you did that, all bets were off. She imagined young Judy Angel believed she could change the world with no repercussions. The consequences of her naivete were the loss of her identity, not to mention hundreds of potential Johnny Macklemore clones walking the Earth.

Judy skidded a chair across the room until it ended up next to her bed. It was identical to the scene in the video her father shown of her working in the facility. When she sat in the chair, the nagging feeling that she was missing something came back, and it frustrated her. *That's why you're doing this*. Yet, there was something she couldn't put her finger on—something simple—something she should know. Judy shook her head and began her process.

233

Both women were afraid of where the night would lead, and neither wanted to worry the other. The chain of events were in motion when Maddie welcomed Johnny into their lives, and everyone knew that the lone way a vampire can come in is if you invite them. Judy wanted to believe that she was a part of the scientific community like Otis Bain, and it was a way of coming to terms with the unnatural things she could do for the injured children.

The more she explored her past and discovered the truth, the less she could call what she did science. Ritual was the word that kept landing in her mind, and it was the word that made the most rational sense. When she discovered she had altered her patients through the years, it shattered her self-delusions and assigned her skills into a category that belonged to—the supernatural.

Armed with a better perspective of her powers, Judy attempted to guide her thinking into the supernatural realm. Johnny stole so many aspects of what made her the person she was. But when she searched deep inside, the one component left untouched by her husband was her reading. All the books she read, even from an early age, were there. If she had to wager—Johnny at least understood that without her experience of reading, she couldn't create books, and he wanted those from her.

That's how I'm a functioning person without my memories, she realized. She drew from thousands of books—devoured them to make a working human being. That's what books have always done throughout history. They create a solid structure of the self from the stories of others. *That is my real gift*. The novels of the supernatural resurfaced for inspiration. The first novel that came to mind was Stephen King's *Salem's Lot*.

In the novel, the lead character Ben Mears returns to his hometown to discover that town was becoming infected by vampires. Although it wasn't altogether the same, she shared a connection with the novel and its characters. Her life skidded into the territory of the irrational. Getting out of the bog meant nurturing the creative side—tapping into the stories that kept her alive.

The rules were different in a supernatural story, and expectations were never the same as reality's harsh light. If Judy's and Johnny's powers twisted the natural world and their laws within, then she had to consider things from that point of view. Would using Maddie's brain to rebuild her brain unlock something in her?

Had Johnny done the same with the people he invaded over the years, spawning creatures like him lying dormant, or infecting others without even knowing it? When she studied her situation from a writer's perspective, the possibilities were horrifying and insurmountable. But the new view also empowered her, and she was sure it was closer to the way Johnny thought. To Judy, her skills were never more than a tool—a hammer that had its limits, but when she broadened her stance, they became versatile.

One skill had the potential of hundreds. Judy's imagination limited the applications of entering a mind and making changes for good or bad. Her car crash and the injury it caused her became the small core of what she was capable of and her limitations. Johnny wasn't playing by those narrow rules, so why should *she*?

After a long while, she heard Maddie's breathing change, transitioning from erratic to deep and uniformed. Her slumber came much later with the prospects dancing around in her, prolonging her wakefulness. It was exhaustion that made her sleep—worn out from the act of trying too hard. Judy plunged into a sleep so restful that she was about to forget the seam she needed to navigate. Her tendrils were there, and she didn't have to think about them or conceive of their existence to make them appear. But what she had to do was imagine using them to make them mobile.

By the time she attached her tendril onto Maddie, Judy was aware of her surroundings. She let the drowse fall off her like a blanket. What she perceived in Maddie was a submissive quality that was so enticing that she understood Johnny's temptation. Her friend was vulnerable, helpless to whatever impulse Judy chose. There was no wonder why Johnny made himself into God as he manipulated those around him. The potential for abuse while inside her host was immeasurable.

She contemplated the things that Maddie had done to her and how she was the sole reason for her wasted life. Her tendril flexed as the anger stirred, causing the unseen appendage to lock down harder. She wasn't sure how to produce damage on purpose, but she understood she had the talent in her arsenal if she so chose. A fire started in her belly—small to begin with and growing each second that she kept her mind on Maddie's betrayal.

If her tendril turned into a wrecking ball, smashing everything in its path, Maddie wouldn't be the wiser. Judy bounced between the lingering notion she remained the young healer and the new idea that she was a supernatural force to reckon with when crossed. Coiling around Maddie's brain, Judy thought of the fragile shell of an egg. An impulse to squeeze hot-wired her faculties. Her unconscious desires tried to hijack her body, and before they could take over, she stopped the trance that tried to win out.

With a renewed focus, Judy went to work restoring the severed parts of her mind. She found they were in the deepest regions of her brain. Logic told her that Johnny cut away her ability, and her defense against him, first. Massaging them back to life was no small feat. Some were missing altogether while others—sliced to the core and needed coaxing into an alternative path, with the help of Maddie's healthy memories. The essence of what made up neurons was the donated material used to reroute her memories. Judy thought of the process as reattaching blood vessels to get the blood flowing, and the image was right, at least in some base chemical way that was unexplainable to her.

The problem, for Maddie anyway, was that using her neurons meant she was losing memories of her own. Healing a person was one thing, but recovering severed memories required the electrical impulses that actual memories contained. It was a metaphysical change that Judy was setting into motion on the smallest level, not unlike the gaining or losing of an atom. What she was taking from Maddie wasn't anything physical or quantifiable to doctors. But even in its minuteness, she was harvesting the true building blocks of what made thought possible or a human life worth living.

The downside to collecting memories from another person was not knowing for sure which memories were on the sacrificial block. She needed so many to make any repairs worth her time that she couldn't access each of

Maddie's memories to decide which to touch and which to leave be. The most efficient way was random, and with that choice, she suspected that part of Maddie would never come back. Her conscience blared its warning equally with a reassurance that karma had the final say in what happens to us all.

Throughout the night, Judy projected serene images into Maddie's mind. She saw her human frailties, but beyond those weaknesses, she related to a friend that just wanted to be happy and wanted to know genuine love. Maddie gave up the privilege of someone loving her for so long that it was a craving she bumped up against while she was working within her interior.

The longer she was among Maddie's secret thoughts, the more she understood she was never a monster. No matter how much she dressed up free will, it was the illusion that people offer themselves to get through each day. The lesson she learned for the second time in her life was that she and everyone walking the planet were slaves to their desires. Some can rise above them on occasions, but none can rise above them all the time.

Time lost its meaning as she worked on through the night. The balancing act of keeping the tendril attached, projecting peaceful images to her friend, and the mental dexterity of rebuilding her mind was wearing her down. She was ready to check in to find out if her work had paid off, except exhaustion masked all her progress. There wasn't more she could do that night, and if she went on as tired as she was, she would do more harm than good to Maddie.

Releasing her bridge from her sleeping friend, Judy pulled back all her mental tethers. Maddie was asleep in her bed. Judy knew her friend gave the ultimate sacrifice and could never calculate her loss. Judy leaned in and kissed her friend on the cheek. Every bit of anger or resentment for Maddie faded.

Chapter Thirty-seven
—You rarely win, but sometimes you do—

Calvin Reed peered down at his hands, except...they weren't the hands he recognized. His fingers wiggled on his lap. Although he watched the motion, he suspected he wasn't moving them. He attempted to close his eyes, and that didn't happen either. The blinking wasn't in sync with his eyelids—he was sure he was breathing. He noted his heart rate went up because of the beating in his ears. *Thank God for that.*

Cal's body lay on a hospital gurney with leather straps fastened across his torso. He noticed his clothes and was making sense of at least *when* he was. These were his teenage clothes. *I'm in a dream.* His pulse slowed, but the surroundings had none of the foggy disconnect that his dreams often possessed. It was clear he was along for the ride which was the best sign that he wasn't awake except...

Why was he locked onto a gurney? The surrounding room was familiar, and when he saw the door with a glass viewing square, it came back to him in a flash. It was one of the examination rooms from the building they broke into in German Village. The same one that Judy worked in as a child. But why was he here? The mind was combining things into a stained-glass nightmare, and he wasn't there at all. He was safe in his bed, and he awakened inside a dream. When the fear subsided, his view changed with the swivel of his head.

Horror captured him as he understood the body—he occupied— was his, but younger. He questioned if this was the right reality. Was he older? He recalled the day before, remembering meeting Otis with Judy and Maddie. Those memories were there if he could trust them. Gazing through his own eyes disturbed him so much that he tried to wake himself more than once. Jerking his body was the logical answer, and he put all his effort into moving—twitching, anything to cause a movement. He had no control of the shell he was in—at the mercy of whatever he was seeing.

The head atop of his body turned, and he lost his breath, not trusting his vision. He was face to face with Judy. Not Judy Macklemore—Judy Angel. By his estimate, she was still a sophomore in high school. *You are so beautiful.*

"I don't want you to worry. I won't hurtcha. We fastened you so you can't fall off the bed," Judy said.

"Thank you," he heard himself say with slurred speech.

"My name is Judy."

"Cccccal," he said with some effort.

"Love that name," Judy said. Cal didn't understand what was happening to him until he remembered what Otis Bain told him. He went on believing that they met in school—when in reality—the facility was where they met. Damaged was the best way to describe the person he overheard speaking. That didn't explain why he couldn't recall knowing Judy until outside of the clinic. These were all fresh memories that he pushed down and tried to avoid. It was Otis's reminder enabling them to bubble to the surface like a magical incantation, setting them free. Judy had described her visions, and as much as he wanted to, he couldn't deny he was amid his own.

"For our younger patients, I create a waiting room, so it isn't as scary. I think for you, this room will do fine. Whatya think?" she asked with a smile a mile wide. Cal smiled back, and it made her repeat her gesture, then brush her hair behind her ears.

"Lay back, relax, and close your eyes," Judy guided. "Go ahead, open them back up." Cal noticed that the room they were in was still the same except each wall, which had worn a dull shade of gray, was now the brightest yellow.

"Isn't that better?" Judy asked. The straps that held him dissolved as if the gurney never had them. "Go for it. Move around," she coaxed. He nodded and slid off the bed and was in wonder of how his body moved.

"How is this possible? Is this really me?" Cal asked.

"Not yet, but when our work is complete, it will be." He sat back down on the bed, and she found a seat next to him. She stared into his emerald-green eyes. She seemed reluctant to turn away, but when she did, she returned with something in her hand.

"What is it?" he asked.

"It's a mockingbird." Judy placed the plush animal on the bed between them. "This was the first gift my father ever gave me. It reminds me that there are good things and people in the world," she said. Judy leaned over the mockingbird and kissed Cal on the lips. They were soft, and he pressed back into hers. When he pulled back, she was smiling.

"Why did you do that? We just met." Her smile remained.

"Because you wanted me too…and I couldn't resist," Judy said.

"I imagined how it would be to kiss you," he said with surprise, "but how did you know?" She leaned in for another kiss, and this time, she parted her lips and felt his lips part. When their embrace ended, he was smiling.

"You asked me again," she said.

"I did. Do you kiss all your patients like this?" Judy laughed.

"You're the first."

"When you brought the mockingbird out, it stirred something in me," he said.

"I know. It was supposed to," Judy said.

"I saw the mockingbird in your mind."

"What else did you see?" He touched her hand with his own, and she let him.

"It's not really what I see…more what I feel there. You are the kindest person I've ever glimpsed. When I have the chance to dive into what's inside someone, they are not like you. Please, most people are good or want to be, but I discover their dark secrets—wicked desires—even when they're young. But you're different, Cal. You have a light that calls to me," she said, and he could tell it was hard for her to say the words aloud.

"I was hurt. Wasn't I?" Cal asked, unsure of himself.

"You were brought here with an athletic injury. You harmed your head, Cal." Sadness struck him, and he turned away.

"I suspected something like that." Cal listened to his younger version and wanted to cry for the sadness that surrounded him as he watched the exchange. The moment was the most precious part of his entire life, and he had no recollection of it at all.

"If you trust me, I can mend you," she said.

"I do. But how?" Judy kissed him, and when she did, she began her work.

Chapter Thirty-eight
—Ugly things in this world—

A banging was so loud on the door that Johnny lurched from his bed and fell to the carpeted floor below. He was deep in a vision—shocked that he stirred from it all. He could count on one hand how many times a noise, of any kind, had the strength to break him from a memory's recurrence. It didn't amount to much but smashing the hold of a vision for any reason was rare and refreshing.

Groggy and with the night's replaying of images reverberating in his head, he unlocked the hotel room door and swung it open. He wasn't sure if he had on clothes, but in his woozy state of mind, it meant little to him—some man in a suit. A manager of some level he wagered, stood in front of him with a scowl.

"What do you want?" he snapped. The attitude didn't deter the manager from his intended course. He placed his hands behind his back, but his glare remained fixed. A couple walked past the room and noticed the two, and Johnny thought the woman recognized him. It was always the woman that recognized the authors.

"Sir..." the manager was rethinking the words he rehearsed on the elevator up, "We at the Renaissance hotel are overjoyed with your choice to stay with us while you are visiting Columbus. We, however, cannot abide by your constant screaming, sir," the manager said. Johnny wiped the sleep from the corner of his eyes, then regarded the man in his doorway with disgust.

"I hardly think I was screaming," Johnny said. The manager turned red, hearing his patron's nonchalant attitude.

"Mr. Macklemore. Even as I arrived at your door, you were in the midst of what I could only describe as a primal scream," the manager corrected.

"Maybe it was one of the other guests."

"Absolutely, Mr. Macklemore. Unfortunately, this is the second night in a row that this has occurred, and I'm sure it won't happen again, by whichever guest is responsible." The manager revealed a knowing smile. The urge to punch the lingering hotel supervisor crossed Johnny's mind.

"Thank you for keeping me up to date with any noises that are happening within the hotel. I hope you have a good night," Johnny said and slammed the door shut before he received any reciprocation. Judy was the one person to fill him in on his night terrors, and it would seem his sleep condition was devolving. He needed privacy and wanted to be away from people like the manager and his condescending attitude.

If he had any hope of going back to his normal life, he had to get Judy back on the rails and back on a plane. He hated to admit that she was the part that made his life comfortable, but it was the truth. Johnny conceded that it would take monumental work to get her back to the Judy he wanted, but he saw no way around the task.

Ridding her of her ridiculous glasses and the dark hair was where he planned to start. Seeing her resemble her old self was unsettling. *Why would she go back to that look? Because she's off the rails*, he told himself. Her disobedience didn't throw him, and in some ways, he considered her a dog that needed to run. Sometimes, a house pet would get past the gate and out of the yard. As a good husband, it was his job to retrieve her so she can't hurt herself or others. So far, she was keeping him from doing his job, and in the aftermath, Judy hurt her mother, father and girlfriend.

He showed her his sweet side, and Judy refused to listen to reason. The last straw was his phone calls that went unanswered.

He was proud of the effective way he removed her ties to the city, and changed how she saw people—but, the moment he accomplished that mission, he found out she took up with Calvin Reed again. *That's her choice—not mine*.

Although he still fumed from the manager's interruption, he was thankful to move again and out from under the visions, at least for the night. His attention turned to the one threat left to him, Cal. He saw her allure to him was strong, and he didn't blame her for gravitating toward him. What threw him for a loop was that she hadn't yet figured out that she had no choice.

Splashing water on his face, slipping a fresh shirt on, and slinking down a baseball cap to his brow, Johnny headed out of the hotel room. He hoped to see the manager on his way out, not to talk with him, but to give him another dirty expression. No manager was in sight by the time Johnny exited the Renaissance. The frigid air against his face was the best feeling he had all day.

Cal's schedule was simple to figure out after a few days. The man was a creature of habit without imagination, and his dull routine proved it. The *less is more* rule had kept him out of trouble and out of jail since he was a kid. Except for a few slips-ups here and there, he stuck to the tried-and-true strategy. Tonight, things changed, and although he was going against the grain with dealing with the officer, the portion of Johnny that craved the chaos, and savored the actions against Becky, enjoyed the rush.

For longer than he remembered, he battled the memory overload. He needed it gone, there were no two ways about it, but to get shit done, he was enjoying the bleeding of thoughts. Sure, there was confusion to which voice to listen to, but there was also a lack of inhibition that made each decision like rolling a die to see how it would come out. He wouldn't deny there were risks involved in allowing the thoughts in without a filter, and when he weighed those risks next to staying sane, he'd take the random thought any day.

His current problem wasn't how far he should go to get Judy back—it was how he would get away with his plans. Staying connected to Bud's mind had been more challenging than he expected. The range he needed to work within and still stay safe was shrinking with every use. A block was the closest he ever wanted to get to his hosts, and that wouldn't cut it anymore. If he weren't careful and strayed from his course, instead of Cal in a body bag, he'd end up in one.

A little voice warned to be afraid of Cal. And getting close to him was the last thing he wanted to do during a showdown. *Get in—pull his plugs. Then get out.* Cal was the last domino that needed to fall, and there was no room to get cute. With Cal out of the picture, Judy would drop right in line. At least that's what he told himself.

Finding the perfect place to enter Cal's head proved more difficult than ever imagined before the evening began. He knew that parking his car in front of a cop's house and falling asleep had the potential to draw some interest, and if the attention he was drawing was Cal's, the game was over. The problem was, the *already* meager distance of one block dwindled further to a couple hundred feet.

Working so close to his victim frightened him. Because he didn't have the time to case the comings and goings of Cal's neighbors, Johnny couldn't use the homes on either side to conceal him while he worked. His options left him pissed. *I've worked too hard in my life and accomplished too much to be in this position.* His train of thought was battling him, and he went with it. He allowed the reckless thoughts, often the most persistent, to hijack the bus—for the time being.

As he circled Cal's neighborhood for the perfect place to park and begin his work, he wished for one of his cars at home. He spent a good amount of money, fitting them with the darkest, tinted windows possible. He told Judy it was for privacy from his adoring fans, and she gave him a sideways glance but went along with it. Why he wanted a blanket and pillow to remain in the back seats of each was a little more difficult to convince, so he had to alter her mind to get that to fly.

The streets were quiet enough, but streetlights lined both sides of the road right up to the curb. Johnny made sure not to park right under a lamppost, but the city did such a respectable job of illumination that wherever his car sat was like daytime.

Judy's relentlessness was one reason that drew him to her. It was her high spirits that beckoned him like a moth to the flame. But after years of trying to control or tame her willfulness, he found himself worn from the task. It was one thing to deal with her stubborn nature from person to person and another thing altogether to bring into him her memories and battle them daily.

The secret, he alone shared, was that the memories he took from others were not just snippets of time like storing a digital recording. With every memory came with it much more contextual data that clogged his gears. If he pocketed an hour of conversation—with it came the person's thoughts—their fears, and their insecurities. Often the recording became duplicated if the person was hiding something. In those cases, there was the usual *inner dialogue* with an additional conversation about what they were thinking underneath.

But when he grabbed someone's memories, he had no choice but to dig deeper into the person's subconscious mind and strip away the root of the thought. This process meant collecting more data than he wanted to store, but he also found that when he didn't harvest things at the subconscious level, there was always the chance that a memory grew back from the root. He, therefore, resolved to reap things that were the most vital, or his storage would become too full. Johnny understood this way too late in the game, and his mind was over saturated with memories.

His frustration bubbled the reckless thoughts to the surface again, but this time he recognized the impetuous ones belonging to Judy. Her thoughts were stronger than the rest, but they also held more danger than the others if left unfiltered. He understood that memories were not a simple slide show when absorbed into another person. But Judy's memories had a purpose beyond roaming around in him, and although he was a slave to their presence, he understood they were combative in the same way a white blood cell sought an enemy.

Was Judy, on some level, adding sentient defenses along with the remembrances he collected? The notion was ridiculous, but it was something that Judy would do if she had the ability. Johnny couldn't think straight, and it heightened the result of paranoia, or at least that was what he told himself. If he wasn't suffering from paranoia, then his collection became infected. His heart raced at the possibilities—even more reason to take care of Cal fast and get Judy back home and sort everything out.

Johnny hopped over the front seat, landing without grace onto the edge of the cushioned back seat, hitting his spine on the hump dividing the floorboard, and came close to cracking his skull. He imagined the newspaper headline if he broke his neck. *Famed Author Dies Climbing into His Backseat.*

He slid back to the center of the seat and pulled his coat over his body. The night air was dropping close to freezing and leaving the car running would draw some suspicion if someone happened next to him. *Another thing to worry about.* Johnny grew tired of the whole situation. Johnny stilled his body, loosened the muscles, and opened his mouth to a slack position. The tried-and-true routine sent his mind into the foggy zone at once.

The vine went out into the night searching as always, and he detected they were within the range of Cal. The vine swayed like an arm weaving toward Cal's home. On its way, he sensed objects in his path— cars, trees, trash cans. He pushed through them in his current plane of existence but recognized their reality all the same. In a few mental twists and turns the vine approached the door he sought.

As he entered Cal's home, he remembered his first encounter with him when he was a much younger man. *Things aren't the same, Johnny. You know a hell of a lot more than you did back then.* A fear from the past burrowed into his courage and threatened to chuck it out of the car. His vine trembled in place, neither moving forward nor back—stuck. His nerves were beyond frantic, and if he didn't get them under control fast, the adrenaline rushing into his system would wake his body, and the opportunity would pass him by like leaves in the wind. *Relax, Johnny.*

He pictured a gentle ocean—waves ebbing—a flag blowing in the breeze. He imagined anything to calm his nerves and soothe the fear that wanted to upend the work he needed to do that night. *Cal is just a man.* His reassurance settled him—if he didn't think about his first encounter with Cal, he would be fine. The vine was under his control once more, and he pushed it back and forth like a billiard stick, assessing its glide.

Johnny's heart rate fell, and his vine was as good as new. He was seconds away from waking up and even saw the veil of slumber dissolving before he gained self-control. With renewed confidence, he darted into the home toward its destination. Without warning, he was aware of the reach, a few hundred feet, was becoming a stretch for his vine. *What the hell is going on?* The miserable range of a few hundred feet shrunk, and his vine was a dog snapping to a stop when its chain ran out of length.

His condition had declined more than he ever guessed. Fury took over his function. *Damn.* He retracted his vine and woke up and caught himself before snapping back into reality. Waking too quick was like leaning back on a chair and jarring yourself. Johnny could wake easier, but it would be impossible to sleep again soon after. He softened his thinking and brought his mind out of the slumber one slow step at a time until he was fully awake.

Johnny shook his head as he sat in the backseat of the rental car. He grabbed his coat, slammed his way out of the vehicle, swung the door shut, and was already dashing toward Cal's home before the car door latched close. On the way, he clenched his teeth and beat the air in front of his path. The length of his range left him feeling ineffectual. While watching Cal come and go, he spotted small hedges decorating the exterior. He climbed behind the hedges and arranged his body snug between the brick of the home and the shrubs.

He lay there, fuming at his predicament. The bushes gave him perfect cover, but the degree to which his ability had plummeted in the last few days appalled him to his core. His time of doing things the nice and gentle way was over. Many images cascaded through his mind. He thought about how to deal with Judy and force her to remove the excess memories from his mind. Johnny rested against the cold ground with a coat draped over him and struggled to find his happy place and allow sleep to come back.

He was back faster than he ever imagined and thrilled that something was going his way. The longer he spent in Ohio—the worse his condition would sink, and the harder it was to get Judy back on the rails. Cal emanated energy, and the vine was strong from such a close distance. He locked onto Cal's location and was heading through his house at breakneck speed. Johnny grasped it was because Cal was so close, but he enjoyed feeling his strength at its highest again.

Within his internal vision, Johnny saw everything in Cal's bedroom. Clothes were stacked in a pile—dresser—television on the wall, and even a cup on his nightstand. The vine searched out Cal like a hungry mouth, and when it sensed the energy of him, it raced to connect with him. When the vine was inches from Cal's skull, a bell rang.

The sound stopped Johnny in his tracks. He sat listening in place until it rang once more in the house. The sound was a doorbell that broke Cal from his sleep and sent him heading toward the door. Johnny screamed in his head when he realized it was his wife who was at the door. *Do you want to see my power?* He bit down on his tongue to stop the scream from leaving his mouth and spilling out into the neighborhood.

Chapter Thirty-nine
—Beginning to understand something—

When Judy rang the doorbell, time slowed to a crawl. Several minutes had passed before she was sure she wanted to push the thing again. She didn't hear Cal stir and gave the doorbell one last chance. *If he isn't here, it's not meant to be.* Judy thought the words but never believed the sentiment—not really. A finger hovered over the button a second before pressing. It was late, but that wasn't her worry. As she was leaning one foot off the porch, she heard rustling in the living room beyond the door. When the door opened, Cal gawked as if he were sleepwalking.

"Is everything okay?" he asked, attempting to focus on Judy. "It's cold—come in." He slid the door open further, then stood behind it before she agreed to enter. Judy smiled at Cal but avoided eye contact until she sat on his couch. Cal picked a spot in a chair across the room until Judy patted the cushion of the sofa. He saw the gesture and sat next to her.

"I'm sorry I haven't returned your calls," she said. Cal was about to speak but leaned back into the couch. "You have been nothing except perfect to me. After Johnny, I don't know how to trust. It scared me to find out you have the same ability as he does," she said.

"You mean the same ability as you, Judy," he corrected.

"Yeah. That's what scared me. This curse I've passed on is a hard urge to resist."

"It's not a curse." Judy was already shaking her head.

"When I see what Johnny has done with it, I feel like a monster," Judy said. Cal cleared the distance between them and grabbed her hand.

"You heard the way Otis talked about the ones I infected—all over the country—because of me," she said.

"Then let's do the opposite of Otis. Let's find these kids and show them what they have and how to control their powers—use them for good," Cal said. Judy turned to Cal as if she never saw him before that night.

"Yes. That is what we should do. I'm sure there was some little girl who grew up not understanding what was happening to them. I want to make things right." Judy stared into the room, drowning in a new chance.

"I'll help you," Cal said. Her thoughts dissolved, and she turned to him.

"You're an officer—you have a career." He smiled and gripped her tighter.

"One way or another—my place is by your side. Johnny kept you hidden a thousand miles away for years—and you found your way back to me. You didn't remember my name—my face or even our past, but your heart distinguished the difference. With all his powers, he couldn't keep us apart. He's not that strong." Judy scrunched up her face.

"He was strong enough to keep me in the dark for a long time. Look around at what he's done to the people I love because I wouldn't go back to him."

"Becky told me he isn't so strong anymore," Cal said, brushing hair from her face. "He's a candle burning down. He won't be in our lives forever."

"I want to believe that—him leaving me—never returning into my life. That's not the way he operates. He will never let me go."

"If he doesn't leave, we'll make him," Cal said. Something changed in her expression.

"What are you saying?" Judy released his hand.

"Maybe it's time we contemplate other options for Johnny," Cal said, avoiding her gaze.

"Options?"

"I know how it sounds—like a jealous lover. He hasn't killed the surrounding people—yet. What if he has killed people close to you over the years—keeping you under his control? Look at your father. We may never bring him back. Can we let him stay alive out there?"

"I guess the idea was there all along," she said. "I don't have many memories of my own. If one of the few remaining is killing Johnny—it will change me—who I am."

"It may come down to you or him," Cal added. Judy sat in a fog of choices without a direction.

"Johnny is too famous. Even the smallest detail about his death—investigators would leave no stone left unturned to find the truth," she said.

"My experience tells me there is always a way," Cal said.

"Would it be better for me? Yes. Do you think I want you to do that? No. I love you just the way you are," Judy said, overcome with a flush using the words for the first time.

"It's been a long time since you said that to me," Cal said, and she saw him lost in the thought.

"If we kill Johnny, there's a chance we'll get caught and an even bigger possibility that it will split us apart. I spent the night with Maddie." The vacant expression she remembered being on Maddie's face when she left filled her with sadness, "and with her help, I can understand my abilities—not all the way, but I think I can use it against him if I have to defend myself," Judy said.

"What does it feel like?" he asked.

"It's funny, it feels like relearning to throw a ball or ride a bike. I feel silly that the knowledge didn't return by itself. It seems so natural—like a part of me I could never lose, even though I had."

"How did Maddie help you?" Tears filled her eyes. "Judy?"

"The shift was subtle—if you didn't know what to spot, you wouldn't realize it even took place. To create something—something else has to be..."

"Is Maddie okay?" Judy shook her head.

"She's less. That's the way I would describe it. It makes me wonder how my father was before he brought me back after my accident. What was he like? I'm sure I took for granted what he gave up for me," she said.

"That's not who you are. And you forced no one to help you—ever. Maddie owed that to you—she owes you far more," Cal said. Judy stared at him, unsure. "Judy? There is something I want to tell you about the locket you once gave me—" A knock on the door startled them, causing fear to rise. Cal moved to the door like he was walking in peanut butter. Judy gripped the arm of the couch as he opened the door wide.

An older couple in their late seventies stood on his porch. Both in well-worn robes with pajama bottoms covering their lower halves. The woman still had curlers in her hair and sported an expression like her house was on fire. The man accompanying her wore the same expression. A tuft of his gray hair fell into his face, and with a stroke of his hand, he arranged the strands back next to the few others he had remaining on his head.

"Are you guys okay?" Cal asked. The couple stood there, not answering. "Please, come in," The couple shuffled inside and was oblivious to Judy's existence in the living room. "These are my neighbors," Cal said to Judy, "Jack and Anne." Judy extended a hand.

"Nice to meet you," Judy said. They never peered her way, and Judy let her hand fall. Anne sat on the edge of a chair with jack standing behind her.

"What can I help you with?" Cal asked. Anne raised her head and gazed at Cal for the first time.

"There was a big bang," Anne said. She peered through them. "It was so loud. Wasn't it, Jack?" Jack swayed with his hands deep in the pockets of his robe, never reacting to his wife.

"We didn't hear any sounds," Judy said. Anne glared over Cal's shoulder.

"When we heard it, we had to come to you right away," Anne said. Judy exchanged glances with Cal. He shrugged.

"Anne, we're fine," Cal said. Jack continued to sway with his hands shaking—minor tremors started in his fingers and slid up his arm. Cal stood up at once.

"Are you okay, Jack?" When Cal moved, he watched their attention follow him as he went. Heads swiveled, keeping the couple's full focus on his face as if connected by an invisible cable. Judy saw their behavior and brought her hands up to her mouth and pushed her frame against the couch.

"It was a bang," Anne repeated. Both of Jack's arms shook out of control.

"I need to get you some help," Cal said, and when he was thinking of where he last left his phone, Jack pulled his hand from the robe's pockets. Cal became still at the sight of a gleaming knife. The blade glistened in Jack's twitching grasp, as if he were shaking a handful of dice.

"Cal?" Judy whispered.

"Don't move a muscle," he whispered back as if the older couple couldn't hear. Cal raised his hand as if he were a traffic cop warning an oncoming car to stop. "Whatever I've done, I'm sure we can talk this over," Cal said to Jack. Anne's face went from a benign expression to rage, as if his words were the catalyst. Jack became personified by the tremor with movements rushing to each limb until he resembled a movie glitching while on pause. "Jack? Relax."

Whatever was building inside, the couple had reached their limit. Jack pumped his legs and moved from behind Anne, running straight for him.

"Run," Cal ordered Judy. If she heard his warning, she never reacted. Jack's movements were not of a man late in his years. Instead, Jack had the actions of a kid with boundless energy and flexibility. Even as he saw Jack charging out of the corner of his eye, Cal saw Anne jump from her chair and join the parade heading his way. Judy thought of her mother and the violent actions her body made as if an invisible puppet master was pulling her strings. Anne and Jack had the same ventriloquist quality that sent terror into her stomach. As Jack was reaching Cal, indecision caught Judy between moving toward the galloping older man to stop him or retreating away from the living room and the imminent confrontation.

Cal watched Jack's hand holding the blade, pushing out any other motion to the peripheral. He intended to grab Jack's hand, but Cal calculated that the older man's momentum alone would be enough to plunge the knife into him. Cal waited for the last instant, sidestepped Jack, and watched as his lunge ended up into the couch.

No sooner had Cal thwarted Jack's attack than Anne careened her frame into his—her intensity caught him off guard. Her head drove Cal backward off his feet and knocked him onto the floor with her landing on top. With air knocked from his chest, Cal saw Jack turning from his collision with the couch and setting his sight on him once more.

Anne was in a frenzy, and although she didn't have a weapon, her nails became knives scratching at Cal's face. He twisted and turned to keep his eyes from taking the brunt of her attack.

"Run, Judy," he begged. This time Judy registered his pleas and took a few steps away from the chaos. Jack was coming at Cal, and for a split-second, he saw his retired neighbor was a ball of tremors. Both his assailants wore a mask of fury.

Cal gripped either side of Anne's robe and flung her off him and onto a coffee table that rested a few feet from the couch. From the force, she spun and hit the wooden table square and solid. No sooner had the wife found the coffee table, then Jack returned knife first. The choices were slim, and Cal grabbed the knife by its sharpened blade to stop it from entering his head. He squeezed tight—the blade sunk into his palms, and with Jack's weight continuing to push toward him, the blade cut deeper into his skin. Cal screamed out in pain.

Jack rocked his body back to get a better lunge forward, and that was the opportunity that Cal needed. As Jack went back onto his heels, Cal readjusted his grip from the blade to his wrists in one motion. This time when Jack's weight fell toward him, his clenching hands held back the load.

Anne was already maneuvering off the table onto him, and this time, she forgot about her nails for the moment. Instead of fingers, Anne bit down on Cal's cheek. Teeth sunk deep. If he let her tear away with her skin still in her mouth, a part of his cheek would go with her. He conceded his battle with Jack and pushed the arms with the knife over his shoulder and grabbed Anne's head before she tore his cheek off the bone.

Anne held in place for the second, but he didn't shove Jack up with enough force, and the blade found a soft spot, driving into and through his collarbone. Cal screamed. He was in a stalemate with Anne, and if he released her, his cheek would follow with her. She was a dog that had clamped down upon a favorite bone and refused to give up her prize as its master tugged.

A forceful blow rocked Cal—but the jolt didn't hit him. Judy found a nearby lamp and swung for the fences, landing the metal body of the light fixture against Anne's skull. With the whack, Anne's jaw opened to a slack position, releasing Cal's cheek, and tumbling her form to the carpet below. Even with the knife deep inside him, Cal breathed in with relief as Anne's biting ceased.

Blood leaked from Anne's head as she got to her feet, and for the first time that night, the older woman saw Judy. It appeared to Judy that Anne went from standing motionless into a sprint within two steps. Gripping the lamp tighter, Judy swung it fast and timed her attack wrong. The swing was way too early, passing in front of Anne's face a hair before she arrived. *Oh, hell.*

The scowl on Anne's face alone was enough to stop Judy's heart. No one ever regarded her with so much anger and outright hatred. George Romero's *The Night of the Living Dead* popped into her mind. Anne was a visceral, mindless killing machine. If the older woman were in search of brains, like in the movies, Judy could believe it. Anne drew back her hand, made a fist, and propelled it forward to Judy's face.

Judy braced for the impact, already expecting the ache. The hit never came, and after a few seconds, she pried her eyelids open to see Anne fight against something invisible. Judy spun around the room for the entity that stopped the old woman and saw nothing.

Anne reconstituted her angry face, drew back, and slammed her knuckles. An inch from Judy—the hand froze in mid-air. She appeared like a dog that ran to the sidewalk, with its chain, jerking it back. With every thrashing movement that failed, Judy saw the muscles and tendons in Anne's body tense as if brakes came alive in her. There was an invisible ally that was helping.

Judy relaxed and stepped closer to Anne, and with the closer distance, the older woman stepped back as if an undetectable barrier controlled her actions. Stepping again, Anne matched her stride with one in the opposite direction. The older woman snarled, not understanding why she wasn't able to get at Judy. The furious woman wasn't considering why there was a barricade but fought with raw brutality to get to Judy. The meaning gelled inside Judy. Johnny had scripted the entire scene. He rewired the old couple with murder in their hearts and blood in the countenance—winding them and sent them like a guided missile to Cal's door. *He's surely miles away in a comfortable bed, enjoying the spectacle.*

The conclusion came slowly to Anne, but she realized she couldn't hurt Judy, so she turned her interest back to Cal struggling with her husband. A knife was sticking out of Cal's shoulder and saw right off that Jack was the real threat to Cal or both if he didn't have any invisible restrictions like his wife. She tested the lamp's weight in her hands and headed for Jack.

In a matter of a few clock ticks, Judy's strategy to defend changed into a plan of attack. Anne gave off the vibe of a woman about to share a recipe and not a lady spitting saliva from her hissing mouth.

The knife inside Cal's shoulder was twisting during the entire struggle with Jack. The older man wasn't trying to inflict pain as much as he was engaged in ending Cal's life. His screams rose above everything else in the living room. The pain of the jiggling knife sent waves of agony, dimming his consciousness. Instead of passing out, Cal let go of the knife and allowed Jack to withdraw it from his body. This action wasn't what Cal wanted to do but continuing a battle with the sharpened blade still in him wasn't worth the fight.

Jack stared at his weapon as it dripped blood onto the carpet close to his bare feet. There was a dreamlike quality in the neighbor's expression, as if he didn't expect to get the knife free from Cal, and since it was his again, he appeared to be contemplating his next move. An internal conversation seemed to continue inside Jack—talking to whatever Johnny had hard-wired into his brain.

The internal dialogue that caused Jack to pause wouldn't last long, and Judy comprehended that if she didn't take advantage of his mental deliberation, the knife he brandished could end up back inside Cal or her. When the frenzied duo first walked into the home, Judy saw them as old and fragile, but their miraculous transformation helped her toss aside her illusions of which package carries death, and which doesn't. The sentiment that pushed others aside and hot-wired her engine was that she wanted to survive.

Cal appeared to be in an agony so searing that his eyes glazed over, looking the way those of a baby doll resembled a human's. She also recognized that any attempt to protect him from Jack from that point forward would be nonexistent. She had two choices that popped to mind—try to break the knife free of the older man's hand and risk failure and watching it plunged back into Cal—or kill him. Judy took him out of the equation, and that meant the possibility of taking his life.

Stepping in front of Cal, who was off in some other realm, Judy pulled back the lamp behind her shoulder as far as her arms allowed. Jack was in a rage, and although he was a genuine threat, she still needed to disconnect the human part that screamed to her not to swing. Cal released a weak whimper, and that was all she needed to warm her limbs and free her conscience.

Judy swung the lamp with the strength she never used before. She pivoted on her heels, and when her rotation was complete, she was spinning on her toes a fraction of a second ahead of the lamp before meeting Jack's head. Even though the lamp's material was heavy steel, Judy saw it give under her force and the sudden end of its travel against the hardness of a skull. At first, she believed the lamp did nothing to his angry state until she witnessed the light in his eyes switch off like the changing of a television channel.

With the mental switchover, she wondered if the real Jack was back in time to feel his body lose all control. He wobbled on two legs that worked more out of instinct than any direct command from his brain.

Anne was undergoing the same rage that sent her charging, but her body became locked into place. Her face curled into a snarl that made her into a feral dog. When she saw the impact on her husband, Anne had a flicker of understanding. Anne turned toward her husband's assailant with an expression that redoubled into a pitiful mask of hatred.

Even if Anne didn't comprehend the reality of the situation, Judy did and sympathized with the woman caught in Johnny's twisted game.

They were nothing more than human torpedoes aimed to take away Cal's life. Human life meant nothing to Johnny, and if he will destroy everybody around her, how could she compete?

With her abilities restored, Judy saw she had the skills needed to cause some harm to her husband if she ever got the opportunity. The problem which returned with every resolution was that she wasn't comfortable with the collateral damage necessary to put a stop to Johnny. *Would I use an elderly couple as a battering ram?* The answer came back to her as a *no*. He would use her weakness against her until he got what he wanted.

Jack slid back onto the couch as if tired instead of getting brained by a light fixture. His knees buckled with the top half of his frame slanting toward the couch cushions. When the furniture entirely held his body, he looked out through vacant eyes, not seeing anything. Anne regarded this with slack in her posture that derived from her former life and went into a gallop right for Judy.

Judy shook her head at the choices left to her and swung the lamp. Timing her swing to perfection—the lamp found Anne's jaw and caused her to fall back to the carpet. A snap was audible, and she cringed at its result even as she felt satisfied that Cal was no longer in danger.

Chapter Forty
—Love could be labeled poison—

The buzz at The Thurman Cafe was so high that it threatened to spill out into the streets. When Johnny Macklemore walked into the café, a roar began—first building slowly but picking up momentum until chatter from every table floated toward their booth. Judy sat across from Johnny, staring at his face.

"What did you do?" Judy asked. Johnny sipped on his iced tea as if she weren't speaking to him. He gazed out into the restaurant and regarded the other patron's conversations.

"Now I know why you loved this place so much," he said.

"You're doing something to make me fall in love with you. Stop it!" Judy screeched through clenched teeth.

"Can I get a picture with you?" a woman in a nearby booth asked Johnny. "My daughter and I both love your books so much. I can't tell you how much they mean to us," she said. Johnny was already plucking the phone from her hand, positioning the three of them inside the camera frame—snapping a few shots for good measure. When the fans walked away, they were grinning and staring at their phones in awe.

"What they don't tell you before you become a celebrity, is you'll become an expert at using other people's phones," Johnny said. Judy plunged into the same swoon when their eyes met—she swiveled away without hesitation. "Have you ever considered the simple truth that you *are* in love with me?" Johnny asked. Judy sat, watching other customers pointing and staring at them. She couldn't catch her breath, but her feeling of admiration dove when she didn't concentrate on his face.

"It must be sad to be so unloved that you have to manufacture the emotion in someone," Judy said, still looking at him. Johnny bristled at her comment.

"Look around you—am I unloved?" Another fan, this time a teenage girl, placed a napkin in front of Johnny, and he signed without hesitation. A waitress sidled up to the booth with a notebook in one hand and pen in another.

"You're Donna—right?" Johnny questioned the waitress.

"Yes," Donna said in shock. "How do you know that?" Johnny handed her his best smile. Judy watched his grin from the corner of her eyes, and it melted her power.

"Judy has told me enough about you—I feel I know you more than her." His smile slid into another easy-going laugh. "Did your sister end up going to London for modeling?" he asked. Donna smiled.

"She did. I can't believe you know that," Donna said. He kept the smile—redirecting it toward Judy and still talking to Donna. "You let her know that Johnny Macklemore is a fan of hers next time you talk. Okay?" Donna was nodding before the words fell from his lips. "My wife and I have way too much to catch up on—can you get us each a Thurman burger and fries? I must have one."

"You got it, Mr. Macklemore," Donna said.

"Please, Donna—call me Johnny." A Cheshire grin returned.

"Your burgers will be right out, Johnny," Donna said. The waitress was downright giddy by the time she walked away from their booth. Johnny wore a satisfied expression when he turned back to Judy.

"I like her," he said, sipping his tea. "By the way, Mike looks like Paul McCartney." Judy wanted to slap the smirk from his face except that every time she saw it, she slid further into admiration for him. *This isn't real—nothing with him is real.* She wanted to believe her words, but there was a separate part that felt a love that deep. Judy had to come to a hard conclusion—her perception of reality was wrong more often than it was right.

"I agreed to meet to tell you face to face—you need to go on with your life—without me," she said. When she practiced the words on the ride over, they sounded more convincing, bouncing off car windows. In the open air of the café, her words sounded empty. Johnny stared at Judy, unmoved by her demand.

"Judy? No one on this planet knows you as I do. Do you think you have some lost connection with Cal? You're confused. I've been in places Cal can never reach—your fears—and your secret thoughts that you have when you think no one can hear. I know them all, Judy. It doesn't *matter* how we got to where we are—we're here. We are close because we are creatures like no one else. You tend to over-analyze situations, and that's something I love about you, but it is also the trait that keeps you from accepting happiness," he said, then sipped his tea.

Johnny's expression had a chemical effect on her thinking, pulling her from the concerns and into a mellow state of mind that beckoned to let her worries fade away. Her mind drifted back to her life in New York— sitting by the pool—enjoying dinners at fine restaurants. They always rubbed elbows with the elite, and that was a forgotten obsession in her life. The best people and the best food became a goal, and although she never chose that path, it filled her days and nights with something to look forward to when there was nothing else.

"Our friends back home miss you so much, Judy," he said as if he read her mind. "We need time together—just you and I. Dinner and drinks—getting back to the basics. I've let my work disrupt us, and that changes. Right now," Johnny promised. His words weren't as strong as his facade, but they were making sense. Her brush with reality, if she called it that, was harsh and hurtful. Every path to understanding Judy Angel led her to heartache. Judy understood that what he was promising was real, not an illusion.

The years she spent with him was comfortable. Comfort was a mild way of describing her existence—extravagant was a better word. Johnny never denied her one luxury, either from asking or otherwise. In that life, not so long ago, she was someone that others around her envied. As a couple, they weren't boastful—flaunting their lifestyle wasn't necessary. Their daily routine did all the talking for them. When Judy abandoned her will into the decadence—it satisfied her. Judy's life was like a rich dessert that captured her body and gave her the sensation that few others enjoyed.

"I'm a prideful man. But I will admit that I can do more to ensure you want for nothing. I have the resources to turn your life into a whirlwind of pleasures if you allow me that opportunity," Johnny said. His lips curled up, revealing a grin full of teeth. The pull was in her chest, expanding outward. A tingling sensation was gentle but nudging in its firmness toward a way of life that had intoxicated her for years.

Judy remembered staring back at her image in pictures and the stark contrast of her appearance. She mixed with the elite of New York but considered herself a hometown girl. *Is that who I am? Were those my choices?* She suspected they were her choices, not all but a lot more than she wanted to confess. Did their relationship devolve into symbiosis like two vampires feeding off each other? Johnny robbing her of her novels, and she sponging the money it made to sustain her outward desires?

The pull from her chest was there, but not as potent as when she gazed upon his face. She was a woman coming up for air after a dangerous period submerged—still seeing him triggered her passions, and they left a negative in her closed eyelids like the after-effects of staring into the sun.

"Relax, Judy. Open your eyes," his voice soothed. Strands of her soul wanted to obey. Her mind tangled reality into a mixture of want and needs—guilt and absolution—and he supplied her with a tainted world that told her it was the rare potential reality. The brilliance of his offering was its imperfection. Johnny was like a shrew, paralyzing their prey and eating them at their leisure over a long time until there is nothing left to feed.

"How many times have you done this to me?" Judy asked. Her hand fell to her side, but she never peered at him head-on, instead, keeping him in her peripheral. He was flashing an ugly smile.

"The truth-finding conversations never help—not you—not me. You bait me into telling you things you don't want to hear. In the end, I feel bad about myself. You may not think I have a heart, but I do, Judy. Let's let the past go. We can make a fresh start. What do you say?"

"How I saw my parents the first time and my friends...you made me see them that way. Didn't you?" Johnny grinned. "How many times have you lured me back?"

"Goddamn it, Judy," Johnny said loud enough to cause heads to turn. A forced smile returned, more for the customers than for his wife.

"Ten years. Twice a year." The restaurant spun around her as if she were on a merry-go-round waiting to stop. "I'll wait for YOU to gather yourself," he said as if he expected the reaction. The truth knocked her out of her body—her mind floated above her scalp like a balloon too full of helium.

"I tried to escape you twenty times?" she was taking in air, but it wasn't sustaining her.

"None of this is constructive, and if you," Johnny paused as Donna slid their plates in front of them, tilted her head, and walked away, "want a happy life—I can give you that. Just let yourself go." His words intended to soothe, and they hit their mark.

With two hands, Johnny grabbed the burger, pushed it into his face with a bite that resembled a lion tearing at its fleshy prey. Juice dripped down his chin and back onto his plate below. "Okay. That is not five-star dining—but damn," he said through a mouthful of food.

"You've painted a pretty picture for me, Johnny. Except...a content person doesn't try to escape their husband or life," Judy said.

"You're a stubborn woman, Judy. Happiness has nothing to do with your little rebellions. It's all about attitude. Come home with me—resign your mind to devoting yourself to me, and the drama will vanish, and I won't harm the people around you. I promise." Judy thought of Cal resting in the hospital.

"How did you get the older couple to attack us last night?" She had a decent idea but wanted to hear it from Johnny. He slathered ketchup onto a handful of fries and shoved it into a wide-open mouth.

"Anyone I want...can come for you. All I do is wind them up and point them in your direction. It could be your second-grade teacher. A driving instructor or maybe the friendly waitress Donna over there." Judy swiveled her head and watched Donna collect empty pop glasses from customers to refill. "It's within my power," he said. Johnny's eyelids twitched, and for the first time that day, Judy studied him.

Judy allowed her gaze to sink deeper than the contours of his face—the facade that triggered a programed response—she watched the subtleties of his countenance. And it thrilled and horrified her when she understood he was keeping it together by the thinnest of margins. Eyes that she believed were ocean waters calling her—darted up and down, then left and right like an addict needing precious medicine to function.

A jerking started in the cheek bones and rippled downward. Judy saw that his head bobbed like the motion of a rooster. Manipulating others was taking its toll. *You're bluffing, Johnny.*

"So, you can go on sending out messengers to do your bidding?" Judy asked, watching his face as he answered. Before he even spoke, she spotted the doubt bubbling in his expression. There was something else she hadn't put her finger on before—he was talking to himself. Or it was more accurate to say conversations were happening in his interior while he sat there in the booth.

Johnny wasn't a novice at dealing with internal dialogue, and she guessed it was a long-running feature that he dealt with because it was difficult to identify unless you could fathom what to watch for in his veneer.

"I can snap my fingers," Johnny said. His words that held so much weight earlier fell flat.

"You're dying," she said as if a veil plummeted from her sight for the first time. Johnny tried to smile and couldn't get the corners of his mouth to cooperate.

"Ridiculous," he said and turned his attention back to the enormous burger. Confidence covered Judy's skin like a warming cocoon.

"You need me to survive. Without me—you're doomed. That's why your attacks have been...so vicious," Judy said. "You're desperate." As if mentioning his predicament inflamed his condition, a twitch, greater than the rest, seized his body. "Someone's talking to you right now...are they not?" she asked.

"You are—always speaking to me," he admitted. "Come back to me. We'll draft novels together. I know that's your dream. I can make it happen for you," he said with hope in his voice.

"Can you even write a novel? Those are my words on the page—my feelings. On the cover of each book may have your name, but it's my creations in the binding that gave you your fame—your wealth and lifestyle. You're a fake," she said with venom that satisfied. Johnny's face turned red, and he went quiet for a long time. "I'm not making this forty-one. It's over," she said, not shying away. "If you don't move on—"

"What will you do?" he asked. An idea came to her.

"I'll find a lawyer or go to a newspaper," Judy said.

"And say what?" His smile didn't return, but it was on the verge.

"I'll tell them you stole my novels." He laughed so hard that people around him stopped to stare at the famous novelist cutting up in their local establishment.

"Let me help. Why not explain to the press that I held you down at gunpoint for each book—six months at a time and made you author my stories? They will laugh you out of any court in the land. How will you afford the legal fees? I left out the minor detail of having you sign a post-nuptial agreement. Are you planning to tell them that was at gunpoint also? If you walk away...it's with nothing—not even memories." Johnny tackled the burger again, getting as much food down him as into him. For the first time that day, Judy gave him a smile of her own, and it unnerved him enough to stop eating. "The only copy of the novels is on my computer—locked away from you," he pressed.

"Is that so?"

Johnny nodded with an unsure expression.

"The funny thing about you taking the novels from my head," her smile widened, "is you didn't try to see when I created them—dreamt them up." She tapped the side of her head. "Were they in the world before I met you?" His mind was chewing the information.

"So what? They're mine now," he said.

"I wouldn't be too sure of yourself, the famous Johnny Macklemore," Judy said as she picked up the burger and took a bite—for effect more than hunger. "I took a tour of the Angel Among Us recently. Guess what I found there—files of every book I wrote. I'd bet all your wealth that a forensic investigator could track down when I wrote those novels from the digital footprints," she tossed a French fry into her mouth, "and decide that every cent you made off of my work belongs to me," she said. His face transitioned from red to white as the blood drained from his complexion.

Judy failed to mention that the computer she created the novels on, brought home by her father, sat in a storage unit for safekeeping—secured right before she arrived at the restaurant. Still, the threat hit him hard, and she saw the reaction. Genuine fear registered on his face. Judy figured he wanted to remove the memories clogging his brain—it was his highest priority until the prospect of money and fame going away entered the conversation.

"Who the fuck do you think you are? You may have written them, but I made the success, and I made you. You are nothing without me," Johnny said.

"I suppose we'll find out—won't we?" Johnny pushed his plate away hard enough to career against Judy's.

"You haven't won anything."

"I forgot to mention it, but my abilities, the ones you attempted to bury, are with me again. If you cross my path I'll make you pay for my life—my family—for everything." Judy stared him down and saw him melt—a bit, but to her, it was precious. She had to throw him off balance— it was the lone card left to her, and she played it. There was no going back into a life of slavery, even if the urge pulled her in that direction. Judy smiled the biggest smile her cheeks allowed, and he reciprocated with a sneer.

With one foot at a time, Judy hoisted her frame onto the bench of her booth. She stood high above the table as if she were greeting the room. She lifted her head high and cleared her throat.

"Excuse me," she shouted above the roar of the restaurant with patrons turning to her voice, "I'd like to set the record straight. My name is Judy Macklemore, and I am the wife of this gentleman sitting right in front of me," Johnny slunk in his seat, "I'm sure most of you know him as Johnny Macklemore and have seen his novels in bookstores across the country. What you don't know is that he's a fraud. He's lied to you. I wrote the novels, and he took credit for every story he's sold to the world." His face turned the darkest crimson shade Judy ever saw on a human. Judy stepped to the floor, keeping her grin.

"I will fucking kill you for that," Johnny said, shaking. Judy walked away from him—knowing she stirred a hornet's nest. A building full of people would never get the word out about his theft, but it felt so damn good.

Chapter Forty-one
—Floated around in his dreamy head—

Judy's abilities were back, and although she understood how to use them, what worried her was whether she should. Without the memories that first accompanied her skills, she was morally rudderless. After witnessing Johnny's disregard for any ethical code, Judy second-guessed her place in the world with such a dangerous talent.

Havoc and mayhem followed her—infecting the ones she tried to help. Since she was a blank slate, she saw a higher authority at work. Denying a power behind the scenes was impossible to ignore, and she wondered if it was there all along. Did she overlook the obvious signs? *It's foolish to think I can control this ability.* And yet, she couldn't walk away from her gifts until she made things right.

Cal was asleep in the hospital—she held his hand tight until she drifted off herself—venturing deep into him. The inside of Cal's mind wasn't much different from his personality, but the doubt crawled back in—curling up in her conscience and roared. Cal lost so much blood that an induced coma was necessary to lower his brain functions, but Judy hoped there was still enough brain activity to reach him. They stabilized him, according to the doctor, but the last thing she wanted to do was push him further into the abyss.

Preparing to pull him toward her, she remained still with mind and spirit. Her newfound mental vision led her to another part of Cal's brain that contained memories—severed from the rest. Could she restore the amputated remembrances? She bet she could manage the task, but for now, she intended to experience them.

When the images flooded her, it took Judy a long time to understand *where* she was until the complete picture emerged. The memory originated in Cal—that was for sure, except—it was a shared vision. The imaginary world had two inhabitants, one was Cal, and the other was...

Judy stumbled onto a vision of Cal and Johnny together. Backing out of it was her first instinct—pretend it wasn't there. But the temptation proved too strong, and she let it unfold like a movie horror scene, sinking into her stomach—she couldn't turn away.

Cal sat on a picnic table in front of an amusement park, sipping on a fruit punch from a small box—straw dangling from a hole in its top. Judy didn't detect fear from Cal as he glanced around his surroundings, trying to decide if they were real or a part of a vivid dream.

When Johnny walked up, he was holding a juice box of his own. The two men, if you could call them that, both under eighteen Judy wagered, stood facing each other. She bet they were close in age, but Johnny was like a boy compared to the features Cal already grew into by his senior year. From feel alone, Judy saw that the constructed world was Johnny's, and he carried himself in it with infinite confidence.

"Hello, Cal," Johnny said. He took a sip of the juice box—the sound of juice and air entered the thin straw.

"Do I know you?" Johnny sat on the top of the picnic table, and the two of them watched a nearby rollercoaster as riders erupted into a scream—the sound dying away as it passed, leaving them staring at one another.

"You don't know me yet—you will," Johnny said and smiled. Cal didn't like the kid's grin, and something was off about his mannerisms. His mind went back to a local play and the stiffness of the actors on stage, recognizing the same movements in Johnny. *He's pretending,* Cal thought. Judy discovered she could hear both of their thoughts.

Cal was unaware, but Judy saw it all—tendrils extended from Johnny's head and latched onto Cal's. The connection alone was ominous and even more disturbing, knowing that, in this timeline, Johnny was close by asleep like a vampire in a coffin—ready to drain Cal of his vital essence.

"Judy will move on from you—thought you'd like to know," Johnny said. Cal studied the young boy.

"Is that so?" Cal wasn't sure what to make of Johnny, but fear wasn't a component of his curiosity. The boldness of the boy off-balanced Cal and Johnny's self-assured attitude reinforced his words, even if they weren't the truth.

"I think I'll wait for Judy to tell me that—if you don't mind," Cal said.

"Suit yourself." Johnny shrugged, but his expression didn't convey his body's indifferent stance. If he was hoping for Cal to cooperate, he wasn't getting his way. Cal took another view around him.

"This is your creation, huh?" Cal asked. Johnny's face showed the shock that Cal had the ability to see through the shroud. Although Johnny was fresh at using his gifts, the illusion he generated was startling in its realism.

"How do you know that?" Johnny asked, surprise still plastered on his face, "You're the first to notice a difference."

"I can't see a difference, but I can feel it," Cal remarked and threw away the juice box when he realized it didn't exist. Judy watched as Johnny's tendril doubled in diameter. He was through talking and ready to finish what he came to do. The tendrils gave the faintest hum as it pulsated, and she was sure Johnny was searching inside Cal's mind. *What is he looking for?* Judy wasn't sure at the treasure Johnny sought but had an idea he meant to remove vital memories—of her.

"What are you trying to do?" Cal asked with Johnny probing deeper. Judy recalled Stanley Kubrick's 2001: A Space Odyssey, with the computer, HAL 9000, questioning while the astronaut fiddled with his insides. Johnny's expression changed from bewilderment to satisfaction when his antenna found the treasure and the purpose of the meeting.

"Relax. This will only take a second," Johnny assured.

"I can see your attachment," Cal said. Whatever Johnny was doing stopped.

"That's impossible." A determined grimace stole Johnny's exterior, with the tendril growing once more. "Goodbye, Cal," Judy observed a yanking movement from Johnny and then nothing. Bewilderment returned to Johnny.

"Something wrong?" Cal asked. A slight smirk transformed his appearance. Johnny jerked the tendril several more times, not receiving the result he expected. *What the hell?* Johnny meant to say this to himself, but Cal heard every word.

"Not working?" Judy saw fear capturing Johnny—his self-assurance melted.

"How are *you* stopping me?" Johnny asked. A tendril, larger than Johnny's, slid from Cal, enveloping the smaller one as it coated it until nothing remained, but the freshly formed tendril. Johnny was a mouse, discovering that a snake had curled around its body with no idea how it happened. Cal held tight as his prey heaved himself—trying to escape, wake up—anything to cut himself off. Cal's tendril was too strong to resist, and Johnny remained there dumbfounded by the trap he allowed himself to fall into without a hint of warning.

"What are you going to do to me?" Johnny asked with terror threatening to take over. Cal walked to the projected form of Johnny, pressing his nose against the boy's cheek.

"What's your name?"

"Johnny Macklemore," he squeaked.

"You're a bully, Johnny. You must hit the bully back. That's what my father taught me," Cal said. Johnny shook. Cal's form remained still, but his mind grabbed hold of Johnny's conscious mind like a giant snatching a person with their huge hands.

"I won't bother you anymore—just leave me alone, and I'll do the same." Cal ignored the pleading. "Where are you leading me?" Cal made a circuit in Johnny's mind to the amygdala area of his brain.

"It thrills you to fill others with fear. I want you to get a taste. The worst part of a human being hides there. I will introduce you to it." Cal gave nothing away with his expression. He completed the circuit, plunging Johnny into the amygdala. Judy sensed Johnny tensing when his residual-self disappeared into the dark region of the mind. Wherever Johnny's body was resting, it was also screaming out for mercy. The act of punishment was as if Cal dunked Johnny into arctic water, but Judy wondered if there was much more involved. She hoped never to know those nightmares.

After a long time, held in the nightmarish world, Cal released Johnny. He knew he would release himself as fast as he could manage. For the briefest of moments, Johnny stared at Cal, unbelieving.

"If you ever give me a reason...I will put you back into that world and never let you out," Cal said. Johnny gave a slight nod and vanished along with the world he created.

Judy realized she was holding her breath and let the air out with a relieved blast. Thoughts were flying at her so fast she couldn't put them in the right order. Seeing the vision gave both her future and past more meaning—a context to understand how she got to where she was.

"An ugly scene—wasn't it?" a voice spoke. Judy spun around in the world she created to see Cal, "This place is something." Cal rotated to see the three-dimensional realm. "You have some talent. It's identical to the garden you took me to on our first date," he said.

"It was a garden my father took me to when I was little." she smiled—tears ran down her face.

"I recall you telling me that. A lot of the past is coming back."

"I had to visit you."

"Why here?" he asked. A stump that didn't exist stood in front of Judy, and he sat anyway—positioning next to her.

"You are...in a coma. The doctor said you will pull through..."

"But you wanted to see me in case I didn't?" She nodded.

"If I ask you a question. Will you answer honestly?"

"Considering this might be our last visit—I'll tell you everything," Cal said.

"At the police station—was that you—controlling the lights?" Cal thought about it for a few beats.

"It was. But I didn't know it then. My memories came back soon after."

"So, you have powers like me?" she asked.

"Not exactly. Mine are a little different." She took his hand into her own.

"If you were in Johnny's world, how did you stop him from manipulating you?" While he squeezed her hand, he contemplated an answer that made sense.

"Our abilities are like," Cal paused, "rock, paper, scissors. You remember that game?" She nodded. "To each other, that's how it is with us who have this talent. We all have strength, and we all have a weakness. When we were teenagers, we spent hours discussing this," Cal said.

"We did?" she smiled and wiped away a teardrop.

"Yeah. My strength is that someone like us can't change anything in my mind without my permission. The most anyone can do is enter my conscious thoughts—the way Johnny did."

"If that's true, then how did I fix you?"

"I didn't know it until we spoke to Otis Bain, but you gave me this ability, and I changed. You don't remember our first moments together—I do, and I'm sure I'd give you permission to whatever you wanted to do to me. I fell in love with you the first time we met, and I think you did as well," he said.

"No. It doesn't make any sense. If Johnny couldn't take memories from you—how did you lose them—how did you not know about your abilities until now?" Judy asked.

"I did it to myself," Cal twisted away. Shame turned his face red.

"Why would you erase your memories?" The answer was close, but she couldn't put the pieces together without his help. Judy could tell he didn't want to answer. "You promised," she reminded. Cal nodded.

"You came to me a brief time after and told me you weren't in love with me anymore—that you had fallen for Johnny..."

"Go on," she said.

"I was so angry—honestly never been that enraged. You betrayed me." It was Judy's turn to avoid his gaze. "My thoughts when that happened were out of control. I was drowning in ideas of lashing out— making the two of you suffer how I was suffering. I started seeing my gift as a tool to make things right. I needed to move on and even came close to giving in to my urges. But I couldn't get rid of my hurt, so I did the only other thing I could do—erase any memory of my powers," he said.

"I'm so sorry," Judy said.

"I was so blinded by anger that I didn't stop to think what Johnny was trying to do when he attacked me. Altering my thought—taking my memories never even occurred to me," Cal covered his face with his hands, "knowing he controlled you and I could have prevented him from hurting you..."

"I would never blame you, Cal, and I don't want you to accept responsibility either. Johnny's done this—to all of us. I have a way to put an end to it all. I can't get back the life you or I deserve, but it will ensure our future," Judy said. Cal turned white.

"I don't like the sound of that. Please wait until I can help you. This has been his goal all along—this whole time, Johnny's been thinning the herd to get you alone," Cal said.

"It's my last chance. He's weak and desperate. Johnny has spent a lifetime doing this to me and others. If I don't jump at this opportunity—who knows what he would do to us—Johnny has to die," she said. Cal wanted to argue but saw the futility.

"Remember one thing," he said.

"Sure."

"We all have a weakness and a strength. If you discover your potency—Johnny can't touch you. Find your strength—it's your edge." Cal held her in his arms and wished it were in the real world. She pulled away, and her creation went with her. The hospital room once again filled her view. She kissed Cal's forehead, hoping it wouldn't be the last time she saw him.

Chapter Forty-two
—Fighting with your head—

When she visited Bud earlier in the evening, she watched him sleep as nurses buzzed in and out of his room like bees in a hive. Her confrontation with Johnny was unpredictable. Whenever she underestimated his ruthlessness, she paid the price. There were too many holes in her plan, and if she looked deep inside, she realized Johnny was smart enough to anticipate her moves—because there were so few to choose.

Emily was asleep by her husband's side, but Judy saw the track of tears, revealing evidence her mother spent the night crying. With her plans swirling around, she needed a mother to talk to, but she couldn't bear to rouse her after seeing her face so peaceful. Regardless of who was at fault, her parents dealt with so much anguish because of her. It weighed heavily on her mind.

If she survived the night, Judy would do everything in her power to bring her father back. With her abilities restored—confidence filled her spirits, and she was never so potent. The trouble, she soon realized, was there were limitations to what she could do to heal her father. Without knowing the precise area of the brain Johnny had targeted and mangled in Bud—she was liable to do more damage than good discovering Johnny's steps to ruin her father. His screams of horror were the key to solving the riddle—it pointed a direction, but without finding out for sure—the risk was high.

Standing in front of the *Angel Among Us* building, Judy thought about the world she created with her first visit with her father—it was so long ago. She searched the neighborhood for any signs of life and saw nothing stirring in the late hour. *The Book Loft*, where she imagined spending most of her childhood browsing, lay dark next to the clinic. The shops connected to the bookstore, shuttered for the night, gave a gloomy abandoned appearance that spread—turning her mood bleak.

Cold steel of the blade pressed against her belly gave her chills and reminded her of the difficulty that lay ahead. The reality that she would end a life was so alien that her intuition kept telling her it wasn't her planning it, but some other Judy—perhaps the Angel she saw in the visions. Her plan that night was to kill Johnny, and although the scheme was solid and locked, Judy struggled with a mixture of conflicting emotions.

Outward, she had no delusions about what Johnny had done to her, but inside, there was a lingering love for him. Hundreds of times, she swore that anything left in the tank that resembled affection, Johnny manufactured. It didn't matter how her feelings got there—they made her choice that much harder. Judy attempted to think of Johnny Macklemore as a cockroach but could not squash him under her shoe. But humanity would be better off without him.

Johnny's fans were another matter altogether after his death. If she had to face the music when the authorities got involved, that was one thing. Dealing with rabid readers of Johnny would never go in her favor. Her public image would be a jealous wife who killed her husband in cold blood. *Shit—half the patrons who heard my ravings in The Thurman Cafe would line up to testify of my premeditation.*

The door of the clinic swung out, and she entered with a feeling of hopelessness. She appeared to walk to an execution instead of the hall of a medical building. Judy imagined her death and the life she would never have with Cal, or her father trapped inside a prison of Johnny's construction. *A few people aside, would anyone mourn my death?* With every step, the belief that she was no match for Johnny scraped at her confidence.

When Judy reached the painting of the garden that hid her private sanctuary—she snapped the latch beneath the painting's frame—the door opened inward. *Does Johnny know about this room?* She wasn't sure, so she left the door wide open for Johnny to discover. She flicked on the light switch and sat on the twin bed in the small room that had been her childhood refuge.

Judy set the trap and prayed he took the bait. Understanding what Johnny's motivations—his urges—were became her last line of defense. There was no doubt that fame fueled him—the money and the success her novels brought him elevated his worth. She recalled his face when she announced him as a fraud in the café. It was more than anger she saw in his features—it was an outrage that someone, especially her, would try to take that away from him. It mattered little how he got his success—to him, it was all about keeping it.

From the moment she met Johnny Macklemore, he was a night owl. And now she saw him for what he was—a nightly predator. It was through sleep that he conquered his prey and took what he wanted, leaving no trace behind. It was his predictability that gave her the edge.

Sooner or later, Johnny would make his way to the clinic to recover her book files—to ensure his way of life. *He will come.* Judy slid the knife out into her hand, turned off the room's meager light, and sat waiting. If it took a week, she would remain there a week. All along, Johnny was one step ahead of her because he knew her well. Although there were holes in her memory, she was ready to play his game.

Judy sat on the bed—holding the knife—motionless for hours, realizing the morning was about to arrive and feeling foolish to think he would behave as she planned—like a character in one of her novels. Johnny contained the same basic rationales as antagonists in the thousands of books she had read, but fiction isn't at all like actual life. The night was a failure, and as she contemplated her next move, if there was one, sleep, with its foggy warmth, ensnared her.

What stirred her from slumber was nothing monumental—a slight nudge of her hands was all she registered the moment her eyes snapped open. Like a grinning nightmare that contained hair and teeth, Johnny was hovering over her on the bed. The nudge she acknowledged was the gentle removal of the knife from her hand. As if by magic, the knife rested in his hand, pointing at her neck.

"Shoot. I was hoping you'd stay asleep," Johnny said with silky words, "It would have gone much easier on you if you had. Why not drift off again?" Johnny coaxed. His words had the opposite effect on her. Judy's eyelids opened as wide as they could, and she was already hurrying away toward the headboard—further from the sharpened weapon.

She was chastising herself for falling asleep when he moved closer—not a lot, but enough to make her squirm.

"Are we done with this dance, Judy?" Johnny asked. He sat on the edge of the bed and rested the knife on bended knee. "If you come home with me tonight, I'll hold no grudges against you. The people you helped me hurt while in Columbus will heal and move on with their lives. I promise you that. They aren't loyal to you the way I am. Did one person try to find you when you left ten years ago?" Judy remained silent. "No one came, Judy—nobody will come this time either. You'll see the truth," he said.

"You'll fix my father?" Judy asked. He studied her face.

"Of course."

"What did you do to him?" she asked, hopeful. He scanned the room.

"I don't see a computer. Was that a lie?" She shrugged her shoulders.

"You didn't answer me. How did you hurt my father?" He grinned and tapped the knife onto his leg in fast rhythms.

"You're smart, Judy. And I know why you're asking. I'll come clean—you've outsmarted me before, through the years. You got it in your head that you will free yourself and unravel the mess I've made of Bud's brain." His smile continued. "Well, you're not killing me, and I'm not telling you my secret recipe that turned his mind to soup," he said.

Judy wanted to punch the smile off his face and count his teeth as they landed onto the bed—but he was right. Judy had no options, and if she were lucky, he would at least make the people she loved whole again. She didn't trust him, but she took the escape plan as far as it could go with one possibility left—him doing the right thing. She remembered his sister, Tessa, and laughed.

"What's so funny?" Johnny asked. She shook her head. *You're an insecure son of a bitch, aren't you?*

"We build relationships on trust," she said.

"So?"

Judy observed his hand—tremors moved his fingers as they curled around the knife's handle. The twitching around in the face, she first noticed in the restaurant, was back and worse than before. She understood his struggle. Johnny could manage until decisions were in order. It was in his times of contemplation that the voices were at their strongest and attempted to take over.

"If you are my husband and you consider me your wife—I should not need a knife—or you for that matter. You're my protection, right?" Judy said, keeping her tone even. The twitches in his cheeks were more pronounced as he considered her comments. He gripped the knife tighter.

"Yes," he said after a long time. "We need to behave like a married couple," he admitted.

"If you aren't willing to grow, then I'm not willing to come back." She motioned to the blade with her head. Johnny gave her a sideways glance, thinking over the alternatives, and nodded. Leaning off the bed, Johnny placed the blade on a nearby desk and returned to the bed in one motion.

"You see? We can get along," she said. His smile returned, but the twitches ran rampant across his face. Judy recalled Cal's warning. *Find your strength—it's your edge.*

"A sign of good faith? Tell me how to help Bud—we'll go back to New York—" He was already shaking his head.

"You have two choices." He leaned closer and slid an amber jar from the inside of his coat pocket. A white rag appeared in his palm like a magic trick, and she recognized by the dexterous gesture, he had practiced it many times. "I can help you fall asleep with this." He presented the bottle like an actor in a television commercial selling the latest product, "or you can fall asleep naturally," he offered.

There was something she had been missing in watching the videos of her healing the children. The harder she tried to make a connection, the further the answer drifted from her. Until the realization came out of nowhere, striking her with an electric jolt of joy. Judy couldn't help but smile. Johnny hovered above her with the bottle in his hand. He shook his head back and forth, and he heard a loud popping sound as if a light bulb exploded in the room. He surveyed the bedroom, found the light fixtures were still intact, then turned back to Judy.

"What was—" Judy thrust her legs out—shoes pounded against the softness of Johnny's mouth and nose. He fell back toward the wall—blood poured from his nose as his back rebounded from the impact. Judy was already up and moving through the doorway, pumping legs as fast as her body would allow.

The kick seemed to jolt Johnny with throbbing pain, causing the static permeating his brain to tumble away, and the twitching on his face stopped for a rare moment. Johnny wiped the blood from his nose with the back of his hand and picked the knife back up.

Although Judy had a head start, she heard his footsteps thundering behind her. Every second was precious, and although she wanted to turn back and gauge her distance, she didn't dare. Moving through the facility toward the exit, she rotated escape routes in her mind like a Rolodex once she reached the crisp air outside. Judy couldn't outrun him for long, and the area was empty of any bystanders that could come to her aid. An idea sprang to mind, and she grasped the concept with both hands.

What little distance that separated the two was shrinking fast. Judy moved to *The Book Loft*, sitting a few feet away from the clinic. In full stride, Judy grabbed a brick off the cement pathway leading to the bookstore's entrance. Without thinking, she smashed the glass door, rotated the lock, and ran inside. She remembered the way Maddie described the layout of the store—its labyrinth-like paths—dead ends and cutbacks. Maddie mentioned she couldn't find her way out of the unusual design once. Judy could now lose Johnny in it, she hoped.

It wasn't the best plan, but under the circumstances, it was the option that was most likely to work. As Judy made it through the opening of the store, passing the register, taking the stairs up two at a time, Judy perceived Johnny's scraping feet on the path just outside. His steps echoed and faded quickly enough to let her know he was already inside with her.

The first path she took was to the right. The hallway—lined with books from the ceiling to the floor, led into a larger room with another doorway opposite the one she entered. She had no memory of the floor plan of the maze-like bookstore, and she couldn't afford the trap of a dead end. If she chose wrong, she wouldn't get a second chance. Judy needed to believe her intuition was guiding her the right way. The path headed four different directions, and her intuition abandoned her.

To her immediate left, Judy spotted the smallest room she ever saw. It had books lining it like all the rest, except it was not bigger than a closet. It was a miracle she noticed it at all, and when she stepped into the space, she prayed for Johnny to pass by without noticing. The sound of Johnny's footsteps changed from a jog to slow, steady steps. He paused in the same place she did, pondering which path to follow. Although it was dark, a slight turn of the head and he would see her form in the tiny alcove. She held her breath and closed her eyes, listening.

For a long time, Johnny stood, listening himself until he chose a doorway, stepping through and away from Judy's hiding spot. She released her breath and started back the way she came—a loud creak exploded in a floorboard below. It was loud enough that she was sure he heard. Sneaking was out the window, so she darted to the right down a long hallway, hoping he would instead head back to the front of the store the same way they entered.

Luck wasn't on her side. The first sounds that found its way to her ears were his bellowing feet. He was in full gallop toward her down the hall and hiding became a faded luxury. There were more winding paths, but he was too close for subtle concealment. Running, Judy scurried into a chamber at the back of The Book Loft's interior. When she got to the far end of the room, she discovered, to her horror, there were no other exits to escape.

Johnny came to the same conclusion, slowing his pace to a crawl as he walked toward her. Back pressed to the shelves—Judy placed her hand in the air like a traffic cop. He was shaking his head and wiping at his still bleeding nose.

"I'm done with you, Judy. You were *never* anything to me other than a vessel I drained whenever I wanted. You'll never stay on the rails, and I can't afford more of these adventures," he said. He moved closer.

"Who's going to write your books for you, when I'm not around?" Judy asked.

"I can take a book from anyone I choose. You were just my lazy way."

"The memories are still choking your mind. Without me—you'll never get them out," Judy mentioned.

"I'll find some way. Besides, I have enough books in print to coast for the rest of my life. I can retire today," Johnny was within a few feet of her.

"I'm warning you. Don't do this," Judy begged. He gripped the blade tighter, lowered his head, and created a scowl that sent chills down her spine. He propelled his body toward her and slid the blade into Judy's heart. Although the knife sunk deep inside her, Johnny detected no blood. He took a step back, withdrawing his weapon from her chest in the same movement. A black crease, made by the knife, smiled back at him, and then repaired itself.

"What the fuck—" Was all Jonny could utter. In a panic, he pierced the blade into her chest again—pulling and pushing back into her several times. The same miraculous healing process took place. "That's not possible," he said with fear. Judy smiled. The knife in his hand vanished, and he looked down with amazement. The bookstore that surrounded them melted like ice on a sunny day.

They both stood inside the hidden room, face to face, buried deep in the clinic. Johnny recognized a vine protruding from his forehead. He thrashed his body to get away, but it held tight. He realized they never ran to the bookstore, and the popping sound was her tethering her mind to his.

"There was something that alluded me. We all have our strengths. Cal told me that, and I never understood my strengths until you reminded me you needed me asleep to take control—your limitation. But my father showed me images of the children I healed, and it didn't occur to me until tonight—my eyes were wide open when I connected to those patients," she said. His mind was working out what she was saying—recognition flooded his features. She nodded.

"My strength...I can be wide awake to enter someone's mind. I could have done it all along if I'd only known." While he stood immobilized, Judy sank deeper into his mind searching for what she wanted.

"He needs the secrets of your ability to survive. He stole your memories...let him drown in them, Jude. Don't let your anger for what he's done to me lure you back to him. Stay safe and stay awake. I love you, Angel." Judy cried when she replayed her father's last words. She replayed the entire night as if Johnny were nothing more than a recorder in human flesh.

"I'll free you, Judy," he said. Judy could taste the fear and desperation from him, "I will walk away from you and everyone you know. You won't have to worry about me again," he begged.

"My father had a clever idea. I should let you drown, but I have a better option in mind." He trembled. "You said it yourself—I was nothing to you, and you kept me alive so you could find out how to clear away all the stolen memories. Do you want to know how to do it?" He stared without saying a word. "Cal scared you away from the solution ten years ago." Johnny concentrated on the surrounding air with the answer evaporating his facade. "That's right. What you call *the Terror*. Visiting that region of your mind destroys the random memories of others—freeing you from them—but you were too afraid to revisit that place, weren't you?" With her tendril secured as tight as ever—she stepped closer.

"Johnny? I will remove any trace of the memories you stole from me—and I don't want any of them back. I'll make new memories," Judy said.

"What are you going to do to me?" he asked.

"I will not kill you. Your punishment will equal your crimes. You banished my father into *the Terror*, and now you will spend the rest of your life there," she said.

"Please, no. Kill me," Johnny said. She shook her head and made the proper connection of his conscious mind into *the Terror*. His eyes were vibrant one second and dead like the eyes of a baby doll the next. As Judy walked away from Johnny, he screamed with all the air in him. The intensity of his howling never waned as she walked out of his life and into her own.

Chapter Forty-three
—I never will be far away—

The press and even the fans of Johnny Macklemore were not as brutal as Judy imagined after such a public tragedy. The outpouring of sympathy with cards and flowers was overwhelming—not for the fate of Johnny, but for the glimpse of human compassion that still existed. They would never know what kind of man he was, and she was okay with that truth. Her reward was freedom, and that made the past manageable.

After she placed Johnny in an assisted care facility, the same one Brice Deville called home, Judy made her last visit with her husband. She didn't make the visit for closure or even to celebrate. Judy wanted to ensure he was safe in the mental prison, where she left him like a monster banished to a forbidden realm. She found out from his doctor that he was still prone to screaming fits if left unmedicated. She did her best to appear sympathetic in all the right pauses of his report, but was happy to find him confined.

Although she could bring back some of her memories, most would never return. Judy had to mourn the loss of her, the recollections that made her who she was. She listened as others were happy to remind her of the past—she would never again remember. She was a clean slate, determined to start again, and avoid the mistakes that led her to someone like Johnny Macklemore. Judy conceded that her gift was a light that would attract Johnny and people like him.

The matter of her mental ability, and what to do about it was still undecided. The threat of spreading her ability to others made her want to lock away her skill from the rest of the world. But in the night's quiet, when she was all alone—the guilt of the children she tried to help, now full-grown, entered her mind. Whatever she unlocked in their minds wasn't their fault. She imagined them scared of who they were becoming, with no one there to lead them away from the darkness.

Cal brought up helping her creations several times, and she smiled. The path to them was clear, but she wasn't ready to open that door yet. Engaging that group, she might discover good-hearted people coming to terms with their transformation. *Just who else might be out there hurting people because of her? What if Johnny wasn't even the worst one?* She craved a time when she could *be* Judy Angel making brand new memories and finding out who that lost girl was.

With every path that lay far ahead, the novels called to her. No matter how unfair it was, Judy had to hide that she wrote Johnny's most popular books. With his ailment taking him from the public, no one would accept her story of his theft. It was enough that she understood they were hers. Within the year, *Desert Lily* would hit bookstores. Judy was preparing for the backlash sure to follow. Critics would compare her style with Johnny's. Others would accuse her of publishing a lost manuscript of the famous author, like she came across it in a desk and attempted to pass it off as her own.

Whether it took her a lifetime to prove she was a legitimate author, or she filled her desk with books that no one would ever read—it didn't matter. It was the writing that she regained, and that was enough. She longed to disappear in a story and forget hers for a while.

Cal was another concern that weighed heavily on her mind. Although Johnny robbed them of their relationship, she couldn't help but think she deserved much more than becoming a woman belonging to someone else—even if that person was Calvin Reed. Who was she without a man by her side? Judy didn't know but was ready to find out.

When Judy entered Bud's hospital room, he was asleep as he always was the past months. The medication kept away the horrible screams even as it kept him from connecting to those around him. It became clear the prison that Johnny buried her father in, but what wasn't clear was if Bud would ever be the same if she brought him back from *the Terror*. Would the time in the nightmare world forever warp his mind? She shook her head to dissipate the negative ideas that tried to push aside her optimism.

She lifted the vintage boom box and placed it on a nightstand close to Bud's hospital bed. Judy slid a cassette from the front pocket of her pants—feeling the cassette tape's plastic body between her fingers. Something was comforting about knowing that music still existed in a solid form. She inserted the Billy Joel cassette in the boom box, closed the window, and clicked the PLAY button.

In the background, music rose—*Goodnight my angel, time to close your eyes and save these questions for another day*—

Judy placed the stuffed mockingbird into his hand.

"I'm going to help you, Dad." Bud's eyes fluttered behind their lids with Judy stroking his hair, "We can do this together. I won't hurt you."

Thank you for reading *On the Tip of Her Tongue*.
For my upcoming novels follow me at:
https://www.jerryrothauthor.com/subcribe/page

If you want to go back and follow Angel's breadcrumbs, keep reading!

Follow the breadcrumbs

If you're reading this, Judy Angel,
you have questions
        — find Maddie Stewart!

- Where Boo Radley hid gifts -
Always Start From The Beginning

-This° is more than meets the eye

- One · Last · Thing

- Did you catch the Lullaby?

To my fans, I hope you followed all the breadcrumbs. If not, go back and find them all. Send me a snapshot of Cal's <u>dollar</u> "In real life" to <u>https://bit.ly/3cSgczW</u> and you will be entered for a chance to win a signed copy of On the Tip of Her Tongue - *Drawing on New Year's Eve 2021*. If not, send a message to my website telling me how many clues you found ☺

ACKNOWLEDGEMENTS

First, I would like to thank my wife for everything she does while I make up my stories and live in an imaginary world. Tricia, none of this is possible without you.

I would like to thank my readers who read my previous novel Bottom Feeders and have decided to join me on this wild ride. Every fan of my books, you make all the demanding work and anxiety worth it—almost.

I also want to give a big shout out to *The Book Loft* for allowing my climactic scene to happen in your great store.

Mike Suclescy and Donna DeVol from The Thurman Café for allowing me to use their business name in my novel. There is nothing like your burger!

A special thanks goes out to my editor Saren Richardson. Her help was crucial and the fact that she shared my vision was the icing on the cake. Can't wait until our next project!

The talented Ross Nischler created the cover and artwork – Thank you.

I want to give a huge thanks to my writing role-model, *Stephen King*. When I was finally old enough to buy my own things, I stumbled across your paperbacks and my world changed forever. Watching your career and reading your books taught me that no matter what genre you write, a remarkable story can break through any barrier.

The genius, Harper Lee's work was the inspiration to this novel. She will never know how many lives were touch by her words.

Above everyone I want to say thank you to my daughter Lea who was the inspiration for this novel. Billy Joel's Lullaby is the song that ties us together as well. If not for the unbreakable love of a daughter, a father is nothing.

ABOUT THE AUTHOR

Photo by Karli Moore Photography

Jerry Roth is a graduate from The Ohio State University studying English Literature. He has written for Ohio newspapers and sports articles for the Disc Golf Pro Tour. His fiction career began as a screenwriter. He currently lives in Ohio with his wife Tricia and his three children Jesse, Lea and Nick. After reading *The Stand* by Stephen King, he became passionate about creating his own work of fiction.

Facebook: jerryrothauthor

Instagram: @_jerryroth_

Twitter: @_jerryroth_